# Seven

## By Susan Renee

*You are my sunshine ♡*

*Susan Renee*

Cover art by Samantha Roth of Grothic Designs

Editors: Nikki Rose and Lauren Brocchi

Formatting: Douglas M. Huston

To Doug.

Now you know why I enjoy our pillow talk.

Thanks for always "loving me okay".

And to Anna and JP

You are my sunshine every day.

# Chapter 1

**January 1, 2013**

"You are my sunshine…"

           *Breathe Peyton.*

"My only sunshine…"

           *Fight for mommy.*

"You make me happy…"

           *Breathe baby girl.*

"When skies are gray…"

           *You can do it Peyton.*

"You'll never know dear…"

           *Please. Please Peyton breathe on your own.*

"How much I love you."

           *Don't you die on me baby girl.*

"Please don't take my sunshine away."

Beep. Swoosh…Beep. Swoosh…Beep. Swoosh.

I sit here next to her hospital bed holding her little seventeen-month old lifeless fingers, so delicate, so small. I think about her first birthday and how adorable she was with cake all over her face, her tummy and in her hair. Peyton is the happiest little girl and so full of life.

Correction.

She *was* so full of life.

Now she lays in a bed that's too big for her, in a hospital gown that's two sizes too big covered in blankets that don't belong to her because her blankie was lost in the accident. EMTs are trained to do all they can to save their patient but they're not trained to search for blankies or favorite stuffed kittens. I'm all she has. My husband, Peyton's daddy, has been in surgery for the last four hours so I'm all she has. I can't leave her. I have to believe she'll wake up despite what the doctors say.

*She'll wake up.*

*She has to.*

"Mrs. Turner?" a voice says to me. I look up and see a nurse in pink scrubs giving me a look of sympathy. I wipe my nose with the sleeve of my sweater.

"Yes. That's me. My name is Savannah Turner. Do you have word on my husband? Is he going to be okay? Nobody has told me anything yet."

"Savannah." She smiles. "That's a beautiful name. My name is Shelly. I'm one of the pediatric nurses keeping an eye on Peyton until her test results are back. I apologize for not keeping you updated but the doctors are still in surgery with your husband. No news could be good news right now. From what I know Shawn suffered several injuries and had a lot of internal bleeding. I'll check in with the surgeons as soon as I leave here and see if I can get an update for you."

Sniffle.

"Thank you. I'm sorry...I...this is all...I..."

"Overwhelming and scary?" Shelly asks quietly, nodding her head as if she understands what I'm going through. She doesn't know anything, but I'm such a hot mess right now I don't even have the energy to fight or yell or scream.

*I just need my family to come back to me.*

"Yeah."

Sniffle.

"I know Savannah and I'm so very sorry. This is definitely not how anyone wants to ring in the new year. Do you have some family that you want to call; someone to sit with you so you're not alone?"

"Umm..." I frown. "No. We're not...we're not from here." I say, shaking my head. "We were just traveling from Knoxville back home to Lexington. Most of our family lives in Bardstown. It would take hours for them to get here and in this weather..." I can't hold back the tears. "I couldn't ask that of them."

*It was the fucking weather that brought us here.*

*Happy fucking New Year.*

Shelly hands me a Kleenex and places her hand on my shoulder. "It's okay, I understand. Just don't lose hope. Your loved ones need all the positive thoughts they can get so for now you hold on to your baby girl. Every baby girl needs her mama. And you let me know if you need anything, okay? You just push that button right there on the side of the bed and I'll be right here."

"Thank you. I will. Actually, the doctors told me I didn't have any serious injuries; just bruising and seven stitches in my knee. They gave me some ibuprofen several hours ago but my head is still pounding. What time is it anyway?"

Shelly looks at the clock hanging just above my head. Oops, I guess I should've noticed it there. "It's just after ten-thirty. Do you remember when you came in?"

"Umm…no. I just remember seeing the clock in car before the accident. It said seven o'clock." I smirk and shake my head at myself. "I just remember it so vividly because I hate the number seven. Everyone says it's a lucky number but for me it's been nothing but a fucking pain in my ass my entire life."

"Ah. I understand. Everyone seems to think thirteen is unlucky so I always make sure to play it on my lottery cards in hopes that not many people use it, which means more winnings for me. I suppose though that you don't see me covered in diamonds so maybe it really is unlucky." She smiles. "Let me pull up your chart and we'll see what we can do for your headache okay?"

"Thank you." I nod, and then lean over to kiss Peyton on her tiny forehead.

I spend the next hour in this same chair holding on to the same tiny fingers and praying, to whatever God will listen, that my family comes back to me. At some point I must've fallen asleep because I'm awakened when two doctors walk into my room accompanied by Shelly.

"Mrs. Turner?"

I jump out of my chair.

"Yes." Shelly is by my side, tenderly holding my shoulder.

*This can't be good.*

"Mrs. Turner, my name is Doctor Shaw and this is my colleague Doctor Spencer. We're the surgeons who have been working on your husband."

"Yes. How is he? He's okay, right? Shelly told me he had internal bleeding?" There are about one hundred questions I could ask right now.

"Mrs. Turner your husband…"

"Shawn." I interrupt in a panic. I heard somewhere that when you give a name to a face, or in this case, to a patient, that it makes everything more personal. My body is getting warmer and I can feel my heart beating harder and faster. Panic is setting in. This is it. Fight or flight.

*Please God, I need some good news today.*

A small burst of tears slides down my face as I hopelessly look at the surgeons in front of me before channeling my inner Sally Field. "Please use his name Doctor. His name is Shawn and I love him. He is my husband and I love him and please tell me he is okay because I love him and I can't do this without him. I can't make decisions about Peyton without him. I need him with me. He needs to see her." I'm crying with fear of what this doctor is about to tell me.

"Right. Shawn. Mrs. Turner, when Shawn arrived here he was unresponsive and had suffered traumatic internal injuries. We did all we could to stop the bleeding and repair the damage, but…"

*Oh God.*

*He said "but".*

*No.*

*Please, no.*

"Mrs. Turner, I'm so sorry, but his injuries were too severe. His heart failed during surgery and we were unable to revive him. I'm so sorry for your loss."

I sit back down in the very same chair I sat down in over four hours ago. Everything leaves my body. There's no more energy, no more soul, no more life.

I don't even have words.

My husband is dead.

I'm staring straight ahead, unsure of what the hell I'm even looking at, and my husband is dead.

The love of my life, the father of my child, my best friend…he's dead.

"Mrs. Turner."

As if my soul returns to my statue of a body I gasp for a huge breath and exhale in an uncontrolled sob.

I cry out in agony. "SHAAAAWN! OH GOD SHAWN! NO! PLEASE GOD DON'T DO THIS TO ME"

"Mrs. Turner…" I hear one of the doctors say.

"WHY? WHY ARE YOU LEAVING ME?" I scream.

"Mrs. Turner…"

"Fuck you!" My extreme outburst makes me gasp in fear. "Oh God, I'm sorry!" I try to cover my mouth realizing, the absurdity of my outburst but there is no way I can control myself right now. I'm tired, my head hurts and the events of this horrible day have beat me down. There's no victory here for me.

"SHAWN! I'M SO, SO, SORRY. OH GOD! SHAWN! I LOVE YOU!" I'm rocking back and forth in my chair unable to move my body from the fetal position I just curled up in. All I can do is cry uncontrollably for the loss of my soul mate, my lover, my best friend, Peyton's daddy.


"Peyton please wake up." I whisper.

               Sniffle.

               Breathe.

               Rock forward and back.

"Peyton, mommy needs you…"

               Sniffle.

               Breathe.

               Rock forward and back.

"Peyton, Mommy needs…"

*What's happening?*

Sniffle.

Breathe.

"Mommy..."

My body is weightless as the darkness consumes me.

*****

Beep...Beep...Beep...Beep.

The steady beep brings me to my senses. When I open my eyes I'm in a hospital room, wires taped to my chest.

*Monitoring my heart?*

I feel the plastic hose of oxygen attached to my nostrils.

*What happened?*

"Savannah, honey." The voice sounds familiar. I turn my head to the left slowly and see my mother at my bedside. Just behind her, light is shining in through a small window. "Savannah, you're alright. You're okay. The doctor said you passed out last night so they put you in a room to monitor you, just to make sure you weren't suffering other injuries."

"What...I...what day is it? How did you get here?" My voice is raspy. I've obviously been laying here a while.

"It's Thursday sweetheart. January second. You were in a car accident. Baby do you remember that? The staff, they must've looked through your purse or phone or something because we got a call late last night to come here and...oh, Savannah." She cries.

*She's crying for me?*

*Was I dreaming?*

*Did I just dream all of this?*

I take the oxygen mask out of my nostrils so that it's not in my way. "Shawn." I whisper to my mother. "Shawn, did he...did...is...did he..."

"Sweetheart, you know Shawn loves you with his whole heart." She says in her comforting southern accent. My mom has lived in

6

Kentucky longer than her hometown of Savannah, Georgia, yet you would never know it from her thick accent. She has the comforting motherly look of Paula Dean. "We all love you so much Savannah but honey…Shawn is watching over you from Heaven, baby girl. He just didn't make it. I'm so sorry."

I watch as my dad walks into the room at the same time that my Mom is wiping the tears off her face with a Kleenex.

"Dad?" I ask.

"Yes Darlin'? I'm here. You're alright. Doc says you're gonna be just fine. You just fainted and were a little dehydrated."

"Peyton. I need to see Peyton. How is she?"

The look that passes from Dad to Mom is the look that says they know something and don't want to tell me. If I didn't know it then, the fact that my mom is crying even harder now tells me that my suspicion is right.

"What's going on? What happened? They didn't take her did they?"

With tears welling in his eyes, Dad holds my hand. "Savannah do you remember what happened last night? Do you remember anything the doctors told you? About Shawn, and about…Peyton?"

I close my eyes briefly and take a long deep breath.

It wasn't a dream.

I'm living a nightmare.

I've gone to Hell. This is it.

"She's gone too, isn't she Daddy? She really is brain dead? There was no change?" I ask resolutely. I feel the stream of tears falling across my cheeks and landing on my shoulder that is peeking through my hospital gown. I don't even bother trying to wipe them away.

"Well Sweetheart," he says softly. "Her little body is still laying in that bed but no…there was no change. The second doctor confirmed that there is no brain activity and hasn't been since she came in here." He's rubbing my hand with his thumb to comfort me, but he's crying all the same. "You have to be the one to set her free. I know you don't want to but she needs her daddy now and he needs his baby girl. You have to be strong and tell her it's ok to stay with him now, but before you do that you have something very important to think about."

"What's that?" I ask, my lip quivering.

"Doctor Turek stopped in to see you this morning after Peyton's condition was confirmed. He mentioned that Peyton could help save the lives of several other people, including a little boy right here in this hospital, that you have the opportunity to turn our tragic loss into a celebration of life for several other families."

*They want to slice open my child and take what's hers?*

*I...I can't.*

"I can't Daddy!" I whimper. "I need her. She's my baby too." My eyes are closed. I feel her with me. I imagine holding her, wrapped in my arms, smelling her strawberry shampoo and listening to her make her silly kitten noises. I feel a smile briefly cross my face before I'm once again overcome with sadness. "I don't think I can do it."

"Oh, Savannah." My mother cries next to my dad. I can't look at them because all I see is the heartache in their eyes but resolution in their body language. The look that says they're overcome with grief for their daughter and son-in-law and baby granddaughter but they know they have to get me through this. Through tears my dad says, "Think about those other families and for just a minute put yourself in their shoes. If there was any way we could save Peyton with an organ transplant, wouldn't you pray for that from those families? Peyton's body can't use them anymore sweetheart, but there are many kids out there who could. We can't make this decision for you, sweetheart, but think about what a hero you and Peyton could be to so many others out there."

"We'll be right there with you if you want us to be." Mom sniffles. "The nurse said we could go see her as soon as you woke up. But Savannah honey, time is of the essence. You were sleeping a long time. It's time for her to go be with her daddy. It's time for baby girl to go play with Jesus."

My mother and father are devout Christians. Their faith is unwavering, always has been and always will be, but mine? Today?

8

I'm not sure what I believe anymore, but I sure as hell hope, beyond all things, that there really is a Heaven that is out-of-this-world-spectacular so that my husband and my baby girl, the flesh of my flesh, have a place to call home until I can join them.

*Why couldn't He have taken me too?*

*I don't want to live a life that they're not a part of.*

*My parents are right.*

*But I wish they weren't.*

Within the next couple of hours, I'm discharged from my room, dressed in a pair of sweats that Mom bought at the hospital gift shop and am wheeled to Peyton's bedside. She's in a tiny individual room, the same from last night, which right now I'm grateful for. I don't need my goodbyes to be a spectacle for the entire pediatrics ward to see.

I sit in the same reclining chair I was in last night, leaning as much of my body as possible onto Peyton's bed. I place my arms around her and hold her snug to my chest for just a moment in hopes that I can feel her tiny heart beat against my body. My parents stand around me, their hands on my shoulders in support. Peyton's lifeless body is warm against my chest but there is no movement in her except for the machine breathing for her. I kiss her cheeks and her head and her hands, letting my lips linger each time. Some of her sweet smell is still there so I take a moment to close my eyes and commit it to my memory.

"You're so beautiful Peyton." I whisper as I run my hands over her soft golden hair. "Mommy loves you so, so, so much baby girl. Daddy loves you too and he's waiting for you." I choke on my words. "He's holding his arms out for you, so be sure to give him a real big hug, okay?" I squeeze her little body tenderly against me and bring my head to her ear so I can be sure that she hears me. At least I hope she hears me.

"It's okay to go with Daddy, Peyton. He'll take real good care of you until I can be there with you. Mommy loves you." I sniffle and feel the pressure of my dad's hand on my shoulder.

"I will always love you, Peyton."

9

With tears streaming down my face I look up at the nurse who is waiting for my go ahead to take Peyton to surgery for the harvesting of her organs. I look down at my daughter one more time and sing the song I've always considered hers.

"You are my sunshine
My only sunshine.
You make me happy
When skies are… gray."
My body is trembling as I fight the battle for inner strength.


"You'll… never know dear
How much I… I love you.
Please don't……take…."

I hold her and quietly sob. My body convulses with emotions but I make no sound. I have no painful sounds left to give. "Please don't take my sunshine away." I whisper to her. "I love you Peyton. Mommy loves you so much. I'm so sorry. Don't be scared baby. I'll see you soon." We watch as the nurse wheels Peyton down the hall until we can see her no longer.

That's it.
I can't be strong anymore.
I have nothing left.
I have nobody left.
It's just me now.

# Chapter 2

**March 17, 2015**

My alarm went off a half hour ago, but I'm still lying in bed. Anyone else would at least be smiling on their birthday but not me. I'm twenty-seven years old today and what do I have to show for it? I've been married and widowed. I've had a child and then lost a child and I moved away from my hometown of Bardstown, Kentucky, years ago, only to end up right back where I started. My dreams are shattered, my future is unclear and my present is in a state of constant flux. Yep, that's cause for celebration.

"Happy Birthday, Savannah. You're really going places," I say sarcastically to myself. I throw off my covers, exposing my legs to the cold air, and roll out of bed. I don't bother turning my heat up much when I'm the only one I have to worry about keeping warm, and lower bills mean more money in my pocket, not that I need it for anything. I'm sitting on a sizeable chunk of life insurance money that I don't ever plan on using. Why would I take death money from my husband and child to turn around and buy stupid shit that I don't need? Insurance companies are assholes. What do they think I'm going to do with all that money? Go on vacation? Buy a new car? Move into a mansion? Who does that? I would give it all back and then some to have them back in my life. Hell, I would switch places with them in an instant if I could. I'm no good to this earth now anyway. I've considered just ending my life so I can be closer to Shawn and Peyton, but unfortunately I'm too smart to know what that would do to my parents. I just can't do it to them as much as I've wanted to for myself over the past couple of years.

For about a year and a half now I've lived back in my hometown with my parents. I thought I could be okay living on my own in Lexington, but after a depressing six months, the house was still filled with Shawn and Peyton's stuff. I just couldn't bring myself to get rid of it. The house still smelled like them every day. I could still hear them around me, and as much as I wanted that feeling, the feeling that maybe I wasn't alone, to never leave, it was driving me crazy and pushing me further down into the Hell of depression. I couldn't get out of bed. I didn't want to eat; I lost no less than forty pounds. I couldn't keep my job because I cried all the time. I guess crying isn't good for customer service or the workplace environment. My parents came to visit me on what would've been Peyton's birthday, took one look at me and the rest was history. I stayed with them until just before this past Christmas. After speaking to my therapist-fuck patient confidentiality I guess-my mom pushed me back out of the nest. She thought it would give me an incentive to get myself out there, meet new people and make friends if I was living on my own. After all, how many twenty-seven-year old girls find love again when they're still living with Mommy and Daddy? I get it, I do. She's right I guess. I've done an excellent job of being a hermit for two years. I don't go many places and only have a few old friends who still live in this town, some single, some not. None of them are widowed, so I'm always the elephant in the room when I'm out…which is why I don't go out often. Who wants to be the Debby Downer when your friends are out for a good time? Fuck love anyway.

Before Christmas I received a call from Rachel about whether I would be interested in a job at Great Lengths, her local salon, cutting hair. Rachel's salon is a nice place, I guess, but not at all what I had dreamed for myself several years ago. I started out very slowly, only working one day a week and not many hours. She's the only one who really knows my past and what it's done to me, and she's fully supported me every step of the way. Now that it's been a few months, I've started coming out of my shell more, picking up more clients which means more hours. I guess for now it pays the bills and gets me "out there" as per Mom's request. Maybe one day I'll fulfill my dreams of owning my own business.

My first appointment of the morning is at nine so I quickly shower and grab breakfast before heading out the door to get to work on time.

"Good morning Savannah!" Rachel exclaims as I walk in the door. She's always so peppy. She reminds me a little of the person I used to be, but she doesn't know that.

That part of me is gone.

"Mornin' Rache." I give her a half smile. My greeting isn't so new to me anymore. I used to wear my emotions on my sleeve but now I carry them in my pocket, never to be released. I give enough of myself away to talk to my customers when they come in. The always useful "How's the weather out there?" or "Do you work around here?" conversation starters get me through the work day without having to reveal too much about myself. Rachel knows me from high school so of course she knows about my immediate past. We weren't the best of friends back then but we weren't unfriendly either. Lucky for me she's become a pretty good friend and knows not to bring it up if she doesn't have to. She seems the type to have a few skeletons in her closet too but since she doesn't ask me about mine, I don't ask about hers.

"Before you get started for the day Savannah, the girls want to take you out tonight for your birthday. You game?" Rachel asks.

*No fucking way*!

"Uh, I don't know." I groan shaking my head. "I don't need any big thing. Twenty-seven doesn't mean much really. I appreciate the thought though."

"No way girl. It's your birthday and you haven't celebrated your birthday in…well…I'm not sure how long, but you've been working here for a few months now and we've never just gone out and had some fun. One or two drinks, some live music. You won't even have to talk much because we'll be listening to the music. What do you say? Let us take you out for a little fun?"

I take a deep breath, letting it out loud enough for Rachel to know I'm not thrilled that she's asking this of me. "Where are you thinking of going?"

"How about over to Wood's Tavern?"

"Wood's? Where's that?"

"It's where the old Brooks Pub used to be. The food is great and the music is fun. You'll like it, I promise. And I'm sure they'll be doing something awesome for St. Patrick's Day tonight!"

13

I mull over the idea of going for a minute. I'm not keen on being out in public for everyone to show me how much they pity me, but the girls here have been so welcoming to me. I know they mean well. I don't want to be the bitchy girl who blows them off forever. "Alright. My last cut is at six. Then I'll give ya'll about an hour or so. A burger and a bourbon and that's it, okay? No surprises!"

Rachel smiles in victory. She knows I usually say no and mean it. "Great! Whatever you want. Promise!"

"Okay then. I need to get ready for Mrs. Tims. She should be here for her cut and color any minute."

"Ok." She's still looking at me like she has more to say but is too afraid to say it. "Savannah?"

"Rachel?" I respond as I pull my apron over my head and tie it around my waist.

"Just…happy birthday." She smiles sincerely at me and for a moment I feel guilty for giving her a hard time about taking me out tonight. She's just trying to be a friend. My old self would've done the same for her if roles were reversed.

*But they're not reversed.*

"Thanks." I pull out one of those fake smiles I'm getting good at in hopes that it appeases her sympathy. The rest of my day is uneventful, although I do receive flowers from my parents and a birthday card from Shawn's parents as well. It's nice that someone is thinking of me today even when I don't feel like celebrating.

Rachel, Heather, Audrey, and I close up shop just after seven and head down the street to Wood's Tavern. The music is already hopping and can be heard from the street, especially as people come and go through the front door. Green lights and St. Paddy's Day decorations are hanging outside the pub and those leaving the pub are all wearing green beaded necklaces like you would find at a Mardi Gras parade.

*Wonder what you have to do to earn those?*

The bar has most definitely been updated from when I used to hang out here during holiday breaks home from school. The walls have been pulled back to their original stone texture, wooden beams have been added on the ceiling, the brass has been polished and the flooring looks brand new. Everything is very clean and almost worldly looking, but still holds the historic feel of the rest of the town. I'm impressed. Whoever bought and fixed this place has done a nice job. I look to the bar and see one bartender talking with a group of women on the other end. Rolling my eyes, I head with the girls to a table near the back corner. If this guy is going to spend time smiling and flirting with the ladies, it could be a while before we get a drink.

A perky little waitress approaches our table with water in hand as we're all studying our menus. "Happy St. Paddy's Day ladies! What can I get ya'll tonight?" The girls all place their orders and then look to me.

"Uh, I'll have a tavern burger and an Old Fashioned please." I hand my menu to the waitress.

"Great. Coming right up ladies! Enjoy yourselves tonight."

Five minutes later we're all sitting around our table with drinks in hand listening to the band playing all sorts of popular covers as we sing along.

Rachel raises her glass to the center of the table and looks at me, smirking. "To Savannah on her twenty seventh birthday! As she slides down the banister of life, may the splinters never point the wrong way!" I snort unexpectedly at her remarks as my eyes snap up to hers. She winks back at me and grins. "And may she take another step closer toward achieving her dream! Happy birthday Savannah!"

"Happy birthday! Woohoo! I'll drink to that." I hear from the girls around the table.

"Thanks girls." I smile and quickly down my drink. I know I told Rachel I would just stay for one drink but fuck it. It's my birthday. I may as well get wasted and erase this damn day from my mind. Two Whiskey Sours and a Kentucky Cousin later, and this birthday couldn't get any better. I feel lighter than I've felt in a long time. It's after ten and I'm still dancing like I'm twenty-one while the band plays their version of Fun's "We Are Young". I turn around with my arms in the air, letting myself go a little more than I usually would, especially in

15

public. For a split second I see the bartender, who is no longer behind the bar, but standing near my table with his arms folded in front of him, watching the crowd with a satisfied look on his face. He's probably looking for his next quick lay.

*Mmm...haven't thought about sex in a long time.*

*It's obviously the bourbon talking.*

The music continues, and I'm laughing with the girls when I feel a hand wrap around my waist. The cologne smell is quite possibly the sexiest thing I've smelled in a long time. His hands are strong against my hips and I can easily tell from his stance behind me that he's strong and well built. Also, I'm a tad drunk. Before I try to turn around and see who it is, his lips nearly brush my ear, sending a spark of God-knows-what to places I probably shouldn't be aware of right now.

"Well on a scale of one to four I would give that little dance of yours a perfect ten," he says softly in my ear.

*What the fuck?*

*Seriously, this guy?*

"Are you crazy?" I ask, trying to push his arms off of me. I'm not going to lie. Being touched by a guy feels kind of good, but no way is this guy going to see any action from me. The widow in me screams to attention.

"Am I crazy?" he asks with a laugh. "You're the one who sits in sugar, princess."

"What?" I ask, looking over my shoulder and brushing off whatever must be on my pants. "Why do you say that?"

"Because you have a pretty sweet ass."

That gets me to turn around, and when I do I stumble backwards, surprised at who I'm looking at. It's the bartender. He's way more built than I could tell when I saw him earlier. He's wearing faded jeans and a fitted green t-shirt that's partly tucked in because I can see his brown leather belt with a star shaped belt buckle. The cuteness of him almost makes me giggle, except when I look up into his brown eyes, he's not smiling.

"Seven?" he whispers, furrowing his brow.

"Seven?" I laugh. "No way man. You said I was a ten. I heard you clear as fuckin' day."

"No," he says shaking his head. "You're Seven. Seven Sanders."

*Fuck.*

*There's a blast from my past.*

*He knows me?*

I jump up out of his reach like I've just been burned by hot coals. Clearly he knows me and I don't remember him, which puts me at a clear disadvantage. I try to place his face but my inebriation is not allowing me to think that clearly.

"My name isn't Seven, jack ass. It's..."

"Savannah. Yeah, I know. But... I always called you Seven."

What the hell? Who is this guy? "Fuck off buddy. Nobody's called me that since..."

"Junior high. At least I think that's when it started." He smirks at me and stands with his arms folded over his chest, clearly having the one-up in this conversation. "You don't recognize me, do you Seven?"

Ugh, the nerve of this guy. "Look asswipe, I'm sorry I don't know who you are. The only thing I know about you is that you're the guy who has helped me forget this night by supplying me with enough bourbon to guarantee that I'll be worshiping the porcelain throne in the morning, so thank you for that. I'm a little drunk off my ass right now, and probably wouldn't recognize myself if I looked in the damn mirror. Now for the last time, my name isn't Seven. I don't know who told you to call me that, and to be honest right now, I don't even care. There was only ever one guy who was douchebag enough to call me that when I was younger, even though I hated it, and you, my fine hunk of a bartender, are not him. So if you'll excuse me, I need to pay my tab and be on my way."

The guy standing in front of me stares at me for a moment just breathing. No expression, he's just...breathing. He's obviously thinking something. Perhaps he's considering an alternative way to get in my pants, or maybe he's deciding that I'm just not worth it. Regardless, I'm just about to say something else when I see his lips widen into a sexy smile. He bites his bottom lip, I think to keep from laughing at me. As irritating as that is, I'm toasted enough to actually be a bit turned on by his mouth. For the first time in years I actually recognize the feeling, the desire to want to kiss someone, but I don't. Ugh, this alcohol trip is causing me to have stupid thoughts. I don't know this guy and he's an asshole for even trying to bring up my past on my birthday. He nods at me silently before saying, "Your tab is taken care of. Happy birthday Savannah."

*That's right it is.*

*Take that, bar man.*

In a huff, I push past him and walk back to my table so that I can rummage through my purse for some Advil. I throw my purse back down onto my seat and head to the bar where Rachel is getting another drink. I ask the waitress standing nearby for a glass of water. At least I can do my part to try and curb the hangover I'm sure to end up with. "Hey, I'm heading out. Thanks for a fun night. You were right. I needed it, but don't be surprised if I'm late tomorrow."

"You're leaving already?" she asks, disappointed. I raise one eyebrow at her in response.

"I said one drink...and instead I've had several...no I mean seven...wait, several...shit." I shake my head irritated. "Doesn't matter, I've had enough for the night. I'm just going to go."

"No way. Not like that. You're in no condition to drive."

"I'm not going to drive, Mom." I roll my eyes at her. Is she serious right now? "I can walk from here. It's only a couple blocks."

"What? That's ridiculous! You're not going to walk home in the dark and by yourself."

*Seriously?*

*It's Podunk town.*

*May as well be a ghost town.*

"Rache, number one, I'm way too drunk to drive my car right now. Number two, my car will be just fine here till morning. Number three, it's a small town and I live the equivalent of about five blocks away;

besides, who's going to hurt me any worse than I've already had it? Seriously, I think I'll be fine. See ya tomorrow."

Rachel looks past me for a moment, her expression perplexed, before she nods her approval.

I scowl at her and watch her for a moment to make sure she's ok. The other girls see that I'm on my way out and join Rachel as I say my goodbyes.

"Happy birthday Savannah!" I hear for the last time before I leave.

"It'll be a happy birthday when I'm alone and in my bed. I may even invite my battery operated boyfriend." I mutter to myself when I walk out the door.

I try to walk quickly towards my apartment building. Not because I'm scared of walking alone at night, but because it's cold outside and I just want to be in the heat...or the mild heat at least. There's surprisingly no snow on the ground right now. Bardstown, Kentucky, is having an unseasonably warm week given the snow we had just two weeks ago, but walking in the mid-forties still sucks. I only live a few blocks away which is good because I really need to pee.

I make it about three blocks before I get that feeling that creeps me out and puts me on instant alert. I sober up faster than I ever have because I feel like someone is behind me, following me. I'm afraid to turn around and check.

*Damnit. Maybe Rachel was right.*

*Why did she even let me leave?*

Someone is definitely following me. At least I'm pretty sure there is, even though I have no evidence to confirm my fear. It's just a feeling I have when I know I'm not alone. I know if I turn around and look to see who is behind me, I could be wasting time, when I could just make a mad dash for my building. I pick up my pace and dart out into the middle of the road. Since there's no traffic, I feel a little safer walking where anyone could see me. My apartment building is in sight, but my anxiety, and perhaps my level of intoxication, are playing cruel games with my nerves.

*Breathe, Savannah.*

*Could be nobody.*

*Could be a neighbor.*

*Or maybe you're going to be killed tonight.*

*Would that be so bad?*

*I could see Shawn and Peyton again.*

My fears instantly subside at that thought and I laugh out loud at my absurdity. Bravely, or maybe stupidly, I turn around while I'm walking to see who's behind me. To my surprise I don't see anyone at all, not even a stray cat. The mind plays evil tricks sometimes, but then again, my instincts are usually correct. I think I need some sleep. When I reach my apartment building, I walk lazily up the steps, making sure to grip the railing tightly so that I don't fall over. Standing outside my door, I reach into my purse to grab my keys, but don't feel them anywhere.

"Damnit," I whisper to myself.

I stop and take a deep breath. My intoxication is clouding my ability to focus on anything right now. I put my purse down on the ground and wobbly scrunch down to have a better look through my purse. My apartment key is on the same ring as my car key and those aren't usually hard to find in my purse. The keychain I have them on is one with Peyton's newborn footprint on it, so it's larger than a normal key chain. I'm clearing random shit out of the way, but my keys are nowhere to be found.

"Fuck this." I stand up, giving my head time to catch up with my movements before pulling my cellphone from my back pocket. So that I don't have to go downstairs only to have to walk back up, I dial the programmed number to Cole, the building superintendent, to ask for help. I've only ever seen him a few times since I moved in. From what I know he graduated college and is interested in getting into real-estate. I guess since I've never had to call him for a repair problem, he must be good at his job, or at least knows how to manage outside help.

"Cole Brookston. What do ya need?" The way he answers his phone makes him sound like the town handyman even though I've never once seen him with a tool in his hand.

"Cole, It's Savannah Turner, in apartment B-7."

"What's up Savannah? You okay?"

"Yeah I uh, drank a little more than I probably should've and now I can't find my keys. I must've left them at the bar or something since I didn't drive home. Could you come let me in please?"

"Sure. I'll be your designated key man." He chuckles but I don't really find any humor in his joke, if he was in fact trying to make a joke. I'm just tired and want to be in my home. "Be up in a second."

"Thanks." I throw my cell phone in my purse and stand along the wall next to my apartment door while I wait for Cole to arrive.

Shit. I just told the single guy living downstairs that I'm not only drunk, but without keys to my home.

*Real smart, Savannah.*

Fuck this day and the horse it rode in on.

# Chapter 3

# *Bryant*

*Fine hunk of a bartender, huh?*

Damn! What are the chances that the pretty girl that walks into your bar, who steals your attention and immediately makes you think dirty thoughts, ends up being someone from your past? She doesn't recognize me at all. I guess it's better off for now. She hated me when we were younger, although I can't for the life of me remember what I did to deserve it. I was probably a smart mouth prick to her or something. God I wish I would've been brave enough to tell her how I really felt back then…but the jocks didn't get to hang out with the brains.

*What I wish I could be brave enough to tell her now.*

She's beautiful tonight. Watching her body move on the dance floor a minute ago, like she didn't have a care in the world, when I know she holds the weight of the world on her shoulders, makes me want to be in her presence all night. Makes me want to grab on to her and protect her, shield her from the pain of her past and of what has to be an inevitable future, and let her continue to dance in her bubble of drunken bliss. I know Savannah's story. Who doesn't around this small gossipy town? I know she doesn't go out much. I know she keeps to herself, and I know she's working down at Rachel's salon. Shit. How lucky am I right now? The girl I always wanted and could never have is back in town; she was just dancing in my bar. I'm not sure at this point if I even deserve a fighting chance with her but how can I not give her everything she deserves after what she's been through?

*And after what she's done for me.*

When she brushes past me and heads to the bar, my chest tightens and I feel that quick stab of anxiety. I wanted to keep talking to her but I blew it. Well, maybe I didn't blow it, but she's drunk enough to not remember me or care one way or another. I suppose for now that's for the best, but if I want to get to know this girl again, I'm going to have to figure out how to keep her from finding out what I know, at least until I'm brave enough to tell her.

I turn to watch her at the bar and spot her purse sitting on the chair she just threw it on a moment ago. It's unzipped and I can see a set of car keys lying right inside. It's too easy. I quickly swipe the car keys and put them in my pocket. She's in no shape to drive anyway. As smoothly as I can, I make my way to where she is standing, careful to make sure she doesn't see me too close behind her. She's talking to Rachel and downing a glass of water.

*Smart girl.*

"What? That's ridiculous! You're not going to walk home in the dark and by yourself," I hear Rachel say.

*Maybe I'll just offer to drive her.*

*I could just tell her she dropped her keys on the floor.*

"Rache…number three, it's a small town and I live the equivalent of about five blocks away; besides, who's going to hurt me any worse than I've already had it? Seriously, I think I'll be fine. See ya tomorrow."

Overhearing Savannah, I quickly wave my hand at Rachel so she looks at me. I show her that I have Savannah's keys and motion to her that I'll walk her home. She won't be alone. I see Rachel nod and watch as the girls all say their goodbyes to Savannah. When she walks out the door, Rachel is quickly at my side.

"You stole her keys?"

"Uh…I might have." I smirk. "Listen Seven and I…Savannah and I go way back but she doesn't remember me, at least not tonight. I'll follow her and make sure she gets home safely, I promise. Then I'll just drive her car to her place for her later tonight and leave her the keys. She shouldn't be driving anyway."

"Dude, Bryant, please tell me you didn't fuck her and chuck her way back when. That poor girl has been through hell. She doesn't need the shit that you've pulled in the past."

Whoa.

"First of all, not that it's any business of yours, but no, I didn't fuck her or chuck her. I never had the chance."

Rachel throws me the you're-a-douchebag look. "Are you serious right now?"

"Sorry, no, that came out wrong. I'm sorry. What I mean is nobody would've thought she was good enough for me…Shit! That's not what

I mean either. I'm messing this all up again." I run my fingers through my hair in frustration. "Look, I'll explain it all later. Just let me make sure she gets home safely. I'll be right back. If Sloan needs me, tell him I just stepped out. He can handle things here while I'm gone."

Rachel's eyes narrow at me as I back out the door. I'm sure the gleam in my eye and my excitement of having Seven back in town has her a bit confused, as she should be. She doesn't know about that part of my life. She knows about my life now, but not how it's connected to Savannah. Nobody knows that but me.

Savannah is not walking very fast. I jog a block up the road so that I'm a little closer to her in case something should happen, but I keep my distance so she doesn't know I'm following her.

"Shit!" I whisper loudly as I trip over the uneven sidewalk in front of me. Maybe Savannah had the right idea walking in the middle of the road, but if I did that I would most definitely look like I'm stalking her. At least this way I can maybe duck and cover if she turns around.

Much to my relief, I watch her slowly walk the stairs to where I can only assume her apartment is. Once she's out of sight, I wait a moment to see if lights come on in one of the darkened windows. When nothing happens in the few minutes I stand there, I assume her apartment must be on the other side of the building. While jogging back to the bar, I come up with a plan. I know the guy who owns the building. He'll help me out. I'm sure of it.

"Did she make it ok?" Rachel asks when I get back.

"Yeah I think so. Listen, I know the owner of her building so I'll drive her car back to her place when I close up here and have him help me with getting her keys back to her."

Rachel narrows her eyes at me again and cocks her head to the side. "What?" I ask.

She purses her lips and shakes her head slowly. "Nothing. I've just never seen you actually pay that much attention to a piece of ass who clearly wasn't interested."

"Shut up Rache. She's not a piece of ass, she's…she's Seven."

Rachel raises both eyebrows and asks, "What the hell is seven?"

"Savannah. Savannah is Seven…at least, that's what I used to call her when we were young." I walk to the back of the bar and through the double doors to my office, not taking notice that Rachel is following me, though not surprised either.

"Hmm…I don't remember you calling her that. So you know her but you've never fucked her? How do I find that so hard to believe? I would've assumed you've had a sample of just about every piece of ass in this town, Bryant."

*This girl is becoming a pain in my ass.*

I turn towards her and raise my voice. "Yeah, well contrary to your ridiculous beliefs, Rachel, I guess I must've missed a few. You didn't know her back then and besides, now that Ivy and I…"

*Fuck.*

*Know when to shut up, Bryant.*

Closing my eyes for a moment, I take deep breath and let it out before looking back to a startled Rachel. Damnit, I probably just hurt her feelings.

"Yeah. Exactly…you and Ivy." She stresses. "I'm glad you're showing a little maturity for once. Maybe you're learning from your mistakes."

*What?*

"Are you calling Ivy a mistake?"

She's taken aback. I actually put the girl in her place for once. "No, I…I didn't mean it like that."

I'm starting to see RED. "You sure as shit better not have."

Rachel quickly raises her hands in front of her in defeat. "I know. I know, Bryant. I'm sorry. I didn't mean it like that. Tell me what your relationship is with Savannah now."

Trying to calm down, I tell Rachel, "There isn't one. And there wasn't one back then either, you know that. I wanted her so badly in high school but we were different people then. Now she's back and just knowing what she's been through…her loss…God." I shake my head. "She's broken Rachel. Shattered, I imagine. You know her story just as well as I do. I don't know how someone comes back from that."

"That's bullshit, Bryant. Take a look in the mirror. You broke not too long ago, and look how far you've come since then. What do you mean you don't know how someone comes back from that? It's just a little different for you. Circumstances were…different." She shrugs.

I nod my head. "Yeah. Yeah I guess. Look Rache, I need to figure things out okay? Just give me a chance to do that and please don't say anything stupid to her, and definitely don't say anything to Ivy. Let me do this on my terms, alright? Please?"

She thinks for a moment. "I'll try not to butt in unless I have to. I'm only thinking of her, and you know what I mean. Just…don't do anything stupid."

Like a perfectly timed episode of Candid Camera, Sloan waltzes into my office and throws himself on the couch against the wall. "Hey man, I saw you talking to that girl that just left. Did you even recognize who she was? That was Savannah fuckin' Sanders! I told you she was back in town." He chuckles as he turns my direction smirking. "I seem to recall you having a permanent boner over that girl, dude! I can't believe you let her leave!"

"Shut the fuck up about it, Sloan, and leave her alone." I come to her defense a littler earlier than I expected, but I know things about her that nobody else knows and I'll be damned if I'm going to let anyone treat her like a piece of meat. Sloan is the only one who knew about my feelings for Savannah when we were young. You can only keep so much information from your best friend. We've been together a long time, Sloan and me, causing shenanigans and working over the women around town, but having Ivy in my life has helped me settle down a little. I'm not the guy I once was. Sloan is still my best friend and business partner, but even he doesn't know all my secrets anymore.

Sliding my eyes in Rachel's direction, I see her eyebrow raise, questioning my motives once again. I get it. She has every right to judge me based on my past actions. I nod my head. "Relax Rache. I have no plans to be an asshole. I promise."

\*\*\*\*\*

The bar closes at midnight and I'm ready to walk out the door by twelve thirty. I send a quick text to my buddy, Cole, who owns the apartment building where Savannah lives. Hopefully he's still awake and can help a brother out.

26

Me: Hey man I need a favor. You up?

Cole: Yep. S'up?

Me: I'm dropping off Savannah's car. She lives in your building. Can you meet me outside in five?

Cole: Sure.

What I need to ask him can't be done in writing since it's basically breaking the law. Hopefully he doesn't think I'm a psycho. We went to college together and were frat brothers, but we weren't necessarily close. I hop in Savannah's car and start the engine. Immediately, I'm being serenaded by Luke Bryan.

*So she's a country girl.*

It's one of his slower songs about loving someone to the moon and back. Immediately I feel like I'm violating a private moment for her; that maybe these kinds of songs are all she listens to. My hand slips down to her key chain. It's larger than normal. I can't see it because it's dark outside, so I hit the inside light above my head for a moment to get a better look at what I'm holding on to.

*A footprint?*

The keychain holding all her keys is a keychain with a footprint on it. No name, no date, no color. Just a metal footprint that clearly belongs to a newborn baby. Damn if I don't feel a quick pang of sadness for her right now. I lay my head back on the headrest and close my eyes for just a moment as I listen to the rest of the song. When it ends I slowly inhale a deep breath, turn off the overhead light, and shake away my thoughts.

*God, she smells like Heaven.*

In two minutes I'm parked in the lot outside her building and walking to the main entrance where Cole is waiting for me.

"You know Savannah?" I nod my head toward the building.

"Of course. Real sweet girl but can be a bitch when she wants to be." He rolls his eyes. "She keeps to herself mostly. I never hear from her except for tonight; had to let her into her apartment. She lost her keys. Was she just at your bar?"

"Shit!" I look down at the keys in my hand. Not only does the key ring hold a car key, but two other keys as well. One is obviously her apartment key. I didn't even think about the fact that she wouldn't have been able to get into her apartment. I'm such an asshole. I roll my eyes as my words from earlier smack me in the face.

*Relax Rache, I'm not an asshole, I promise.*

"Yeah, I imagine she does keep to herself mostly and yeah, I have her keys right here. I drove her car back here for her. Anyway, look. I didn't want to ask you this via text because, well, I know it's breaking the law a little."

Cole's eyes light up ever so slightly at the mention of breaking the law, like I'm about to ask him to streak through the building or something like in our college days.

"I'd like to leave her car keys in her apartment with a note. I promise I won't touch her or wake her and if there's any sound coming from her apartment I won't even go in. I'll just leave the keys with you. I just want to make sure she's safe. She had a little too much to drink tonight." Good God what the hell am I asking here? I want to walk freely through her apartment and I expect him to say yes? Is it still breaking and entering if I have a key? Maybe there's a loophole. Maybe she won't get pissed and chop off my balls.

"You just want to drop her keys off in her apartment? Why don't you just shove a note under her door that you have the keys so she has to come see you to get them?"

I cock my head at the dumbass standing in front of me. "And how is she going to get to me tomorrow morning to get the keys to her car when I live miles away from here and she won't have a car? And how will she lock her apartment tomorrow when she leaves?"

"Oh, yeah." Cole nods. "Okay. Let's do it. But if there's any sound whatsoever coming from her apartment, I'm not doing this. And if she calls the cops, you totally stole the fucking keys from me."

"Deal." I nod. "Let's go."

I follow Cole to her apartment since I have no idea which one it is. When we reach her door he puts his ear against it to listen for any evidence that Savannah may be awake. I can't help but smirk and chuckle softly to myself when I see that she lives in apartment B-7. Seven must be her lucky number.

"I don't hear anything. I'll wait close by in case she starts screaming."

"Thanks, man." I half smile. I can feel my hand shaking slightly as I insert the key into the lock and open the door. Once I'm in I notice the chain lock she has for the door but obviously didn't use. I hope it's

28

because she was too drunk to think of it and it's not something she does all the time. It's not safe to leave it unlocked.

*Obviously.*

I lay her keys on the small table inside her door, assuming that's probably where she keeps them. On the table already is a traveling coffee mug, a stack of post-it notes, and a pen. I quickly leave a note for her next to her keys so she realizes that someone brought her car back for her.

*Savannah is in this apartment.*

*I can smell her.*

*Sleeping?*

*I should check on her.*

*I should absolutely not check on her.*

Against my better judgment I continue into her apartment and turn to quietly close her door. I make my way into her kitchen and look around. It's dark but she's left a light on over her sink. She must wake up throughout the night and need a drink.

*A drink.*

*Perfect!*

I search the cupboards until I find her glasses and quietly take one out and fill it with water. It won't be cold but it's still water. I place it on the counter and look through more of her cupboards, hoping to find some Advil. Many of her cupboards are bare. She doesn't keep much for herself around here – just a few dishes, glasses and mugs. My heart melts for her a little more.

*She deserves so much more than this.*

A-ha! I find a bottle already open sitting farther down on the counter. I pull three of them out and lay them next to the glass of water. Going back to grab a post-it note, I scribble a quick note to her in hopes it'll help with the hangover she's bound to have in the morning. I want to check on her so badly but I just can't risk being seen. She doesn't ever need to know I was here, that just seeing her again has brought back feelings I had forgotten I had. Life gets in the way sometimes and we forget about things until they're presented to us a second time and in a different circumstance. Wishing this were a happier circumstance, I make my way back to her door, pulling it closed behind me and watching as Cole locks it from the outside with his key.

"Thanks, man. I owe you one."

"Anytime, Bryant, and your secret is safe with me."

"Thanks." As much as I wish I could just sit outside and wait for her to wake up so I can make nice, I know that's a ridiculous idea. This is going to take time. I'm going to have to play it cool if I even have a half a chance with this girl's heart. She's not going to throw it out there very easily, that I do know. Somehow, I'll have to make her see that she needs me.

*Chapter 4*

I don't feel nearly as bad as I should, having just woken up from a night of pretty heavy drinking. It's almost disappointing. Maybe I'm just not the lush I thought I was, or maybe that asshole of a bartender was watering down the drinks. Sitting up in bed doesn't cause the room to spin as I expected it would, and my head isn't hurting worse than a dull ache. Regardless, I make my way to the kitchen to grab some Advil and orange juice, and maybe even a quick bowl of oatmeal. I walk into the kitchen towards the sink to grab a glass from the cupboard above except…there is already a glass of water sitting out on the counter, a bottle of Advil right next to it. A yellow sticky note lies next to them that reads,

**Take two and make some toast.**
**You'll feel better.**

"What the fuck?" I say aloud.

*This isn't my handwriting.*

*Who the hell was in my apartment? Are they still here?*

*Shit!*

"Hello?" I say a little louder than usual for someone who lives alone. Still holding onto the note, I quietly tip toe through the kitchen to my living room, shaking a bit with every step. Nobody other than my parents and Cole has a key to my apartment. I don't know why I'm just now deciding to go all silent ninja once I've already said hello. Not one of my brighter moments. A quick and silent walk through every room in the apartment shows no evidence of someone having been here.

*Was I that drunk that I don't remember?*

I walk to my door and confirm to myself that it is indeed locked but laying on the table right inside the door where I usually throw my mail is my car key with another note.

**It's parked out front. You're welcome.**

"What the…?" I mumble.

Quickly I dash to the front window where I can clearly see my red Ford Fusion parked in the lot.

*I didn't drive my car back last night.*

*I walked.*

*Nobody has my car keys.*

*Who the fuck moved my car?*

*And why?*

Having absolutely no clue how any of this matches up, I walk back to my room and grab my phone. I send a text message to Rachel asking her if it was her that moved my car. She doesn't answer right away so I gather that she must still be sleeping off last night as well. Needing to hit the grocery store before I go to work, I make my way to the bathroom to get myself decently ready for the day. The shop doesn't open until noon, so I have just enough time to get what I need for the next few days.

Ten minutes later, I'm making my way through the aisles of Save-A-Lot, throwing my necessities into my cart. Since I spend a lot of time alone, I've become a good cook. It's easier to learn to cook for myself than it is to be spotted around town eating by myself. I suppose I could live off of ramen noodles and Spaghetti-o's like the college students do, but who can eat that shit as an adult? Yeah it sucks sometimes having more left overs than I know what to do with, but at least it provides me with a decent lunch the next day. I get through the produce section, picking up my favorite vegetables, and turn down aisle four for a few other ingredients for tonight's dinner.

"Seven Sanders...it's good to see you up and at 'em this morning." I hear the male voice say. I turn my head from where I just grabbed a bag of noodles with my mouth hanging open.

*Fuck. Not the bartender again.*

"Looks like you're making it through the morning just fine huh? The alcohol didn't do you in, I guess." He smirks.

"It's Seven *Turner*. Savannah Turner, I mean." I say shaking my head. "My name isn't Seven..."

He leans effortlessly against the shelf in front of me. "Yeah well my name isn't Jackass or Asswipe but you seemed to have no problem calling me by those names last night, sweetheart."

"Hey, if the shoe fi..." My voice fades away when I finally make eye contact with the guy speaking to me. The short soft hair, the deep brown eyes, the most likely very sexy body under those clothes...it takes my breath away for just a moment. There's something about him though that I can't place.

"Do I know you?"

"Apparently not."

"Should I know you?"

"I would've thought."

*What the hell...*

"Do you always talk like Dr. Seuss?"

He smirks. "Is that what you now deduce?"

*Hmm. He's good.*

"Ok, point for you. Now how do you know who I am? Are you an old client?"

He tries to hold back a smile but can't.

"Nope, I'm your old friend Bryant."

*Har har.*

"My old friend Bry..." I narrow my eyes. It can't be.

"Wood," he says quietly. "Bryant Wood."

I gasp loudly. "Bryant 'The Giant' Wood?" I ask. "That Bryant?"

He winces and throws his head back in a hearty laugh. "Touché, Seven. I guess I deserved that. Nicknames can be brutal. So you do remember me then." He grins, crossing his arms in front of him, an action that causes his biceps to bulge in front of me.

*Holy hell.*

"Remember you?" I raise an eyebrow before rolling my eyes. "How could I ever forget 'Mr. Climb-my-stalk-and-free-the-giant' Wood?" I cast my eyes quickly over the body standing in front of me, surprised that I could actually see it as desirable, if it didn't belong to Bryant

Wood, the biggest asshole of my high school class. "I can't believe I didn't recognize you. You've uh... changed." I try not to notice how his shirt sleeves tighten at his biceps when his arms cross, but sometimes a girl can't help it. Football obviously agreed with him. Bryant's body reminds me of a young farmer in a way: hard around the edges from days of hard work, but built and warm enough to want to snuggle up next to.

*Whoa.*

*Where the fuck did that come from?*

I shake my head, blinking quickly and hoping that Bryant isn't perceptive enough to know what I was thinking just now. The smirk on his face tells me I'm probably wrong.

"Doesn't everybody?" he asks. "I mean look at you, Seven. You're...beautiful." His eyes drag leisurely down my body and back up, resting on the mounds of flesh attached to my chest, making it very clear that like most men, Bryant is a boob man. I watch as he licks his lips like a lion about to pounce on his lunch. Think again, buddy.

*Yeah, I'm not the little fat girl anymore douchebag.*

"Yeah? Well, I guess people change as they grow up don't they Bryant? Maybe I should say thanks...except I don't really feel that grateful. You certainly did a bang-up job of telling everyone how much I was changing back in the day." I roll my eyes again and shake my head. "If you'll excuse me I just need to finish my shopping and get home before I have go to work."

Bryant looks caught off-guard for a second, tilting his head in confusion. He shakes his head slightly and says, "I'm sorry. Did I...offend you in some way?"

Ugh. It's not worth the argument and will only make me look like the petty one. He doesn't even remember that far back. "No." I roll my eyes. "Don't worry about it."

I watch as he inhales deeply, not saying anything, before he looks in my shopping cart. I suddenly feel violated, like someone just peeked into my medicine cabinet.

"Carrots, celery, peas, noodles...looks like someone's making homemade soup," he says to change the subject.

"So what if I am?"

"I like soup," he says.

"I don't care."

"Maybe we should have soup together sometime."

*Like Hell.*

"I don't think that's necessary."

"Why not?"

"Because I didn't like you then, and I don't think I like you now." I spit out.

"Ouch." He chuckles. "Why don't you like me now?"

"Because I don't like men who push themselves on women."

"Is that what you think I'm doing?" he asks.

"Isn't it?"

"Not at all, Seven. I'm just trying to have a friendly conversation with an old classmate who, yes, happens to be attractive, and like myself, also happens to like soup. Is that such a bad thing?"

The dimple in his cheek is a cute feature. I hadn't noticed it before.

"The jury's still out on that one."

"Well, when the verdict is in, please do let me know. Chicken soup is good for the soul as they say; I mean, I hear they write books about it and stuff." That tickles my funny bone enough to finally chuckle out loud. Damn him and his smart mouth.

"Yeah, I guess they do." I nod my head towards his shopping cart, taking stock in what he's purchasing. "Didn't you know 'Trix are for kids,' Bryant? I'm pretty sure the age limit on that sugar intake is like twelve or something."

He chuckles but doesn't seem too affected by my teasing him. "Yeah. I guess you caught my guilty pleasure. Could be worse though, huh?"

"Yeah," I say quietly. I glance at him one more time with a tight smile. "Look it was nice to see you this morning and I appreciate the catch up, but I really do have to get home. I work soon."

"Yeah. It was nice to see you too *Savannah*." He says with annunciation so that I acknowledge that he indeed used my real name. For a fleeting moment his smile fades and he looks at me with what appears to be sincerity, though I'm sure it's an act. "I'm glad you made it home safely last night. I'll uh…I'll see ya around."

"Sure. See ya." I half smile and continue down the aisle, turning the corner into the dairy section, telling myself over and over to not look back over my shoulder to see if he's watching me... because I'm not interested.

*He's no good for me.*
*Don't fall into the trap Savannah.*
*I'm not interested.*
*I don't care.*
*'Cause I'm not interested.*

# Chapter 5

# *Bryant*

Oh fuck. I must've called her "fat", and from the way it sounds I did it on more than one occasion. That's why she finds me repulsive? Because I called her fat when we were in junior high? How do chics remember that shit? Does she not see, quite literally, that people change? I doubt there's much use in apologizing. I sense a grudge that's not just going to go away with a "Sorry about what I said, but you look beautiful" almost fifteen years too late. I watch her continue down the aisle and disappear around the corner. I tell myself repeatedly in my head not to go after her. It won't do any good. This is going to take some time.

All I remember of her is the chunky seventh grader I had swimming class with in middle school. I remember her from some of my elementary school classes but it's not like we were ever really close. We were as close as kids are at that age I guess for the sheer fact that all the homeroom moms knew each other. Other than that she was a froo-froo girl and I was a boy with cooties. She changed over the summer after eighth grade and many people noticed, but in high school she was the numbers nerd and I just focused on how to score…on and off the field. I was the typical high school boy letting my dick make my decisions for me. Savannah Sanders took my breath away back then but I didn't stand a chance with her. I wasn't her type and by all school stereotypes she wasn't mine. But now? Now, she has eyes that pierce me, hair like the softest chocolate silk and a body any guy would be crazy not to want to lose himself in. God I have my work cut out for me with this girl.

I try not to think about her, but everything about her has me twisted up from the inside out. I shouldn't get involved with someone who has walls as high as I'm sure she does. She's not going to open up to me very easily, but damn if I don't want to try. I can't believe I didn't recognize her before she walked into the bar. All I cared about last night was flirting with the ladies in order to make a little more money for the bar. Once I realized who she was I fell for her all over again immediately. Fuck if I didn't want to embrace her and tell her how sorry I was for everything she's gone through in the past several years. She's been like an urban legend around Bardstown. Not many see her around socially.

I have to help Savannah see life outside of the shell I'm sure she's living in. To show her that there is still life to live, and people to live it with…people who want to see her happy. With any luck Rachel will be on my side and willing to help. If there's one person in this town that I need with me on this, it's Rachel. I need to talk to her about it before she blabs to Savannah. She could ruin everything for me.

I drive through town and walk into Rachel's salon in less than ten minutes.

"Mornin' Rache."

I'm greeted with a double eyebrow lift and a doubting look as she organizes her tools and supplies for the day.

"So? You're not in jail, so I'm guessing you didn't get arrested last night for stalking, or assault, or grand theft auto."

"Very funny, and no, none of the above. I returned her car just like I said I would, dropped her keys off in her apartment, and made sure she had water and Advil for this morning. I was the perfect gentleman, thank you very much.

Rachel's jaw drops. "You went into her apartment? What did she say? Did she throw your ass out?"

I shake my head, shyly smirking. "Uh, not exactly. She was asleep. Didn't even know I was there."

"WHAT?" Rachel's eyes grow huge. "You were in her apartment while she was there but she didn't KNOW it? Are you fucking nuts? Wait. Don't answer that," she says with her hands up in defense. "You are fucking nuts."

"Yes I suppose I am, but she was taken care of, and that's all that matters. More than I can say for you. You just let the poor drunk girl walk home in the middle of the street by herself."

"Only because I knew you were watching her and keeping her safe."

"A-ha!" I say with a smile. "So you DO trust me and you DO like me!"

She shakes her head, failing to hide her smile. "I'll never admit that so don't brag. But for what it's worth, thank you for helping her. She needed last night and I'm glad she was able to let her hair down a little."

"Yeah. Yeah, I know. Listen, speaking of Savannah, there's something I need to talk to you about."

"You have my undivided..." She gazes up at the clock on the wall. "At least until Savannah walks through the door in about ten minutes."

"I want to help her."

"What do you mean help her?"

"She's not living her life Rache. She's hiding in her apartment."

"You don't know that. Do you know anything about her?"

"Well for starters she's never been in my bar before and pretty much everybody in this town has been to my bar. Secondly, you told me she never goes out, and thirdly, I know all I need to know right now." I know I'm right about Savannah and damnit, I know Rachel knows that I'm right about her too.

She looks at me. "And you think you're the guy who can bring her out of her shell?"

"You think I'm not? Cause that's not what you were preachin' last night."

"I didn't say that."

"Then what are you thinking?"

"Actually, I'm thinking several thoughts. One, you definitely have an uphill battle. She's not easy to please and the walls she has up may as well be the thickest cement walls you've ever seen. She's like a damn panic room. Two, it'll be fun watching you try to be a gentleman when

I've seen you as the bad boy flirt machine in the past, and three, what about...?"

My eyes snap up to hers. "What about what?" Looking at her stern eyes staring me down I know exactly what she's referring to and I don't want to go there right now. "It's not a big deal right now Rachel. I can handle it."

Rachel pulls scissors out of her apron and lays them on the counter in front of her. She's quiet for a moment, hopefully contemplating my game plan. She exhales loudly before turning to face me again. I'm staring at her like a puppy hoping for his next treat.

"Okay look. I want to see Savannah happy just as much as you do. She's my friend and I care about her. But you make one stupid mistake...even one time, and it's over, do you understand? I'm in this for everyone's happiness. I'm just not sure how you plan to work this out."

"I'll make it work. I owe her that much. Just...don't tell her anything okay?"

Rachel slowly shakes her head. "You know I won't interfere with your life, Bryant. I just hope you're doing the right thing and not just for yourself...and why on earth do you think you owe Savannah anything when you barely even know her?"

*Fuck. Think fast Wood!*

"I just..." Shaking my head, I try to come up with an excuse for my slip fast. "I was a douche to her in high school so you know, I owe her. I'm not the same person I was back then."

Rachel nods and I smile, relieved that she's being supportive. "Look, I'll get out of your hair and let you get the shop opened. Thanks for the talk. I'll catch you later, okay?"

She shakes her head in defeat. She knows I always get what I want. I don't take no for an answer if I don't have to. "See you, Bryant. Have a good one."

# Chapter 6

# ᗡ *Savannah*

The drive from my apartment to the salon takes only a few minutes but in those moments Bryant Wood causes my mind to travel back to seventh grade, the year I began to hate the world and all boys in it…or maybe I just hated Bryant.

I don't know whose bright idea it was back then to make middle school kids take co-ed swimming classes, but it happened. There definitely weren't many kids happy about it. On one hand, there were the girls who were forced to wear bathing suits right out of the nineteen fifties, except that they were a nasty worn out red color with numbers written in permanent marker in the corners, and were assigned to each of us. Why we couldn't wear our own one-piece bathing suit is beyond me. Every girl hated locker room time. It was the time we sized each other up. Whose boobs were growing? Who was wearing a bra? Who shaved their legs? Who didn't shave their legs? And on top of all that drama, there was the mystery of who was on their period each week. Didn't want to swim that day? We just told Mrs. Farabee, our gym teacher, that it was shark week. No questions asked, although that also meant we sat on the bleachers watching everyone else swim. We may as well have been wearing a huge scarlet letter on our foreheads.

On the other hand, the poor middle school boys were forced to wear tight red banana hammocks that not only rarely fit right, but allowed everyone to see the instant hard-on each of them had watching the girls in their less than attractive bathing suits. At that pubescent age it didn't matter what a girl was wearing. Boys got boners constantly just imagining what was under those things, and God forbid one of those girls be a little more blessed in the chest.

Our first day back in the pool after summer break was a day that will forever be etched in my mind. It was the day my schoolgirl crush on Bryant Wood ended, the day I secretly wished he would uncontrollably shit his pants every day until the end of the year, so that he would understand the embarrassment of being judged by a member of the opposite sex.

I had just jumped off the diving board and into the pool. The water was a refreshing change from the steamy stuffy natatorium. Bryant was next up to jump so I swiftly swam out of his way toward the ladder on the wall so that I could exit as he jumped. I was just hoisting myself up the ladder and out of the pool when Bryant swam over to where I was. He watched me for a moment before giggling and saying "Man, someone got fat over the summer."

*What?*

*Did he really just say that?*

I didn't even know how to respond. How do you respond to a comment like that, especially when it's coming from the one person you have had a complete and utter crush on for the past several years? "Shut up Bryant," was all I could say. I walked away completely defeated, but I had to hide it from everyone else for the rest of the class period. If that weren't bad enough, that afternoon on the bus, for whatever reason, his relentless teasing just wouldn't stop.

"Savaaaaaanah," he would sing. His tune was completely made up and stupid.

"Savaaaaaanaaaaaah…Hey, Savannah, did you know your name sort of sounds like you're saying Seven-ah? Anyone ever call you that Savannah? Seven? Seven Sanders?"

"Shut up Bryant. Leave me alone."

"Okay Seven. But I'm going to call you Seven from now on because your name sounds like Seven. Do you get it? Sev-an-ah?" He annunciated each syllable so everyone around us heard him. Some of the kids would giggle but I just stared ahead of me. I didn't want to give him the satisfaction of knowing that what he was doing was bothering me. In reality, he was breaking my heart, and making me angry with myself for ever liking him in the first place. Stupid fucking love.

\*\*\*\*\*

"Hey Rache," I greet Rachel as I enter the salon. I head to the back of the shop to store my purse and keys and grab my apron. My first client should be here any minute. Rachel is already working on Mrs. Wither's weekly style.

"Well good afternoon' to you too birthday girl!" Rachel smiles.

*Oh yeah…it's noon already.*

"It's not my birthday anymore. That was yesterday. Today is today."

"Yeah well it looked like you were having a great time last night. Thanks for letting us take you out. Glad you made it here safely this morning."

"Thanks. Yeah, I did have a pretty good time. And speaking of making it here safely this morning, were you in my apartment last night? Did you get my text earlier?" I whisper to her. "Was I that drunk that I don't remember letting you in?"

Rachel shakes her head. "Nope. Wasn't me."

"Huh. What the hell then?"

Scrunching her eyebrows at me, Rachel asks, "Why do you ask?"

"Well…because my car was parked in the lot outside my building, my keys were waiting for me on my front table, and there was a note on the counter with some Advil and water. I know I wasn't that trashed that I would forget doing all those things. I mean, I certainly wouldn't write myself a note."

I look over at Rachel just in time to see her roll her eyes and smirk to herself as she curls another piece of Mrs. Wither's hair.

Narrowing my eyes at her, I step towards her and quietly say, "You know something."

She's quiet for a moment, most likely contemplating how to respond. The shit-eating grin on her face tells me I'm right.

"I might know something." She closes her eyes tightly and laughs, almost like she knows she just got caught with her hand in the damn cookie jar.

"If it wasn't you, then who was it? Heather or Audrey?"

"Nope." She giggles.

"Damnit Rache. You let someone break into my apartment last night? I gave you that key because I trusted you! You're the only one who…"

"Whoa whoa whoa!" She smirks. "Stop right there. One, I didn't *let* anyone break into your apartment. I was nowhere near your apartment. I was at the bar last night until it closed. Two, I also didn't give anyone your key, so slow your roll there sister. It wasn't me."

"Okay it wasn't you, but you know who it was, and I'm going to assume that you at least thought about my safety in knowing that someone was going to break into my apartment, so out with the details Rachel!"

"Well…" She puts down the curling iron she was using and begins to comb out the curls in Mrs. Wither's hair. Mrs. Wither looks just as confused as I do in getting to the bottom of my mystery visitor. "You were getting along so well with Bryant Wood last night…"

"Bryant Wood? Bartender last night Bryant Wood? That Bryant Wood?" Something in my chest flips.

Rachel nods her head slowly, smiling. "The very same."

*What the fuck?*

*No wonder he asked how I was at the grocery store.*

"Rachel! Why the hell would you allow that guy in my apartment?" My mind is going a mile a minute. How the hell could she think that was a good idea?

"What's the big deal? He said you knew him."

I throw Rachel an exaggerated huff and almost shout, "Yes, Rachel…KNEW would be the operative word here. I knew him. We grew up around each other and went to school together. He was a douche back then and he's a douchebag now."

*Albeit an attractive douchebag.*

*Did he see me sleeping?*

*Did he watch me?*

She smirks again, not hiding her amusement of the situation at all from me. "Well anyway, for the record, I didn't *allow* him anywhere. I didn't know he was going to enter your apartment. How he did that is beyond…no, wait. He went to school with your apartment supervisor, Cole. I'm guessing that's how he got in. But Savannah, before you get all pissy about it, think about something first."

"I'm all ears," I say, deadpanned.

"He followed you home last night to make sure you made it safely into your apartment. He said you walked down the middle of the damn street!"

"Yeah because I was creeped out. I thought someone was behind me. Guess I was right." I cross my arms over my chest and tilt my head, staring at her as she continues.

"After he followed you home and made sure you made it in, he came back here. He already had your car keys Savannah." She laughs. "He showed them to me behind your back last night when you were telling me you were going to walk home. He must've gotten them from your purse or something. I don't know. The guy is slick, I'll give you that. But he drove your car back to your place for you and he made sure the keys were returned for you. So, um, I'm guessing he's also the one who left you the Advil and water." She raises her eyebrows in my direction and I see the suggestive notion all over her face.

*Why would he do that?*

*For me?*

I feel my expression change from one of irritation to utter confusion. I don't understand at all why a guy like that would do that for me and not come knocking for a booty call. That's what all guys want. I roll my eyes at the thought and remind myself that I'm pissed at Bryant for…whatever it is he did.

"Ugh! Wait till I get my hands on Cole for being Bryant's accomplice and giving him a key! I might have to kill him."

The bell above the door dings when my first client of the day comes in.

"Good morning Mrs. Bently. How are you this mornin'?" I say a little too bitterly towards a customer undeserving of my attitude.

"Fine, dear. Just a cut and style this morning, please."

I smile to reassure her that I'm okay and not upset with her or anyone else. "Sure thing. I'll meet ya right at the back sink. Come on back."

I look over at Rachel, who is watching me in her mirror as she sprays Mrs. Wither's hair. I quickly wipe the smile from my face so she knows how serious I am. "This convo isn't over Rache. I'm so not okay with this."

"Yeah, yeah. I hear ya, but Savannah, listen." Rachel turns around to watch me walk back to the sinks.

"What?"

"He may have been a douchebag then, and I'm not defending his past, but the Bryant Wood that I know is actually a pretty decent guy. Cut him some slack, ok? You don't know his story."

I roll my eyes. "Oh please, enlighten me. Tell me his story."

She shakes her head adamantly. "It's not my story to tell. He'll tell you when he's ready."

*What does that mean?*

"Okaaay." I say slowly. My mind spins frantically as I try to come up with some sort of horrific story of his past that he must've suffered through, but quite frankly, none can come close to mine. Besides, he seems like he's doing just fine now.

# Chapter 7

# ⮾ *Savannah*

I don't see Bryant around much at all the next week, except for the awkward moment in the drug store a couple days ago. I had just stopped by to pick up some more Advil and a new tube of toothpaste when he almost ran right into me on his way out of the store. He had been checking his phone and not paying much attention. Oddly, he apologized and without saying much of anything, told me he was running late, and left. I wouldn't have given it another thought had it not been for the no less than four prescription bags in his hands. Well, that and the fact that when he saw me he seemed a bit flustered...like he wanted to talk to me but...couldn't.

*Is he sick?*

*Is someone in his family sick?*

I know it's none of my business, but four prescriptions at one time is a lot. That coupled with the fact that Bryant Wood was not his usual charming, flirty self was odd. Needless to say, I've been thinking more and more about him after seeing him that day. Rachel's words are etched in my brain about Bryant's story.

*He'll tell you when he's ready.*

What could it possibly be? Cancer? A sick wife? Is he missing a leg? I don't know, but I allow all possible scenarios to play out in my head.

The following week I'm walking down the street to The Java Joint to get lunch for Rachel and me when I see him again. Bryant Wood is just a few store-fronts down from where I'm standing, walking out of Peirson's Gifts. I probably wouldn't have even noticed him if it weren't for the fact that he's carrying a gift box wrapped in red and silver paper, and a small bouquet of pink and yellow roses. I stand there momentarily wondering who he would be purchasing a gift like that for. Obviously it's for the girl in his life; maybe it's for his mother or grandmother. Maybe he has a sick cousin or something. I take a deep breath and shake the thoughts from my head.

*Does he have a girlfriend?*

*I'm sure he has a girlfriend.*

*I don't even care.*

*I'll ask Mom.*

There's no way he's not committed. As much as I don't want to admit it because of the negative feelings I harbor for him, the guy is, indeed, attractive. Working as a bartender, I don't doubt that he has girls all over him pretty much every night. I remember seeing him in action a couple weeks ago at the bar, though I didn't know who he was at the time.

Bryant walks out to the street and gets into a black truck. It doesn't surprise me at all that he drives a Chevy Silverado pick-up truck. I roll my eyes as I open the door to the restaurant, shaking my head at my own thoughts. "It's probably for his flavor of the month," I mutter to myself in reference to the gift he's carrying. "She's probably a skinny bitch."

"May I help you miss?"

I turn my head away from the store-front window to see the girl at the counter looking at me with raised eyebrows and a smile waiting to take my order.

"Oh yeah, sorry. I called an order in for Savannah Turner."

The girl behind the counter turns and grabs a bag sitting behind her. She lifts up the tag attached to the take out bag to read it back to me making sure my order is correct.

"One Gobbler and one French Pig?"

*Well, nobody's ever called me a skinny bitch…*

"Yep. That's the one. Thank you." I pay for our lunches and walk out the door, trying very hard not to crack up laughing.

*****

*Can this day be going any slower?*

As the afternoon wears on my energy starts to drain, and my body aches, mid-afternoon slump I guess. I'll be ready to get home and curl up on my couch for the night so I can continue binge watching episodes of *Boston Legal* on Netflix. It's an old show, yes, but something about the relationship of Alan Shore and Denny Crane gets me every time. Really, I think I'm just a huge James Spader fan.

"Hey Savannah, would you mind closing up this evening? I need to leave a little early to get to a dance recital on time."

"A dance recital? Who's dancing?"

Rachel smiles and scrunches up her nose. "My cousin, actually…she's like, my second cousin or something but whatever, we're a close family. She's so stinking cute in her little pink and purple tutu. I'll have to show you pictures tomorrow. She's three and a half and you can only imagine what watching a group of little girls that age trying to dance around on a stage looks like." She giggles.

*Peyton.*

*Peyton would be three and a half.*

*I'll never see her in a pink and purple tutu.*

*I'll never see her dance on a stage.*

"Savannah, are you okay? I lost you."

"I…I'm sorry. I guess I just stared off for a minute." I force my face to smile so that I don't worry Rachel, and so that I don't have to have a conversation that I desperately want to avoid at this very moment. "Sure, I'll close up. No problem. That sounds cute. I can't wait to see pictures tomorrow."

"Great. Thanks so much. I really appreciate it."

"No problem." I walk quietly back to the bathroom and take a quick look at myself in the mirror. My face is ashen and my eyes look tired. My stomach turns slightly and I think for a minute that perhaps I'll regret eating that French Pig panini for lunch. I take a minute to splash some water on my face and just focus on breathing in and out instead of on losing my lunch.

I make it through the end of the day and close up the salon, saying my goodbyes to Audrey and Heather, who had come in for the afternoon. I can't get back to my apartment fast enough. My blanket is calling my name, as are my favorite oversized sweatshirt, and my thickest socks. Damn if I'm not freezing my ass off right now, which I see as a bad sign. There's no way I don't have a fever.

I don't bother to stop anywhere on the way home. I just drive quickly the few blocks it takes to get there. When I enter my apartment I throw my keys on the table and head for the kitchen where I remember seeing the bottle of Advil. I grab three pills and a tall glass of water before heading to my bedroom. Grabbing a fresh towel from the pantry, I slip around the corner to the master bathroom. I always get a shower after a day at the salon. Undoubtedly, I have hair, other people's hair, all over me, and I feel nasty if I don't get it off of me before getting into my bed. Tonight, I'm happy to be able to stand under a scalding hot shower in hopes that something, anything, warms me up.

Unfortunately, it's not quite the heavenly escape I was hoping for. My body aches and I'm exhausted. I'm obviously coming down with something but I can't figure out yet what it is. Something just isn't right, but I just want to go to sleep. I'm sure I'll feel better in the morning. I pull on my pajamas and my thickest socks. Mom always told me when you're cold at night, socks do the trick and she was right. I roll into bed. deciding to not watch *Boston Legal*. I know I'll just sleep through it anyway, and I don't want to miss anything. It's lame that I'm going to bed with no supper at seven-thirty on a Wednesday night, but with any luck I'll feel much better in the morning.

*I miss Shawn.*

*He always took care of me when I was sick.*

*He would be keeping me warm right now.*

*Why do men always feel so warm and comfortable?*

I dream of him, of his arms wrapped around me, of his kisses running down my neck that make me shiver slightly. He lies behind me, my back to his chest, holding me in his arms, gently stroking my hair as I drift in and out of sleep. The sound of his voice humming to me soothes the ache in my body as I lay happily in his arms. I've missed this feeling, being held by a man. He makes me feel safe and loved and cherished.

His hand moves to my stomach and gently glides under my t-shirt. I know where he's headed and I smile to myself as I lay there with my eyes closed until he reaches his destination. The moment his hand brushes over my breast I feel the spark of electricity shoot through my entire body, like he's just flipped a switch inside of me. My breath hitches and I moan softly. I can feel his excited body next to mine. His breath is warm against my ear and I'm eager for more of him, more of his hands, more of his body, more of his kisses, more of his warmth. I feel his lips near my ear just before I hear him say "Baby, on a scale of one to four…I love you Seven."

Bryant?

WHOA!

My eyes open and I jolt up in my bed. I take a minute to look around to make sure I'm alone before closing my eyes and taking a very deep breath.

"What the fuck was that?" I ask myself.

*I did not just have a damn dream about Bryant Wood.*

*I must be sicker than I thought.*

*****

My cellphone is ringing. It's not on my night stand as it usually is. Sounds of the strumming guitar ringtone continue to fill up my room so I know it's nearby, I just don't know where. I crawl out of bed and hit the floor with a thud. My body feels unusually heavy, like I've been in bed for a whole day with the stomach flu, except I don't have the stomach flu. When I turn my head I spot my cellphone laying just under my bed and grab it to see that it's Rachel calling. I swipe the screen to answer her call.

"Hello?" The words almost don't make it out of my mouth. What happened to my voice? "Hello?" I say again.

"Savannah? Is that you? What the hell, are you okay?" she asks.

"Rachel?" I lean my body against my bed from where I'm sitting on the floor. My head falls back against my mattress. I have zero energy and just want to go back to sleep. "Yeah it's me. I'm sorry, I was just..." I can't think of what to say. I'm so tired.

"Savannah, you sound terrible. No wonder you're not at work."

"Huh? What do you mean not at..."

*What day is it? I'm not even sure anymore.*

I look at the clock on my night stand. It's eleven o-clock in the morning. I was supposed to be at work at eight. "Oh shit. Rachel, I'm sorry. I've been sleeping since about...I don't know...seven thirty last night? I went to bed with a fever and now, I just... I don't know what's wrong with me."

"Whoa. Savannah, that's awful. Do you need anything? I can stop at the store when I break for lunch."

"No, no. It's ok. I think I just want to sleep. Maybe I'll feel better in a few hours. I'm really sorry Rachel. I must've slept through my alarm...or maybe I just forgot to set it." I mumble.

"Totally okay babe. Audrey will clear your clients for today. Don't worry about it. You just get better okay?"

I clear my throat willing myself to sound somewhat normal. "Great, yeah. Thanks. Oh hey, how was that umm, dance thingy last night?"

Rachel chuckles lightly. "It was adorable as expected. I'll tell you all about it when you're feeling better. Maybe I'll bring some soup over this evening so you don't have to bother doing anything. Would that be okay? I'll just check in on you."

I smile at Rachel's request. She's so motherly I often wonder why she doesn't settle down with someone and have kids of her own. It's nice that she thinks of me though. "Yeah, that's fine." I yawn. "I'll see you later then Rache."

"Okay. See ya soon. Bye."

I hit the button on my phone to end the call and climb back into my bed for a few more hours...or days, of sleep.

# Chapter 8

# *Bryant*

"I got this," I mutter to myself in the mirror. That hot shower was great and the late morning run felt good, but it's done nothing for my nerves. What twenty-seven-year-old guy still gets nervous at the thought of seeing a girl? This is bull shit. Except it's not. She's the one that got away. Strike that, she's the one I never had the balls to try for, and now that's she's back, she's broken. At least she thinks she's broken, and damn if I can't blame her for thinking that after what she's been through. This is my one chance though, to fix my past, right my wrongs, and show her that I can be the one she needs to help guide her through the world of hurt that she lives in and bring her through to the other side. I owe her that much.

*I owe her everything, but she can't ever know that.*

I just have one thing I need to figure out.

Ivy.

How the fuck am I going to make this work?

Ivy's been my world for almost four years. I love her. She loves me, there's no denying that, but Savannah was my first crush, and damn if I'm not feeling the pull of her all over again. I'm all of a sudden pushing everything and *everyone* else aside for a just a minute. I know I have responsibilities…big responsibilities that I need to be focused on, but I can't get Savannah out of my mind. Her body, the way she felt when I touched her at the bar, the way her hair glistened under the bar lights. She's clouding my damn mind. Against my better judgement, I pull on my clothes, make sure I don't look like a slob, and head to the salon. Maybe if I catch Savannah having a good day I can get her alone at some point to just talk to her and show her I'm not the douchebag she mistook me for last week.

Fifteen minutes later I'm out of my car and entering the Great Lengths Hair Salon with a chocolate milkshake in my hand that isn't for me.

*Girls like chocolate milkshakes, right?*

"Hey Bryant. What's up? You need a quick cut this afternoon?" I raise my eyes to search for the voice speaking to me and see Audrey smiling at me from her station. I take a quick survey of the salon but don't spot Savannah. Maybe she's in the back.

"Uh, no, not today anyway. Is Rachel around? Or Savannah?"

"I'm right here!" I hear Rachel yell from the back room of the salon. "Come on back Bryant."

I nod to Audrey and head back to find Rachel mixing some goopy mayonnaise-like solution together in a bowl. It looks like pudding but it smells like shit.

"Whoa." I crinkle my nose and try not to breathe in too hard. "What is that stuff?"

Rachel laughs. "It's for coloring Mrs. Swanson's hair. What's up? You were lookin' for me?"

"No." I say quietly so that the other girls can't hear our conversation. "I'm actually looking for Seven. She not in today or what?"

Rachel eyes my chocolate milkshake. "Nope. Talked to her a few hours ago. She's actually pretty sick so I cancelled her clients today. I'm going to drop by later and check on her, make sure she's okay. She said she's been sleeping since early yesterday evening. She sounded terrible. Is that for me?" She nods to the milkshake in my hand before raising an eyebrow and smirking at me.

I tip the milkshake slightly in my hand. I had almost forgotten I was even holding one. "Uh…it wasn't, but it certainly is now. If she's sick, a milkshake is probably the last thing Seven needs."

Rachel shrugs. "Her loss is my gain then. Thanks."

"So you think she's really sick? With like, the flu or something?"

"Don't know. She said she had a fever and she said she's been sleeping a lot. Other than that she honestly didn't say but she definitely didn't sound like herself."

"Maybe I should check on her, make sure she's okay."

Rachel leans on her hip and crosses her arms in front of her. "Why would you do that?"

*What the fuck Rache…*

"Well why not? You were going to, weren't you?"

"Yeah…and I'm her friend, Bryant. And her coworker. What are *you* to her besides the creep that entered her apartment a couple weeks ago while she was sleeping?"

*Damn. She has a point.*

*I don't care. This is my chance.*

*I can do something nice for her.*

"I'm the guy who would like to enter her apartment and see her while she's awake so she can actually witness me being a nice guy instead of having to creep around."

Rachel looks exasperated. "Bryant, she's sick! She's not going to be up for company. Have you not been listening to me?" she shouts.

"For Pete's sake, yes Rache. I heard you loud and fucking clear. I'm fully capable of being a nice guy who takes care of a sick girl, you know."

Rachel looks at me like I just smacked her in the face with extremely hurtful words. Fuck that. She doesn't get to judge me. I know how to take care of a sick girl. I'm a goddamn pro really.

"I know, Bryant," she says. "I know you are. Sorry, I didn't mean it like that."

"And if I'm not mistaken, I've come to your aid a few times with a hot cup of…" I stop talking when the idea hits me right in my face.

*That's it!*

"Rachel, I'm doing this. I got this. Don't worry. Just text me later and I'll let you know how she is. Are you still on for tonight with Ivy? Cause this morning she was going on and on about manicures and pedicures and shit like that."

Rachel laughs and shakes her head. "Yes we are definitely doing girl's night. Don't worry, I've got it covered. Just don't mess this up."

I release the breath I was holding before I nod and give Rachel my victory smile. "I won't. And thank you for doin' this, Rache." I start to retreat from the back room of the salon so I can head to my next destination.

"Yeah, yeah, I hope I don't regret this." I hear her mumble as I head towards the door.

"Later, ladies." I nod to Audrey and Heather and hear their farewells as I leave the salon and hop into my truck.

*****

Putting the truck in reverse and heading out onto the road, anxiety creeps up at what I'm about to do. I know I told Rachel that I can take care of a sick girl, and I can, but this is a make-or-break situation for me. Either I'll win her over with my compassionate heart or I'll creep her out and forever be known to her as Stalker Number One. What does a twenty-seven-year-old woman want when she's sick? Does she just have a bad cold so she wants a warm blanket or is she in the constant state of puke and just needs a washcloth and a sturdy bucket? A guy needs to know these things and I hate to admit that I just don't. If she could just make it easy on me and tell me she wants to me to hold her, let her snuggle up next to me and sleep, that could make this day a victorious one. I doubt I'll get that lucky.

I pull into the nearest drug store and walk slowly down each aisle, hoping that my eye will catch something great that Savannah might really appreciate. I figure some Advil and Tylenol are good choices, along with plenty of Gatorade, just in case she's feeling dehydrated. Since I don't know which one is her favorite, I pick several different flavors. I steer clear of the lemon-lime one though because who drinks that shit? It tastes like cleaning solution…or at least what I think cleaning solution would taste like if I ever had to try it. I also spot a box of crackers and some Jell-O. When I was a kid, my grandmother used to tell me that there's always room for Jell-O. I believed her until she tricked me into eating spinach by putting it into her lime Jell-O. Never again Grandma, never again. I quickly add a few more things (and by a few I mean a lot more things) to my basket. I figure it's better to be safe than sorry.

"Whoa. Someone must be really sick. Are you sure you got everything?" The girl at the counter, the one with spiked purple hair and a nose ring hanging out of her nostril that I feel the urge to pull, pops her gum and smirks at me. I'm pretty sure she's making fun of me for buying what looks like all of aisle six but fuck if I don't give a rat's ass what she thinks.

"Well Princess, why don't you tell me since you seem so concerned with what I've chosen. She may be a little sick or she may be a lot sick. I won't know that until I see her so back up the sarcasm truck and help a guy out, huh?"

*And chew with your mouth closed. I'm sure your mother didn't raise a cow.*

Spikey cashier girl narrows her eyes at me and pops her gum one more time. She releases a loud sigh when she sees that I'm not in the mood for her sarcastic bullshit and chews on the side of her mouth for a moment while she surveys the products I've chosen. She grins and shakes her head, I think trying to stifle a laugh, and says, "A magazine."

"A what?"

"A magazine."

"A magazine? For what? What kind of magazine?"

"Look, when girls are sick they want to cuddle under a blanket and either sleep, watch TV, or read quietly. So go with something like *People* magazine."

"Why *People*?" I'm intrigued by her logic.

She sighs again before she speaks. I think I'm putting a kink in her day, but I'm sort of proud of myself for it. "Okay look, if you get an *Inquirer*, she'll assume you think she believes the shit they make up. If you get her *In-Style* magazine, she'll assume you think she needs help in that department. Does she need help in that department?"

"Not as far as I'm concerned."

"Okay well if you choose *Cosmopolitan*, you're basically telling her you want to screw her and whether you do or you don't, it's just not the right choice to make for your first time."

"Uh…this wouldn't be my first time, Princess." I smirk.

"You've purchased magazines for girls before?"

"No."

"Well then it's your first time Mr. Magazine Virgin, so just take my advice and get *People* magazine. Info about celebrities, stories about real people and it's not fully loaded with Oprah-spiration."

"Okay, okay. Just…give me whatever you think girls like." I like this girl. She's got spunk and definitely looks comfortable in her own shoes. Gotta give a girl props for that, but it's time to get to my gir…to Seven. I gather up my bags and throw them on the seat beside me in the truck and head down the road towards Seven's complex. She has no idea I'm doing this. The closer I get the more I feel those damn butterflies in my stomach. I don't know why I'm letting her make me so nervous. The poor girl is sick as shit. She needs me.

She just doesn't know it yet.

I gather up all the bags of stuff I purchased for my sick patient and head up to her apartment. Being that we're in a small town, I don't have to worry about getting buzzed in to her building, which is good because she would most likely tell me to go away. At some point she'll at the very least have to open the door.

*She'll open the door right?*

*I can't fuckin' break in again.*

I knock loudly three times in a row.

# Chapter 9

# Savannah

I must be dying. If I'm not dying, someone needs to just shoot me. Like a pathetic moron, I'm all wrapped up in my fleece blanket on the couch watching a TLC marathon of *Say Yes To The Dress*. I don't even know why I'm watching it. It's not at all a favorite of mine but there's something about it that keeps me watching. Maybe it's these girls who walk into a salon with a set budget and every damn time they fall for the dress that's way outside their comfort level. It's just a dress, bitches. It's one dress, sometimes two, that you will wear for a few hours on one day of your life. Put that sixteen thousand dollars towards a down payment for a house for Christ's sake. I roll my eyes one more time before I feel myself slipping away back into dreamland.

I'm startled awake when someone knocks loudly on my door. I lift open my eyelids to see that the stupid bitch on TV did, indeed, throw her budget out the window and purchased the sixteen-thousand-dollar dress.

Knock, knock, knock

There it is again. Someone really is at the door. Damnit.

*Oh yeah, Rachel said she was stopping by.*

I grab the remote and turn the volume down as I slowly stand up off the couch. "Don't know why you spent so much money honey. He'll probably die on you anyway."

*God, I have a headache.*

I reach for the door knob and swing the door open coming face to face with Bryant "The Giant" Wood.

*Son of a bitch. Now?*

"You're not Rachel."

"No ma'am, I am not," he says, half smiling. Actually, I'm not quite sure what to think of the look on his face. It's almost cautious. Something in my chest just did that flippy-thing again.

"What do you want, Bryant? And since when do you knock anyway? Don't you have a key?" I raise an eyebrow and give him my biggest "yeah I know what you did" expression. He coughs a little at my question. I must've caught him off guard.

"Ooh. Busted." He cringes. "And here I thought maybe I was just being a gentleman watching out for you in an inebriated state on your birthday, Seven. You're welcome by the way."

I stare at him deadpanned.

"Can I come in? These bags are getting heavy."

"What's in them?"

Bryant cocks his head to the side and smiles. "Why don't you let me in so I can show you?"

"Because I didn't invite you here, and in case you haven't noticed, I'm all sorts of sick. I'm pretty sure I have the plague and I..."

"Savannah," he interrupts me.

"What?"

"Trust me, okay? I'm here for you. I know you're sick. That's why I'm here. I came to help you."

"I don't need your help. Rachel is..."

"I am here in Rachel's place. I told her I would stop by and I was even kind enough to stop at the store to pick up a few things to help you feel better."

I eye the *three* paper bags he has in his arms. "A few things?"

He shrugs. "Well...I wasn't exactly sure how sick you were or what you might want...so I improvised."

I narrow my eyes at him. I'm losing this fight. I can feel my body wanting to go back to the couch. "How do you know Rachel?"

Bryant stares at me for a moment, dumbfounded. "Did you forget that we all went to the same high school, Seven? You left but she didn't, and neither did I for very long. It's a pretty small town you know. Plus, we're like...second cousins or some shit like that. Does that answer your question? These bags aren't getting any lighter."

I release a huge sigh and let the door continue to swing open. On any other regular day, I would tell him to take a hike but frankly, I feel like shit and the sooner I let him in, the sooner he leaves and I return to my couch.

Bryant steps in the door and kicks it closed behind him. "Thanks," he says softly. He checks me out from head to toe before he says,

"You're cute when you're sick. The comfy look suits you." He tries to smile at me but I don't quite return the smile.

*Is he really trying to flirt with me when I'm sick?*

"Gee, thanks. I think." I roll my eyes and head towards the kitchen where Bryant puts down the three bags of groceries. I watch him unload them from the bar stool I'm sitting on and can't help but feel slightly entertained by the variety of items now sitting on my kitchen counter. A chuckle escapes me for the first time in days. It feels good to laugh a little even though I feel like hell.

"What? What's so funny?" Bryant asks.

I pick through the items on the counter. "Well, let's see. We've got crackers, Gatorade, Tylenol, ibuprofen, a baby thermometer, fuzzy socks, ice packs, a heating pad, Vicks vapor rub, a small bucket, Lysol wipes, Lysol spray, a Neti Pot, crayons, and…tampons? Wow. I guess I really *do* have the plague. You've definitely thought of everything." Laughing hurts my stomach but the items he has here for me are damn funny…and kind of sweet.

"Okay, okay, laugh all you want. I've never done this before…shopped for a sick adult female, and I don't know what you girls like. But the very nice girl at the counter schooled me on all things girly magazines. She was sure you would like this one." He says, handing me a magazine out of the last bag.

"Ooh. *People* magazine. Good choice."

*This really is thoughtful.*

"You know, Bryant, you really didn't have to go to all this trouble but…"

"It wasn't any trouble, Seven. And you're welcome."

He knew exactly what I was going to say. All I can do is smile softly at him.

"You're shivering," he says to me.

"What?"

"You're shivering, Seven. Don't you feel that? I can see you shivering sitting right in front of me." He looks past me into the living room for a moment before walking swiftly to the where I left the throw blanket on the couch. Bringing it back towards me, he wraps it around my shoulders and rubs my arms from behind me to try and warm me up. My body jolts when I feel his hands touch me, like an electric spark just shot through my body. Bryant stops moving for just an instant. It's then that I have a feeling he felt it too.

"You should go lay down for a bit. You must have a fever. I'll make you some tea and a cup of chicken soup. You need something in your body and by the looks of you, you haven't been eating much."

"No. It's fine Bryant. You don't have to do that. I can handle it." I wrap myself tighter in the blanket he laid over me.

"Hey." He turns me around on my stool so I'm facing him. "I'm here aren't I? I wanted to be here. I wanted to help you. Just trust me a little, huh? I can handle some tea and I make a mean chicken noodle soup. I think I told you that the other day."

"You said you liked soup. You didn't tell me you knew how to make it."

"Yeah well there's a lot you probably don't know about me, Seven." He places the back of his hand on my forehead and gives me a worried look. "You're burning up. Come on. Let me get you settled on the couch."

"I need to use the restroom first. I'll be right back."

"I'll get you some Tylenol and water," he says.

When I finish in the bathroom, I brush my teeth quickly. I don't know why. Maybe I haven't brushed them all day or maybe I'm just paranoid that there's a guy in my apartment and my teeth don't feel clean. Come to think of it, none of me feels clean. I probably smell like shit. Bryant is at least nice to not mention it if I do. I should get a shower later. I walk back down the hall to the living room and see Bryant sending a text message on his phone.

"Is that Rachel you're talking to?" I ask him.

"Hmm? Oh... uh, it's nobody." He slides his phone back into his pocket.

"Oh."

*It's a girl.*

*He has a girlfriend?*

*Of course he does. He had a gift in his hand the other day.*

*Why didn't he say something?*

"Hey, Bryant. Please don't feel like you need to stay or anything. I know you must have other plans. Don't break them on my account. I can take care of myself."

"Nonsense. Here, take these and then lie down for a few while I get a pot of soup going. At least it'll be ready for when you feel like eating. Let's see if we can get that fever to break." He hands me three Tylenol and a glass of water, which I devour quickly. Dang. I must be thirstier than I thought.

Bryant chuckles. "I'll refill your glass ma'am."

"Thanks Bryant."

He helps get me situated on the couch, and covers me with a second blanket to cover my cold feet. The urge to ask him to sit with me and keep me warm is so strong, but I remind myself that he isn't Shawn. He's Bryant. That would just be hellaweird. Bryant picks up the television remote to turn up the volume for me. He turns his head back towards me and crinkles his nose.

"Really? Wedding dress shows? I guess I didn't take you for a girly girl the other night, Seven. I'm surprised."

"Yeah well…" I yawn. I can feel myself slipping fast. My eyes are heavy. "There's a lot you probably don't know about me Bryant." I give his words right back to him. I drift off to sleep but not before I swear I hear him say "…then I can't wait to learn."

I have no idea how much time passes as I slip in and out of consciousness. I hear the moving around of pots and pans in the kitchen and at one point hear the kitchen sink running. I think Bryant was washing the dishes. The next time that I even slightly awaken it's because I'm being lifted. All wrapped up in my blanket, Bryant has lifted me up and is carrying me down the hall to my bedroom.

"Bryant," I whisper as my head curls into his chest.

"Shh, it's okay, Seven. You've been sleeping pretty hard. I just wanted you to be comfortable until that fever breaks."

He lowers me to my bed and covers me with my comforter. I'm so exhausted that I don't even question what he's going to do now that he's helped me to bed. I know he'll just see himself out and lock the door behind him. Hell, I don't even care if he just takes my key tonight. I think I can trust that he'll bring it back.

"Thank you, Bryant," I say half asleep. "I'm sorry I wasn't good company." My eyes open just long enough to see him kneel down next to me. He smiles shyly and smooths a wisp of hair away from my face.

"I don't know, Seven. On a scale of one to four I would say you were great company. Cute, genuine, accommodating, not pushy at all," he says quietly, his voice lulling me back to sleep. "I would say you were a perfect first date."

I want to say to him that this was absolutely not a date in any way, that he's merely wasting his time if he thinks otherwise, but I can't fight the pull of my body forcing me back to sleep. I give in to the temptation and trust that Bryant won't be a douche and try to take advantage of a sick girl.

# Chapter 10

# *Bryant*

**August 25, 2003**

On the first day of school I would usually be just as pissed off as any other boy having to put away the bike and the video games in exchange for a back pack and shit loads of homework, but this year is different. I'm finally a freshman in high school. I'm no longer a stupid junior high dweeb with unkempt hair and braces. My looks matter now if I want to score with the older girls and dang, I want to score with the girls. My older brother told me once that the cheerleaders put out pretty regularly, and that if I want to get some good head one day, I need to find a cheerleader to be friends with. One day soon, I'll be a big shot in our school, the girls will be all over me, and I'll be prepared for each and every one of them, but until then, it's training time.

Sloan and I are seated half way back on the bus when it stops to let the next small group of students on. I don't pay much attention to them until she appears. The most beautiful girl I've ever seen. In pink shorts and a flowery top, I notice right away that the top three buttons are open, leaving way too much to my imagination.

*She has tits. Nice ones.*

*I wonder what she looks like under there.*

Her long brown hair is pulled back a little bit and clipped somehow in the back. Thin silver earrings dangle from her ears. She smiles at the girl seated a couple rows in front of me as she lowers her back pack to her lap and sits down. In this moment I'm grateful to have my backpack already sitting on my lap.

*That girl…*

*I wonder if she's a cheerleader.*

"Dude, you catching flies or what?" Sloan asks next to me.

"Huh?"

"You got a thing for Savannah Sanders?"

I laugh almost too loudly at his joke. "Dude, what are you talking about? That wasn't Savannah San...." My voice trails off as I try to get another look at her. There's no way that's her. Or is it?

Long hair.

Brown eyes.

I gape at Sloan who is looking back at me with one eyebrow raised. "Uh, dude, check again. It most certainly is Savannah Sanders. Damn...summer was good to her, huh?"

I'm so busy trying to watch her that it doesn't even register what Sloan just said. Savannah Sanders...the pudgy little girl from middle school...the girl I used to tease on bus rides home...she looks like an angel now. How could I not have recognized her?

"Do you think she's a cheerleader?" I ask Sloan.

"Don't know. Why?" he asks.

"No reason."

"You think she's hot?" he whispers to me. I'm still watching her as she talks to the girls sitting next to her.

"Yeah." is all I can answer.

"Hmm." Sloan looks out the window for a moment before turning back to me. "On a scale of one to four – one being *I-would-rather-kiss-a-Troll*, and four being *I-would-do-her*, how hot is she?"

The ridiculousness of Sloan's question isn't lost on me, but I'm so enthralled with the sheer beauty that is Savannah Sanders sitting just a few rows ahead of me, that I can't help but answer his question unequivocally.

"On a scale of one to four..." I say. "She's a fuckin' seven."

*****

I watch her breathing even out as she falls asleep so peacefully. I could watch her sleep all night long, but I don't. Quietly, I rise to my feet and slip out of her bedroom, leaving the door cracked so I can hear her in case she needs something while I'm still here.

*I'm still here.*

*She didn't make me leave.*
*What do I do with that?*
*Does she want me to stay?*
*She probably doesn't know what time it is.*
*Should I go?*
*I should go.*

I feel the twinge in my chest that I can only assume is my heart growing again as it makes room for Savannah…or maybe it's guilt that I wasn't with Ivy tonight. I stand and walk back to Savannah's kitchen, quickly sending a text to Rachel, hoping she's still awake.

> Me: Hey. Is Ivy mad at me?
> Rachel: Not that I know of. Should she be?
> Me: Guess not except I wasn't with her tonight.
> Rachel: How's Savannah?
> Me: Pretty high fever that won't break. I just carried her to bed. She hasn't eaten.
> Rachel: She's in bed and you're still there?
> Me: She didn't kick me out and I need to clean the kitchen. I made soup.
> Rachel: Stay there tonight.
> Me: Come again?

Whoa. What? Did I just read that correctly? Rachel is telling me to stay here? I mean standing here right now in Savannah's kitchen, I sure as hell don't want to leave, but I'm still a respectable guy. I would never take advantage of her like that.

> Rachel: Let's not talk about who's coming and who's not ok? She might need someone and depending on what she may have she could be contagious anyway. Just sleep on the couch.
> Me: You really think she would be ok with that?
> Rachel: What's her temp?
> Me: Dunno.
> Rachel: Go take it.
> Me: Are you serious?
> Rachel: Yes

I look around for the thermometer I purchased earlier today. Mixed in with all the items I purchased, I pull it out of the pile. "Damnit," I whisper. Obviously I didn't even notice that I had picked up a pediatric thermometer. No wonder she was laughing at me earlier. I'm such a dumbass sometimes. Ripping open the packaging, I quickly scan the directions and walk back to Savannah's room, pushing her door open and slipping inside.

"Savannah…" I whisper to see if she's awake, but she doesn't answer me.

Thankfully she's out like a light and doesn't even budge when I stick the thermometer lightly in her ear to take her temperature. I cringe and take a deep breath when the thermometer beeps loudly several times in a row. The color on the screen is red and the temp reads 103.1.

*Damn.*

*No wonder she's miserable.*

I step outside Savannah's bedroom to send a reply to Rachel, letting her know Savannah's temperature and that she's sleeping heavily.

Rachel: Stay there. She may need you.
Me: What about Ivy?
Rachel: Don't worry. I'll cover for you.
Me: You sure?
Rachel: I can't believe this is all my idea but yes I'm sure. Savannah has nobody.
Me: But what about Ivy?
Rachel: Don't worry about her. Things will work out however they're meant to.
Me: Thanks Rache. That means a lot coming from you.
Rachel: Yeah yeah. Keep me posted.

I spend the next hour or so cleaning the mess that I made in the kitchen and try to figure out where I might put the things I bought for Savannah earlier today. One bag will just need to sit in the bathroom until she decides where to put it all. I'm not the kind of guy who rummages through a woman's bathroom cabinets looking for tampons and girly shit like that. I'll leave that for her to do. Once everything is in place for the night, I turn out most of the lights, leaving a small light on above the stove in the kitchen in case she needs a drink. I make my way to the couch, kick off my shoes, pull my shirt off and get as comfortable as I can get for the night. I would much rather be curled up behind Savannah holding her until she feels better but this time, the couch will have to do.

# Chapter 11

I'm a sticky mess.

My stomach is growling.

The clock says 6 AM but I'm not sure I can go back to sleep right now. Clearly my fever broke overnight as I'm now lying in a puddle of sweat-soaked sheets. I'm still wearing the sweat pants, sweatshirt and heavy socks I fell asleep in and they're all now clinging uncomfortably to my skin. I feel gross. I spot a bottle of Gatorade on my bed stand and immediately open it, drinking almost the entire thing. Parched doesn't begin to describe my present condition. Undoubtedly I'm dehydrated; I'll have to fix that today and force myself to drink more. Eating more shouldn't be a problem, though, as hungry as I feel but first, I have to get a shower and scrub all this nasty off of me. Rolling out of bed slowly, I gather my robe and head down the hall to the bathroom.

Snoring.

I hear snoring.

My nerves send my body slamming back against the wall frozen in fear.

*What the fuck? I thought I was alone.*

I'm too scared to speak. If it's an intruder, waking him could mean danger for me. I slip into the kitchen and grab a knife from the block by the stove. I've never in my life had the urge to stab someone, but at least it's something just in case. Walking quietly down the hall, I turn my head to peer into the living room where the snoring is coming from and holy hell…I wasn't prepared for that sight so early in the morning.

Shirtless.

Asleep on my couch.

Bryant Wood.

Though a feeling of relief washes over me, my eyebrows shoot up and I immediately find it difficult to swallow when I catch the sight of

Bryant on the couch. Feeling guilty and a little afraid of getting caught staring, I look away. I can't help myself though. I have to look again. His left arm is hanging off the couch but his right is resting peacefully across his stomach. He has one of the throw blankets draped over him so I'm not getting a full view but from what I can see, he has broad shoulders. So many thoughts run through my head. I don't know whether to be pissed off or…sort of…grateful that he's still here?

*I didn't ask him to stay, did I?*

*I don't remember telling him to go home.*

*He didn't try to sleep with me.*

*He stayed…for me…?*

I bite my lip to hide the very quick smile that forced its way onto my lips, and turn back to head to the bathroom. I need to get a shower before Bryant wakes up and see me gawking at him looking like the nasty sick beast that I am. Actually he doesn't need to see me gawking at him at all. Looking at myself in the bathroom mirror confirms my thoughts. I look like sick shit. I feel a lot better this morning though, so it's time to wash the sick away. Stepping into the shower I let the scalding hot water burn away whatever it was that made the last day and a half feel like the end of the world. Immediately my thoughts turn to the man asleep on my couch. It dawns on me that I'm naked and less than fifty yards away from him right now. I'm not sure how I feel about that.

*He stayed…*

*For me…*

*He carried me.*

He could've woken me up and sent me to bed. Hell, he could've left me lying there and left…but…he carried me. He's stronger than Shawn was. Shawn never carried me a day in his life, not that I hold that against him at all. He's warmer than Shawn was. His warmth, he felt like the security blanket I've been missing for several…

*No.*

*Stop thinking about Bryant.*

*He's not Shawn.* I remind myself as I turn off the water and open the shower curtain. I grab the towel off the rack and hold it to my body, continuing the battle between my own damn thoughts in defense if Bryant.

*But he was just trying to be nice.*

*He's not Shawn.*

*He gave up his night for me.*

*He's not Shawn.*

"Of course he's not Shawn, Shawn is dead, and I'm alone," I say to myself as I step out of the shower, glaring at myself in the mirror. I throw my towel on the floor in a huff and give my reflection the evil eye.

*Am I going crazy?*

The problem is, as nice as Bryant has been to me, I can't trust that he won't turn back into the douche he was years ago. Anyway it doesn't even matter. I'm alone and that's the way it has to stay. Once a douche always a douche, right? I mean…right? Isn't that how it goes? Bryant hasn't changed that much, I'm sure. I'll bring the douche out of him eventually and that will prove to myself that I'm right.

I clear my throat quickly and clean up the bathroom around me. Within minutes I'm wrapped in my robe, teeth brushed, and head wrapped in a smaller towel to dry my hair before heading out to the kitchen so I can find food and do something about my hunger pangs.

*May the odds be ever in my favor.*

Oatmeal. I really want oatmeal. Trying my best not to wake the sleeping giant, I grab what I need to start a pot of oatmeal, fill the tea kettle with water and place it on the stove. Call me old fashioned, but I don't need a machine that I have to plug in to make my hot tea for me. Plain old hot water from a kettle will do just fine. Once everything is mixed, I leave everything to heat up on the stove while I run back to my room to get dressed.

I slip on a pair of comfy black yoga pants and my favorite pink oversized sweatshirt that hangs off of one shoulder. I don't plan on going anywhere today, so comfy clothes it is for the day. Releasing my hair from the towel round my head, I grab my comb but am interrupted by an unfamiliar whistling sound. It grows louder and louder until I finally remember that I had the tea kettle on to boil water.

"Shit, shit, shit!" I whisper loudly to myself as I run back to the kitchen. I'm too late though. There he stands, in his jeans and bare chest, pouring my hot water into the mug I had sitting on the counter. Holy cheese and rice…he has…

"Abs."

*Oh my God.*

*I said that out loud.*

Bryant looks up from his pouring. "What?"

*Shit!*

"I…"

*Holy shit Savannah, make words come out of your mouth, and for the good of all that is holy stop staring at his chest!*

Bryant clearly notices my stare. He looks down at his own chest before smirking back at me. He chuckles lightly.

*Is he chuckling at me?*

*He's totally chuckling at me.*

"You okay, Seven?"

I shake my head out of the trance that is Bryant's abs and look up at him wide eyed. "I'm good. Yeah. I'm fine, Bryant."

*Dear God, Savannah, you are so not fine.*

I clear my throat and gather my wits before speaking again but when I do I practically spit all my thoughts out at once. "Um, you're still here. Did you sleep well? Where is your shirt?"

*Really Savannah. Just go back to bed.*

Those questions earn me an outright laugh from Bryant. Seriously, my face must be seventy-seven shades of red. "Well, let me think here for a second. Your fever was pretty high and I was worried about you and since you didn't specifically ask me to leave I figured I would stay in case you got worse. I slept pretty well, thank you, considering I slept on a couch all night long and what was the last one?" He smirks. He's teasing me. He's going to make me say it again.

I release a larger than life sigh before saying "Your shirt, Bryant. You know, 'no shirt, no shoes, no service'?"

"I don't think I asked for any service," he says. His head tilts as he looks from the tea kettle he's holding to me standing in the doorway of the kitchen. "In fact, I'm pretty sure it looks more like I'm *servicing* you." His eyebrow raise tells me he very much meant the innuendo. I wince internally, trying very hard not to let him know what those words just did to my body.

*How does he do that with just one word?*

"Back the truck up there, flirt-face. Nobody is *servicing* me, thank you very much. I'm sorry the tea kettle woke you up. I tried to get to it before the whistle went off but I was..."

"Too late," he interrupts. He shakes his head and says softly, "It's okay, it's just tea and I don't mind pouring it. Now, show me where the wooden spoons are so I can stir your oatmeal before it burns in the pot."

His response actually makes me feel slightly guilty for purposely being so harsh. I walk across the kitchen and reach for the drawer that's practically in front of where Bryant is standing. "It's...here." I say quietly as I reach for the handle of the drawer. Bryant backs up slightly so that I can reach the drawer but the proximity of him makes my heart beat just a little faster.

"You smell good," he says. Distracted by his compliment I drop the spoon from my hand and jump when it falls to the floor with a thud.

"What did you say?" I ask innocently, although I'm pretty sure I heard him loud and clear.

He clears his throat before he repeats himself. "I said you smell good, like vanilla." His gaze is overwhelming to my senses, let alone the nearness of his half naked body. I just hopped out of the shower but the way he's looking at me now makes me feel...I don't know. Pretty, I think...or dirty...or pretty dirty. Damnit. How does he do this to me? I'm sort of at a loss for words here. All I can do is thank him with a small shy smile. He bends down to pick up the spoon while I pull another from the drawer.

"I'm sorry, Seven. About my shirt I mean. I took it off to sleep last night. I didn't think it would really bother you. I'll go get…"

"It doesn't!" I exclaim, maybe with a little too much emphasis. I shake my head but look away, embarrassed by my outburst. "Bother me, I mean. It doesn't bother me. I was just…curious. That's all. It's fine. Whatever. Can I um, get you some tea, or I think I have orange juice or milk?"

Bryant gives me what I think is a sincere smile. "Yeah. Orange juice will be fine. Thanks."

A few awkward moments go by where neither of us says anything. I wonder to myself what he's thinking as he stirs the oatmeal and I pour his OJ. I steal a quick glance his way as he stirs and take in the specimen standing in my kitchen. Well defined is an understatement; he looks rock solid from head to…well…who knows. I try not to smile when I notice how his veins sort of pop out around his arms like vines on a tree. I've always had a thing for those type of arms, and speaking of vines…he has one. I'm full on staring now as I take notice of the tattoo on his left shoulder. It looks like a vine of some sort, though perhaps unfinished. I only see one little leaf hanging from it. A green leaf that looks like it should be amongst a patch of them, like a patch of ivy. I don't quite understand the meaning behind such a bizarre tattoo but I'm pretty sure I don't want to ask about it. Then again, curiosity killed the cat.

"What's with the tattoo?"

Bryant looks up from the stove before glancing down at this shoulder. Continuing to stir our breakfast, he's silent for a moment. I think that maybe he's ignoring my question, but then he quietly answers, "It's nothing."

"It's definitely something," I argue.

"You wouldn't understand."

I narrow my eyes.

*Is that a challenge?*

"Try me. How hard can the understanding of a tattoo be?" I tease.

"It's my existence, the symbol of my life."

75

I study the design again.

*Okay…he got me.*

"I'm not sure I...It's a vine, right?"

"Yes. It's a vine."

"So you're saying your life is a vine."

"All of our lives are like vines, Seven. We all grow when and wherever we're given room to grow. We thrive on life, and no matter how many times our leaves are pulled or our stems are cut back we can regrow."

"…Like an ivy vine." I say, trying to comprehend the meaning behind such a strange tattoo. It's not every day you see a well-built man with a string of ivy tattooed on his skin.

"Exactly."

*Interesting.*

"That's pretty deep for such an early hour of the morning," I smirk.

Bryant laughs. "Well that there is your fault, Sev. You're the one who asked."

*Ooh 'Sev'…not sure if I like that or not.*

"Yeah. Yeah I guess I did."

*What is it about him?*

*Why isn't he being the douche I know he is…or was.*

We're standing in the kitchen staring at one another. It's an extended silence between us for a minute before I hear him clear his throat to break the silence.

"How are you feeling? You look better."

"Yeah, thanks. I actually do feel a good bit better. My fever broke at some point last night so I just needed to wash all that nastiness away. I really am sorry if I woke you. I didn't know you were still here. I thought I was…um…" I clear my throat. "Alone."

"It's really not a problem at all. I was happy to be here for you. I *am* happy to be here for you. And you don't ever have to be alone. Believe it or not there are people in your life who care about you, myself included."

*I don't get it.*

"Why?"

"Why what?" He frowns.

I watch as he hands me a bowl of oatmeal and makes a bowl for himself as well. "Why do you care?" He sits down at the breakfast bar with me and holds my eyes as he eats a spoonful of oatmeal.

"Why shouldn't I care?"

"Oh, I don't know." I shake my head, and fling my arm slightly, almost flinging my spoonful of oatmeal across the room. "A few nights ago you had your hands on me like you were praying for a booty call until I turned around and you saw my face. It was like you saw a ghost."

Trying to hide a shy smirk Bryant shrugs and nods his head slightly. "Yeah. I guess I did. A ghost of my past."

"What's that supposed to mean?" I watch him swallow his bite before he answers me.

"It doesn't have to mean anything. Look, all I meant was that when I saw your face I recognized you immediately. I haven't seen you in years and when I saw you I just…"

"Just what?"

He shakes his head to dismiss my question but I stare him down until he answers. "It was just really good to see you, Seven. Really good. I…forgot how pretty your smile was."

*What?*

*My smile?*

"Yeah? Well, I guess I don't smile much these days."

"No? And why's that?"

*Is he stupid?*

*Is he really going to do this now?*

I let my spoon fall into my bowl, annoyed with where this conversation is going.

"Are you really that obtuse?" I ask him.

He's taken aback by my accusation. "No, Seven. I…" I watch as he shakes his head slowly and exhales in defeat. "I didn't mean to sound like an ignorant douche, I'm sorry. I just mean that, you know, sometimes life hands us a shit ton of…" he exhales. "Even worse shit than we could ever imagine, but…that doesn't mean we have to let it destroy us."

"You think I'm letting life destroy me?"

He shakes his head. "I didn't say that, no."

"But it's what you're thinking."

Bryant looks up from his oatmeal, his brown eyes piercing me with resolve. "It is what I'm thinking, yes, but I'm also thinking that I would never blame you for feeling that way."

*The nerve.*

"You don't know anything about me, Bryant," I huff. I take a bite of my breakfast, refusing to even look at him.

"I know more than you probably think, Seven."

OK now he's just pissing me off. I throw my spoon into my bowl and lean back in my chair, crossing my arms in front of me. "Oh really? So you've lost your wife and kid and you're all alone in this world too? I'm so sorry, I didn't know, Bryant. I might have sent flowers." I feign compassion as he watches me but all I feel right now is sadness and confusion and…growing anger. "Tell me why you're here, Bryant. I mean seriously…if you're going to talk to me like an ass and pretend to know all about me then why are you even here? Did someone put you up to this? Are you trying to right some sort of wrong from the past?" I stand up from my seat and place my bowl in the sink. I can't think of eating anymore. "'Cause I don't need your pity or anyone else's for that matter."

"Do you want me to go Savannah?" he asks softly.

"I…" I bite my tongue immediately because as much as I want to scream at him to get the hell out of my apartment something inside me wants to yell 'PLEASE DON'T GO!' I feel befuddled as I stand here trying not to look at him, not because I can't stand to look at him, but because I don't want him to see how lonely I really am. "No." I shake my head and mumble quietly. I grab the hand towel in front of me and pretend to wipe off my hands. "I mean, whatever. I guess I don't mind the company. It's pretty quiet around here most days."

*Am I really that lonely?*

*Geesh, get a grip Savannah.*

"Well…" I hear him exhale. "I can't go home now anyway so I'm all yours for the day. You're stuck with me."

I whip around from the sink to look at him. "What? Why?"

"Because you've most likely infected me with your plague and there are people in my life who don't need to be exposed to your infectious diseases." He chuckles.

"Oh."

*People in his life?*

*He doesn't live alone?*

I gasp when I realize what Bryant is saying. "Oh my God!"

"What?" He sees the alarm on my face and stands up to be at my side.

"You're married?!"

"What? No." He smiles and shakes his head. "It's not like that."

"What do you mean it's not like that? You said you have people in your life…so I'm going to assume that means you don't live alone."

He pauses for a moment. I'm guessing he's deciding how to answer that question without giving me more information than what I asked for. He shakes his head slowly. "I don't always live alone, no."

"What the hell is that supposed to mean Bryant? Oh, no, wait. I was right…you *do* have your flavors of the month. Different girls from the bar a few days a week huh? What's the matter, no good piece of ass to take you home last night so you came here?"

"Watch it, Savannah." He warns.

*My stomach hurts.*

*My heart is beating faster.*

*Why do I feel like we're breaking up when there was no getting together in the first place?*

"Jesus Christ, Savannah. Do I really have MAN WHORE written in blood on my forehead or something? I mean, is that what it looks like? Is that what you think of me?" Bryant actually looks offended. He runs his hands up and down his face, clearly aggravated with me.

"Well if the shoe fits…" I mumble, shrugging my shoulders.

"Well the shoe doesn't fit, Seven." He sneers. I watch him walk away from me before turning back around. "You're wrong. I live alone every other weekend because every other weekend my daughter visits her grandparents, okay?" He turns back away from me and exits the kitchen, leaving me standing alone looking like a deer in the headlights.

# Chapter 12

# *Savannah*

*Whoa.*

*Did he just…?*

*He said daughter, right?*

*Did he say daughter?*

*Bryant has a kid?*

Exiting the kitchen, I find Bryant in the living room pulling on his shirt. "What? I mean…wait…you have a daughter?"

"Yes."

"You're divorced?"

"No." I watch as he rolls his eyes as if he's irritated that I'm not getting it.

"So you are married then?"

"No, Seven. I told you already I'm not married," he says calmly. "But if I were married, I would now be a widower." Bryant's eyebrows raise and he watches me until his words sink in. For once I'm speechless.

I have no words.

She's dead.

Oh.

"Oh…God…I…"

Can my foot enter my mouth any farther than it is right now?

Nice goin' Savannah.

"You know what? I should just go. I'm sorry, Savannah".

"No! Bryant, I'm sorry." I reach out to touch his shoulder, shaking my head in disbelief, and trying to remind myself not to leave my mouth hanging open. "I didn't know."

Who's the douchebag now?

"It's okay," he says quietly. "I know you didn't know, or at least I didn't expect you to know."

"Do you…" I swallow unsure if I really want to broach what I know to be a sensitive topic myself. "Do you want to…you know, talk about it?"

Bryant shakes his head and shrugs. "There's really not much to tell." He says, sitting on the arm of the couch. "Samantha and I were never an item. We were a one-night-stand accident. She came into the bar one night with her sister, drank a little more than she should, and I…" He sighs and shakes his head in defeat. "I took advantage of the situation. I knew she wouldn't say no. A month later she comes back to tell me she's pregnant and that she's absolutely sure it's mine."

"Oh Bryant…"

"Ivy's beautiful though, Seven. Absolutely beautiful. She's my sunshine on a rainy day, my sugar and spice, she's…everything to me now. We take care of each other and I wouldn't want it any other way."

My heart is melting. Damnit to all hell my heart is melting.

He has a kid.

"What happened to her mother?"

"Pulmonary embolism. Three of them, actually, in her lung following child birth. She died three days after Ivy was born. The doctors didn't catch it in time."

"Ivy…" My eyes move to Bryant's shoulder. "That's why you have the tattoo. It's Ivy."

"Yes," he says quietly.

"I don't understand."

"Don't understand what?"

"Your tattoo." I say. "I mean, I get it. It's an ivy leaf…but, it's a beautiful green leaf hanging on…why does it look like a dead vine?"

"Because it signifies resiliency, strength, and courage. All the things Ivy is; all the things she's had to be in her short life."

"What do you mean?" I ask him.

"She doesn't remember Samantha's passing obviously, and lucky for her she doesn't remember much of anything she's had to endure in the past couple years."

"Like what?" I ask.

"Like traveling to Louisville Children's Hospital a few times a year. Like enduring the never ending sting of a needle every time she has to get bloodwork done."

Oh Jesus. She's sick.

Poor Bryant.

Poor baby girl.

"Cancer?" I ask.

"No. Liver transplant. She was diagnosed with Biliary Atresia when she was a couple months old. Her poor body has been to hell and back, but she has a new liver and has been on the upswing for a while now, thank God. She's on constant meds and is watched closely. So yeah, I guess we celebrate life any time we can because…well, she almost lost hers."

Bryant's words cause my past to flood my brain with memories of a horrible time. I'm listening to what he's telling me but I'm not hearing a damn thing. All I can think about is Peyton.

*"You have the opportunity to turn our tragic loss into a celebration of life for several other families."*

*"…Put yourself in their shoes. If there was any way we could save Peyton with an organ transplant, wouldn't you pray for that decision from those families?"*

"Savannah?" I feel a hand on my arm. "Savannah?"

"Huh?" I shake my head releasing my brain from the trance I was just in. "Yeah. That's great, about Ivy, I mean…"

What the fuck did I just say?

"I mean, no, it's not great that she went through all that and had to have a transplant. That's not what I meant…shit!" I mumble. "I'm sorry, I'm just not getting my words…"

"Seven," Bryant interrupts.

"Huh?"

"It's okay." He smiles meekly. "You just spaced out on me, and I'm about seven hundred percent sure I know where you went and what you were thinking about just now and I apologize. I didn't mean to bring this all up. It's not my intention to hurt you."

I shake my head. "You're not hurting me, Bryant. It's okay, I mean, I would be lying if I said I never felt the stabbing pain in my heart when I think about my Peyton, but at some point I have to pull up my big girl pants and realize that if it weren't for kids like mine, kids like yours wouldn't have a life to celebrate, right? Life goes on…until it doesn't anymore."

Bryant winces as he tilts his head and watches me try to hold back my tears. "Why do you say it like that?"

"Because Peyton was an organ donor." I cross my arms in front of me and look away so Bryant doesn't see the tear slipping down my cheek. I take a slow, quiet deep breath before swiping the tear away as inconspicuously as possible. "I didn't want to. I wanted to take my baby girl and run from that hospital. I wanted to wish her back to life but…my heart knew what my head didn't want to admit. She was already gone. Shawn's organs couldn't be donated because of the damage but Peyton…she was able to be a hero to a little boy in the same hospital that day who needed a kidney, and little girl from another hospital who needed her heart." Several tears now run down my cheek and I decide to let them run free. "I mean how could I say no to those families ya know? Those kids are alive and well and growing up in a healthy body all because of Peyton."

"You've talked to them? The families Peyton helped?"

"No. Well, yes, I guess, in a way. I wasn't going to. I sort of didn't want to know, ya know, where all of Peyton's pieces went." I cringe at the thought. "But my therapist encouraged me to write a letter to help me heal so I did…but it didn't. He mailed the letters out on my behalf and since then I've received a few replies from grateful families. It took me a while to want to read them." I can't hold back the tears now. I know I should be happy for what Peyton has been able to do but this hurts. One look at Bryant's pitying expression and I'm a goner.

"It's harder than any hell I could ever endure to know that my girl is alive but in someone else's kid. I'm supposed to feel happy for those kids, happy for those moms and their families and I do, but I so totally don't at the same time," I sob. "I don't get to hug her or kiss her or feel her heart beating next to mine. Those moms get that, but I don't." I reach for a Kleenex to wipe the steady tears from my face. "God, I'm sorry Bryant. I don't mean to be a blubbery mess."

Bryant watches me for a second without speaking before slowly walking towards me. Our bodies are now inches from each other and I gasp slightly when I feel it. That spark. I haven't felt it in a long time, and maybe it's because I'm just feeling down and drained and lonely but it's there. When I raise my head to look at Bryant's face I can tell he feels it too. I want him to kiss me so badly right now, but everything about that seems all sorts of inappropriate. Slowly his arms envelop me as he pulls my head to his chest with his hand. As he's holding me in this warm, comfortable hug, his hand glides down my hair and smoothes the damp tendrils over and over again. This is nice. I haven't been hugged like this in a long time. I allow my arms to embrace Bryant in return as my head lies softly in the crook of his shoulder blade. The smell of Bryant's day-old cologne from the t-shirt he's wearing wafts through my nose, a calming essence to my emotional state. Without hesitation Bryant kisses the top of my head. I don't react; not because I didn't like it, but because I'm not totally sure that he's aware that he did it. He's achingly gentle and...compassionate; definitely not the Bryant Wood I used to know.

I'm not the Seven Sanders he used to know.

He lets go of me just enough to raise my chin up to his face with his finger. "Savannah, there is nobody in this world who gets to tell you that you're not allowed to be sad or feel sad whenever you damn well please. You're a mother, Sev. You were, you are, and you always will be because a piece of you now lives in a piece of those children. It's okay to be a little sad for all the reasons you mentioned...but...as a father of a baby girl whose life was saved by the life of another, I hope that one day you'll be at peace with knowing what a hero your daughter was and is to this day for so many kids, and that you'll be able to celebrate her life instead of mourn it."

"Thank you, Bryant," I whisper. "I hope for that too." He wipes the tears from my cheek with the swipe of his thumb. The simple act of compassion makes me feel warmth in places I don't usually pay much attention to anymore. The spark between us is definitely there and damn if I don't want to ignite it. With his fingers in my hair, our foreheads touch, I look up to see that Bryant's eyes are closed. We stand together like this for what feels like many long minutes each of us trying to calm our rapidly paced breathing.

"Seven," he whispers.

"Yeah?" My lips part slightly in anticipation.

"I really want to kiss you right now. Like, really kiss you. I've wanted to kiss you so badly since high school…and even more so since you turned around in my bar the other night." I don't know what leads me to do it but I close my eyes and raise my head just a little bit to let him know I'm okay with a kiss. In fact, I'm hungry for the connection.

"But I'm not going to."

What?

I hold my breath instantly, not sure of how to react, but before I can even say anything Bryant has my face in his hands. "I can't in good conscience kiss you right now because I would be taking advantage of the moment we just shared and I don't want to be that guy anymore. I'm not that guy anymore and I want to show you that, so just know that…that when I do kiss you…and yes I promise, I *will* kiss you…that it won't just be because I'm a single man and you're a smoking hot woman who just happens to have my pity because you have the plague." That makes me laugh and bite my lip to keep from laughing all at the same time. "It'll be because I've wanted to kiss you the way I want to kiss you for years and damnit, it's going to mean a whole hell of a lot…okay? Is that okay with you Seven?"

"You've wanted to kiss me for years?" Why didn't he ever tell me that?

"I've wanted to kiss you since our first day of our freshman year of high school." Bryant swallows then smiles as he reminisces. "You walked up the steps of our school bus looking like an angel…and you never once looked at me. You never knew I was watching you the whole time." A small dimple appears in his right cheek as he smiles. "Good thing I had a back pack, too, because I had to hide my hard on for the entire bus ride."

Oh my God!

"I don't remember that, I'm sorry. I just remember you as a…"

"Complete dickhead. I know. Believe me, I know. The asshole that I was back then said many less than nice things to many undeserving girls, including you, but I was young, and so very stupid, and I'm so damn sorry." He touches my cheek with his hand. "Savannah, I promise you I'm not that guy anymore, and if it's okay with you, if you'll let me, I would really love to show you the man I am now."

Damn if he didn't just ignite my spark. Maybe it's his semi-southern twang but his voice is captivating and calming all at the same time. I find myself not wanting to say no to him, and at the same time I feel guilty for not feeling guilty about saying yes. Am I finally moving on with my life? What would Shawn say? Does it matter? He's gone. I'm alone and that's not how I want my story to end. And deep down, I don't think Shawn would want my story to end that way either.

"Yeah Bryant. That's okay with me."

"Okay…good…yeah…okay." He says in between heavy breaths. We both try to calm ourselves down. His warm lips place a soft kiss on my forehead. "So, what do we do with the rest of our day 'girl-with-plague'?"

"Um, well, I'm feeling better but probably shouldn't go out and do too much so…umm, I guess if you're serious about staying for the day we could watch Netflix and chill or whatever."

Bryant gives me a devilish grin before busting up laughing.

"What? Why are you laughing?" I can't help but smile at him because his laughter is contagious, but I don't get what just happened.

Through his laughter he asks "Do you even know what you just said?"

"Umm..." I think for a second. "Didn't I just say we could watch Netflix or whatever?"

"No Seven, you said 'Netflix and CHILL'...do you not know what that means?" He's got a serious case of the giggles.

"What do you mean? It's Netflix...like on the cable box you know? Like, movies, or binge-watching episodes of *Breaking Bad*. Why? Does it mean something else?"

"Hahaha! Yes, it means something else. You really don't know?"

"Obviously not douchebag, so tell me. What did I say?" I swat his arm as I begin to laugh with him.

Bryant shakes his head in amazement...at my naivety I'm sure. "Seven, 'Netflix and Chill' is code for 'let's have sex'."

I gasp and try to hide my embarrassment. "It is? Since when?"

Bryant chuckles and runs his hand down the back of my head. "Since you clearly don't get out much."

"Well you're right about that."

"Yeah well as soon as you're feeling better we're going to rectify that situation. I'm going to take you out and you're going to have fun. Just you and me."

What?

"You mean like a date? Are you asking me out on a date?" I ask playfully.

He narrows his eyes slightly. "If I did, would you say yes?"

I shrug teasingly, but try to remain as serious as possible. "I guess you won't know until you ask me."

Bryant smirks but shakes his head knowing that I'm playing with him now.

"Seven, will you go on a date with me?"

I give him a seductive look. As seductive as one can be in sweatpants and a tank-top. "Because you want to 'Netflix and Chill'?"

My joke backfires though when without hesitation Bryant pulls me into him, our bodies as close as they can be to one another. I squeal in surprise.

Damn…his body.

"Baby, I'll 'Netflix and Chill' with you anywhere, anytime…" He tilts his head just enough so that he's speaking softly in my ear. Mother trucker…this is…he is…I'm melting like butter in his arms. I can feel myself giving into the temptation that is Bryant Wood and I'm not even feeling guilty about it. What the hell?

Oh my God, this is hot.

Please just lay me down right here right now.

"…But I really think we should kiss first and I can't kiss you until I've taken you on a proper date so please, for the love of my now fifty shades of blue balls, will you please do me the honor of joining me on a date?"

That earns him a hearty laugh and a confirming, "Yes, Bryant. I think a date sounds nice. I would love to."

If there's one thing that the last eighteen to twenty-four hours has taught me, it's that Mr. Bryant "The Giant" Wood is not at all the douchebag I remembered from my childhood. I guess people really can change. At least I hope I'm right. I guess it's time to take that leap of faith that Mama talks about all the time.

*Chapter 13*

## *O'Bryant*

**January 2, 2013**

After a relaxing morning of snuggling on the couch with Ivy, watching episode after episode of *Mickey Mouse Clubhouse*, I make my way to the kitchen to get us both some lunch. It's time for Ivy's medication as well. I open the refrigerator door when my cell phone rings loudly in my pocket. I don't usually jump and fumble for my phone when it rings, but this ringtone is different. Motley Crüe's "Doctor Feelgood" only plays when one person calls. It's a sound I haven't heard in a while and now that I'm hearing the hard core guitar sound, my adrenaline is pumping. Ivy's doctor, and surgeon at Kosair Children's Hospital, is calling me. It's now that the thought crosses me mind that my daughter's life or death may be one finger swipe way.

"Hello?" I answer quickly and quietly so I don't alert Ivy in the next room.

"Hello, Mr. Wood?"

"Yes. Speaking."

"Mr. Wood, it's Dr. Fellgud from Kosair Children's Hospital. I'm calling with some great news that I think you need to hear."

*Oh shit!*

*This is it.*

*Is this it?*

*Please, God let this be it.*

I can't swallow. My mouth has gone dry. I'm backing up in my kitchen until the backs of my knees feel the chair against the wall telling me it's okay to sit down. I can't make words come out of my mouth because me entire body has been overtaken with nerves.

"I…oh…is it…um…?" I clear my throat hoping to be able to focus more on saying actual words.

*Please save my baby girl.*

There's a pause on the other line that feels like six hours when really it's probably only been six seconds. A very faint chuckle comes from the other line before I hear "Mr. Wood. Are you there?"

"Yes! Yes, I'm here. I'm sorry." I clear my throat again. "What is your news, sir?"

"Mr. Wood I'm happy to report that we have a liver for Ivy."

HOLY SHIT!

*This isn't happening!*

*It's happening!*

*He said a liver!*

"A liver, right? You said a liver?" Damnit I'm choking on my own fucking tears. "You have a liver for Ivy? This is really real? I'm not having another fuckin' dream, am I? Oh sorry about that Doc., excuse my language. I just…oh God." I try to catch my breath when I lean over and place my elbows on my knees. One hand shaking as it tries to hold the phone, the other on the back of my neck.

"Yes sir. I did say a liver. It's a perfect match for Ivy and lucky for us, it's close by and won't take long in transport. We would like to have Ivy with us this afternoon for pre-op testing and preparations. Can you do that?"

*Can I do that?*

*Is the Pope Catholic?*

"YES!" I shout way louder than need be, and nod my head, wiping the tears that are flowing like a damn river down my face. "I mean, yes. Yes of course Doctor. We'll leave right now. Holy…I…oh my God this is happening. You're going to save my little girl."

I'm crying like a baby and don't fucking care.

I can tell Dr. Fellgud is smiling on the other end of the line. "Yes Mr. Wood, we are definitely going to do our best. As long as this liver is accepted by her body we should see a good future for young Ivy. I'll see you when you arrive. Please drive carefully."

"Yes, yes sir. Will do. Goodbye."

Words cannot explain the emotions going through my head at this very moment. Elation that finally, after such a painstakingly stressful wait, my baby girl is going to get what her body needs to survive. Fear that the girl I love the most, the girl I've committed my life to, the girl that my world revolves around is about to undergo a huge surgery that could end with her little cold body left alone on a table.

*What if she doesn't make it?*

*What if her body doesn't accept the liver?*

*What then?*

I jump up from my chair and make it just in time to the sink before I lose everything I've consumed so far today.

*She has to make it.*

*Lord, please, this has to work.*

*Don't take my sunshine away.*

On top of the excitement and the fear, there's the knowledge that my kid is getting an opportunity to live because another set of parents out there just lost their reason for living.

I can't stop the tears from welling. My baby girl has gone through hell in the last fourteen months and now, now she's finally going to get a damn fighting chance!

"Daddy, sad?" Ivy walks in holding on to her favorite Minnie Mouse doll. "Daddy, sad? Minnie bettew."

"No Ivy, Daddy is not sad. Daddy is so happy!" I pick her up and squeeze her little body in my arms. I kiss her cheeks so much that she giggles wildly. She holds Minnie out to me and says "Bettew, daddy. Daddy aaaall bettew."

Laughing at the ridiculous piece of cute I'm holding in my arms, I grab Minnie Mouse and squeeze her extra tight as well. "Thank you Minnie for making me feel so happy. Minnie, I need your help finding Ivy's shoes because we have to go for a ride to the big doctor place now."

She gasps and her eyes grow three sizes before I hear Ivy exclaim "Pwize? Pwize?" She's referring to the huge toy box filled with toys donated by local area organizations from the area. The nurses make sure that each patient receives the toy of their choice while staying in the hospital; a little something to bring a smile to their faces, when some are there for not-so-happy reasons.

*Oh you sure are getting a prize this time.*

"Ivy we're going to go get you the biggest prize of all. Let's go get your stuff."

The doctors and my family had always told me to have a bag packed just in case, for the good or the bad. Finding a donor for Ivy means that somewhere out there another family has lost a family member and since nobody knows when that will happen they tell us to be prepared for anything at any time. I keep an extra bag packed in the truck as well, in case we're out when we get the call. I don't even have to check them since it's what I do every night before I go to bed. I help Ivy into her shoes and winter coat, grab her favorite stuffed animals and favorite pink blanket and we're out the door.

*****

## Friday, April 10, 2015

It's been a week since I've gotten to spend time with Savannah. Business is picking up at the bar with the late spring season. Tourists are starting to roll in to visit all the distilleries in the area. Between having to cover hours at the bar and life with Ivy, I haven't gotten to see her this week at all. We've communicated via text a few times, enough times to confirm that today is the day, our first real date. I couldn't be more nervous but excited at the same time. The music of Blake Shelton is on a constant repeat in my head. "Gonna" is a catchy song and he's damn right when he says I'm gonna hold her tight all night long, one day, or in my dreams at least. I have no intention of overstepping any boundaries today but damn if I'm not praying that this first date is followed up by a second, and then a third, and then a seventh, and one day, a seventy-seventh. I'm beginning to forget how she felt in my arms when I held her in her apartment. I can't wait to have her hand in mine for the whole afternoon.

Since Savannah hasn't really gotten out much in the past few years I decided today will be spent completely outdoors. She'll either love it or hate it, but it's supposed to be a beautiful day with plenty of sunshine, so I'm taking advantage of it to show Savannah a nice day with an even nicer guy. I'm just putting my arm through the hole of my t-shirt when I hear the movement of little feet outside my door.

"Daddy!" she exclaims in her biggest princess voice. "You in there?"

With a smile on my face that can't ever go away when I hear her little voice I reply, "Sure am Princess!" I walk over to the door and in true royal butler fashion open it to see my baby girl all dressed in her sparkly blue Princess Elsa nightgown. Her messy head of curls hangs loosely around her face. It's probably time for a haircut but I just can't stand cutting those beautiful curls. She has her mother's pretty hair but those big green eyes are mine. I see myself every time I look at her.

*God, she's just a beautiful little Princess.*

Clearing my throat, I try to rid my voice of any country accent I may have to make way for my poor attempt at sounding like Sven, the Reindeer.

"Good morning Ivy-Elsa. I was just heading out to work on the ice."

Giggling, Ivy bounds into my room leaping onto my bed. "Silly daddy. There's no ice out there today. Look," she says, pointing out my bedroom window. "It's super sunny outside today."

"Oh. So you don't want to build a snowman?" I sneak up behind her and tickle her until she falls over in a fit of giggles. "No daddy. I get to see Pappy and Nana today. Pappy said…he said…umm he's gonna make me pancakes for SUPPER!" I watch as her arms flail out to her sides like she's showing me the entire world, but then I playfully gasp in horror as if I don't approve. "He's what? He didn't ask me if he could make you pancakes for supper! I'm going to have to have a talk with that man…"

"NO DADDY!" She says covering my mouth with her hand. She whispers, "Conceal, don't feel! It'll be ok. Princess Elsa says I can have pancakes for supper."

Shaking my head in awe of my flesh and blood I grab Ivy and swing her around in my arms. "Well if Princess Elsa says it's okay, then it must be okay. I hope you have the yummiest pancakes ever. Eat one for me too okay?"

"Okay but Daddy, where are you going?"

"I'm spending some time with an old friend. Her name is Savannah."

"Subannah..." I watch Ivy's expression as she thinks about that name. "Is Subannah a boy or a girl?"

"Savannah is a girl. We used to go to school together when Daddy was young."

"Does Subannah like Princess Elsa, Daddy?"

"Oh...yes! I'm sure she loves Princess Elsa, but just in case you're not convinced, maybe you can ask her yourself someday."

"Yeah. Maybe when I'm bigger like you I'll be friends with Subannah too and we'll be princesses together." She jumps up and down on my bed in excitement and even though I shouldn't let her, she's so damn cute I can't stop smiling at her. My heart grows about ten sizes bigger at the thought of Savannah running around my house with Ivy as her princess.

*Let's not get ahead of yourself, cowboy.*

"That's right Princess. Maybe you will be friends with Savannah one day. Now let's go get your clothes changed and your shoes on so we can go see Pappy and Nana. Pappy's gonna need your help mixing up those fishcakes."

"No, *pancakes*, Daddy! Pancakes!" She giggles.

"Oh yeah. Right. Pancakes. I forgot." I wink at her as I shuffle her down the hall to her room.

As we walk down the hall to Ivy's bedroom, she grabs my finger and wraps her hand around it. "Do you love me okay, Daddy?"

I stop walking and crouch down to be at her level so I can look into her beautifully happy eyes. "Princess Ivy Lynn, on a scale of one to four I love you…one hundred and ten! So of course I love you okay! Do you love me okay, Princess?"

Her smile grows larger as she wraps her hands around my neck and places the sweetest wet kiss on my chin. "YES Daddy! I love you one hundred and eleventy nine!"

"Whoa! That's a lot of love Princess. Are you sure you can handle that much love at one time?"

"Yeah Daddy. Can I wear my Elsa nightgown to Nana's house for pancakes?" A three-year-old can't focus on one subject for too long. Her response makes me chuckle.

"Well I think that's the perfectest idea I ever heard, Princess Ivy-Elsa. Now let's go get your shoes."

*****

Once Ivy is easily settled at my mom and dad's place for the day, I get back in my truck and head back into town to pick up Savannah. My nerves are running wild now with every mile I drive closer to her place.

*Do I look alright?*

*Do I smell okay?*

*Is my truck clean enough?*

It's been a damn while since I've really tried to impress a girl. My past is admittedly splattered with an array of different women over the years. I wouldn't say I was an addict back then but damn if I didn't like to fuck a nice piece of ass whenever one walked into my bar. Looking back, I know I should've said "no" to Samantha the minute she waltzed into the bar, but something about her just said I wouldn't have any trouble helping myself so I did, and a month later I received the biggest damn cock block a man's ever seen. "Pregnant," she says. "It's yours," she says. Fuck.

Who knew that day my biggest nightmare and my wildest dream were all going to come true. I knew one day I wanted to be a daddy

96

and settle down with a family, but I wasn't ready just yet. Regardless, I wanted to do right by Samantha and my soon-to-be child. I worked my ass off to finish the bar renovations so I would have steady income to help her out with the baby. I wasn't going to let her be a single parent, even though we both knew marriage wasn't an option for us. We didn't love each other and in my future I want to be married to the girl I can't live without. A girl I'm head over heels for. I want to marry for love, not out of obligation.

I pull into the parking lot of Savannah's complex and hop out of the truck. It's mid-morning so there's still a bit of a chill in the air, but the sun is shining brightly and promising a beautiful afternoon. We should be plenty warm enough by the time we get there but I try to remind myself on the way up the stairs to make sure Savannah brings a sweater or a jacket. I knock on the door three times and wait for her to answer. "Coming!" I hear her yell excitedly from inside. Sweet Jesus, hearing her voice yelling that word does something to my insides.

*Maybe not tonight darlin' but soon, when the time is right, you'll shout that word for me.*

*Chapter 14*

# Savannah

I've been ready for an hour. I don't know why I let him talk me into this, but I couldn't sleep a wink last night knowing today was coming. I haven't been out with anyone of the opposite sex since Shawn, and even though our marriage was spectacular, the butterflies-in-your-stomach feeling had dissipated over time. I imagine that's pretty normal in any long-term marriage, but now, I have to do this all over again. I've had butterflies in my stomach all night. No, not butterflies, moths! Big, ugly, obviously nocturnal moths since they wouldn't go away, and so here I am ready to go way early because…moths.

I see his truck pull into a spot out front but try not to pull the curtain back too much to watch him in case he looks up to my window. I may be anxious about today but I certainly will not be letting him know that. I get to hold the cards today. The moments we shared last week in my apartment were intense, and I never meant for any of it to happen, but it's been a week. Who knows what he may be thinking now. Maybe he's the super great guy that he was here last week or maybe as I get to know him he'll show truer colors and I'll see the old Bryant Wood emerge, the douchebag looking for a booty call. He'll be dialing long distance if that's the case.

*Except I almost kissed him a week ago.*
*I would've kissed him back had he followed through.*
*Will that opportunity come today?*
*Do I want it to?*

As Bryant emerges from his black truck, I watch as he takes a big breath and looks at himself in the driver's side mirror to make sure he looks okay. It's cute to watch a guy care about the impression he's making. He only looks for a second though, so at least I know he's not too vain.

*He's perfect.*

He knocks on the door three times and even though I knew he was on his way up, I still jump at the sound of the knock. I take a step toward the door and then cringe and slap my hand to my forehead.

*Stupid girl! Don't be in such a hurry.*

*Make him wait!*

*You're not desperate.*

So that my voice doesn't come across too clearly I tiptoe as quietly as I can back down the hallway toward my bedroom.

"Coming!" I shout.

*One one-thousand, two one-thousand, three one-thousand, four one-thousand…*

I take one last look in the bathroom mirror even though I know I look fine. I've looked at myself every ten minutes for the past hour. I chose my favorite skinny jeans that are faded, with a few small holes in spots, a pink, blue, purple and yellow plaid button down shirt unbuttoned halfway, layered over a pink tank. Not knowing where we are going today except that I was told to dress casually, I left my layered hair down. I like the way it frames my face but still hangs past my shoulders. I throw a ponytail holder in my pocket just in case I need it later. I'm ready to go. I'm ready to answer the door.

Calmly and quietly I open the door and cast my eyes on Bryant standing in the doorway.

*Holy hell.*

Looking at him standing in front of me makes me feel like I'm about to fan-girl on the red carpet of some cheesy awards show. He looks like he could be the fourth brother in the family if Ryan Gosling, Bradley Cooper, and Chris Hemsworth were all related. He has the eyes of one, the body of another, and the shit eating smirk of another. He's dressed perfectly casual in worn denim jeans, a blue t-shirt, with a blue plaid shirt over top. One might think we coordinated outfits. It's almost ironic how well we complement each other. I remember what he looked like the morning he stood shirtless in my kitchen. Though his shirt sleeves are slightly rolled I can still see his strong arms. They definitely look bigger today even under his clothes...I wonder if he worked out just before coming over.

*To impress me?*

That thought makes me almost giggle out loud.

"Good morning Seven," he says with a smirk as if he knows I'm thinking about him naked, which I'm not...okay I might have for just a second, but I absolutely am not now.

I nod my head up to make notice of his face. "You left somethin' on your face there, Bryant."

"You like it?" He says rubbing his hand over the stubble on his face.

*YES!*

Nodding slightly, I respond, "It's not bad. It suits you."

"Good. Ivy likes it. She says I have sprinkles on my face and it just so happens that I like sprinkles so I figured what the hell."

"Sprinkles. That's cute." I can't help but smile at the thought of a little girl telling Bryant he has sprinkles on his face.

"You look great, Seven. Not having the plague suits *you*." He winks at me and I smile back, shaking my head.

"Thanks, I think."

"You ready to go? Do you need anything?"

I shake my head slowly. "Don't think so. I'm good." I check to make sure my phone is in my back pocket, grab my small purse and keys off the hook by the door and step out into the hallway.

"Great. Let's go. It'll take us a little while to get there." Bryant watches while I lock the door behind me and then guides me to the stairwell with just the slightest touch of his hand on the small of my back. It's weird, but not uncomfortable. Uncomfortable should have been Bryant almost kissing me a week ago in my apartment, but that felt...eerily not uncomfortable.

"Where are we going?"

Bryant turns his head once we've reached the ground floor and shrugs. "You'll see. Hop in." He holds the door open for me and waits as I grab what I call the 'Oh Shit' bar above the door in his truck and hoist myself in. These pickup trucks sit so high up. A trampoline would be a much more fun way to get in.

Within minutes of our drive I see that we're headed east on I-150. Obviously we're not going somewhere local, which now has me stumped. Where on earth could he be taking me?

"Are we headed to Springfield?" I ask.

"Well, we're gonna pass through Springfield eventually, but that's not where I'm stopping." He looks over at me through his sunglasses and sees the perplexed look on my face. "Relax, Seven. We'll be driving for about an hour, but I promise you'll like it...well..." He turns on his signal to change lanes before looking in his rearview mirror. "At least I hope you'll like it. I just thought somewhere peaceful and quiet might be nice and it's supposed to be a beautiful day."

*An hour?*

"Sounds great." I smile shyly...because at this moment I actually am a little apprehensive. It'll be a long shitty car ride home if today doesn't go well. I don't want this hour to be awkward; it would be nice if I could find something to talk about so we don't sit in silence for the entire ride. I don't really want to know about all the women Bryant has dated and I don't particularly want to talk about my dead husband when I'm supposedly on a date with another guy. Ugh! Why is this so hard?

"Hey," Bryant's voice causes me to turn my head in his direction. He's looking back and forth between me and the road.

"Yeah?"

"Where did you go just now?"

"What do you mean?"

He smiles at me. "I mean you haven't stopped twiddling your thumbs since you got in the car, you look tense and if that doesn't give you away, I just watched you exhale rather largely looking out your window. Are you okay? Do you not want to do this?"

"No, no! Yeah, I do. I'm sorry. I...haven't been on...a...umm..."

"A date?" he asks. I'm grateful that he's saying it so I don't have to. Why does this make me so nervous all of a sudden? I wasn't like this a week ago.

*Maybe because I actually care?*

"Yeah, a date. I haven't done this in a while, Bryant. I'm just being stupid. I'm sorry." I shake out my hands quickly to try to brush off the nerves. "Just make me talk so I don't sit here wondering what to say or what not to say."

Bryant tries not to smile or laugh at me but I notice his small chuckles and see his cheeks rise under his sunglasses. "Okay, umm...well, tell me something I don't know about you."

"Dude, that could be a lot of things. You don't know much about me at all...but then again, it sort of feels like you know everything." I answer quietly.

"I know you like to lay on the couch and watch silly television shows about girls trying on wedding dresses, and I know you like oatmeal."

I shake my head in partial embarrassment over his reference to *Say Yes to the Dress*. I suppose it could've been worse. I could've been watching old reruns of *Full House*.

*Have mercy.*

"I know that your bathroom is blue and white, which I liked very much by the way...not too girly, but not too plain. You can tell a lot about people by looking at their bathrooms."

"Yeah? So you were snooping through my bathroom? Hope you got a good look at my hairbrushes and tampons."

Bryant lets out a loud laugh. "Tampons? No, but I did assume that you're not someone who takes forever to get ready for something...you don't have enough products on your counter to justify the time."

*Wow. Perceptive.*

"Ten points for you, Bryant. You would be correct with that assessment."

"Want to know one other thing I know about you?" he proudly asks.

"You don't have to say it."

*My husband is dead.*

*My daughter is dead.*

*I'm alone.*

"You're cute when you sleep."

"WHAT? What the fuck? You watched me sleep?" I shout. "Oh my God, are you a creeper or what? How long did you watch me?"

"Only for a few minutes, Savannah. You were so peaceful."

"Oh shit, did I snore?" I ask. "Because if I did, it has to be because I was sick, you know."

*Ugh, how embarrassing.*

Laughing at my outburst he replies, "Relax okay? I watched you sleeping hard enough to know you deserved to sleep in your bed for the night and not on a couch. That's when I carried you back to your room, remember?"

"Oh…yeah." I breathe. "I remember now."

*I felt comfortable in his arms.*

"Anyway, you're beautiful when you're awake and every bit as beautiful when you're asleep too."

"Oh, God! That can't be true." I scoff lightly. "I probably looked like Medusa on steroids or something."

"Nah, nothing like that. You look…peaceful. Content. Beautiful…" He trails off.

I look down for a moment sliding part of my hair behind my ear so it's out of my face. "Thanks, I guess."

"You're welcome. Now answer my question and tell me something I *don't* know."

Without thinking I just blurt out, "Ranch flavored Doritos are my favorite. I can't ever eat just one. Your turn."

Bryant nods in appreciation of my answer, however random it was. We'll see if two can play at this game.

"I don't like the sound of Saran Wrap when it crinkles together," he says with a disgusted look that makes me laugh.

*Yes, two can play at this game!*

I almost bust a gut laughing. "What? Does that even make sense? Is that a thing? That's not a thing."

He looks at me playfully insulted by my words. "It is most definitely a thing. You know how when it sticks together and you try to pull it apart it makes that gross sticky sound? Or what it feels like when you're wearing it and it sticks to itself…ugh, no."

I can't stop laughing! "Bryant Wood, when have you ever worn plastic wrap in your life?"

"Quit your giggling. They wrapped my arm and shoulder in it when I got my tattoo, just to keep the bandage on. It was the most disgusting feeling ever and when it would rub together…" he pretends to shiver in disgust. "Ew. No. Never again. I hate the stuff. Your turn."

I take a deep breath to compose myself and try to think of something interesting about me. "Okay, okay, I used to spit my lima beans into my milk and then pour them down the drain after dinner. I hate beans. All beans. The texture of them is disgrossting."

Bryant cocks his head to the side. "Did you just say disgrossting?"

"Yeah…disgusting and gross…disgrossting."

"Disgrossting…" he lets the word roll off his tongue and then nods. "I like it. You know what else is disgrossting?"

*He's using my words.*

*This is fun.*

"What?" I ask.

"Mustard."

"Mustard? Why the heck don't you like mustard? Isn't mustard like…one of the American staples of all condiments?"

He shrugs. "Maybe it is, but when your mom puts mustard on your grilled cheese sandwiches as a kid, and refuses to make you one without mustard simply because you don't like mustard, which let me remind you would be one *less* step for her in making dinner…I just couldn't ever learn to like the yellow smelly goop. It kinda looks like baby poop on bread anyway…disgrossting."

This conversation makes me smile. I don't know why I was so worried about talking to Bryant. Words just flow easily from both of us. It's comfortable in that get-to-know-you sort of way. "Okay…mustard is disgrossting. I'll give that to ya, but it's still your turn since you just piggy-backed on my turn."

"Alright…I've got a good one…but no judging."

Already I get a case of the giggles. I wonder what this could be. "Okay," I say holding my hands up in defeat. "I promise. No judging."

Bryant takes a moment to look in the rearview mirror and changes lanes again so that we can make the exit onto 55-S. "I can pee and brush my teeth in the shower at the same time while washing my hair with my non-tooth-brushing hand."

Okay, I can't. Oh my God, I need to laugh so hard that my eyes are watering as I bite my lip to keep from laughing out loud.

"Hey!" Bryant yells at me laughing. He points to me as if he's trying to parent me. He's totally trying to adult me right now. "Don't think I don't see you trying not to laugh. You said you wouldn't judge."

In the best effort to not laugh out loud I quickly pretend to cough and wipe my nose with my hand. "I'm not laughing, I swear. I just…have…something in my eye."

"Uh huh…I've heard that one before, Seven. You wouldn't believe how much time it saves me though when I need to shower and Ivy is awake by herself. I try to wake up before her but when the sky's awake, she's awake."

"Ah, so she's a *Frozen* fan is she? Who does she like better, Anna or Elsa?"

Bryant rolls his eyes but smiles which tells me he's not really that annoyed by Ivy's obsession with Frozen. "Elsa *and* Sven if I had to pick one other character. You know, she asked me this morning if you liked princesses and if you liked Elsa."

*What?*

"You told her about me?" I gasp.

"Yeah. Well…yeah I guess. I mean, she asked where I was going today and I told her I was hanging out with my friend, Savannah."

"Oh. Right. Yeah. Okay."

"Anyway," he continues. "One of these days she'll want to tell you all about her love of princesses. It's your turn, Seven."

My mind drifts to another place – another time, when I would dream of my little girl playing dress-up and being her daddy's princess. Every now and then I think I can handle talking about someone else's kid or even knowing that another friend of mine has kids, but right here, right now, but I can't. I'm stuck here in this truck with a man who doesn't understand yet that sometimes talking about children can be a trigger for me. I'm not ready to tell him though, so instead, I look out my window and say the words before I even realize I've said them.

"I hate the number seven and sometimes I wish I could live someone else's life...even just for one day."

*Silence.*

*More silence.*

*One one-thousand, two one-thousand, three one-thousand...*

"I'm sorry Sev...Savannah. I...I didn't mean to hurt your feelings or anyth..."

"No, no. It's okay. You didn't," I interrupt. "I shouldn't have said that."

"No. You said it because you mean it. There's no fault in that. So tell me whose life you would want to live for even just a day? If it could be anybody...who would it be? Jennifer Lopez? Carrie Underwood? One of those Kardashian girls?"

"It doesn't matter. Some days I wish I could just wake up and have a completely different life, you know? Like a restart."

"Yeah...I understand. Life likes to throw tons of shit our way and it would be nice to step out of it for just a while. I wished that for Ivy so many times, and I would be lying if I said I never wished it for myself."

"Yeah...I know that feeling," I whisper. "I read this book once, called *What If* by Rebecca Donovan. It's a story about having a second chance to meet someone for the first time."

"Yeah...go on..." Bryant says.

"Well, so this girl goes missing in high school and this guy sees her over a year later in his college town and is convinced it's this missing girl, only she doesn't recognize him at all."

"Sounds eerily familiar in a way," Bryant says winking at me.

"Yeah?" I ask. "How so?"

"Well…you didn't recognize me when you saw me in the bar that night, so I guess that sort of gave us a second chance at meeting each other for the first time."

"Yeah, I guess, but I never went missing. And I certainly don't come with a satchel full of secrets. At least it feels to me like I'm a walking open book for the world to read at their leisure."

"Hmm…" he murmurs. "So what happens in the end?"

I shake my head. "Can't tell ya that."

"What? Why? You just told me what it's about and now you can't tell me how it ends?"

"Nope."

"Why not?"

"Because that would be a huge spoiler. If you want to know how the story ends, you should read it for yourself and find out."

"Ugh, you women and your books! I don't even know the last time I picked up a book and just read."

"Well maybe now you should consider it."

"Yeah, maybe." He smiles. We're quiet for a few minutes, both lost in our own thoughts. I jump slightly when I feel Bryant's hand on my left leg. He squeezes just enough to get my attention.

"For what it's worth, I'm glad I got the second chance to meet you. I enjoy hanging out with you, and I've really liked getting to know you all over again."

*That was sweet of him to say.*

*Warm and fuzzy.*

"Thanks, Bryant. For what it's worth, I'm enjoying hanging out with you too. Sorry for being the Debbie Downer for a minute."

"Hey," he says placing his hand over mine. I can feel him rubbing his thumb over the top of my knuckles. "You don't ever, EVER, need to apologize to me. I understand, and when I don't, I'll try really hard to so that you don't have to feel anything but happy. You deserve that. I just want to show you a nice day outdoors in the beautiful weather."

I watch him from my side of the truck. If the Bryant of years past were sitting here beside me I'm pretty sure his hands would be trying to get in between my thighs right about now; he would have a ball cap on backwards and would be trying to impress me with his big bad truck. His face would be insincere and his body would be so aloof because he used to never give a damn about anyone but himself, or so it seemed to those of us on the outside. The Bryant I see today is different. He's older, wiser, a little more weathered in the face. I can tell life hasn't been parties and shots of whiskey all these years for him, and even though it's unfair of me to say so, I like that about him. At least he has even a little bit of something I can relate to.

"Bryant?"

"Yeah?"

"I never take the last bite of my food, no matter what it is. It's just a thing with me I guess."

"Never?"

"Nope. Never."

He watches the road for a minute, nodding his head, taking in my words. He smirks before looking over at me. "Well it's a damn good thing I like to eat. I'll always take your last bite for you, okay?"

"Okay." I nod and smile as I rest my head on the back of my seat. I'm still somewhat facing Bryant so for a moment I just watch him drive. He's really done an outstanding job making me feel comfortable when I'm with him, I'll give him that. I'm excited to see where we're going today. I don't have to wait long as I see us head west toward the big sign that says GREEN RIVER LAKE.

"For real?" I exclaim. "Green River? I've heard great things about this park but I've never been here before!"

"Well, good! I used to come down here with my family in the summer time, do some fishin', hikin', that kind of thing. I thought it would be nice to just be out in the sun, maybe walk one of the trails or something? And I packed us a picnic lunch if that's okay?"

*How perfect.*

*He really planned this out.*

*Just for me.*

"Yeah, Bryant. That sounds wonderful. Thank you."

We park the truck and he comes around to open my door. He first takes my hand to help me out but then moves his hands to my waist to help steady me as I jump down from my seat. I'm not five years old and can certainly make the jump on my own but I let him hold me anyway. I don't want to spoil these moments of our date. Immediate sparks of warmth shoot through my body when he touches me. I didn't expect that feeling at all and wobble just slightly when my feet hit the ground.

*Because my mind is somewhere in the clouds.*

"Thanks."

Bryant takes my hand and leads me towards the lake. "Come on, let's see what we can get into."

# Chapter 15

# *Bryant*

Damn she feels good. Her hand in mine as we make our way across the parking lot feels natural, like we've been doin' it for years. What doesn't feel natural is the feeling that someone just jumped into a ball pit inside my stomach. Damn if I'm not nervous. Bryant Wood doesn't get nervous. What the hell is making me feel this way all of a sudden? I can't remember a more enjoyable car ride with a woman. Savannah makes conversation so easy. It's been years and although I had my eye on her in our high school years, we definitely didn't talk often so there's so much I have yet to learn about her. Walking the trails here at the park, in the fresh air where she won't feel trapped, is the best place I could think to bring her. There's nothing like the natural beauty of the outdoors.

*And nothin' like the natural beauty of the girl whose hand is in mine.*

We start out along one of the easier hiking trails, making small talk and taking a minute every now and again to marvel at the beautiful environment surrounding us. Leaves are growing back on the trees, and the robins are obviously having a family reunion somewhere close by.

"Do you know these trails well?" Savannah asks me.

"Uh, not like the back of my hand but I've been up and down this one several times as a kid. It's one of the easier trails and not too long. I didn't want us to have to work too hard, hope that's okay."

I watch as her eyebrows raise and she shakes her head. "Yeah, absolutely. Besides, trying to remember all the new things I learned about you in the car will be hard enough."

I feel the slight squeeze of her hand that lets me know she's teasing me.

*She squeezed my hand.*
*That means something right?*

*Why do I feel like a fucking teenager?*
*Damn this girl.*

"I don't know, but I have a strange feeling you're going to remember every damn thing I told you about myself."

She doesn't answer me, but when I look at her she's blushing and hiding behind her smirk.

"So why the bar? Have you always wanted to do something like that? Own your own business I mean?"

"You wouldn't think so. Since my last name is Wood it was preached to me for years and years that I would take over my dad's distillery one day. I mean, when in Bardstown, drink the bourbon, right?"

"That's not what you wanted? Not that I would blame you, but I don't remember you as the rebel child."

*Not with a grandfather on the school board.*

"Nah, I was a pretty good kid. Did what I was told. Studied in school, was good at sports. That kind of thing. I just spent too many years playing around the distillery ya know? I didn't want to spend my life doing the same damn thing, not that I don't have tons of respect for what my dad does. I do, it's just…"

"I get it. There's a whole world out there so why not take a risk, right?"

"Yeah. I mean, that's what I wanted. I never thought it would be a bar though. I used to spend my evenings at that bar before Jerry retired. That's where I met Samantha, Ivy's mother."

Savannah's head whips up quickly as if she's shocked by that news but nods in understanding. "Right. Yeah. I forgot you said you met her at a bar."

"Yeah. Well…I already told you what happened after meeting her. When she told me she was pregnant I really wanted to step up and try to do the right thing. I was already a disappointment to my family at that point for knocking up some girl I barely knew so you know, why not take the plunge and leave the family business too."

Savannah stops walking. I feel the slight tug on my arm from her hand still in mine. She's looking at me with disbelief in her eyes.

*Or is that pity?*

"You okay?" I ask her.

"Yeah. I didn't know your family saw you that way. Do they still? I mean, it looks like you've been pretty successful and all. I would think your family would be proud of you."

*Yep, it's pity.*

"Hell, now…now I can do no wrong because I have Ivy." I shake my head almost in disgust at my family. "It's funny really, how my family can go from seeing me as a disappointment because I got someone pregnant, to thinking I'm the best damn dad in the land for doing what I've done for my little girl. For giving up all that I have for her, and why wouldn't I? I mean she's my kid for Christ sake. What parent wouldn't walk on fucking water for their kid if they could, ya know? That's just being a good parent. That's all I want for her."

"You are a good parent Bryant." She smiles at me but the smile doesn't quite reach her eyes. "I can tell that from the way you talk about her. She's a lucky little girl to have a daddy like you."

Shit, she just took my breath away. I'm staring at her. For whatever the reason I've lost my ability to say coherent words. I'm just staring at her, nodding my head like I hear what she's saying. I want to tell her everything on my mind. I want to tell her everything in my heart.

But I can't.

"I'm the lucky one" is all I can whisper at the moment. Sensing my unease, Savannah takes a step forward so that we can continue up the trail. The smell of pine infiltrates my senses. It damn near smells like Christmas in these woods. The moment I look up ahead of me though I stop suddenly and pull Savannah back. I catch her off guard and she ends up falling backwards into me. Swiftly, my arms fold around her to steady her on her feet.

God, she feels good.

And smells good.

"Look!" I whisper pointing ahead of the spot where we're standing.

"What?" She whispers back, paying no mind to the fact that I'm holding her.

"A doe...see her? She has her babies with her. Looks like two little fawns there. See them?" I whisper in her ear.

*I would rather be whispering something else in her ear.*

*Her hair smells like vanilla and the outdoors.*

I feel her gasp slightly when she lays eyes on the deer about one hundred yards from us. We stand as still as we can so that we don't scare them off. As we watch for a few minutes they make their way through the woods, munching on leaves along the way. At one point we both strain to hold in our laughter when one of the fawns playfully jumps towards the other like it wants to play. I feel Savannah's body stiffen as she tries not to laugh out loud.

*She's so close to me.*

*I can feel her.*

*If I could just...spread my hands across her stomach...*

I take in a deep breath, committing her smell to memory. I can tell she feels me behind her and to my surprise she leans ever so slightly more in my direction. Her breathing has quickened, like she's waiting for me to make the call. I could do it. I could turn her around right now and kiss her. I could kiss her neck from where I am right here and something inside tells me she wouldn't stop me. I could make her feel good. I could give her what she needs, what she deserves.

*But I can't.*

*I won't.*

I promised myself I wouldn't take advantage of her. We're thirty minutes into our date minus the drive. A gentleman wouldn't jump so fast for someone he really wants to keep at his side. I have to be patient. Sliding my hands down her arms I make sure she's okay before letting go. Like a shy dumbass I throw my hands in my pockets and clear my throat before walking on with her right beside me. Her look tells me she's not exactly sure what just happened between us.

*I'm not sure either.*

*Stupid fuck.*

*Maybe I should've kissed her.*

"So what about you, Seven?"

"What about me?"

"Your hopes and dreams? What did you want to do before…"

*Fuck! You had to bring this up didn't you?*

*Fix it, Bryant! Say something else!*

Too late. She beats me too it. "Before my life fell apart in front of my eyes and I was forced to move back home alone?"

Shamefully, I shake my head. "Fuck. Savannah, I'm sor…"

"It's okay. Really. It is what it is, right? I mean, it's been two years. If I don't saddle up and move on I may as well spend the rest of my life in a house filled with hoarded shit and a load of cats right?"

*Ummmm…*

"Well, that's…uh…that's a way of putting it I guess." I'm totally at a loss for words. What do I say to that?

"Sorry, I'm not making a joke of my life. I have shitty days where I want to crawl under a rock and die and then I have days where I think I see sunlight on my horizon, that maybe there is more to my life than being alone and feeling sorry for myself." She chuckles to herself, an inside joke?

"What's funny?"

"You were talking about Ivy earlier and her love of everything *Frozen*." She shakes her head slightly. "I know it sounds stupid and really cheesy but there are days I feel like 'Let It Go' needs to be my theme song ya know?"

"Nah…you need something more like…'Fight Song'."

"The Rachel Platten song?" My suggestion makes her smile.

"Yeah…if that's her name. I hear it all the time and it's on that car commercial…it suits you."

"Yeah," I watch as her smile widens. "Yeah I guess it does."

"Okay," I start. I want to keep her talking as much as I can. I want to figure out what makes this woman tick on the inside. "So if your days were filled with sunshine and rainbows and shit like that, what would make Savannah Turner a happy woman? What's your passion?"

She takes in a big breath and releases it while looking around the trail. We've made it to the top of the hill and from here we can see the water of the lake shining like a pool of diamonds as the sun's rays hit the surface. It's beautiful up here. You can see for miles.

"My plan was to own my own spa one day." She kicks her foot lightly into the loose dirt at her feet. "I guess that sounds a little stupid now huh?"

I shake my head. "It doesn't sound stupid at all. Why would you say that?"

"I don't know. It was a lofty goal way back when. I made this plan of going to college for business, and then going to beauty school so that I could learn the trade. I was determined to learn all there is to know about what goes into a great spa. I wanted to have the best."

"Impressive," I say to her.

She continues. "So I accomplished that goal, but after Peyton was born I took time off to just be mommy for a while. We figured once she was ready for preschool I would look into starting the business. It would give me something to do while she was in school, so I didn't miss her too much…but then…"

"Yeah," I interrupt so she doesn't have to say it. I get it. Then Peyton died, and so did Shawn. And then she was alone.

"How did you end up at the salon with Rachel?"

"Well, oddly enough her mom and my mom are good friends…Red Hat Society or some weird shit like that." She laughs. "Once I came back to town I was in a huge depressive funk. Didn't go anywhere. Didn't talk to anyone besides my family. Slept a lot, that sort of thing."

"Understandable."

"Yeah, so my mom must've mentioned it to Rachel's mom who mentioned to Rache that I was back in town and had my license. She was looking for someone new to have at the salon, well, either that or she was just showing me some pity, so she called me. We were never besties in school but I remembered her from back in the day and she remembered me. She's been great for me though, ya know? Someone to talk to. Someone who may not always understand but helps me through the rough patches. I owe her a lot. I suppose it was the right call…got me out of my parents' house and on my own again."

"You ever think about starting that spa now?"

She shrugs. "I don't know what my life is doing right now. I guess I'm just along for the ride until I figure it out."

"Never say never Savannah. You're too young to give up on your dreams." She gives me a sad look but doesn't respond right away. Silence falls between us as we make our way closer to the lake shore. There's a slight breeze in the air but it's warm and inviting.

"It's beautiful here, Bryant. Thank you for bringing me. It's nice to be outdoors, taking it all in." She smiles at me and my heart flips. Damn if I don't feel like a middle school boy around her. She's causing feelings to stir in me that I don't remember having before. Maybe everything is different now. Maybe I'm older, wiser, stronger…ready to love her. Or maybe I just feel the need to protect her, to hide her from inevitable truths, truths that now I fear could crush her. Never in a million years did I think this would happen, Savannah and me, together. Now that we're doing this…whatever it is we're starting, my deepest secret is bubbling at the surface, waiting to break free. What if what I think are romantic feelings are really just feelings of guilt or shame? I wish she would never have to find out, but at some point the truth will be revealed, and then what the hell do I do when she finds out? Will she look at me the same way? And will she even be able to look at Ivy at all?

# Chapter 16

# ⹂ Savannah

"It's not much. I just made us a few sandwiches and packed some fruit salad, some pretzels, and last but not least," he says as he pulls everything out of the cooler. We're seated on a large woolen blanket spread out on the ground, face to face so that we can easily talk to one another. "A couple of damn fine double chocolate brownies if I do say so myself."

"Oh I don't think you'll be saying that yourself for long. Maybe I should eat dessert first."

Bryant tosses the brownie wrapped in wax paper in my direction. I eye him questioningly after turning the wrapped dessert over in my hands. "You know most people would use plastic wrap or even a baggie…why wax paper?"

The look on his face makes me laugh. He's annoyed with my question though not really at all. I really wasn't trying to be funny but once the words fell out of my mouth I realized what I had asked. "Did you forget that I can't stand the sound of plastic wrap? Jesus, woman, you're supposed to remember those most important things about me. I'm hurt!"

"Oh, I'm so sorry," I playfully console him. "I guess I've been trying to focus too much on how you could possibly wash your hair, brush your teeth and pee all at the same time. I forgot about the plastic wrap."

"Yeah, keep it up there, Seven. Karma's a bitch ya know." Joking with Bryant feels so easy. Like we're flirting but not really. This day has been a perfect day so far. Our walk through the trails was breathtaking. The water was beautiful and now this simple quiet lunch together. For not having to plan much, Bryant went all out. It feels good that we can both just be ourselves, and not have to dress up and try to be people that we're not. I suppose if he's already seen me a sweaty sick mess and still wanted to take me out, he can't be a bad guy at all. I like him. And I get the impression that he likes me. I'm a little surprised that he hasn't tried anything yet other than holding my hand. Not surprised...sad maybe.

*Maybe he's changed his mind.*

*Maybe he doesn't want me like he did before.*

I take a deep breath telling myself that even though my mind flip-flops back and forth when it comes to talking about kids, I need to buck up and get to know Bryant, the dad. If we're going to spend time together eventually that will have to involve Ivy. I can't beat around the bush or hide behind my past anymore. The world doesn't revolve around me.

"So tell me more about Ivy." I say nonchalantly as I take a sip of my Diet Coke. "What's she like? Do you have a picture of her?"

Bryant looks at me cautiously, almost as if he's unsure of how to react to my questions.

"What is it? Did I say something wrong?" I ask.

"No." He shakes his head. "I just...we don't have to talk about Ivy if you don't want to, if it makes you uncomfortable. Today isn't supposed to be about putting you through the emotional ringer." He says with compassion in his voice that makes my heart skip.

*Damnit. I must be all over the place today.*

I try to smile to assure him I'm okay. "I'm sorry. I know I'm hot and cold when it comes to talking about children sometimes. It's been a problem for me and sometimes I don't have control over it. A memory hits me or something strange makes me think of Peyton, and every now and then it just takes my breath away for a second, you know?"

"Yeah. I get it," he says.

"My therapist told me back then that it could happen. A form of PTSD, I guess, but that I can't let it control me. Anyway, I don't want you to think I don't want to know all about you, Bryant the Dad, because I do. I want to know about Ivy. She's your life and you light up when you talk about her and that spark of energy in you is..."

"Is what?" he asks.

"It's attractive." I can feel myself blush. God, I just told him I think he's attractive.

With his fingers under my chin he lifts my head so that he can see my eyes. "You'll tell me if it's too much?"

I nod. "Yeah. I promise."

Bryant smiles while pulling his phone out of his back pocket. "Then yeah, I have a picture. Sorry I didn't think to show you before." He swipes his finger across the screen, and staring at me are a pair of beautiful green eyes. She's an adorable little girl with light brown hair and a smile that would brighten anyone's day.

"How did you get her hair braided like that? You can do that all the way around her head?"

"Me? Hell no." He laughs. "Rachel did it that morning. I had taken Ivy into the salon for some girly time. Rache always does her hair up real nice and sometimes paints her fingernails if she doesn't have a busy day."

"Oh. I didn't know Rachel knew Ivy."

"Yeah. Actually Rachel and I are cousins…well, second cousins I think? Her mom and my mom are cousins so…however the hell that works out."

I laugh understanding perfectly well the confusion of a large family tree. "Wow…I don't think I ever knew that…and I'm a little surprised that she never mentioned it to me before."

Bryant raises his eyebrows. "You mean you talk about me often in the salon?"

Smacking him lightly on the arm I say, "No, wiseass, but your name has come up in conversation before…" I think back to one we had not too long ago. "Wait…the dance recital…Rachel said she was going to her cousin's dance recital. Was that Ivy?"

Bryant chuckles. "Yeah. Damn…Ivy looked so stinkin' cute in her little tutu. It was her first dance class recital and she was beyond excited. I bought her some flowers and a new princess nightgown to give her that day. Even had the store clerk wrap it up with bright pink paper. She loved it. We spoiled her rotten."

Wrapped gift.

Flowers.

"That's right…I saw you that day. Walking out of Peirson's."

"You did?" He cocks his head. "Well why didn't you say hello?"

I roll my eyes at my own stubbornness and stupidity. "Well, because that was just after I had learned that you snuck into my apartment so you weren't exactly my favorite person at the moment and…" Silence falls between us.

"And what?" he asks.

"And…I thought the gift and the flowers may have been for…you know…" I'm blushing. "Not a three-year-old girl. Let's just put it that way."

"Ahh," he says, smiling. "You thought I had another girl in my life eh? Well gee, Seven, I have to say I sort of think green looks good on you."

I throw a pretzel at Bryant to try and hide my embarrassment. "Shut up. It does not."

"Uh huh…" I watch as he picks the pretzel that I threw at him off his shirt and pops it in his mouth. "On a scale of one to four just how jealous were ya?"

*Oh my God, this is embarrassing.*

*He's right though. I was jealous.*

"On a scale of one to four I was a shut the fuck up, Bryant Wood. That's what I was. Now quit teasing me!"

Through our laughter he says "Okay, okay. I promise not to buy anymore gifts for the women in my life without lettin' you know."

I push Bryant in the chest with my right hand so that he falls backwards, but he's too quick and grabs a hold of my hand, pulling me down with him. My weight shifts as he pulls me, but rather than falling on top of him he grabs me and immediately rolls so that I'm the one looking up at him.

*Holy shit.*

*What the hell just happened?*

*What was that noise?*

*What am I laying on?*

*Pretzels?*

I look up into Bryant's eyes. The humor that I saw in them a moment ago is gone. Instead he almost looks worried. "I'm sorry Rachel never told you about Ivy. It's my fault. I need you to know that I asked her not to tell you until I was ready."

*What?*

*Why on Earth would he do that?*

"I don't...understand. Why is it such a secret? Have I done something wrong?"

"No, no, no." He shakes his head. "God, no. Savannah I just...I needed time, I guess."

"Time? For what?"

"To see you again. To get to know you again. To..." He releases a huge breath. "I'm not explaining this very well, but...Savannah I've known you were back in town for a while now and...well..."

"Well, what?" I ask softly.

"You were the one that got away," he whispers. I wait as he takes a deep breath before continuing, "I liked you a lot when we were in high school, Savannah. Like an idiot I did nothing about it, but here you are and here I am and I'm doing something about it now. I just needed to do something about it without the stigma of being the single dad. I wanted to protect you and I needed to protect Ivy. And I needed to be me."

I'm still stuck on that first part.

"You're doing something about it now?" I almost can't get the words clearly out of my mouth. The butterflies in my stomach are fluttering around so damn fast I can barely catch my breath. I feel the heat rising in my cheeks and I'm nervous to hear what he has to say.

"I like you Savannah. I've liked you for a long time and I still like you. I know..." I watch as he swallows again. "I know we don't know each other that well, but you're so damn easy to talk to and I like who I am when I'm with you. You're beautiful and you're funny, and you're beautiful and, damnit, I know I said that already." The fact that he's flustered softens my heart and gives me the giggles. Bryant Wood is cute when he's trying to be sweet.

"Savannah, I know I said last week that I wasn't going to kiss you until you knew it was going to really mean something, but I'm really not sure how much longer I'm going to be able to look at you and not taste those beautiful lips that are always sitting there waiting to be kissed, because on a scale of one to four I…"

I quickly place my pointer finger on Bryant's lips to stop his nervous ramble. It's cute and I completely understand the feeling. "Bryant?"

"Yeah?"

"I don't care about your scale right now. I like you too," I whisper.

"You do?" he whispers back.

"Mmm hmm."

"Oh thank…" He closes his eyes momentarily. I watch his Adam's apple move up and down as he swallows again. I smile at how cute he is right now. "Does that mean I can, umm…" He looks down at my face, my lips, and back up at my eyes, asking permission. I know he wants to kiss me right now. And after an entire day of wondering why he hadn't done it yet, I'm eager to let him.

I nod my head from underneath him. "Yeah, I think that would be okay."

He nods. "Good. Yeah, good."

I smile shyly as I watch him lower his face to mine while still holding me underneath him. With one hand he brushes back the hair from my forehead and cradles my face in his hand. He looks down at my lips one last time and back up to my eyes before I feel the warm soft contact. His kiss is ever so gentle. His lips are soft and meld to mine with perfect ease as he kisses me once and then twice. The third time my breath hitches when I feel his fingers on my cheek holding me to him while our kiss deepens. My eyes closed, I try to breathe in this moment. His lips aren't Shawn's lips and although I half expected to freak out over that – I haven't kissed another man since before marrying Shawn – there's something about Bryant's kiss, the way he holds my face, the feel of his body hovering over mine that just feels comforting and good and safe. A soft moan escapes me as my desire for more strengthens. My lips part slightly bolstering Bryant's confidence as his tongue slowly entwines with mine.

Good God, the man can kiss.

Bryant pulls away a moment later and smiles down at me. Leaning down once more he kisses my forehead and quickly rubs his nose against mine. He says my name quietly as he sighs.

"Was that everything you thought it would be?" I ask, smiling up at him.

"And then some. I'm half tempted to do it again, but I'm afraid I won't be able to stop." Watching his face, I can tell that he's trying to reign in his control. This is a man who is used to being the horn-ball, the player, the man who always gets what he wants. It's oddly sweet to watch him try to be respectable, and compassionate, and gentle. That says more to me than he realizes. I push myself up just enough to kiss his cheek.

"Thank you, Bryant."

"For what?"

"For taking your time. For being gentle. For showing me that you're not the cocky douchebag I always took you for."

He laughs. "I probably deserved that, but you make me want to be better, Savannah. I've wanted it for years. I just never had a reason to want it until you came along. You're worth waiting for."

I place my hand on his cheek and look into his eyes. "Was I worth a completely smashed bag of pretzels?"

"Huh?" He raises an eyebrow and I giggle at his response, turning my body just enough to grab the bag of pretzels that was underneath me.

"When you flipped me over I landed right on the pretzel bag. I think we killed it." I frown as I hold up the bag of now crushed pretzel pieces. We laugh together as he helps me up from the ground. He takes the bag of broken pieces and tosses it back in the cooler nearby.

Winking at me he explains, "Well now you don't have to worry about taking the last bite."

It's been a perfect afternoon with Bryant, but we need to head back home. He needs to be at the bar tonight, so we can't be away for the entire day. It's okay though; I have more than enough to do to keep myself busy for the evening.

Holding Bryant's hand, we make our way to the end of the trail to where his truck is parked. He helps me in and I wait as he loads the cooler and our blanket into the back. The truck is pleasantly warm after spending the morning sitting in the sun. All the fresh air from this morning coupled with a nice warm truck is the perfect invitation for an afternoon nap. I resolve to stay awake for Bryant's sake though. It probably doesn't bode well for a girl if she falls asleep on a first date.

The windows are slightly down, causing my hair to blow in the warm breeze. We both have our sunglasses on, hiding the fact that since that kiss up on the trails, we've both been a bundle of smiles. It's like kissing me has finally put a spring in Bryant's step and if I'm being honest with myself, it has taken a small weight off of my burdened shoulders. I didn't realize how much pent up tension I was carrying around with me until I was able to release a little bit of it. They say that kissing someone for more than fifteen seconds releases endorphins, like a shot of adrenaline to the body.

*Maybe I should kiss him more often.*

Bryant turns the radio on and immediately starts singing. I can't help but laugh watching him. I'm not familiar with the song but it's obviously one of Bryant's favorites. He knows every damn word. He reaches over and squeezes my knee while he sings to me.

*Damn his voice.*

*How did I not know he could sing?*

I'm catching phrases like being all over the road and not being in control because of the girl sitting next to him. It's cute and quite catchy. "What's this song? I don't know it!" I smile. I don't want it to end because I like the feel of his hand on my leg. I lay my hand on top of his to let him know I'm okay with him keeping it right where it is.

"It's Easton Corbin. You don't know him?"

"Nope. But I also don't always listen to country music."

"Oh yeah? What do you like? You can change the station."

"No it's fine," I purse my lips. "I'm eclectic. I like a little of everything really."

Thinking he's going to call my bluff, Bryant smirks and says "Bullshit."

I gasp but laugh out loud at his response. "What? What do you mean 'bullshit'?"

"There's no way you're a rap girl."

"Oh no?"

"Nope." He's adamant that he knows enough about me to know my musical preferences.

"Suit yourself smarty pants." I shrug my shoulder and smirk as I look straight ahead out the front window of the truck.

"You should come by the bar tonight. Bourbon Creek is playin' and they're doing live karaoke night," Bryant says over the radio.

"Oh yeah? Karaoke huh?"

"Yep." He nods. "There's always a crowd on those nights. Blake Browning, he's the lead singer for the band, always knows how to get people up on stage for a good time and I swear he can play just about anything. He's genius! You should come. I promise you won't leave unhappy. That's for sure."

"Hmm...maybe I will. If I come, am I going to be forced to stand up on stage?" I ask a little frightened at what Bryant's going to say...but not that frightened. I can think of a song or two that would surprise the shit out of the guy sittin' next to me.

*He thinks he knows me!*

Bryant let's out a chuckle. "Would you like to? Because I can arrange that."

"No. I'm not saying that. Just curious. Maybe I'll call Rachel and see if she wants to hang out."

"Good idea. She'll come for sure. She loves karaoke night."

125

I take my phone out of my pocket and shoot a quick text to Rachel to see if she's available to go with me tonight.

Me: Hey girl. I need your inner Jennifer Hudson tonight. You game? #karaoke

Rachel: Sure! Does Bryant know?

Me: Nope...and it's gonna stay that way.

Rachel. Shit! This ought to be good! I'm in.

Immediately a long list of songs plays through my mind of what I could perform and oh, how shocked Bryant would be. The thought causes the grin already on my face to widen. I look down for a moment and pretend to pick non-existent lint from my jeans. The ride back home is warm and comfortable. With my body turned slightly toward Bryant I've been able to talk with him, laugh with him, and just watch him as he drives us home. Sometime during the ride, I close my eyes for a second listening to Bryant's voice as he sings softly.

*Is that a Brad Paisley song?*

*It's sweet.*

*Is he singing to me?*

I hear him sing the words "She's everything to me" and how I'm a warm conversation, a fighter when I'm mad and a lover when I'm loving. I keep my eyes closed so that he thinks I'm sleeping, and because the sound of his voice when he sings does things to parts of my body that I wasn't sure still worked.

*I could get used to this.*

# Chapter 17

# *Bryant*

I've been driving for an hour and a half. Not because it took us that long to get home but because the beautiful angel sitting next to me in my truck fell asleep and I don't want to wake her. She looks comfortable and peaceful and damn, if she isn't a vision to look at. I'm easily falling for her. How can I not? She's perfection. She's everything I always wanted but couldn't ever hold on to. The life I have, living with Ivy, being her superhero, is one I never thought about having in the past, but I'm content. I can be Dad and still have time to be Bryant. I can work hard at the bar and know that Ivy is taken care of, that I'm doing all of this so that she'll never want for anything. I can keep her healthy and happy and safe. That's all that matters, it's all that has ever mattered. But all of that changed in one damn instant, the moment she turned around that night in my bar. Savannah Turner took my breath away, made me weak in the knees and immediately hungry for something more. She makes me want to pull this truck over to the side of the road and make out with her until our lips are raw, but instead, I continue driving in circles around the outskirts of town, while she sleeps. Not only does it mean extra time spent with a beautiful girl in my presence, but the quiet time gives me time to reflect on how I even got here.

*****

**January 2, 2013**

The waiting room feels cold even though it's painted in vibrant primary colors. I thought waiting rooms were supposed to be calming, but this room, with blue and green and red striped walls with yellow curtains around the windows, is anything but. I get it. It's a children's hospital. Everything is happy and cheery. Maybe I'm just going crazy because my little girl has been laying on a surgical table for two hours now and I haven't heard anything yet. Dr. Fellgud said it would take a while; I just expected to hear something by now.

"You should stop drinking the coffee, honey. It's making you jittery." My mom says calmly. She likes to think she's the calm one, but I've been watching her for the past hour twiddling her thumbs with Olympic speed, and if her head isn't sore from constantly turning and looking at the door expecting someone to walk in, I will be shocked.

I'm pacing the room for what has to be the one hundred and twenty fifth time. "Yeah I know. I just really thought I might hear an update by now. I don't know whether to worry or not."

"No news is good news, Son. It'll all be fine. Ivy is a fighter. She'll pull through this with flying colors." My dad says from behind his newspaper.

"I know, Dad. I know." I roll my eyes hearing his words go in one ear and out the other.

*No news is good news, my ass.*

*What if there's no news because they're arguing over which one has to tell me that she's gone?*

Exasperated, I throw myself in a waiting room chair. Before I go stir crazy I pull my phone out of my pocket so that I can text Sloan. At least checking on the bar gives me something to do.

> Me: Hey Sloan, is everything ok there?
> Sloan: Hey! Is Ivy out of surgery? How did it go?
> Me: No. Still in surgery. Hoping to hear something soon.
> Sloan: No news is good news man! Yeah the bar is fine! Pretty light afternoon.
> Me: Good.
> Sloan: Hey did you hear the news about your girl, Savannah Sanders?
> Me: Asshat. She was never my girl and no. Why?
> Sloan: I heard she was in a bad accident last night. Lost her husband and child.

*WHAT?*

"Holy fucking shit." I mumble covering my mouth in shock.

"What is it?" My mom asks anxiously.

"Sloan just told me that Savannah Sanders was in a car accident last night. He said her husband and child were killed."

"What? James and Margie's daughter? Oh Lord, have mercy!" Mom cries. "That poor girl. I'll need to send them a card right away. I can't imagine what they're going through losing that grandbaby that they loved so much." She dabs at her cheeks with a tissue while I sit and stare at the text from Sloan on my phone. I still haven't replied to him. I don't even know what the fuck to say.

> Me: Thanks for letting me know.
> Sloan: Uh, sure thing. You ok?
> Me: Yeah. I can't think about it now. Ivy comes first.

It's the only reply I can think of right now because it's true. Ivy comes first. She has to. But damn if my heart isn't crumbling for the girl I was in love with all those years ago.

*****

## September 30, 2013

Ivy is finally asleep after a fussy battle of having to take new medicine that she doesn't like. Why do those pharmacies tell us that it's a yummy grape flavor when in reality they all taste like Robitussin? It's just gross. I feel bad for my baby girl, but taking that medicine is important. She'll get used to it. The weather is still mildly warm this evening so I grab a beer and the baby monitor and head outside onto the deck off the kitchen. May as well enjoy some peace and quiet and fresh air while I can. The solidarity after a rough day is nice.

I'm two sips into my beer when my phone rings in my pocket.

*So much for solidarity.*

It's my mom undoubtedly calling to check in on Ivy. "Hey Mom. What's up?" I greet her.

"Hey Honey, I was just calling to see how my little princess did tonight. Did she like her new medicine?" Mothers can be so predictable...or in this case, grandmothers.

"She did alright after a nice screaming fit. They should make that shit dye free. She took one look at the purple color and wanted no part of it. I got it in her eventually. An extra Hershey kiss did the trick."

Mom chuckles on the other end of the line. "Smart thinking, Daddy. Good job."

"Yeah, whatever gets the job done at this point. How are you and Dad? Everything okay?"

"Oh yes. We're fine. We had a nice day out antiquing this afternoon and we took a drive down to the lake."

"Sounds like a nice day." Retirement is obviously treating them very well. We talk for another ten minutes before a quick silence falls between us.

"Oh hey, did I tell you that I ran into Margie Sanders the other day?" she asks.

*Savannah's mom.*

*I haven't heard anything about her in months.*

"Nope. Why? Is she okay?" I ask.

"Of course. She's fine. It's her poor daughter that isn't doing well I guess."

*Savannah?*

I sit up a little straighter, not that anyone can see me. "What do you mean not doing well? Is she sick?"

"Depression I would guess. Margie mentioned that she was in therapy but still pretty despondent over her loss. Who wouldn't be, really? But anyway, Margie said they moved her back home so she's staying with them now. Hopefully that helps her a little bit."

*She moved home?*

*She's closer now?*

*If only we had been closer in high school.*

*I could go to her.*

*I could help her.*

*Anything.*

I try to sound nonchalant even though my heart breaks again for Savannah. "Yeah. She probably shouldn't be alone. She'll do better being around people."

"You guys were friends in school right? Maybe you should check in on her sometime," Mom suggests.

*There's nothing I would love more, Mom.*

"We knew of each other. I wouldn't say we were friends. Not that we weren't friends…" I correct myself. "We were just in different social circles. Maybe if I run into her I'll see how she's doing."

"Good idea," Mom says. "It wouldn't be a bad idea for you to have some company either."

"Yeah, Mom. I hear you."

"I love you, Honey. You sleep well and give a big hug to Ivy for me in the mornin'."

"Love you too, Mom. Will do. G'night."

\*\*\*\*\*

## July 20, 2014

The day is shaping up to be the steamy hot day that all the weather stations warned us about. I took Ivy to the park earlier rather than later in the day so that we could avoid the heat during the afternoon. I even surprised her with an ice cream cone before lunch which put me at Best-Daddy-in-the-World status as far as she's concerned.

"Mail Daddy! I get the mail okay?" If there's one thing Ivy likes to do, to make her feel like she's a big girl, it's pulling the mail out of the mailbox.

"Sure thing Princess. Let's walk down and get it together." I take her hand as she leads me back down the driveway where our mailbox sits near the road. I lift her little body enough that she can pull down the lid and grab today's mail. "Biws biws biws." She says as she looks at each envelope in the small stack. "Nuffing fun. Here, Daddy." She hands me the mail and skips back up the driveway where she waits for me on the porch. It's the same response she gives every day, but I laugh anyway. Through my laughter I finger through the mail one envelope at a time. It seems Ivy is right. Medical bills, medical bills, medical bills. The cycle never ends as far as those are concerned, but I don't give a rat's ass. I would come up with a million dollars to pay for Ivy's care if I had to. She's worth it. Her body went through hell seven months ago and I'm so proud to see her doing okay now. The around-the-clock care, the strict timing of her medicinal needs, the constant worry as her parent, it's all worth it to see her on days like today. It's like that liver inside her was made for her.

There is one envelope in the stack of mail that I don't expect to see. Addressed to Ivy and me from the Donor Family Services Coordinator at Give Life, an organization that aids donor and recipient families in communicating with one another. I tear open the envelope and pull out the letter inside.

> Dear Mr. Wood and Ivy,
>
> We received this letter from the family of Ivy's organ donor. We hope that this letter brings you joy and peace and finds you both well, and healing happily. If you would like to send a response to this family, please follow the instructions in the attached brochure. I am also available to help you in your communications in any way I can.
>
> Sincerely,
>
> Mary Ellen Duffler
> Donor Family Services Coordinator
> Give Life

It's a letter from Ivy's donor family.
*Well I'll be...*

*I never thought about writing one myself.*

*Man, do I feel like an asshole.*

Who goes through this painstakingly emotional process and doesn't say 'thank you'? Me, that's who. I never gave it a moment's thought. I just focused on Ivy and her needs. Shaking my head at myself and resolving to write an immediate reply, I swallow a huge piece of humble pie before opening the envelope that on the front says,

## Donor Recipient

Eager to learn more, I rip open the envelope and pull out a neatly handwritten letter.

*Dear recipient,*

*My name is Savannah. My daughter, Peyton, was the little girl who donated one of her organs to you. She would have celebrated her second birthday on July 7th. Although she is no longer with us, I know Peyton and her Daddy are smiling down on you from Heaven and watching you grow in strength and peace. I hope you...*

"Oh God, no..." I gasp.

My hand starts to shake. It doesn't take long for me to figure it out. Bardstown, KY is a damn small town. News travels fast, and when it's headlines like "Hometown Girl Loses Husband and Daughter in Car Accident," there isn't a person alive not talking about it. I still remember the text I got from Sloan that day in the hospital waiting room. I knew Savannah had a husband and a little girl named Peyton. I knew she lost them both the day before in an accident. I don't even need to read the entire thing because the person writing the letter states that her name is Savannah and that her daughter, Peyton, was the donor of Ivy's liver.

*Holy shit.*

*No.*

*Just, no.*

*Never in a million years.*

*What are the odds?*

*Of all the fucking livers in the world…*

*How many Savannahs and Peytons could there possibly be?*

*It has to be.*

*Fuck.*

"Daddy, I need my Mickey!" I hear Ivy whine, standing at the front door. My hand continues to shake as I pull my keys out of my pocket to unlock the front door.

I clear my throat and wipe the sweat off my forehead before looking up at Ivy. "Go ahead Sweetness. I'll be right there." I open the door and let it swing all the way open as Ivy waltzes in, making a beeline for her favorite Mickey Mouse doll.

The weight of the letter in my hand is too much for me. I stumble in the doorstep and sit down quickly on the bench inside the door.

*What do I…?*

*Who do I …?*

*I…where…?*

I don't even know where to start. There's no way in hell I can tell anyone about this. Not one fucking person. Damnit! Gossip flows through this town just as fast as the bourbon does. There's no way I can ever risk Savannah finding out, not that there's anything she can do about it really but if it were me…I don't…even…know.

It could break her even more.

I can't be the cause of her pain.

Because the hurricane that was my life at the time wasn't shitty enough, on top of it all, I now have to hold on to the fact that my daughter's liver once belonged to the daughter of a girl I wanted when I was young. A girl I wouldn't mind having a second chance with. What the hell am I going to do with this information? I can't write her back. I can't tell her who I am. I haven't seen her in years, but I know she's living with her parents. I know she lives on the outskirts of town. We live not even fifteen minutes apart for Christ's sake. I know she's alone. I know I would love to see her but how the fuck can that happen now?

*"Oh hey, Savannah. Nice to see you again. Oh by the way, sorry about your kid but thanks for the liver! Ya want to grab a drink sometime?"*

Double fuck.

That's a weight nobody ever imagines themselves needing to carry. Certainly not me, but fate can be a cruel bitch.

*****

## December 21, 2014

I have a truck load of Christmas presents for Ivy and not enough time in the world to get them all wrapped. To top that off, if there's one thing I fucking suck at during any time of the year, it's wrapping presents. How do women make them look so pretty with bows and glitter and shit? And isn't the kid just going to rip them open anyway? Why spend all the time and money on shit that's just going to be purposely ripped up and then thrown away? I'll never get it, but I'm Santa Claus and that's the way Santa does it…as long as this Santa has an elf's help. I tap the quick dial number on my phone for Rachel. She can cut hair, surely she can wrap gifts.

"Hey Bryant," she says.

"Hey. What are you up to tonight?"

"Uh…not too much. Just finishing up some Christmas shopping. Why? Is Ivy okay?

"Yeah she's fine. I just put her to bed. Now Santa has a shit ton of presents to wrap, and Santa has to tie pretty ribbons and bows on his gifts, except Santa doesn't fucking know how to do that kind of stuff so he's going to need a little help. You cut hair, so that makes you a ribbons and bows expert right?"

Rachel laughs into the phone. "Ribbons and bows expert I am not, but I do enjoy making presents look pretty. Don't ask me why the hell I enjoy it when people just rip it off and throw them away. I know it's stupid, but yeah. I can help you. Want me to stop by on my way home?"

"Would you? I'll feed you and I'm sure I have a few beers in the fridge," I plead.

"Sure thing. I'll be there in about forty minutes."

I look at the clock, noticing that it's not quite time for the salon to be closed yet. "Are you not working tonight? I mean, it's okay if you need to stay there to help close."

"Nope. I'm good. I left early. Audrey and Savannah are closing up tonight."

Savannah…

"Savannah?" I ask innocently. "Who's that? A new girl?"

"Oh, yeah. I haven't talked to you in a while. Remember that girl from high school? Savannah Sanders?" she asks.

What the fuck? Is she serious?

My heart rate immediately starts to elevate. "Yeah. She lost her family in that car accident a while back," I answer.

"Yeah that's her," Rachel confirms. "Anyway my mom and her mom are in the Red Hat Society together and got to talking about Savannah. I guess she's really had a hard time getting over everything. I mean, not that I can blame her, but anyway, my mom told her in passing that I was looking for new people and her mom mentioned that Savannah actually had her Beauticians license. She thought maybe if Savannah got herself a job, she would start to brighten up a little. I really felt for her, and she was such a nice girl back in the day, so I called her and offered her a job."

Holy shit. She's working right down the street from me.

How the hell am I going to make this work?

She can't ever find out what I know.

"Bryant?" Rachel asks.

"Huh? Yeah. I'm here."

"Sorry I thought I lost you. Anyway, I'll see you in a bit okay?"

"Yeah. Thanks Rache."

All this time I've been able to keep my distance from Savannah, even with us both in the same tiny town. Why do I feel like no matter what I do, fate is going to force our paths to cross eventually? And what the ever living fuck am I going to do when it does?

Her deep breath tells me she's waking up. I look over at Savannah as her eyes open and she shifts in her seat, stretching just slightly. I catch sight of the side of her torso when she reaches her arm up to fix her hair. Thoughts of my hands on her body, my lips on her skin; they consume me, but I'm forced to swallow them back. She deserves to be treated like a damn queen and I can give that to her. But I'll be damned if I let her think for even a minute that all I want is a one-night stand.

"Sleeping Beauty awakens."

She looks at me with a just-fucked smile, the smile that says she's comfortable and happy and not embarrassed one bit. Her confidence turns me on even more.

*Damnit this girl.*

"Yeah, sorry-not-sorry about that." She chuckles. "I guess this truck is more comfortable than I thought. I wasn't out long though was I?"

I clear my throat and shake my head "Nah, only a few minutes. Not nearly enough to drool on my shoulder or anything."

"Hmm." Her lips purse.

"What?"

"A few minutes huh?" She smirks when she leans forward and taps the digital clock on the dashboard. "I would believe you if the clock didn't say three-thirty!" She laughs.

I suck in my breath and scrunch my face. "Busted. Okay. Okay, you slept most of the way and you snore like a damn troll. Does that make you feel better?"

Savannah slaps me on my arm. "I do not snore like a damn troll, you big liar!"

I love it when she laughs. I could listen to her laugh all day.

Taking my hands off the wheel for a second I raise my hands in defeat. "Alright. You got me. You weren't out that long and I selfishly enjoyed every minute of watching you sleep. That's my story and I'm stickin' to it."

Within minutes I'm pulling into Savannah's apartment complex and helping her out of the truck. I'm at a little bit of a loss because it's the middle of the day. This isn't the end of the night where I kiss the girl and then walk away thanking God that I never have to see her again. This is completely different. I want to kiss this girl. I want to lay her down and make love to her in the middle of the goddam afternoon, but I have places I need to be if the bar is going to be ready to go for the night.

"Penny for your thoughts?" she asks quietly as we walk up the steps together.

I feel the heat rise in my cheeks. I vowed to handle this girl with every honest thought I had except for the one thing I can't ever bring myself to tell her. "Well Seven, I was thinking about how I was going to kiss you before I left you. I mean, it's not the end of the night so hopefully I'll get to show you a proper good night kiss a bit later, but I am leaving you for now so…you know…"

"Yeah…I guess you'll have to try a proper goodbye kiss then…"

Fuck! This girl knows how to turn me on.

If the blush on her face doesn't give her thoughts away, her body language does. She stands in front of her apartment door with her hands hanging on her back pockets, causing her chest to push forward, closer to me. I try to remain calm, focusing on taking one breath and then another.

For a moment we don't speak. I make the mistake of letting my eyes travel down her body one last time but they come to a quick halt. The swell of her sweet breasts peek out of the tank-top underneath her button-down shirt. The way she stands in front of me, it's like she's offering them up to me, free for the taking.

*Soft and gentle or rough and hard?*

*Focus, Bryant!*

*Soft and gentle or rough and hard?*

I don't know which way to go. I want to be gentle with her, but when I finally make eye contact with her she's biting her bottom lip and I'm gone. I can't hold back any more. I step into her, immediately grabbing onto her so my weight doesn't slam her into the door. With my right hand I hold tightly to the hair on the back of her head, pulling just slightly enough so that her face reaches up to mine. Being taller than her has dominant advantages. I slide my left hand under her chin and around her ear, holding her face as I bring my lips to hers with vigor and force. She rewards me with a relieving sigh, happy to have her breath taken away by my lips. She moans when I press my body harder against hers. The feel of her chest pressed against mine, our breathing in tandem, it's all I can do to not lift her up and wrap her legs around my waist.

I lick her bottom lip slowly, savoring the taste of her mouth, wishing I could taste more of her. The desire I feel for this woman is like nothing I have ever felt before. I want to slow down. I want to take my time and savor every fucking minute with her, but when her tongue reaches out to meet mine, we find a rhythm that I don't ever want to break.

"Bryant." My name said breathlessly between kisses.

"Seven." I slow my pace until our lips separate. I kiss her lips softly again before kissing her cheek, and her nose, and finally her forehead, all the while trailing my arm down the side of her body until my hand rests just underneath her chest. I could do it. Holy fuck I want to slide my thumbs softly across the front of her, so I can feel the hardened peaks; I want to see her aroused. I want to know that it's me that makes her feel that way. I want to help her let go. I want to make her mine. Her eyes are closed as if she's waiting for me to make that move, but damnit, the hallway is no place for that and I can't stay now.

*Another time.*

*It's okay.*

"I should go," I say quietly. I feel like a shmuck walking out on her after what we just did in this hallway. What I wouldn't give to keep going. "I have to get to the bar so I can be there when the band arrives."

"Yeah. Okay," she says, watching my every move.

*What is she thinking?*

I kiss her forehead one more time, letting my lips linger at her hair line, breathing in her scent and committing it to memory.

*As if I could forget.*

With a hand on each of her shoulders I softly say to her "I...I had a wonderful day with you, Seven. Every single moment with you was...perfect."

She slowly smiles. I feel her hand on my bicep rubbing back and forth.

*She could do that all damn day.*

"I had a perfect day with you as well, Bryant. Thank you...I really did enjoy myself, and you." She blushes. "I'll see you tonight though right?"

*Yes! She's coming!*

*God, I hope she'll be coming soon...*

"Absolutely. I'll be the guy at the bar serving all the hot ladies." I wink at her so she knows I'm just teasing.

"Oh yeah? Well I guess I'll be a hot lady then."

"You already are, Seven." I shake my head eyeing her body one more time before I leave. "You already are."

# Chapter 19

# *Savannah*

As soon as I shut the door, I run to the window to watch Bryant walk back to his truck. I stand back from the window just enough that he won't know that I'm watching him. I see him appear in the parking lot and immediately my body responds. The heat, that tingle in my stomach, the blush in my cheeks…that good-bye kiss was…hot! I could've stood in that hallway all afternoon, not giving a damn who saw us. I bet Patty Prude next door could learn a few things if she watched for a while.

I watch Bryant walk back to his truck, open the door and then turn to look up toward my window. Instinctively I gasp and step back, afraid of just being caught ogling at him. I watch his head fall back as he takes a deep breath, releasing it with a huge smile across his face. He touches his lips with his hand before sliding his hand over his face and slipping into his truck.

*He's happy.*

*With me?*

I almost wish he could see that my expression matches his at this very moment. He made feel happy today, special, like my life mattered to someone. That's a feeling I haven't had in a while and it was nice to feel it again. I was so wrong about Bryant Wood. He's not at all the douchebag I once thought he was. I guess life changes people. I'm a testament to that as well, and now that I've had a taste of what Bryant is offering, suddenly living doesn't sound so bad.

*****

Once I'm out of the shower I send a text to Rachel making sure she's good to go for our girl's night at Wood's tavern.

> Me: Are you ready for a little Jennifer Hudson action tonight?
> Rachel: Woot! Hell yeah I am, girl! What time?

Me: Tell the girls eight? I need to do my hair and rethink my outfit. Want to come help?

Rachel: I would LOVE to! I'll be over in an hour. Girl, when I'm done with you, Bryant's not gonna know what hit him.

Me: Counting on it!

Rachel is right. Bryant has no idea that the girls and I have these break-into-song moments at the salon. I'm usually the girl who keeps to herself, but every now and then the old me seeps out and I want to do something carefree and fun. Together Rachel and I have worked up quite the song list…but Bryant doesn't know that. Karaoke and a few drinks tonight will be perfect. Now I just need to focus on looking like the hot lady without looking like the desperate hussy.

I decide on a flirty plum colored strapless tunic dress covered with my denim jacket and, of course, my trusty cowgirl boots. Rachel helps pull my wavy curls up into a loose ponytail to expose my neck since "guys love that" she tells me. Big dangly earrings and a long necklace complete my look for the night and for the first time in years I look at myself in the mirror and approve. I look good. Really good. In the next two hours, we're walking into the bar ready for a good night.

Like a moth to a flame my eyes immediately find Bryant. He's standing at the bar pouring a beer for a few customers. When he looks up, he sees me walk in with the girls. At first I'm not sure he notices that it's me and not just some other girl, except he's staring.

*He notices.*

"Dude what are you doin'?" I hear the guy at the bar say. Bryant blinks and looks back to the guy talking to him and immediately I see what happened. Bryant jumps back and laughs, shaking his head, before looking up at me and winking. Beer from the tap is overflowing the glass Bryant is filling.

"Sorry about that, man." I hear Bryant say to his customer. He chuckles to himself, grabbing a towel to clean up the spilled mess. "I guess I was just distracted for a minute there. Here ya go." After wiping down the glass quickly, he hands the customer his beer. Once the customer rejoins his party, Bryant looks over to me. I step over a little closer to the bar so I can say hello to him.

"Hey!"

Bryant lifts the countertop door and walks out from behind the bar, his towel draped over his shoulder. My breath hitches at the sight of all of him. His light denim jeans distressed in all the right places, paired with a form fitting black t-shirt. Damn the man can dress himself, that's for sure. As he walks slowly over to me and the girls, I see his lips twitch. I can't tell what he's thinking but he's not smiling like I expected him to be.

"I thought you said you were going to be one of the hot ladies tonight?"

*What?*

I'm completely taken aback.

"Come again?" is all I can think to say, although I certainly don't want him to say it again. I heard him loud and clear the first time.

Bryant shakes his head eyeing my legs, my chest, my neck, and finally meets my questioning eyes. "On a scale of one to four, I would say you're drop dead sexy."

*Oh, thank God.*

Bryant leans over, holding my head with his left hand so he can whisper in my ear. "I've got to make you come a first time before I can make you come again, Seven, but that is definitely something we can talk about. You look fantastic tonight." He kisses me lightly on my neck right below my ear and I nearly go weak in the knees. The girls giggle behind me and for the first time in a long time, I feel shy.

"Thank you Bryant," I say quietly. Clearing my throat, I look behind me and proclaim to the group, "Let's drink ladies!"

"Are we going to see you in action tonight, Bryant?" I ask, raising my eyebrows in a challenge.

*I hope so.*

*He's got the sexiest voice.*

"We'll see." He grins. "We'll see how the night goes. What'll it be ladies? Your drinks tonight are on the house."

We all place our orders and find a good sized table near the front so we can watch the band. Both Bryant and Rachel have said that Bourbon Creek is a fantastic band with a lot of talent. There's definitely a level of excitement in here that I've never experienced. I'm looking forward to watching the action.

Two cranberry Old Fashions later and I can officially change my name to Tipsy. The music is great, the laughter with the girls feels fantastic and the constant flirting with Bryant throughout the night is ramping up my hormones. The alcohol I've consumed is definitely making me brave.

"He really likes you, I can tell," Audrey says across the table.

"Oh, I completely agree." Rachel raises her hand like we're in a damn classroom. She's obviously feeling the buzz as well. "He's smitten. He hasn't taken his eyes off you all night."

"You mean tits and ass!" Heather shouts. "He hasn't taken his eyes off her tits and ass." My eyes nearly bulge right out of my head but I giggle nonetheless.

"Not true!" I try to defend him but who I am kidding? I've noticed him cast looks my direction several times throughout the night. Tonight I feel sexy and important, like I matter to someone. It wasn't too long ago that I stood at that bar and watched Bryant flirt with other women. Women who were clearly prettier than me. Women who were obviously looking for a free drink in exchange for a booty call, but that's not the Bryant I see tonight. Tonight I see him not pay a second's notice to any of the women who try to throw themselves at him. He only has eyes for me. It's endearing.

Rachel gives me her best smug smile, like she knows me better than I know myself. "Whatever you say Savannah, but there's no denying there's something there between you two. I mean, if you don't see it…"

"I see it," I assure her. "I don't know. Right now, we're two adults, who have been through hell, and just want to have some fun together. He's not the guy I remember him being back in high school.

He's...sweet...and protective...compassionate." I shrug. "I don't know, I like him."

I look around the table and the girls are all smiling at me in that "aww she's falling in love and it's cute" kind of way. Rolling my eyes at all of them I motion for our waitress so I can order another drink. It's then that I hear a familiar strum of a guitar playing what sounds like the intro to a song everybody knows since it's played on the radios around here many times a day. I turn to watch the band once again, thinking to myself that the voice of Bourbon Creek's lead singer wouldn't be able to sound as much like Sam Hunt as others might want him to. The introductory chords are played over and over again to the point that I'm assuming I'm wrong about the song selection until I spot him in the corner of the room. Bryant Wood with a microphone in his hand.

*Oh God he's not...*

He walks up to the small stage where the band is playing softly and says "So I spent some time with a girl today..." The entire bar hoots and hollars, shouting cat calls and "Get 'er done's". Obviously it's no secret that Bryant knows his way around the ladies.

"No, no, no...it's not like that," he says with a wave of his hand. "This girl is a special girl and spending the day with her was the best thing to happen to me in a long time. I've had this damn smile on my face all day." He shakes his head, chuckling partly to himself before looking up to find my gaze. "Anyway, she told me she likes rap music and I called bullshit. I don't believe her...but just in case, this is the best I can do, so here goes."

Bryant starts into the beginning of Sam Hunt's "Take Your Time". The song is about not wanting to steal my freedom, not wanting to come on too strong, but just wanting to take some of my time. If I wasn't drunk I might actually tear up a little bit because Bryant makes no hesitation of singling me out in the crowd. If this town didn't know that Bryant and I spent the day together, they do now.

He finishes his song, thanks the band and turns to the crowd. "Who's next ya'll? It's Karaoke Night LIVE with Bourbon Creek!" The crowd in the bar cheers as several people raise their hands and make their way to one of the band members to check out their repertoire list. A quick wink and nod to Rachel and she knows just what to do. I watch as she hops up from her chair, swallowing down the rest of her drink, and makes her way up front.

"Well, what did you think, Seven? Was that rap enough for you?" Bryant appears at my table and wraps an arm around my shoulder.

"Well I don't know if I would constitute talking in the middle of a song as rap, but not bad. I can give you props for that performance."

"Ah well thanks. That was all for you. I promise the next one won't be so mushy." I feel his lips on my head as he stands above me.

"You don't do mushy? Cause I would beg to differ if you said no."

"Oh Seven, I can do mushy with the best of them but this crowd doesn't need to see that. That can just be privately for you," he whispers in my ear so the girls don't hear him either. The closeness of his breath on my ear makes me close my eyes and inhale to try and take control over my body. Maybe it's just the alcohol, but having Bryant around me, watching him tonight as he watches me, knowing what we both probably want but are too shy to take, I'm aching. It's been a long time but I'm going to need some relief, sooner rather than later. This man makes me want to step out of my comfort zone but I'm not sure how comfortable I am going there with him just yet. He makes me want to forget my past though. Maybe not forget it, but live past it.

"Uh huh...just for me you say? Is that how you earned the nickname Bryant...*the Giant* Wood? You know, privately with the ladies?" I whisper back to him using his nickname so he knows I'm purposely flirting. I flip my loose ponytail over my shoulder and take another sip of my drink, making sure to keep eye contact with him the entire time. Lowering my glass, I lick my lips before biting my lower lip in a smile.

*I think I'm turning myself on.*
*You're being a tease, Savannah.*
*Meh. You only live once...or in my case...sort of twice.*

I watch as Bryant swallows and tries not to react to the obvious signs of attraction I've just displayed. It's fun to watch the player become flustered. "Nah, that's just the nickname the guys on the football team gave me. You know how it is. Guys being guys…but I'm sure you could wrestle the giant anytime you wanted, Seven. You just say the word."

*Yes, please.*

"Hmmm I don't know…would I have to wear one of those WWE costumes?" I ask teasingly.

Bryant closes his eyes and bows his head. I can tell he's smirking but I'm not quite sure what he's thinking.

"Damnit woman you know how to make a guy question his control. To answer your question, no. You don't have to wear a costume, but fuck if you wouldn't look fantastic in one of those tight little numbers."

I hear the keyboard start to play and look up to see Rachel standing on the stage waiting for me. This is my cue. It's time to play. Bryant watches as I boldly shoot the rest of my drink down my throat and wipe my mouth with the back of my hand. "I'll keep that in mind, Mr. Wood. In the meantime, I have somewhere to be." I hop up a bit unsteadily from my chair.

"Savannah where are…"

There's not time to answer him. I wink at him before making my way to the stage. Rachel hands me the microphone just in time for me to turn around and look at a very shocked Bryant watching us. I try to hold in my laughter so that I can keep in character. He thinks I can't rap or that I don't like it, but shit, I'll show him. Alcohol is freely flowing through my veins and encouraging me to let go of my inhibitions as I point to Bryant, channel my inner Iggy Azalea and begin to rap.

> "I should'a known that you were bad news,
> from the bad boy demeanor and the tattoos…
> …and a little trouble only makes for a good time,
> so all the normal red flags be a good sign…"

Rachel is the Jennifer Hudson to my Iggy. Raising her arms as she belts out the chorus, I stand back and dance behind her, allowing all the troubles of my world to melt into oblivion around me. This song has meaning to Rachel and I. We both see it as one of those situations when you realize you're meant to be friends because of a moment you both shared.

Working in the salon one day, I was trimming up one of the local high school cheerleaders who seemed a way more down in the dumps than she ever had been. I don't remember if she ever told us what the problem was but when "Trouble" came on the radio, my motherly/BFF instinct kicked in and I immediately knew how to make her smile. I started rapping and to everyone's surprise, I knew every word Iggy said. All Rachel could do was laugh, grab a round hair brush to use as her microphone and sing along to Jennifer's part. We've been good friends ever since.

Our song finishes and the roar of the crowd in the bar is even louder than it was for Bryant. Rachel and I give each other a high five and a big hug before handing the microphone to the next performer. As we proudly walk back to our table, Bryant is standing next to my chair with a shit eating grin on his face, shaking his head back and forth. "How was that Mr. Wood? Did that pass your 'Savannah can't possibly rap' test?" I raise my hands back to fix my hair that had started to fall out of my ponytail and the moment I bow my head slightly to reach back he grabs me.

Pressing his body against mine with one hand on my back and one holding my hands on the back of my head, Bryant kisses me hard. Electricity shoots through me all the way to my core. I feel the pulse of my heartbeat in places I didn't know a pulse could be felt. Bryant's warmth, his fiery passion, and his apt for surprise make me hunger for more of him. I match his kiss with the same intensity wishing to God we were anywhere but standing in a public bar being whistled at by more people than I probably care to notice.

*Sober me would care.*

*But I'm not sober.*

*So I don't care.*

When Bryant pulls back, softly kissing my nose, I peer up at him with a desire to tug his hand and take him in a back room somewhere.

*There's always a back room somewhere, right?*

"I think that performance was…the hottest, sexiest, most arousing thing I've ever seen a girl do in this bar and I've seen some pretty…rare things."

"Hmm…well I thought about doing 'Like a Virgin', but I'm glad you approve."

"Yeah well I almost sang about checking you for ticks so we're even, and I'll always approve of you dancing, Seven. You can move your body around this bar any fucking time you want on one condition."

I raise my eyebrows at his proposal. "Oh? And what condition is that?"

"I have to be here to watch. Every time. I don't know if I could stand it knowing that you were here without me dancing while other guys were here watching you so please, just make sure I'm here so I can watch, and then protect you from the fuckin' sharks."

Why does that make me blush? Damn, this guy knows how to say all the right things. Not that I feel the need to be protected. God knows I can obviously handle myself just fine, but it's nice to know there's a man looking out for me again. Females can be strong, independent bitches, but in the end, none of us mind knowing that someone is there for us, looking out for our safety. It's what I find attractive in Bryant. Well, that and his strong arms, and nice ass.

"Deal." I wrap my arms around him and kiss him sweetly one more time. Kissing Bryant could be my new hobby.

I turn my head to look at the girls who are all now seated at the table around me. Audrey and Heather both try to nonchalantly pick their jaws up off the table while Rachel squeals loudly, clapping her hands in approval. Audrey pours us all a glass of water from the pitcher sitting on the table. Scooting a glass in my direction she says, "Soooo I guess your date went pretty well today then, huh?"

That earns Audrey a round of laughter from the rest of us.

"I should go check on the bar. I'll check in on ya'll in a bit. Let me know if you need anything. I'll send over another pitcher of water." The girls all smile at Bryant, thanking him for his hospitality. He looks to me before walking away. "Did you drive here tonight?"

"Nope." I shake my head. The room spins around me a little bit but nothing I can't handle with a few more glasses of water. "We came in Rachel's car."

Rachel chimes in, "And since I'm the DD for the night, I only had one beer and that was when we got here. I'm good."

Bryant nods but looks seriously between the two of us. "All the same I would like to make sure you get home safely. That okay with you Sev?"

*Alone time with Bryant? Uh… yeah.*

"Yeah. That would be great. Thanks Bryant."

"Don't mention it. I'll check on ya in a bit." He kisses my head lightly and walks back to the bar.

"Phew girl, he's got it bad," Rachel teases.

"Nah, he's just being a nice guy. I guess I'm new to the nice-guy treatment these days so I'll take it while I can even if it means I'll get hurt in the long run."

Rachel tilts her head in my direction, confused. "Why would you get hurt? Bryant *is* a great guy. You don't know him like I do. I think his feelings are legit. I've never seen him like this around a girl before…like, ever." Rachel raises her eyebrows before winking at me. "Face it, Savannah. You have yourself an admirer."

I gulp down my water, hoping to God that I really can handle this.

*What if Bryant's the one who ends up getting hurt because of me?*

# Chapter 20

# *Bryant*

I didn't think I believed in second chances at life until I met Savannah Turner. I resigned myself to thinking that I would forever be a single daddy to the world's cutest little girl, feeling grateful for the gift of her life and living with the guilt of knowing where her new liver came from and never telling a damn soul. But then fate had a way of answering my long-awaited unanswered prayers when Savannah moved back into town. I knew then that no matter what happened, I owed this woman my life and would do whatever I could to make sure she was cared for. I can't explain what's happening now between Savannah and me, but whatever it is I'll take it. I'll take all of it and I'll hold onto it for the rest of my life if she'll let me.

This might be one of the best days and nights I've had in my adult life. Sun up to sun down I'll remember this day for as long as I live. It's the day I started falling hard for a girl I don't deserve. I don't even know how it happened but watching her tonight, seeing her smile, her eyes as they lit up when she performed with Rachel, feeling the desire in her kiss, the warmth of her hand in mine...she's the one. She has to be, but something about that possibility feels so damn impossible to me. I'm lying to her by omission...because I have to...but at some point in our future, maybe next week, next month, next year, or ten years from now, the truth is going to make its way out and when it does...

I have to tell her before it does.

But not tonight.

Tonight is not that time.

She probably wouldn't remember anyway.

"Hey? You okay? You're quiet." Savannah bumps my shoulder gently as we walk the steps to her apartment. She stumbles a little bit so I wrap my arm around her waist to steady her. I'm not judging this girl at all for her intoxicated state. She needed a night like this to let go of her demons, and what better place than amongst friends and in my bar where I could watch her, take care of her.

"Yeah Seven. I'm great." I smile warmly at her as I basically lift her up the steps. I can still smell her perfume as she leans into me. It's intoxicating. When we reach the top of the steps Savannah pulls her keys out of her purse. I watch as she tries to put the key in the door to her apartment and can't. It's humorous and endearing all at the same time. She's a cute drunk.

"Son of a bitch, it won't go in," she says loudly before giggling and exclaiming, "That's what he said." I shake my head laughing at her as I gently take her key chain out of her hand.

"That was your car key Seven. Here, let me help you." I find the correct key on the ring and quickly unlock the door, but not before the door next to her apartment opens. A petite woman who looks to be in her late sixties, dressed in a zipped up bathrobe and fluffy pink slippers stands in the door. She doesn't look at all pleased with what she sees in the hallway.

"What's going on out here?" she asks.

"Oh, hi Patty," Savannah leans back and waves to her like the two of them are across the room from each other. "Sorry. I was just having trouble with my door. It's okay now. Bryant got it for me. You can go back to your *Golden Girls*. Sorry to bother you."

Patty sneers at the both of us before running her eyes up and down my entire body.

Is this old lady checking me out?

Eat your heart out lady.

I nod politely to her before wrapping a hand back around Savannah and lead her inside. "Good night ma'am."

Once we're finally behind closed doors Savannah announces, "I gotta pee. Make yourself at home, Bryant."

While she's in the bathroom I take a minute to get us each a glass of water. The bottle of Advil is still on her kitchen counter where I had left it the last time I was here, so I shake a few out for Savannah.

Hopefully I can help her morning be a little more bearable. At least her head won't be in a toilet.

Savannah comes back down the hallway carrying her denim jacket and the boots she had on tonight. She throws her boots on the floor in the hall closet and hangs up her jacket. She's now dressed only in her strapless purple dress, walking quietly to where I am in the kitchen in her bare feet.

Even tired and drunk she looks amazing.

I hand her the glass of water I poured for her along with the Advil which she takes immediately. "Thank you," she says.

"You're welcome; that should help come morning," I wink at her.

I watch her drink her water as she watches me. She blinks her eyes and all I see are the longest, softest eyelashes I've ever seen. I can feel the knot in my throat as I try to swallow. I don't know what she's thinking about but she's studying me silently.

"Will you dance with me?" she asks softly.

Her question almost catches me by surprise. "Dance with you? You mean now?"

"Yeah. Right here. Right now." Her eyes are seductive yet...pleading.

I look around the room for a radio or CD player but don't see one.

I shrug my shoulders slightly and nod. "Of course I'll dance with you. Do you...want some music?" I ask.

Who needs music?

Savannah pulls her phone out of the pocket of her dress and slowly slides her thumb up the screen a few times. When she stops, she lays her phone down on the counter. Music starts to play as she steps closer to me. I don't know the song and I don't care. I'll take any excuse I can to hold her in my arms.

I take her hands in mine, holding them both near my shoulder so I can wrap my arm around her waist and pull her close to me. She looks up at me and smiles contently. We sway back and forth to the rhythm of the music before I slowly lead her in small circles around her kitchen floor. I don't usually pay attention to sappy music but with this girl in my arms and my heart starting to attach itself to her I can't help but hear the words of Lady Antebellum and wonder if this is what she's really feeling or if it's just the first slow song she came to. Maybe it's her favorite song. I have a lot to learn.

Seems like I was walking in the wrong direction…
Not scared of love but scared of life alone…
It must be time to move on now…
Without the fear of how it might end...

There's no way she randomly chose this song.

I slowly slide my hand up her back until my hand is touching the skin of her upper back and shoulder. I glide my fingers across her back, lightly causing goosebumps to rise up on her soft skin. She sinks into me, leaning her head on my chest right at the crook of my shoulder; she fits there perfectly. I could hold her like this all night, but as the song ends Savannah looks up at me again, her eyes searching mine. For what, I don't know. Permission maybe? Perhaps she's trying to decide if she's brave enough to do what her body says she wants to do. Before I can even consider that thought, her hand is on the back of my neck and her lips are on mine.

Like long-distance lovers finally reunited, I feel the adrenaline of arousal shoot through me to my core when she kisses me. It's anything but delicate. Her lips are strong against mine as she takes what she's hungry for, taking over all of my senses. Her tongue, swirling with mine, tastes of bourbon and cranberries. Her body leaning against mine…shit, I haven't felt something this good against my body in a long time. Her skin is silky smooth, but the tension in her body as she presses herself into me gives her desire away. She works her lips against mine, and I feel the warmth of her palm when she places her hand on my cheek. My stubble is not a deterrent for her. I wrap my arms around her thin frame, squeezing her tighter against me. The give and the take of her kiss has my mind running wild.

*I want this girl.*

*And I'm pretty sure she wants me.*

When I hear the gentle moan of desire escape from the back of her throat I can't stop myself. My hands make their way to her waist, enjoying the feel of her curves along the way. Fervently, I lift her body and turn us both around until she's seated on the kitchen counter. Immediately she wraps her legs around me as I stand in between her thighs.

*Jesus, Mary and Joseph, I'm standing in between her thighs.*

*How does a guy get this lucky?*

Music is still coming from her phone on the counter but I'll be damned if I'm even listening to it. Whatever it is, it's slower in tempo which only fuels the flames between us.

My lips leave hers as she slowly rolls her head to the side, granting me access to her neck. Like an animal pouncing on his prey my lips are on her without a moment's hesitation. I carefully brush her neck with my tongue before sampling the same spot lightly with my teeth. Savannah gasps before releasing a satisfied moan, making my dick scream for attention.

*And it's right there…*

*Between her thighs…*

*Blocked by my damn jeans…*

Her hands hastily make their way to the hemline of my t-shirt. She tugs at it fiercely until I help her pull it up and over my head.

*Dear God, this is happening.*

"Bryant…" I hear her whisper as I continue my trail of kisses across her neckline. She folds into me, hugging my head and holding me against her chest. I take that as my cue that it's time to move her. I kiss her chest lightly right at the top of her dress while moving my hands slowly up her legs. I'm about to go where I've never gone before with her and fuck if I'm not enjoying every minute of it. My hands glide underneath her dress as they slide eagerly up her thighs. I'm trying so hard to slow down and take it all in but this girl is hungry and I want to be the one she feeds on.

"Hold on to me, Baby, I've got you," I tell her. She wraps her arms around my neck as I lift her and turn to walk down the hallway toward her bedroom. She continues to rake her fingers through my hair as I carry her, causing a desire-filled moan to escape me. She gives me her best cat-ate-the-canary grin before tugging my hair slightly.

*Fuck me…she just pulled my hair.*

I stumble back a step when her lips smack into mine. My breath hitches but I meet her challenge head-on, pushing my tongue into her mouth, pulling it back and grazing her bottom lip with my teeth. When we enter her bedroom, I sit on the edge of her bed, her body now straddling my own. Time slows down. We slow down. Our kiss slows until it ends. When I finally open my eyes she's watching me, gazing at my chest as it rises up and down with each breath. Her hands glide up and down my upper body and all I can do is close my eyes and take in the heady feeling. I realize I'm panting but, it's the best feeling in the world to have her hands touching me like this, like she's memorizing the feel of me. It's like she can fucking see me…see all the way into my soul and for a minute, that scares the shit out of me.

*What am I doing?*

My eyes move with hers as they roam up and down my body with her hands. When her gaze finally reaches mine she takes my hands in hers and moves them up her body until she's holding my hands on her chest. I've wanted to go there since this all started but I'm trying as hard as I can to be a gentleman with Savannah. I need her to know that I'm not the guy she thought I was.

"Touch me, Bryant," she says.

Immediately my dick stirs underneath her. I feel like a damn virgin, like this is the first time I've ever touched a pair of tits. Maybe if I just keep telling myself they're just tits, I'll be okay.

*But they're Savannah's tits.*

*Fuck.*

I squeeze her breasts lightly as they rest in my hands. I can feel her hardened peaks underneath the material of her dress. Damn if I don't want to explore this part of her body a little further.

*I can still be a gentleman.*

Slowly I pull the elastic top of her dress down over her chest and come face to face with an exquisite black lace strapless bra.

*Oh fuck.*

*Black lace is my kryptonite.*

"On a scale of one to four, you're Goddamn beautiful, Seven," I tell her. She smiles in response as she pushes her chest forward slightly. I reach in front of me to touch them again and as I do, I lightly run my thumbs over her most sensitive peaks.

"Oh my God, Bryant!" she cries out. Her breathing is hard and fast. Sitting astride me she grinds herself into me. Her body is speaking to me. I know what she wants. I can feel her warmth even through what I know are soft silk panties. It would take nothing to make this happen. A snap of a button, a tug of a zipper and a ripping of a small piece of material and I could be inside her, feeling the heaven I know she has underneath this purple dress.

But this isn't right.

I can't do this.

Not to her.

Not yet.

"Savannah…" I whisper.

"Yes, Bryant. Please." She's kissing me, my lips, my neck, my cheek, my forehead. Her hands are gliding smoothly through my hair and it feels so damn good.

"Savannah…"

"Touch me again, Bryant."

"No, Savannah, stop. We have to stop."

*Enter sounds of screeching record here.*

I feel her body stop as she sits back and looks at me. "Are you okay? What's wrong? Do you want to be on top?"

I chuckle lightly only because there's nothing I want more than to be on top…entering her…pushing myself into her again and again. I can feel the pulse just thinking about it. "Savannah, there's nowhere I would rather be, believe me, but this isn't right. We shouldn't do this." I shake my head slowly as I watch her face. I don't want to let her down, disappoint her, but I don't want to take advantage of her either. Especially if she's still a bit inebriated.

*I can't believe I'm cock-blocking my damn self.*

*When did Bryant "the Giant" Wood become such a pussy?*

"What do you mean we shouldn't do this? Did I do something wrong?"

"NO! God...NO!" I say shaking my head faster now so that she understands this is in no way about her. I take her face in my hands and explain, "Baby, you did nothing wrong. In fact, you almost made me lose control way sooner than I want to, and believe me when I tell you, I want to, but..."

"But...what?" She looks sad. Suddenly I'm praying that I'm doing the right thing here. Making the right call. I'm doing it for her. She has to realize that.

"Savannah, we just spent our first full day together, and I had...the most...absofuckin'lutely fantastic day with you. I just don't want you to feel rushed into anything. I don't want to be that guy for you."

"What guy?" She shakes her head confused at what I'm trying to tell her.

"The one-night-stand type of guy. That's not me, or, it's not who I want to be with you. I want to have two nights, and then ten nights, and then a hundred nights with you, Seven. When we're ready I want to take my time with you. I want to give you everything you need and everything you deserve, but it doesn't have to be tonight. I can wait."

"But it's been so long...for both of us," she says. "Isn't this what you want?"

I nod my head, my eyes hungry with desire. "Oh Savannah. Yes. I want you. I've wanted you for so long and believe me, it's giving me the biggest case of blue balls a guy's ever seen to stop what we're doing right now..." She smiles sympathetically. "But if I laid you down and took what I wanted from you now I would be just like the douchebag you always thought I was and I'm not that guy. We'll get there, I have no doubt about that, but it doesn't have to be on our first official date."

Self-consciousness setting in, Savannah starts to pull up the top of her dress, but I immediately grab her wrists. "No, Seven. Please don't feel like you have to cover yourself. You're..." I shake my head, studying every detail of her black lace bra. "You're stunning, and I enjoy looking at you, and I enjoy touching you. Don't feel like you ever have to cover up with me. I'll never hurt you. I promise you that."

She looks at me silently for what feels like minutes. Quietly she slides backwards off of my lap. "I'll be right back," she says.

"Okay." I'm not sure what's happening now but I watch as she walks back down the hallway toward the kitchen. I hear movement but can't see what's happening. When she walks back into the room, she's wearing nothing but my black t-shirt.

*Have mercy.*

She walks over to me and grabs my hand. "Do you have to go home tonight, Bryant? Is someone at home with Ivy?"

"No. She's with Samantha's parents this weekend. It's my weekend off," I tell her.

"Good."

She walks to the side of her bed and pulls down the covers. "Will you hold me?"

*Is she serious?*

*She's asking me to spend the night?*

*Is this a trick?*

"There's nothing I would rather do, Savannah. Are you really okay with that?"

"Please Bryant. Please don't make me beg. I don't want to be lonely anymore." Her expression is filled with something I can't quite read but nevertheless I understand; sadness mixed with need. We're both adults. We've both experienced a loss that has changed our lives and finally, after all this time, she's back in my life. I'm here with her and she's asking me to hold her as she falls asleep...something I wanted to do weeks ago when I watched her sleeping on her couch and carried her back here to this bed.

I kick my shoes off and walk to the opposite side of her bed. She watches me as I unbutton my jeans, pull down the zipper and slide my pants off. She tries to hide her smile but can't as I stand beside her bed in nothing but my navy boxer briefs. "I'm sorry I can't wear a shirt to bed, but it looks a hell of a lot better on you anyway."

"I figured if I wore it to bed you couldn't say no to staying here with me tonight."

I release a breath in slight defeat.

*She was afraid I would say no.*

"Savannah, I don't ever want to say no to you. I just want to make sure I'm doing right by you. Whatever this is between us, I don't want to let it go. I won't be able to let it go. You should remember that."

"Point made," she says resolutely. "Now get in here and keep me warm."

I slide into the bed laying on my left side so I can see her. She turns her body and backs up into me so that the swell of her ass is snuggled right up next to the part of me that doesn't seem to know when to calm the fuck down.

*This could be a rough night.*

Carefully I slide my left arm underneath her neck and my right arm over her hip, and pull her into me as tightly as I can. This feeling is foreign to me. Completely new, overwhelming, yet peaceful all at the same time. I'm not a snuggler. I never have been. I've always been that one-night stand guy. 'Fuck'em and chuck'em' as my friends would always say. Have my way and never stay...but not with this girl. Holding her in my arms like this, my body wrapped around hers, protecting her, this is what heaven must feel like. Her breathing evens out as she falls into a peaceful sleep. Lightly I kiss the back of her head before closing my eyes and dreaming about the two most important women in my life.

# Chapter 21

# *Savannah*

Today's the day. I'm meeting Ivy today for the very first time and I have to admit, I'm nervous. Normally I wouldn't be bothered except two things run through my mind constantly. One, she's roughly the same age Peyton would've been and that's harder on my heart than I want to admit to anyone. Two, what if she plain old just doesn't like me? It's been a few years since I've spent any length of time with young children. Since Peyton's passing I haven't wanted to put myself in the environment where I would have to interact with young kids, especially young girls, but today is the day.

It's been a three weeks since my first official date with Bryant and although we're moving a little slower than I had expected, it's been nice. We've met up for lunch a few times during the work week and he's taken me on a few more dates when he can get someone to watch Ivy. We've met up a few times to take a walk around the park and he's driven me home from work a few times. I very much respect the decision to not involve Ivy right away. Who knows where this thing between Bryant and me is going. I certainly wouldn't want to hurt Ivy, or myself, by either of us getting too attached too early.

Bryant told me to dress for comfort since we would just be hanging out for the evening with Ivy. I chose a pair of black leggings and an oversized pink button-down shirt. I slip on a pair of black ballet flats and I'm ready for an evening of playtime with a new friend.

*I hope she likes me.*

It takes approximately fifteen minutes to get from my apartment in town to Bryant's quiet ranch. I didn't realize he lived so far out of town, but I like it. It's peaceful here, calm, beautiful. Driving out I saw one field after another lined with sprouting crops but when I turn onto Bryant's road all of the fields around me are lined with wooden fences.

*He never said anything about a farm.*

Seven

I pull up to a larger sized ranch house than I expected. The exterior is a mix of stone and wood siding, almost like a log cabin with a little extra flair. The front porch wraps around the side of the house which overlooks a small wooded area. I imagine it's quite peaceful at times to sit outside and listen to the goings on around you. There are great big windows to the right of the front door. The great room, or living room, must be on that side of the house. On the other side of the front door is a smaller set of windows as well as the attached garage. I don't see Bryant on the front porch and I don't see him watching out any of the windows of his house, so I get out the car and make my way to the front door. I ring the doorbell and then stand in anticipation for Bryant to answer the door. I don't know why I'm so nervous. It's not like I didn't just spend the night with Bryant the other day. Obviously the nerves are for the young human I'm about to meet for the first time.

I take another step back from the door when I see them. Two small hands pulling back the white curtains in the window of the great room. Soon I see two green eyes staring at me. She's not moving. She's just staring…and smiling.

*Oh thank God she's smiling.*

I bend over slightly so I'm more her height and wave gently to her. I don't expect her to answer the door, I am a stranger to her after all, but she smiles back at me and waves as the door swings open. When I stand up I'm looking into the eyes of an almost panic-stricken Bryant holding a hairbrush and a comb in his left hand.

"Hi," he says with a huge sigh.

"Hello," I smile at him questioningly. I'm not so sure I understand why he looks so panicked but as soon as the little girl from the window steps out from behind Bryant, I see it. The beautiful curls I remember Ivy having from the picture Bryant showed me are gone; pulled back and frayed in some sort of…braid? Is that what it is? Not knowing how I'm supposed to react because perhaps this is the very first time Ivy has ever done her own hair, I put on my widest friendliest smile and crouch down again to Ivy's height.

"Hello. You must be Ivy."

"Yep. And you awe Subanna" She says my name loudly and with pride, as if she's known me her whole life. "My daddy talks about you lots. She is pwetty, Daddy, just like you said. Like an angel."

*Be still my heart.*

"Well thank you very much, Ivy," I chuckle. "You know what? Your daddy talks about *you* a lot too, and you are a beautiful little girl. I think Ivy is a beautiful name."

"Tanks. Do you like my dwess?" I watch as she twirls around in her beautiful blue Elsa dress.

"Oh Ivy, you are most certainly the prettiest princess I've seen today."

She stops and rubs her head vigorously with her hand. "Daddy can't bwaid vewy good. It doesn't look like Elsa..." She looks at me and jumps up and down. "Can you fix it? Girls can bwaid and boys can't bwaid so you can fix it wight?"

My eyes glide quickly over to Bryant who is still standing in the doorway watching Ivy and me with a sheepish smile. I smirk at him as he sighs and shakes his head in defeat.

"I can make the world's best chicken nuggets and the yummiest chocolate milk, but there's no chapter on Elsa braids in the Daddy handbook."

I nod, understanding what obviously must've transpired right before I got here. I look at Ivy's cute scowl toward her father and back to Bryant who almost looks embarrassed to have even attempted the challenge and now know exactly why I am here. I clear my throat and in my best Mary Poppins voice I say "In every job that must be done, there is an element of fun. I think I know a great way to start off our afternoon." I turn towards Ivy and say, "How about I teach Daddy how to make a beautiful Elsa braid. It just so happens I do know a lot about braiding hair."

"YAY!" Ivy cheers. "Come on Subanna! Come in, come in!" Her little fingers wrap around my thumb as she charges toward the house, eagerly pulling me behind her. As I step through the doorway Bryant leans in and kisses me on my cheek.

"I'm really glad you're here," he says.

"Me too," I respond.

"Me thwee! Let's go Daddy! Subanna is gonna teach you things."

I spend the next half hour sitting next to Bryant on the couch as Ivy sits patiently in front of him watching an episode *of Mickey Mouse Clubhouse.* With her hair between his fingers I show him several different types of braids. He's a fast learner, better than I expect him to be, and in no time, Ivy's hair looks just like her favorite snow Queen, Elsa.

"Thank you for the braiding lesson, Savannah. Phew, you saved me from the wrath of a Queen Elsa tantrum just in time."

I laugh as I bump into Bryant's shoulder slightly. "You're welcome. It was the least I could do. I mean a princess can't spend her day doing princess things with terrible daddy hair."

Bryant stands up and turns to me. "Can I get you a drink?"

"Sure." I hold my hand out for him to pull me up from the couch. "Give me a tour of the kitchen?"

"Absolutely. Come on." Bryant nods his head towards Ivy whose eyes are transfixed on the television. "We'll be back before the hot dog dance."

"The what?" I ask as he pulls me from the room. As soon as we're around the corner and in the kitchen Bryant pushes me against the kitchen island and kisses me with so much force, I have to grab onto his biceps to steady myself. In no time though, I'm returning his kiss with equal fervor knowing that we could lose our moment of privacy at any minute.

"I missed you Seven," he whispers between kisses. Bryant's hands hold on to my hips but begin to slowly slide up the sides of my body igniting sparks in me from head to toe. Damnit, if there weren't a kid in the house I would lay myself out for him right here on this kitchen counter.

"I missed you too." I wrap my arms around Bryant a little more as his hands continue northward, grabbing my face and holding it in his hands. His lips retreat, leaving me panting and famished for more of him. He lays his forehead against mine closing his eyes as our breathing evens out. "I'm sorry Seven."

"What? Sorry for what? What's wrong?" I'm confused. One minute he was sucking my face and now…

"I'm sorry I have a kid in the other room and I can't lay you across this kitchen island and finish what we started the other night. You just, smell so damn good and I couldn't wait any longer to kiss you, to touch you."

"Mmm…I'd like that too," I whisper.

"Stay with me tonight." He's not really asking but I can tell by his inflection that he doesn't want me to say no.

*What about Ivy?*

"Do you really think that's a good idea?"

"I wouldn't be asking you to stay if I didn't."

I smirk even though he can't really see me with our foreheads still touching. "Oh, was that you asking me? Because…"

"Savannah?" He interrupts my teasing.

"Yeah?"

I watch him swallow the knot in his throat as he thinks for a minute before staring me square in the face. "I don't want to be alone anymore either, but I don't want to be with just anyone. I want to be with you."

I don't know why my stupid face chooses this moment to betray me but hearing my words echoed back at me causes a small tear to slip out of my eye and trail down my face. I watch Bryant's eyes follow it down my cheek before he lifts his thumb to swipe it away.

*He wants me?*

*He remembered what I said?*

"How do we do this with Ivy…?"

He kisses my lips quickly before wrapping his arms around me, shaking his head. "I don't care," he says. "We'll figure it out. I'll sleep on the couch if I have to Savannah. I'm just so damn glad you're here, but now that you're here, I don't want you to go. Don't worry. I'll handle Ivy, okay?"

I smile shyly. "Okay. I trust you."

I watch him turn away from me toward the cupboard above his head. He opens it and reaches for two glasses.

"Oh, shit," I mumble to myself, acting defeated.

"What is it?" Bryant turns around quickly, waiting for my response.

I give Bryant my best provocative smile and shrug my shoulder slightly as I explain, "I didn't bring anything to sleep in." That's a lie. I totally packed a small duffle bag with pajamas and toiletries because a girl never knows where she might end up, but I'll be damned if I'm going to tell him that.

Bryant places both glasses from his hands onto the counter and then spins around toward me. His head comes in close to me so I bend my head back. He smiles as he leans in closer laying feathery kisses along my neck. "It's settled then. Fuck the couch. Someone has to keep you warm if you won't be wearing any clothes. I volunteer as tribute." He closes his lips around my earlobe, earring and all, and I'm a goner.

"OH TOOOOOOOOTLES!" Ivy shouts from the living room. Bryant stops his torturous exploration of my neck at which point we both burst into laughter.

"Fuckin' Tootles…" he says. "That thing has terrible timing."

I kiss Bryant's cheek and place my hand in his. "Come on, you promised we would be back in time for the hot dog dance."

*****

"Subanna!" Ivy gasps and jumps up from her chair in the kitchen. In the last couple of hours, we've braided hair, done the hot dog dance, put together four different princess puzzles, read six different books, and held ourselves the best princess tea-party a girl could ever have, complete with crowns, pink feathers and only our very best British accents. If I didn't already know, I would never believe that Ivy was a little girl who has endured terrible medical issues. She is nothing but a ball of energy.

*This sweet pea is so much fun.*

*Peyton would've liked her.*

"What's wrong Ivy? Are you okay?" I ask, surprised by her sudden gasp.

"Do you wanna see my woom? It's BEAUTIFUL! My Daddy made me a biggest huge castle bed. Do you wanna see? Come on! It's so big you won't even bewieve it!"

I look to Bryant whose eyebrows are up in excitement as he watches his little girl talk to me. He returns my gaze and shrugs his shoulders. "Frankly I'm surprised it's taken her this long. She loves that bedroom."

"Oh yeah?" I turn back to Ivy. "Well then, darlin', this is something I just have to see! Show me your biggest huge castle bed."

Ivy takes me by the hand and leads me, literally skipping down the hall, and up the stairs to her bedroom. She opens the door and runs into her room twirling and smiling all over herself. "See? It's my biggest huge castle and it's all for me but I share it with Daddy sometimes and I'll share it with you all the time because you're a princess girl like me."

I almost don't hear a word she says because my eyes are floating in wonder around this little girl's bedroom. Yes, it definitely looks like pink threw up in here, but it's the most perfect little girl's princess room I have ever seen. Straight ahead of me is a beautiful bay window with bench seating, pink of course, and billowy white ruffled curtains. The window overlooks the field in the back of the house. It's breathtaking. To my right sits a ridiculously large castle complete with steps on one side, and a sliding board on the other.

*Damn, she wasn't kidding. "Biggest huge" is right.*

I watch as Ivy walks up the steps and jumps on what must be her mattress. I walk over to the castle and laugh as she rolls around above in her bed. Her giggle is the most joyful sound. I can't not smile when I hear it. The front façade of the castle has two towers. One right next to the steps, and one next to the slide. In between the towers is a pink sparkly curtain of sorts.

"Ivy, what's inside under here?" I motion toward the sparkly curtain.

"I show you Subanna! It's a supwise!" She slides down the slide and runs over to me, pulls the curtain back, and reveals the space within. The floor inside is filled with fluffy pillows. Ivy immediately springs forward and lays down on her back inside. "Come in Subanna, come here. Lay down." She pats the pillows next to her.

A little surprised I turn around in time to see Bryant nod at me to follow her inside. It's a little small for adults but I manage to crawl into the space and turn over onto my back. Ivy and I are now both laying under her bed looking up at the platform where her mattress lies. It looks like any old piece of wood except that it appears to have tiny holes all over it.

*For ventilation?*

*So her mattress doesn't stay wet if she has an accident?*

*Is that a thing?*

"Do it Daddy! Do the thing! Do it!" Ivy shouts.

"I've got it Princess. Are you ready?" I hear him say from outside the castle. I feel his presence close to me but I can't quite see him.

"Yes Daddy! Weady!" She's so excited, but I'm not sure what we're supposed to be looking at.

And then it happens.

Bryant flips a switch and the entire under carriage of the castle lights up. Tiny white lights appear in all of those tiny holes and they're all sparkling softly. I gasp in amazement as my eyes light up. This is a dream come true bedroom for a little girl. What I wouldn't have given to have a room like this when I was young.

"Oh, Ivy...it's...it's beautiful!" I exclaim.

"Mind if I join you?" Bryant asks. He's asking Ivy but he's staring at me.

"Yes Daddy, come in! Make a wish wiff us!"

Bryant slowly crawls in and lays directly next to me. I would think he was trying to make the moves on me except there really is no other room under here. Ivy is practically laying on me as it is. We lay quietly for a moment just taking in the soft pink beauty surrounding us. I could spend hours in here just staring...thinking...

"I go first!" Ivy says. "I wish…no more puple medicine and I wish evewyday I get to see Subanna. You go next Daddy."

*This girl just melts my heart.*

I feel Bryant take my hand beside him on the floor and squeeze it tight. The gentleness and secrecy of my hand in his releases butterflies throughout my stomach. I return the gesture not letting on to Ivy that anything has changed whatsoever.

"Okay I'll go next." Bryant says. "I wish that my Ivy would grow big and strong no matter what kind of super power medicine her body needs. And I wish I could see Subanna every day too. Just like Ivy." He squeezes my hand again but I can't return the gesture this time. I'm too busy holding my breath, trying not to overreact by either crying like a baby or smiling so big I end up giggling like a school girl. I simply hold my breath quietly as I listen to Ivy and Bryant's wishes.

"Your turn," Bryant says softly.

"Yeah you go now Subanna. You make a wish," she turns her head back to stare up at the stars. It must be what she and Bryant do pretty often as she seems to have this routine down to a science.

"Okay…ummm…I wish…"

*I wish I could see Peyton again.*

"I wish that I had a biggest huge castle just like this one so that I could lay here every night, next to my friends and family, and make my wishes over and over again. And I wish that only good things would happen to people. Never bad things, so that nobody would ever have to be sad again."

"Yeah me too." Ivy says. "Only good things. Not bad things like big pokes from the hopsital."

*The hopsital. Kid language is the greatest.*

"Yeah," Bryant says softly. "Only *good* things. Never bad things…ever again."

I'm pretty sure he's talking to me.

After a brief moment of silence Ivy swings her legs over onto me and sits up. "Daddy, can Subanna have a sleep over?"

"Well, why don't you ask Savannah if she would like to have a sleep over. She might be really busy." I turn my head toward Bryant but he's not looking at me. He's still staring up at the sparkling lights above us.

*I wonder what he's thinking about.*

"Subanna? You want to sleep over right? Daddy makes pancakes with chocolate chips in them."

I gently gasp as I play along for Ivy. "He does? I LOVE pancakes with chocolate chips in them! Do you think he can make me a smiley face out of chocolate chips?"

"YES! He can! He can! He can!" She bounces up and down excitedly.

"Then I think I might have to stay because I have to have pancakes with chocolate chips in them in the morning."

"YAY!!!" Ivy screams and runs out of her biggest huge castle to jump and twirl around her room. Bryant and I laugh as we watch her.

"See? That wasn't so hard at all. I knew she'd want you to stay."

"Oh yeah? And how did you know that?"

"You mean beside the fact that she's been at your side pretty much since the moment you walked through the door?" He chuckles quietly.

"Okay, you have a point. She's a great little girl, Bryant. You should be very proud of yourself. You're a great daddy."

"Thank you. I appreciate that. I just do what I can when I can and pray for the best."

"Subanna will you tuck me in tonight at bed time?" Ivy asks from across the room.

I turn my head back to Bryant and smile before responding to Ivy. "Of course, Princess Ivy! Whatever you want."

*****

Ivy comes skipping down the hall from the bathroom to her bedroom wrapped in her pink butterfly towel. The hood over her wet hair even has little green antennas on the top. She makes an adorable butterfly.

"Was that a fun bath?" I ask her.

"Uh huh!" She exclaims. "I spwashed Daddy even! He got all wet!"

"Oh my goodness." I giggle with her. "Good girl! High five!" I raise my hand up in front of me and she happily swats at it as she jumps up and down. This girl has so much energy, though I can tell she's tired because she doesn't want to stop moving. Somehow kids always know if they stop moving they're done for.

As she starts giggling we both hear Bryant stomping down the hallway. "FE, FI, FO, FET...I AM A DADDY WHO GOT SUPER DUPER WET!" He steps into Ivy's bedroom and I can't help but smile. Bryant has wet spots all over his t-shirt and jeans. Clearly, Ivy got him good!

"Whoa! Hahaha...thatta girl Ivy! You got him good! Double high five!" I raise both hands in front of me this time for her to excitedly slap them. Just as fast as she jumps in excitement, she stops and shivers.

"Daddy, I'm cold."

"I know, Baby. Here, let's get your jammies on so you can snuggle up under your covers." I help Bryant get Ivy's PJs on quickly before getting her into her bed surrounded by all of her stuffed animal friends. Recognizing a familiar sheep that she squeezes tightly, I walk over to her bookcase and pick one of my favorite bedtime stories to read to her.

"How about a little *Russel The Sheep* before you go to sleep? Would that be okay?"

"Yes!" she smiles.

"Perfect," Bryant says. "Savannah can read that to you while I go get your medicine." He winks at me and slips out of the room quietly while I begin to read.

After reading the final pages, I close the book as Ivy yawns. "Ivy, thank you for letting me come play with you today. I really had a great time."

"Me too. Wait, where awe you sweeping tonight? I don't want you to go home." Her eyes are saddened.

"She can sleep in my bed." Bryant answers as he walks in and hands a small medicine cup to Ivy. "I'll sleep on the couch."

*I don't want him to sleep on the couch.*
*I want him to sleep with me.*
*But I understand.*

Ivy swallows her medicine and snuggles up with her Russel the Sheep as tightly as she can. "Okay. Sing my song, Daddy. Bye Subanna." She says softly. She's not long for sleep now.

"Good night, sweetheart. See you in the morning." I place a soft kiss on her forehead before heading out of her room. I would stay and listen to Bryant sing her to sleep but I don't want to invade their privacy any more than I already have today. I head downstairs to the kitchen to grab a glass of water while I wait for Bryant. Alone in the kitchen for a few minutes I can't help but think about today and what it feels like to be with Bryant on a daily basis. I don't understand why I'm falling for him, but I am. Seeing him today, as a daddy and not the guy who needs to woo the ladies, was heart-warming. It makes me think about what life could be like...what it would feel like to have a normal life again with a husband and a child.

*Even though she isn't mine.*

I'm standing at the large kitchen window, sipping my water and thinking about how beautiful it is outside even at night when I hear it. Recognition dawns on me as I hear Bryant's voice singing to Ivy. There's a baby monitor, here in the kitchen somewhere, that I wasn't aware of. From that little machine come the all-too-familiar lyrics.

"You are my sunshine
my only sunshine.
You make me happy,
when skies are grey.
You'll never know dear
how much I love you.
Please don't take my sunshine away."

*Please don't take my sunshine away.*
*Ouch!*
*I can't...*
*Breathe, Savannah...*

*I can't catch my...*

Breathe...

I can't catch my breath. The room is getting smaller around me and I'm doubled over with my hands sliding down the large windowpane in front of me. I feel the incredible urge to vomit but the only thing my body is doing is hyperventilating.

*Maybe I need fresh air.*

I slowly make my way outside to the patio off the kitchen and lean against the railing, trying my best to inhale even a few tiny breaths. There's a stabbing pain in my chest that's beginning to scare me. Before I can even think of figuring out what's happening to me, my body starts to violently tremble, I lose feeling in my legs, and sink to the ground, landing on my hands and knees.

*Am I okay?*
*What's happening?*

*Should I be crying?*

*Screaming?*

*Bryant?*

*Shawn?*

*Peyton...*

# Chapter 22

# ⌒ *Savannah*

"SEVEN??" I hear him but I can't see him. I've covered my face with my hands. I don't even know if Bryant sees me or if he's calling for me because he doesn't know where I am, but regardless, I can't yell to him. I try and I try and I can't make any sound.

"SAVANNAH?" I hear him again. He's closer to me now. Did he open the door? I didn't hear the door open.

*Did I even shut the door in the first place?*

"Bryant." A tiny whisper of his name squeaks out of my mouth.

*Why can't I talk?*

*What's wrong with my voice?*

"Savannah, what is it? What's wrong? Are you hurt?" His hands are immediately on me, checking my body for signs of distress. He's throwing questions at me one after another and I can barely even hear what he's saying. I start to wring my hands together but something feels weird. I look down at them in confusion.

*My hands…I don't understand.*

"My hands," I speak in a voice that I don't recognize. "Bryant, my…hands… are… wet. What's happening?"

*I dropped my water.*

*Where's my glass?*

*Did the glass break?*

"Baby…" his voice is gentle and soothing. "You're crying. That's why your hands are wet, Savannah, you're crying. Something's wrong. What's going on? Are you sick? Let me help you."

I blink my eyes, I think for the first time in minutes, and when I do, I finally feel the small rivers of tears floating down my cheeks. I can't speak anymore. I squeeze my eyes shut for just a moment and when I do all of my thoughts hit me at once like a slap to the face.

*Shawn.* I see the car flipping over in the median.

*Peyton.* I'm holding her hand in the hospital singing to her for the last time.

*Bryant.* He's picking me up, carrying me to my room.

*Ivy.* So full of energy and joy.

*Sunshine.* God took my sunshine away.

I cover my face once again to hide my sobs. This is all so embarrassing. "I'm sorry Bryant. I'm so sorry. I'm sorry." I shake my head back and forth, my expression forlorn. It's all I can say to him.

Bryant is on his knees grabbing my body and wrapping his arms around me, protecting me. "Shhh, Savannah it's okay. You're okay Baby. I've got you. I've got you. I've got you." he repeats to help soothe me. "I need to get you in the house okay? I'm going to pick you up. Hold on to me."

He picks me up and cradles me as he carries me out of the evening air, back through the kitchen to his bedroom. He sits down on the oversized chair in the corner holding me to him all the while. I focus on breathing in Bryant's scent to help calm me down, and try to match my breaths to his, slowing my pace in between hiccups and sniffles of my earlier sobs.

We sit in relative silence for the next few minutes, me trying to control what's happening to me and no doubt Bryant trying to figure out what the hell just happened as he gently rubs his hand up and down my back.

"Savannah, I need you to tell me what's going on. Did I do something?"

"No," I say quietly.

"Did I hurt you?"

"No."

"Did Ivy say something?"

"No," I shake my head. I know he can feel me even though he isn't looking at me.

"Did you fall? Can you tell me?" He pleads and I feel so damn guilty. I hate my body for betraying me. I thought I was strong enough.

"There's no way you could've known," I whisper to myself and to Bryant. "I'm sorry, Bryant. I…I'm not strong enough."

"Strong enough for what?"

"For you…for Ivy." I sniffle.

"I don't understand," He whispers.

"That song," I take a deep breath before I can continue. "I used to sing it to Peyton all the time. I sang it to her when…" I can't finish my sentence. My breath hitches as I feel another sob coming on, but Bryant feels it too and squeezes me even tighter. His embrace is warm and comforting and it's the only place I want to be right now.

Softly in my ear I hear him say, "Oh God, Savannah, I'm so fucking sorry. I didn't know. I'm sorry, I didn't know."

"I know. It's okay," I reassure him. At least I think I'm reassuring him and not just myself. "It's not your fault. I just…thought I was fine. I didn't know I would react that way to hearing someone else sing it, and…I didn't know there was a monitor in the kitchen, it just…literally…took my breath away." I try to wipe the remaining wetness off of my face and compose myself.

Bryant is observing me. "Have you ever had a panic attack or an anxiety attack before? Like this, I mean?"

My lip quivers. "No. You must think I'm a fucked-up nutcase."

His smile is sad yet endearing. "Not at all." He says placing a kiss on my head. "I don't blame you one bit. Savannah, you're stronger than you think. You were so strong today. I'll be honest, I wasn't sure how the day was going to go but you were like a pro with Ivy. She loves you already."

"She really is an amazing little girl," I whisper as I choke back my tears. "You should be so damn proud of yourself. This house, your life, your beautiful little girl. She has all she could ever want and then some with you."

"She's been through a lot in just a few years." He runs his knuckles lightly down my cheek gazing into my eyes as he does so. "And so have you."

I bend my head to avert my eyes from his but he immediately takes my face in his hands rubbing his thumbs back and forth along my cheek. "Savannah, look at me."

Slowly I lift my gaze back to his. He catches one tear as it escapes down my face. "Grief is…it's a fickle thing. It never ends. Never. It just…changes over time…and we learn to adapt our lives to it. It comes when we least expect it and sometimes it's not there when we think it should be. It's not a sign of weakness or a lack of love on your part. Intense grief means there was an intense love and to me, that's the greatest gift you could give anyone. Grief just means your heart is working."

I take a deep breath, trying to retain the words he's saying to me. "Sometimes I feel guilty because I forget to think about them all the time, or like just a while ago, in the kitchen, when I wasn't thinking of them at all until I heard you singing that song. It was like…" I shake my head not knowing how to describe my feelings to him.

"I understand. Sometimes grief swings in and takes your breath away. And that's okay. Don't minimize your pain and your loss because you think you should. Grief will come and go for the rest of your life…and if I'm lucky enough," he brushes my hair back off of my face. "I'll get to be here with you to help you through it every single time."

"Do you…" I start to ask what's on my mind but I chicken out.

"Do I what?" He asks.

I chew on the inside of my mouth for a second…a nervous habit. "Do you…ever feel guilty for…you know…"

"Feel guilty for what?" He tilts his head, still watching me.

"For being…physical. With other women, I mean. Or…with me.?"

*Would he be with Samantha if she were alive?*

Bryant's eyes meet mine immediately as if he knows exactly why I'm asking. He confidently shakes his head. "No, not at all. But, it's different for me. Samantha and I were a one-night-stand. There wasn't love there to begin with. I mean, don't get me wrong, I grieved when she passed away. She's still Ivy's mother and we had become, at least, good friends in the eight months we spent together planning for Ivy's arrival. But..." He shrugs slightly and quietly says, "I didn't love her."

"Oh."

"Savannah?" He says after a minute of semi-awkward silence.

"Yeah?"

"Do you feel guilty? About what we've done?"

I wait a moment before answering him to be sure that stab of guilt isn't there.

"No."

"Good." He nods. "Okay, good."

"But I do feel guilty for not feeling guilty. I don't want to be alone anymore. I know I've told you that before. I miss them both so fucking much, but I'm smart enough to know that no amount of grief or loneliness is going to bring them back. So why do I feel so damn guilty about not feeling guilty about wanting to be happy? Does that even make any sense?"

"Yeah it does. It makes all the sense in the world, but I don't have answers for you. It's just the way grief works. I think you just have to live and allow yourself to love and know that what happens, happens. Cross bridges when you come to them, you know? If there's a silver lining to grief, it's that grief gives us a choice of what we do next with our life."

"What do you mean?"

"Well, do you sit at home alone forever, never allowing yourself to find love again, or do you hold those memories close to your heart so that you can celebrate life with those you love in your future? And you're the only one who can make that choice. Your heart will know the answer when you're ready."

*Make the choice Savannah.*

*You're ready.*

I release a huge sigh and wipe my face one last time with my hands. "God, this is the last thing I wanted to be doing with you tonight, talking about our grief."

He chuckles lightly and sits back, rubbing my arms to warm me up. "Well then what was the first thing you wanted to do?"

*Oh God.*

*There's no way I'm saying that out loud.*

"Umm…nothing." I shake my head shyly averting my eyes from his. "I want to do whatever you want to do."

"Hmm…really?" He raises an eyebrow playfully. "Because I know what I *want* to do…but I'm not sure if you're up for it." He leans in closer to me, laying soft kisses on the side of my neck, just under my ear. I don't know how the hell he does it but immediately my body wants to respond to him.

Shyly I glance at him and say, "Well…I'm pretty sure what I want to do is probably what you want to do."

"Hmm…and what is that?" He teases.

"You're going to make me say it?" I laugh.

*Could this be any weirder?*

Throwing me his orneriest grin he laughs and says, "Hell yeah I am. A man has to be sure of his girl's intentions." He moves his mouth to the other side of my neck echoing the kisses he's already left.

I stare at his face for a few seconds pumping myself up to say what I want to say.

*You can do this girl.*

*You got this.*

*Just say it.*

*It's what he wants too.*

"I want you to make love to me, Bryant." There I said it.

I feel him stop as soon as I say the words. He slowly leans back and looks at me, his expression somber. He swallows slowly. His forehead creases and his eyes soften.

*Oh God, he doesn't want this.*

"I can't do that, Seven."

I shake my head briskly trying to brush off his rejection even though my heart feels like it's just been sliced in half.

*How embarrassing.*

"It's okay, Bryant. I...I don't know what I was thinking. You're right, you have Ivy here and we've really only just…"

"No." He interrupts. "That's not what I mean. That's not why I can't do it, Seven."

"I don't understand."

*Does he have a problem that I don't know about yet?*

He studies my face for a full minute at least before letting his eyes trail down my body. A little fearful of what he's about to say I feel the tear forming in the bottom of my eye. Blinking will give my feelings away, but he sees it before it escapes. Immediately his eyes are large.

"Savannah, I can't make love to you without telling you first."

"Telling me what?"

"Telling you that I love you."

"Oh."

*But he's not ready for that yet.*

*What do I say now?*

*Maybe I shouldn't have said "Make love to me?"*

*I should've just called it sex.*

I have to try to figure out a way for this moment to not be awkward for him. "You don't have to do that, Bryant. I mean, it's just sex, I should've said…never mind…it's no big deal anyway…"

"No, Seven. You're not hearing me." He pushes me back slightly so that he can hold my face in his hands. "It's not just sex with you, and it *is* a big deal, so you need to hear me say it."

I raise my voice a tiny bit to speak over him grabbing at his hands to pull them off of my face. I get it. He thinks I need all this lovey dovey stuff…

"No, Bryant I really don't. It's totally fi…"

"Seven, I love you! Do you hear me?" A chuckle escapes him and he shakes his head. All I can do is stare at his handsome face. When presses his lips against mine I can feel them lips form a small smile. "Savannah Turner, I love you. I've had a crush on you since high school, and I have a crush on you now."

I'm still staring.

I can't bring myself to say words.

He continues. "I watched you leave town and knew I would never have the girl of my dreams, but now…" His knuckles lightly graze the side of my face. "Damn…you're back here and you're in my life…" He breathes. "I know it's not the way either of us would've wanted but the reality is you're here. I'm here. You've brightened my days, excited my nights…given me a reason to want to live…really live…to love with my heart and not just my dick. To want to show you that there's more to me than just the douchebag you knew in high school, or the flirt who tends the bar in town."

*He loves me.*

*And I think I…*

*Is that okay?*

*It's okay, right?*

"Seven, I've been in love with you since I carried you to bed that night in your apartment. I wanted to lay next to you and hold you all night. I loved you then and I love you now, Seven. Do you hear me?"

I'm frozen in place. My eyes are wide, and my mouth hangs open as I try to say the words my heart wants me to say.

"I…"

*This is it.*

*Time to let go.*

*Forgive me, Shawn.*

"I think I might…" Christina Perri's voice rings though my head.

> The scariest part is letting go.
> Love is a ghost you can't control.
> Let the words slip out of your mouth.

"I think I might be in love with you too, Bryant."

I watch as his eyes close and he inhales a large breath. A satisfied smile forms on his lips when he releases his breath, as if he has just eaten the most delicious meal. But just as quickly as his smile appeared, it's gone, replaced with a fearful expression.

"Savannah," he whispers quietly, my name rolling off of his tongue. "I need to…"

"Make love to me Bryant." I don't care what he was about to say and I don't know what compels me to do it, but I take his hand and place it on my breast, my hand over top of his. "Please."

His gentle squeeze says all the words I need to hear. He touches me and my body flutters with an intense need for him. Still seated on Bryant's lap, I tilt my head back as he trails seductively slow kisses up my neck and under my chin. His lips are warm and soft and caressing. I gasp when he nips at my neck and then sooths the same spot with his tongue. He makes his way back to my mouth but when our lips meet neither one of us moves. He doesn't move to kiss me, instead, we breath each other's rapid breaths, knowing that when the dance finally begins, there will be no stopping either of us. His tongue lightly brushes my bottom lip, asking permission to enter and I am eager to invite him in. When his lips finally entwine with mine they move together like crashing waves. A pleasured moan escapes from the back of his throat making me all too aware of the desire pooling in my body.

Bryant slowly pulls back from our kiss and holds my gaze before lowering his eyes to the buttons on my shirt. My breath hitches when his cool fingers touch my warm skin. I look down to see him slowly releasing the buttons one by one. When he reaches the last button his left hand slides up against my skin near my collar and gently pushes my shirt off of my shoulder revealing a black lace bra similar to the one I wore the last time we were together like this.

He shakes his head in defeat but he's smirking when he says "Jesus Christ, Seven, you're killing me with your beauty. Black lace…" He shakes his head again. "You're so damn beautiful." Without saying another word, he pushes down the other side of my shirt. I lower my arms one by one, releasing them from the sleeves and letting the shirt fall to the floor behind me. His hands are intoxicatingly slow as they explore my upper body, gliding down my sides and just slightly coming in contact with the sides of my breasts. It's agony waiting for his hands to touch other parts of me. My pulse throbs as desire heightens inside me. Still, he is quiet. Unusually quiet.

*What is he thinking about?*

Without hesitation, Bryant leans forward and kisses my shoulder while gradually sliding my bra strap down my arm. He echoes his movements on the other side, trapping my arms within my straps.

"You okay?" he asks gently. Good God I think I just fell for him again.

"Yes," I nod. "I'm more than okay."

Bryant holds my now clouded gaze as he reaches behind me and unclasps my bra. Delicately he pulls my arms through the straps and lets the black lace fall from his fingertips to the floor. I'm still sitting sideways across his legs but my body is turned toward him in anticipation, aching for his touch. Quickly before he can touch me again, I lift the hem of his shirt up over his head. Leaning in closer I place a soft kiss in the middle of his chest. A sincere, reverent kiss to let him know that this means something to me.

*More than he will ever know.*

He grabs my arms with his right hand, holding them behind my back, causing me to sit up straighter, my chest thrusting forward just a bit more. Steadily and deliberately he glides his left hand down my neck, to my chest, and directly in between my breasts. His skin is so damn soft but scorching as it touches me now. Feeling the palm of his hand over my heart and seeing his eyes cast directly on what he's doing…it's like he's seeing right into my soul.

Like he knows everything I fear.

Everything I desire.

Everything I need.

*I want this man.*

*Like I've never wanted anyone before.*

"Bryant…" I whisper.

"Shhh," he says. "I've waited…so long…to touch you, Savannah. To hold you, to kiss you." He breathes. "I just…need a minute. We'll never get this back, this moment, and I want to make sure that whatever happens we will always have this moment."

He closes his eyes, relishing the feel of my heart beat beneath his palm.

"Please Bryant," I whisper. "Please tell me you've never said those words to another woman before, because I've fallen for you...real hard, real fast, with every word you've said...and it will destroy me to find out later that you say things like this all the time, to all the girls."

"This might surprise you to know, Savannah, but you're the first girl that isn't family to ever be in this house."

*Whoa!*

*I am surprised!*

"You're the first girl to ever be in my bedroom with me." He slides his left hand underneath my legs and stands up with me in his arms. Two steps later and we're at the side of his bed where he gently lays me down. "You're the first girl to ever be in my bed."

"I'm a lucky girl, I know," I say.

"No, Baby, I'm a fuckin' lucky man who is not going to take this night for granted." Bryant leans over to kiss me and when he does I trap him in the softest, slowest, full blown kiss I think I've ever had. My tongue dances with his tasting the inside of his mouth. While he's distracted with our kiss I lightly scrape my fingers down his bare chest, exploring every line, every muscle, memorizing his body until I reach the top of his jeans. I tug on them just enough so that Bryant understands that I want him to join me on this bed.

Our kiss intensifies when he crawls over me and lays his body half on top of me and half on the bed beside me. Our skin to skin contact is electrifying. Immediately his hands are moving down the side of my body, grabbing my waist firmly and pulling me closer to him. A consuming moan escapes me as I tilt my head back gasping for air. The slowness of his movements is torture on my body.

I close my eyes to revel in the escalation of my arousal and the moment I do, Bryant's mouth is on me, circling his tongue again and again around my hardened peaks. Several whimpers escape me.

"I've got you, Baby," he croons. "You're irresistible. I couldn't wait any longer."

"No, God, please…don't…stop," I gasp. My body hasn't been stimulated like this in so long I've forgotten what it feels like. I don't remember it being this way before. I always just viewed sex for what it was – just sex. Two people giving in to their natural primal feelings. But this, the emotions I feel, the electrifying passion between us, he makes me feel like he's worshiping my body. And I don't ever want him to stop.

Bryant's lips explore my stomach, stopping every few seconds to brush my skin with their warmth. I feel him move lower and lower until his hands are sliding up and down my legging-covered thighs, stopping on the waist band just under my bellybutton. He looks up at me, his eyes not asking permission, but telling me that he's about to take what he wants. Arching my back slightly, I moan in response.

Slowly he pulls my leggings off and drops them to the floor, all the while staring hungrily at the black lace panties I'm wearing.

"Fucking kryptonite," he mutters softly.

How can he seem so calm? My body is on fire for him, my core swollen and begging for him. "Bryant," I whimper between pants.

"Just breathe, Baby. Breathe, and know that I'll take care of you. I want to take care of you." As he speaks, he slowly slides my panties off before his fingers explore every inch of my legs. He reaches the apex of my thighs and I'm grasping at the sheets around me as Bryant's finger delicately invades the nerves inside me, sliding in and out, coating me in my own arousal.

"Oh God!" I whisper as quietly as I can. I want nothing more than to scream his name, but remind myself over and over that we're not alone in this house.

"Savannah, good God, you're so warm and soft and…" he takes a deep breath and blows it out to steady himself. "Damn, you're going to make me lose control way before I want to."

"Bryant, please." My body is growing anxious and impatient. It's been too long and I'm raging inside with the need to feel his body against mine.

"Watch me, Baby. Watch me taste you."

Keeping my eyes open, let alone on the man who is torturing my senses, is harder and more erotic than I ever thought it would be. His tongue as it slides up and down the most sensitive part of me has me throwing my head back and moaning loudly in a fit of passion. "Mmmm…Bryant…I can't…"

"Yes you can, Baby. It's okay. Let yourself go. I've got you." He continues his slow assault on my body as I grab at the sheets. I hold my breath knowing I'm on the brink of ecstasy, as soon as I let it go my body will lose all control. Finally, I feel his tongue on me one last time, making me gasp for one more breath, and then I'm free as my body explodes inside me. The blissful feeling of flying high and floating on air envelops my senses. Every nerve, every muscle relaxes as my mind comes down from euphoria.

"It's not fair, how sexy you are," Bryant whispers quietly against my ear. Though my eyes are closed, I smile shyly at him knowing that my body is splayed out in front of him, yet his jeans are still on. "Your body is so alluring, Savannah. I want to make you mine so damn badly and then I don't ever want to let you go."

My smile fades as I open my eyes. "Then don't." I whisper leaning up to trap his lips in mine. My hands wrestle with the button of his jeans. Once open I pull my legs up to Bryant's hips. He raises his body just enough for me to remove his pants and his boxer briefs with the help of my toes. He sits up between my legs to pull his pants off the rest of the way and tosses them to floor. There he is in all his glory.

Finally, after all this time, I understand the nickname, Bryant *the Giant* Wood.

*Sweet Jesus.*

Bryant leans over me, to the bed stand next to us, and pulls a silver foil packet out of the drawer. Immediately I feel a pang of guilt for not having thought of protection for myself. I certainly thought of the black lace bra and panties but it's been so long since I've had to worry about birth control it never even crossed my mind. I watch in anticipation as Bryant rolls the condom on.

"I need to feel you, Seven. I need to make you mine. Do you trust me?"

"Of course I trust you."

"I don't want to hurt you, Baby."

"I'm not made of glass, Bryant. Kiss me. Touch me. Take me. I want to go on this adventure with you."

*I hope he hears what I'm saying.*

Bryant leans forward, resting his forearms on each side of my head. He kisses my forehead, my nose, my cheek, and my neck before teasing my mouth open with his tongue. His kiss is passionate and hungry. I feel the tip of him at my entrance.

"I love you Savannah." The look on Bryant's face melts my heart. Yes, his body tells me that he's blinded by passion and hungry for carnal intimacy, but his eyes tell me that this moment right now means more to him than anything. That I mean more to him than anything. That I really can trust him to protect me.

"I love you too, Bryant." My body relaxes as he kisses me again. Bryant's lips part as he exhales in blissful satisfaction. He slides into me with ease, holding himself there until my body relaxes around him.

"Savannah...you're..." He finishes his sentence with an "Ahhhhhh yeah" as he pulls out and thrusts back in, this time a little more forcefully. Within minutes, I wrap my legs around his waist, holding his body close to mine. He nuzzles my neck as his tempo accelerates. Little grunts escape him with each push.

"So...fucking...good..." he says between thrusts. I'm shocked when the heat in my body begins to rise again, the pleasure furiously taking over every nerve inside me.

"Bryant..." I pant as our speed increases. I grab onto his shoulders, digging my nails into his flesh. Bringing his body down slightly so that his mouth is directly in line with my chest, he looks at me briefly giving me his sexiest smolder before playfully biting my nipple.

"Oh God…I'm going to…" Before I can even finish my thought my body responds to the savage beat of Bryant's sensual frenzy. The fire running through me rocks me to my core causing my world to shatter within me. My muscles pulse around Bryant, pushing him over the edge as I feel him come apart inside me. His head nuzzling my neck he releases several grunts as he rides out the wave of ecstasy.

Our foreheads touching.

Our lips parted.

Our breathing in tandem.

"Savannah…" My name rolls eloquently off his tongue.

"Bryant…" I'm crying. I'm not sobbing but I can feel the tears run down my face as my body trembles lightly. I can't control them or make them stop, and in all honesty, I'm not sure I want to. I'm both shocked and proud of myself at the same time.

"Are you okay?" he whispers.

"Yeah," I say, trying to catch my breath. "Yeah. I'm okay. Bryant, I promise these are…incredibly happy tears because that was…" I try to catch my breath. "That was…I've never…sex in my past life was always just sex. Two people, desire, needs…but this…"

"Yeah." Like he's reading my mind he responds immediately in between pants of breath. "I know. For me too…like nothing I've ever experienced before."

*That can't be true.*

*He's just saying that so I'm not embarrassed.*

I smirk doubtingly at him. "Ah come on, you don't have to say that to make me feel better."

He looks at me with hurt in his eyes. "You don't believe me."

"Well…you told me about your past lifestyle." I place my palm on his cheek. "I'm not blaming you at all. Please don't take my words the wrong way."

Bryant pushes himself up so that he can see my face. With a disappointed-in-himself expression he says "Savannah, not that you really want or need to know this, but Ivy was conceived on the couch in my shit hole of an office at the bar."

"What?" I chuckle slightly but I am caught off guard. I guess I expected it was more than just a quickie.

"It's true." He takes a breath before continuing his explanation. "I meant what I said when I told you that you're the first woman to be in my bed, or in my house for the matter. You're right. I told you that Bryant 'the Giant' Wood was the 'fuck'em and chuck'em type. It's not something I'm proud of now and I'll regret the way I treated women for the rest of my life but you..." He shakes his head bewildered. "Savannah, you're the one my heart has been waiting for since I can remember. I've always wanted to make love to you, to taste you, to touch you, to smell you....to protect you...to hold you. I've dreamed of making you mine but you've always been just out of my reach."

"I'm here now." is all I can think to say.

"You are...and as much as I don't want to thank God for that because of the circumstances in which you're here...I'm thanking Him anyway...for bringing you back to me, for allowing me one more chance." Bryant kisses me softly holding my cheek with his right hand. "I love you Savannah Turner. I loved you then and I love you now and I want you in my life for as long as you'll stay. Whatever you want, it's yours. I want to be the man who takes care of you."

He's so sweet. I didn't expect this much sincerity from him but since he's offering, I decide now is the time to make one little request. "Bryant." I place my hands on his chest, his warmth emanating from his body. "I don't need anything from you. Just knowing you're in my life makes me happier than you could imagine. And sweet, little Ivy...you both are so special..."

"Why do I feel a 'but' coming on?"

Pursing my lips, I continue. "But while we're on the subject there is one thing you can do."

"Anything. Name it and it's done."

I lean up quickly to kiss Bryant's cheek and say, "I think your office may need a new couch."

"Hahaha!" He laughs grabbing me in a bear hug and rolling me on top of him. "Done! You can even help me pick one out." His eyes grow as they roll up and down my body. "Maybe I need a pin-up poster for my wall while we're at it." He raises both of his eyebrows quickly in succession.

"In your dreams Wood. In your dreams." I laugh along with him as I lower myself down to his chest. I kiss him one more time, but as I try to sit up he traps me in his arms, rolling us both onto our sides. Our kiss deepens once again as we enjoy exploring each other's bodies, making the most of our time together.

# Chapter 23

# *Bryant*

"Savannah I need to tell you something. It's really important so I need you to hear me." As I look down and to the side I see Savannah's head tilt up towards me from where she is lying in the crook of my shoulder. Her soft hands glide against my chest. Her expression is one of comfortable satisfaction and that makes me a very happy man; nevertheless, what I'm about to say scares the shit out of me. My pulse quickens and my anxiety is growing with every passing second.

"I'm right here, Bryant. What do you need to tell me that's so important?" She kisses my chest and my shoulder before rolling up towards me and softly kissing my lips. She leans back and watches me in anticipation.

"It's about Ivy."

"Okay."

I swallow slowly, "And Peyton."

She smiles endearingly like I'm about to tell her a story of what great friends they are. "Okay. What is it? Tell me."

"Well, umm, you know how I told you that I hadn't been in contact with Ivy's liver donor? How I had never written them to say thanks or to give an update on Ivy or anything like that?"

She smiles again, which is unnerving. "Yes. I remember. You really should find her donor though, Bryant. I'm sure the other family would want to know that their child's life benefited someone else's."

"Savannah…"

"What, Bryant?" She chuckles softly smoothing her fingers down my cheek. "What is it you need to tell me?"

"I'm uh…I'm telling you now, Savannah."

"Telling me what?"

"I'm telling you now...that um...Peyton's life..." I hold Savannah's arms in my hands so I can help her when she hears the news. "It benefited someone else's."

She laughs.

*What the fuck?*

*Why is she laughing?*

"Of course it did, Bryant. I received several letters last year..."

"Not from me, Savannah." I shake my head adamantly. "You didn't receive one from me."

She stops laughing and looks at me, her head tilting in confusion. "I don't understand."

Closing my eyes quickly I inhale one last big breath before simply spitting it out so she understands. "Savannah, you didn't receive a letter from me because I was way too afraid to write one. I didn't know how to tell you that Ivy was the recipient of Peyton's liver. I didn't know how to tell you because I'm in love with you, but the guilt of not telling you is eating me alive so I'm sorry you didn't receive a letter from me but please, Savannah. Please know that Peyton's life...it means more than the world to me. It meant life for my child and for that I will be forever and ever grateful."

I look at Savannah's face as she sits astride me in my bed. Her face soft but void of expression. We're both vulnerable in this state...naked, together in bed. I'm not sure what she's thinking. If only her face would give me a clue as to what she's thinking I would know which way to go but damn, if she isn't just starting at me.

"Savannah..."

"It's okay, Bryant. I love you," she says softly.

I release a breath and wrap her in my arms, relieved that she didn't just chop off my balls for keeping the truth from her. When I open my eyes I'm shivering. Confused as to why I'm suddenly so cold, I let go of Savannah and lean back slightly.

"WHAT THE?" I shout as I jump from my bed. I feel guilty for a quick second that I just threw Savannah off of me except that what I tossed wasn't Savannah at all. When I leaned back I was hugging Olaf the snowman.

What the ever-loving fuck?

I watch in shock as his head rolls to the side and he giggles. "True love means telling the truth…let it go, Bryant. Let it go."

*****

I startle awake, gasping for air.

I look around the room and remember that I moved out to the living room this morning to lay on the couch in case Ivy woke up early.

*Damnit.*

*It was just a dream.*

*I haven't told her yet.*

Shaking the absurdity from my head I put my face in my hands and am rubbing my temples when I hear her singing. I must've heard it in my head while I was dreaming.

"Let it gooo…let it goooo…Subanna slept ova last niiiight." I smile at the cute voice that I recognize as Ivy's and am surprised to hear the laughter of Savannah's voice right along with her.

*Ivy must've woken up Savannah.*

*Shit. I hope she doesn't mind.*

*I should go get her in case Savannah wants to sleep.*

*But listening to them giggle is a nice way to wake up.*

That was a fucked up dream if I ever had one but I understand it now that I've had a moment to process it. I love this girl, I've wanted her for so long, but the guilt I have for keeping the truth from her is constantly on my mind. I have no idea how she'll really react. I'm not convinced she'll be the same Savannah from my dream when I tell her…and I'm not sure I would want her to be.

Quietly I make my way back down the hall toward my bedroom where I hear my two ladies singing and giggling. I stand outside the door and listen for a while as Ivy tells Savannah all about her love of Elsa and Ana and all things *Frozen*. As much as I would love to join them, they sound like they're having a great time together. I make my way back down the hall to the kitchen. I promised a certain little girl I would make pancakes for breakfast.

It's not ten minutes later that I hear the pitter patter of little feet hopping down the hallway toward the kitchen.

"Come on! Come on Subanna! I smell PANCAKES!"

"Mmm! I love pancakes!" Savannah laughs. I can see her smile in my head. The gorgeous curve of her lips and the blush in her cheeks when she smiles is forever ingrained in my brain. I like to make her smile. That one little expression can warm my body every single time I see it on her face.

*She deserves to smile.*

*She deserves to be happy.*

The picture of Savannah in my brain is an exact reflection of her as she turns the corner into the kitchen, Ivy's hand in hers. My little princess is tugging Savannah's arm excitedly toward the kitchen island where I'm preparing breakfast. Our eyes finally meet and my world stops. It just freezes. Holding my spatula in mid-air, I stop what I'm doing at the stove and stare at her, trying to memorize this moment in time. The moment when the woman of my dreams walks into my kitchen, looking carefree and gorgeously sexy. No makeup, unkempt hair pulled haphazardly to the top of her head, she's confidently stunning. When I left her last night she was naked in my bed. She obviously found her bag I brought in from her car last night, though the grey cotton t-shirt she's wearing is still mine. Damn she looks hot in my clothes, and her holding the hand of the most important other female of my life makes an indelible impression on me. The picture in this kitchen right now is like that of a normal Saturday morning with any other normal family.

*But this isn't our normal.*

*I have to tell her.*

My dream…it hits me like an arrow to my heart and I gasp audibly causing Savannah's expression to change to one of worry.

*Fuck! My dream…*

*I can't tell her.*

*I don't want to lose her.*

"Are you okay? Did you just burn yourself?" Savannah asks as she helps Ivy up to her stool in front of the island counter where I have our place settings ready.

"Uhh, yeah." I lie. "Just touched the pan accidentally. I'm good." I try to play it off and hope that Savannah doesn't pick up on my distraction. I smile at her and Ivy both sitting across from me. I want so badly to kiss Savannah but I haven't done anything like that in front of Ivy yet...I'm not sure how she'll react to that. She's never seen me kiss a girl before. Instead I clear my thoughts from my head, and offer up some morning beverages.

"Would you lovely ladies like a drink? Milk? OJ? Coffee?" I direct that last suggestion to Savannah.

"Pwincesses Daddy! We're Pwincesses!"

"Ohhh, well excuse me then beautiful princesses." I try to use my best British butler voice. "Would either of you care for a cold, or hot, beverage to go with your pancakes this morning hmm?"

Ivy scrunches up her nose and giggles before lifting her chin to respond in her version of a British accent, "I fink I will have miwk Mista Daddy if you pwease."

"Perfect darling. Yes of course Princess Ivy needs a healthy glass of milk with her pancakes. How about you, Princess Savannah? What can I get for you to drink Madame?"

As if she's played this role a thousand times Savannah turns on her dramatic British charm. If I didn't know better, I would swear I was standing in the middle of an episode of *Downton Abbey*. "Coffee in England, are you mad? Everyone knows it's tea we drink, but I'll settle for a tall glass of milk to go with my flapjacks. Cheers." She looks to Ivy as they both break into a fit of giggles.

*How does she do it?*

*Perfectly fits into our little family dynamic?*

Shaking my head in humorous defeat, I pour my girls their milk before walking around the island to hand Ivy her sippy cup, and Savannah her glass.

"Cheers darling," she says, smiling. Quickly she kisses me once on my right cheek and then again on my left. I'm frozen in place having not expected that display of affection. What I also don't expect is the look of passion in Savannah's eyes as they stare back at me. Like pancakes is the last thing she wants for breakfast.

I clear my throat and swallow before speaking. "Hungry?" I ask her softly.

Blinking slowly, she holds my gaze. "Mmm hmm."

I watch as she takes another sip of her milk and licks her bottom lip just lazily enough to hold my attention.

*Have mercy.*

*If I could just take her back to my…*

My eyes quickly divert to where Ivy is sitting.

*Shit.*

*Don't do anything stupid, Wood. Your kid is in the room.*

I try to smirk in triumph knowing that as hungry as she is, she now has to wait. Little does she know that I'm not the triumphant one at all. She's already won.

"Pancakes are coming right up…would you like…sausage with that?" I wink at her when I ask so that she knows I'm not talking about Jimmy Dean.

Wearing her best shit-eating grin, she chuckles softly. "I do enjoy the taste of a good strong sausage."

*Good Lord she can make my dick twitch.*

Immediately I turn around and walk back to the stovetop to continue my work with our breakfast. "Coming right up."

*Fuck if it isn't.*

*Control yourself Wood.*

If there's one thing I've learned for sure in the past few weeks, it's that Savannah Turner is my kryptonite. She's caught me hook, line, and sinker and damn if I don't want to swim in her waters for the rest of my days.

But I have to tell her. I have to tell her about Peyton and Ivy before whatever it is we have gets any tighter. I vow to myself that I will tell

Savannah the truth when it's time, although, who the hell knows when that might be. I'm hoping it'll just come to me and she'll be okay when the truth comes out.

*The truth sets you free right?*
*Will I ever be free from the guilt?*

# Chapter 24

# *Savannah*

"Holy shit you spent the night there? At his house? With Ivy?" Rachel hammers me with questions one after the other.

"Yes, yes, and yes," I say, trying to remain as nonchalant as humanly possible. I'm sure she can see through me. She's always good at picking up on my feelings.

"Well how was it then? Did you guys...you know...with Ivy there?" Her eyebrows raise in excited suspense.

I continue washing my combs and brushes as I think back to Friday, playing with Ivy, putting her to sleep with Bryant, the time we shared together afterwards. "It was..." My anxiety attack floats through my brain and my stomach turns, wiping the smile off of my face.

"It was what?" Rachel asks noticing my mood change.

"It was nice. I had a great time."

Rachel's eyes narrow. She knows something is off. "No, no, no, no, no." She waves her finger at me. "You don't get to tell me that it was just nice. A minute ago you were all smiles and now you're not so what the fuck happened and how badly do I need to kick Wood's ass?"

"Not at all...that's not..."

"Then what is it? Did he hurt you?"

"No," I say immediately. "He didn't hurt me at all Rache. I just...had this moment on Friday night that I can't explain."

"Okay...try," she prompts.

I dry off the combs and brushes I was washing and place them back in my drawer so that I'm ready for the day. The clock on the wall tells me we're opening in about five minutes so I take a second to sit in my chair as Rachel takes her cue from me and sits in hers right next to me. I can tell she's concerned.

"Okay, Ivy wanted me to help put her to bed which I did. I kissed her good night and left Bryant alone with her so that they could have their regular nightly routine together. I didn't want to be in the way, so I excused myself to the kitchen."

"Alright, I can understand that. Then what?"

"So I'm standing in the kitchen and all of a sudden I hear Bryant start singing to Ivy. I didn't know there was a monitor in the kitchen and I heard it all loud and clear."

Rachel tilts her head slightly. "I don't get it. Why is that a bad thing? Did he sing some sort of inappropriate song or something?"

My head turns to the top of the mirror at my station. Above the mirror is a small painted canvas that reads "You Are My Sunshine." I've had it there since the day I started. It brings me peace on those days when I just miss my family. Rachel sees me looking at the canvas and a lightbulb flashes in her head.

She gasps softly. "Savannah did he sing that song to Ivy? 'You Are My Sunshine'?"

I nod.

"Did he know?" She asks.

"Know what?"

"Did he know that was your special song for...Peyton?"

"No. He didn't know. He found out really quick though when he found me outside on his porch doubled over in tears."

"What? Oh God! Savannah, you poor thing!"

"I can't even tell you how it happened Rache. One minute, I was standing in his kitchen, and the next moment I couldn't breathe. I had tears pouring down my face and didn't even know it. It's the weirdest thing to happen to me in a long time."

"So what did you do?"

"I didn't do anything. Bryant found me like that, picked me up and carried me to his room, held me, talked to me, you know. He felt terrible. I felt terrible for causing him to feel that way. I should've just gone home but he didn't want me to be alone and to be honest, I didn't want to go."

"Girl, I've heard that grief hits you when you least expect it. Sounds like that song just triggered something for you. Are you okay now? Do you need some time off?"

"No, no, no. I'm totally fine. Thanks though, I'm good, I promise. After that, our weekend was fantastic. Really."

"Okay good." Rachel's eyes fall to the door when the bell rings and Audrey walks in.

"Mornin' ladies!" Audrey says in her usual perky tone.

"Good morning Audrey," I reply.

"Well ladies…" Rachel looks down at her watch. "I hope you're ready for what this day has to throw at us so early this morning. Just don't hate me alright?"

Detecting a bit of trepidation in Rachel's voice I have a bad feeling I know what's about to happen. "Why would we hate you so early in the morning Rachel?" I ask sternly.

I no sooner ask the question than three ladies waltz into the salon, all looking every bit the bitches I know them to be. Jamie Henders, Jody Westin, and Brooke Lilt, three best friends from high school who never left town to grow up. They're the same now as they were back then, spoiled rich girls always sticking their precious noses in other people's business. If there were a cast for *The Real Housewives of Bardstown*, these girls would be the stars.

I turn quickly to Rachel before the ladies have a chance to see my expression. "Make ya a deal, Rache. I won't hate you if you don't hate me for accidentally knocking my fist into one of their beautiful sets of perfect teeth."

Rachel chokes on her coffee but tries to hide her smile. She deserves it for starting my day this way. These girls were the bane of my existence in high school and I can't stand them now. They walk in dressed to the nines on a Monday morning wearing their perfect designer jeans, high heeled pumps and carrying their Coach purses. Even Brooke, who is at least seven months pregnant, is sporting designer maternity clothes. They definitely put my black leggings and yellow tunic to shame.

*Seriously, does she know one day her water is going to break and ruin those pants?*

*Maybe I should ask her about her mucus plug.*

*This isn't Rodeo Drive ladies.*

Nevertheless, I plaster a brilliantly fake smile on my face and welcome them in with open arms. "Good morning ladies! How are you all this morning?"

Jody eyes me up from head to toe before answering sympathetically in her best southern twang. "That's right. I forgot you were working here now. My mom told me you were back in town. It's good to see you." Ugh, the way she drags out the word 'you' with her southern accent makes me really want to punch her in the teeth. She sounds like a two-faced church girl trying to be nice to the devil.

"Yes. I've been here for a few months now. It's good to be back. What are we doing for you today?"

"Oh yes, well umm, I definitely need to have my eyebrows waxed and then I'm thinking just a cut and style. No need to go overboard today."

"Okay. That's no problem. Let's head back to the sink and we'll get started on those brows."

As I lead Jody to the back of the shop Audrey and Rachel both make their plans with the other two girls. These bitches always seem to travel in packs. I would like to think that alone, one wouldn't be so irritatingly pompous, but then again, getting one of them alone for any length of time is next to impossible. Jody and I used to be relatively friendly with each other growing up. She lived near me in my neighborhood and we often rode the bus together. As we grew up though, we definitely started growing apart, she became a high school cheerleader and I was the school nerd. I had goals and ambition, a passion for the arts. From what I heard she and her little besties had a passion for penis and every guy knew it.

*Maybe I should ask Bryant…*

*No…don't ever ask Bryant.*

*Some things I don't want to know.*

Eventually all three girls are seated next to each other in their salon chairs clucking away like gossiping hens. Hair salons are definitely where you hear everything about everybody whether you want to hear it or not. In the twenty minutes they've been here, I've learned about Robyn Small's drinking problem, and the affair her husband is having with their babysitter. I listened intently while Brooke talked about the six kids Michelle Timely has because she can't keep her damn legs closed, and they all laughed while discussing Ben Garster's rise to fame in the corporate world only to be sent to jail for three years for embezzling.

I can only imagine what they all had to say about me not too long ago.

"I heard that now that Ben's back home and his wife left him, he lives with his parents again and spends his nights at the bar," Jamie says, filing her nails as her hair is being cut.

"Too bad. He was hot back in the day. Nobody will ever want a piece of that now," Jody says.

"Didn't you have a little fling with him back then Jode?? That one summer during college? Wasn't that him?" Jamie asks.

Jody laughs. "Little fling would be a good word for it if you know what I'm sayin'. God, he was such a mistake. I'm glad it didn't last more than a few make-out sessions that summer. He was a sloppy kisser too. Blech."

"I'm sure by now he's got his one-way tickets to Alcoholicville with as much time as he spends at the bar." Brooke says. "Speaking of the bar, Savannah…"

*Huh? What?*

I was able to drown them all out by thinking about my weekend with Bryant and Ivy, but as soon as she says my name I'm all ears.

"I heard you were having a little fun with Bryant Wood at the bar a few weeks ago."

*Is that a question?*

*Does she expect a response?*

"Uh, yeah. The girls and I went to have a few drinks. He was there. It was karaoke night."

Brooke nods her head slightly. "I hear you gave a stellar performance. You always were quite the singer in high school."

"Bryant Wood huh?" Jamie's eyes narrow as she looks across to me through the mirror in front of her. I can only imagine what she must be thinking. "He's definitely a looker now isn't he? He's grown into his body quiet well I would say."

"Um, yeah I guess. I don't know. We didn't hang out much in high school." I try to play off my feelings. The last thing I need is this group of gossip girls running their mouths around town.

"He sure gets around from what I've heard - flirts pretty heavily with the women who go there. I hear they're all over him. They always were in high school too. Bryant Wood definitely is a ladies-man." Jamie says. I look at her expression in the mirror just fast enough to see her wink at Jody.

She's goading me.

I decide not to reward her with a reaction to what she just said. Instead I pretend to be focused on my work with Jody's hair, meticulously snipping in the appropriate places and wishing I was buzzing it all off.

"Did he kiss you?" Jody asks me.

"That's what I heard." Brooke announces in a high pitched sing-song voice.

"My brother, Joe, saw the whole thing. Said you two were making out right there at your table, in front of all your friends," Jamie raves.

I feel the red.

I'm seeing red.

I'm thinking red. How I would love to slide the blades of these scissors across all three of their fucking little necks. I smirk to hide my pissed off expression. What Bryant and I do is none of their damn business.

"That's bull shit. They never made out. I was right there, sitting at the table." Audrey comes to my defense, not that I needed her help. I appreciate it anyway.

"So he *did* kiss you then?" Jamie asks again.

I slide my scissors into the pocket of my apron and pick up the blow dryer and a brush. "Not that it's any of your business Jamie, but yes, Bryant kissed me…and I kissed him back. Is that what you want to know?"

Before there's time to hear a response from either of the three bitches seated in front of me, I turn the blow dryer on high and begin to glide my fingers through Jody's hair, praying it dries in record time and I can get the hell out of here. I know the girls are still chatting because I can see their lips moving, their eyes landing on me as they exchange winks and smirks.

*Stupid catty girls.*

*Time hasn't changed for them.*

*They're still ugly, inside and out.*

Immediately I'm smiling to myself as I begin to hum the tune to the one Pink song that makes me unequivocally think of these three ladies. "Stupid Girls". Almost five minutes later I'm shutting off the blow dryer and grabbing the hair spray to finish Jody's hair.

"You know he has a kid right?" Jamie asks.

I've had enough of this bitch. Who does she think she is? Who do any of them think they are?

Throwing my hand on my hip I cock my head to the side and stare her down through the mirror in front of me. "Why are you telling me all this exactly? Why all the questions? Is there a problem you need to talk to me about or are you still the high school gossip queen lookin' for her next headline?"

Jamie's jaw hits the floor momentarily. Even Audrey and Rachel stop to look at me. Oops, I guess I said all that out loud.

Jamie clears her throat and with the most diva-like attitude I've ever seen in a young adult white female says "I don't know who you think you're talkin' to Savannah Sanders, but you should understand a few things. Bryant Wood isn't the shiny white night you probably think he is. He's nothin' but a loser with a big ass douchebag of secrets and if you're not careful, he'll knock you up too." She purses her lips and rolls her eyes before checking her make-up in the mirror in front of her.

"You don't know what the fuck you're talkin' about Jamie Lynn," I say with all the calmness I can muster using her middle name just as she used to be called when we were kids. "And my name is Savannah Turner."

All of a sudden Jamie's expression changes to one of complete remorse. I actually start to feel guilty for being a bitch to her just now. She tilts her head, her eyes filled with sadness. "Of course…maybe that's what you're looking for then…someone to knock you up to replace the dead kid you no longer have. How could I have forgo…"

"GET THE FUCK OUT OF MY SALON YOU CRAZY FUCKING BITCH!"

Those words didn't come out of my mouth.

Rachel…it was all Rachel.

I don't even know what to say. The wind has just been knocked out of me. The room becomes a tilt-a-whirl for a full minute.

I don't…even…know…what to do right now. Vacantly I look around the salon, catching every flabbergasted or snide expression staring back at me.

"Ex…" I clear my throat. "Excuse me." I mumble. I'm not even positive the words come out of my mouth but my feet are moving toward the door.

"Savannah, no, wait!" I hear Rachel call after me but I don't turn around. Not even once. I head out the door into the warm morning sunshine, not even sure of where I'm going. I just can't be here.

Not now.

# Chapter 25

# *Bryant*

I hate Mondays. It's always a slow night at the bar, but yet I have to spend most of the day doing inventory and running around town to make sure we're stocked with everything we need. As the months pass and the weather grows warmer, Bardstown starts hopping with out-of-town tourist groups. They don't call us the Bourbon Capital of the World for nothing. Everyone likes to come to town to sample what our local distilleries have to offer. My dad loves this time of year. I guess I sort of like the quiet months when it's just the locals and I know I can take more time off to be with Ivy…and now Savannah too. But business is business and money is money so I'll take everything I can get.

"Hey, Wood!" Sloan calls back to where I am in my office from the bar. "Add Baccardi Gold and Buckeye Vodka to the list if you're working on it."

"Will do!" I shout back to him. Inventory time is tedious but having my friend and business partner, Sloan, around makes things much easier and a bit more enjoyable. I add the needed drinks to my list and run another check to make sure I haven't missed anything. Sloan walks into the office carrying a case of beer, setting it on top of the others I have against the wall.

"So…"

"So what?" I ask.

Sloan nods to a picture I have on my desk of Savannah and me from a few days ago. "You two make it official of anything? Cause everyone's been talkin' since you put your tongue down her throat a few weeks ago in the middle of our bar."

"Oh yeah?" I try to seem uninterested but hell if I don't think about putting my tongue down her throat every damn day. "Who's everyone and what are they sayin'?"

"Just the guys that practically live here…Cliff, Woody, Norm…they haven't seen you so fucking stupid over a girl in a long time, man."

Sloan and I gave a few of our regulars nicknames to match the characters from *Cheers*. Seemed like the right thing to do at the time, and we were all pretty plastered, but it stuck.

"Yeah? When has anyone ever seen me 'fucking stupid' over a girl in my adult life?" I know I've been known to flirt with the female customers and all but I'm pretty damn sure nobody has ever seen Bryant Wood in love.

"True that. I guess just Sam…" he starts.

"I was never 'fucking stupid' over Sam, it was one night and we were both…fucking stupid."

"So Savannah is different then? 'Cause usually you're an open book about the women you hang out with but this time it's the silent treatment, so what gives? You were all about wanting her back in the day and now you're tight-lipped about it. You got something with her?"

"Yeah I got something with her. That okay? I mean not that I need your damn approval or anything 'Papa Sloan' but you're sittin' here askin', so is that okay?" I'm annoyed, but only because for the first time since I can remember, I'm in love with a girl and I don't need the whole damn world knowing our business. I'm pretty sure Savannah would feel the same way if she were here.

Sloan's smirk turns into a huge celebratory smile. "Hell yeah that's okay Bry! I'm happy for you, man. Really…you deserve to be happy." He rocks his body up off the couch and slaps his hand on my shoulder. "But if you don't want people diggin' on you, you may want to think about where you are when your tongue is playing hockey with hers." He chuckles.

I look up from my desk and smirk at him. I suppose he has a point. It's my fault everyone knows about us. "Yeah thanks for the advice, Douche."

He laughs, stepping towards the office door when my cell phone rings on my desk. My caller ID says it's Rachel. I assume she's calling about meeting up with Savannah for lunch so I swipe my finger across the screen to answer the call.

"Hey Rache. What's up?"

"Is Savannah with you?" she asks quickly.

"Uh…no. She's supposed to be working today. Where are you?"

"At the salon."

"So she never showed or what?"

"No she was here but left about ten minutes ago." The panic in Rachel's voice alarms me.

"Wait, wait, wait." I say. "What do you mean she left? Is she okay?"

*Why the fuck would she just leave?*

"Because Jamie Henders and her bitches came in this morning."

"Oh shit." I mutter. Jamie Henders is known in this town for knowing everything about everybody. She's also known for throwing her spoiled rich married body at any man who looks at her, and yes, that included me at one point. I fucked it and chucked it many years ago and she's never forgotten. I have no doubt that she's heard about Savannah and me, which means I'm one hundred percent sure she was out for blood this morning.

*And again, it's all my fault.*

I hold my head in my left hand slowly rubbing the stress out of my temples. "What did she say, Rachel? Tell me what happened."

"She was being her regular damn self, Bryant. You know, certified grade-A bitch and her girls were just as harsh. It was like we were in an episode of *Glee* and Savannah ended up with a verbal slushie to the face. I finally had enough and told them all to go fuck themselves and to get the fuck out of my salon, but it was too late. The damage had been done."

"Fuck," I whisper.

"Yeah. So Savannah quietly excused herself and walked out. I have no idea where she went, because her car is still parked outside, and she's not answering her phone. I thought maybe she would've walked down the street to see you."

*Where could she have gone?*

"No, she never showed here. I haven't heard from her. Maybe she just needed a time out for a few minutes. If she left her car there, then she has to come back at some point to get it… I'm sure she'll come around eventually."

"Bryant?"

"Yeah?"

"Jamie told her that the only reason she would want to be with you is so you'll knock *her* up too, and give her another kid to replace the dead one she no longer has."

*Oh…*

*Fuck…*

I'm up out of my chair in a split second. I get it. Savannah is strong-willed and can take a beating to an extent but a comment like that…from a bitch like Jamie Henders…I'm sure it broke Savannah into pieces. She could be anywhere…I have no idea where I'll find her but I'm waving to Sloan and am out the door in a minute. "I'm on my way out the door Rache. I'll look for her. I'll find her. Let me know immediately if you hear from her. I'm getting in my truck right now! I'll drive around a few blocks and see if I can find her."

I don't even wait for a reply. I disconnect the call, throw my phone onto my dashboard, and practically peel out of my parking spot from the back of the bar. The first place I need to check is the park. We've been there a few times together, always stopping at the same secluded spot where we bring our lunch to eat and spend some time alone. It's beautiful piece of land where we can talk quietly and not have to worry about other people. I head down the alley and smoothly pull into the public parking lot. If she's upset, I would rather she not know I'm coming. She didn't run to me initially so…shit.

My feet freeze on the pavement.

*She didn't run to me.*

*She knew I was here.*

*She could've come here.*
*But she didn't.*
*She doesn't want my help.*
*Or she doesn't want me.*

Son of a bitch, if I ever see Jamie Henders or either of her two bitches again, it'll be way too soon. That girl has fucked with me more than once and I'll be damned if I'm going to let her get away with it this time. She's got me doubting myself and Savannah's part in my life and that doesn't sit well with me at all. Just the thought of breaking Savannah's heart into pieces has me immediately nauseous. If she doesn't want to see me right now it's okay, but I still need to find her, watch her...make sure she's alright. I can't do nothing when I know she's upset. Swiftly I jog to our little spot in the park where I expect to see her curled up under the tree, but she's not there.

"Where are you Seven?" I whisper to myself. She could easily be walking any of the several nature trails the park has to offer but there's no way I could possibly search all of them at once to find her. Pulling out my phone I quickly send her a text to see if she'll respond to me.

Me: Hey. I'm at the park, you here?

No response.

Maybe she turned her ringer off. Rachel didn't say she left it at the salon. I slowly start to make my way back tto my truck, looking all around for her just in case I missed her the first time. Eagerly anticipating her reply, I text her again.

Me: Babe, are you ok? I can't find you.

No response.
*Damnit.*

"Come on Sev. I need to know you're okay." I mutter to myself again. Knowing she can't have gone too far on foot, I drive around a couple blocks through town in hopes that I'll find her sitting on a bench or something. After another five minutes of driving I still haven't found her. I check the flower gardens near the historical museum, I ask the drivers of the town carriage rides if she's stopped by, and even drive out to the elementary school to see if she's there watching the kids play.

*Where the fuck can she be?*

Me: Seven I just need to know if you're okay. Please.

No response.

The way I see it, I have two choices. I can go back to work and pray to God she makes her way back to me when she's calmed down, or I can go back to town and stop in every store on Main Street to see if she's been in. Unless she took a cab, and there aren't many of those in this town, there's no way she's far away from town. My head says go back to work, but my heart unequivocally wins out as I turn my truck around to head back into town. Peirson's is my first stop. I step into the gift shop and look around quickly for anyone resembling Savannah. I don't see anyone in the store at all except for Mrs. Peirson who is smiling at me expectantly from the register.

"Good morning Bryant. What can I help you with this mornin'?"

"Mornin' Mrs. Peirson." Although I know her first name is Linda, I can't ever get myself to be on a first name basis since Mrs. Peirson was my seventh grade math teacher. Her family has always owned Peirson's gifts, so since she's retired from teaching she's made herself available to help at the store. "I'm sorry ma'am, I was just stopping in looking for someone this morning. That's all.

"Oh, well who might you be lookin' for? Jamie Henders perhaps? She was just in not too long ago with her girlfriends."

Fuck no. Anyone but her.

"No, actually I'm looking for Savannah Sanders...uh...Turner. Savannah Turner. Has she been in at all this morning?"

Mrs. Peirson immediately gives me the sympathetic I-know-all-about-Savannah's-loss expression before she says "No, I'm sorry. I haven't seen her at all today, but if she stops by I'll certainly tell her you're looking for her."

"Thank you ma'am. Have a nice day."

"You too Bryant," she waves as I back out of the store.

I head to the next place on the block, Bardstown Books, but don't see her in there either. As I step back out onto the street my cell phone buzzes in my pocket, alerting me to a text.

Sloan: Savannah's here for you.

*Oh thank Christ!*

Me: Is she ok?

Sloan: Don't know but it does look like she's been crying. She's been here for about fifteen minutes. Didn't want me to tell you she was here.

*What the hell?*

*Why not?*

*She really doesn't want to see me?*

Me: DON'T LET HER LEAVE! I'll be right there. Keep her safe!

Sloan: She's fine, Dude, what the fuck? Did something happen?

I don't even bother to respond to his last text. I jump in my truck and speed down the next few blocks. Standing outside the back door to the bar, I stop and force myself to take a deep breath to calm myself down. If she's feeling beaten down and is overwhelmingly upset, I can't run in there upset with her. I'm not upset with her. If anything I'm pissed at myself for what she's gone through this morning. In one way or another, I'm directly related to the problem. This is all my fault and I now all I can do is hope that she'll forgive me. Quietly I pull the door open and step inside. Sloan is standing against the wall outside my office fiddling with his cell phone, ready to ambush me with questions.

"Hey man. Is everything okay? What's going on? Did she get hurt?"

My eyes grow large at the thought of someone physically hurting Savannah. "What do you mean did she get hurt?" I whisper so she doesn't hear me. "Does she look like she got hurt?"

"NO. No, calm down Bry." Sloan shakes his head. "She looks fine physically…just a little tired and like she had been crying. She got here and didn't know you were out. I wasn't sure where you went so I told her you would most likely be back soon. She didn't want me to bother you so I didn't text you. But dude, you gotta see…"

"You should've bothered me, Sloan. I was out looking for her! Rachel called and told me she ran out of work upset and she couldn't find her. I've been looking everywhere."

"Oh…fuck. I'm sorry, man. Really I am, but if it makes you feel any better, it seemed to me like she got the therapy she was apparently looking for."

"What the fuck is that supposed to mean?"

Sloan smiles and nods toward my office door. "See for yourself." He turns and heads back to the bar to continue his work. I watch him walk away, completely unsure of what he's talking about. I want to be livid with him for not fucking calling me but I can't. He didn't know why I left in the first place. At least she's here. She came back.

*To me.*

Curious as to what Sloan meant about her finding therapy, I slowly turn the knob to my office door and step inside. I never knew a heart could feel so strongly - that one minute, one event, could cause a heart to burst into tiny floating pieces that immediately and lovingly connect to another person. I thought I loved her then, years ago, but I see her laying there peacefully asleep on a brand new charcoal grey leather couch wrapped in what looks to be a new throw blanket, and I've completely and irrevocably fallen in love with this girl all over again.

I want to laugh out loud. I want to laugh with her and tell her how absofuckinlutely charming it is that she remembered what I had told her about my old couch. I want to tell her how astonished I am that she would even consider doing something like this for me, especially given the morning she's had. I want to tell her how flattered I am that she obviously did this to stake her claim and I'm one hundred percent okay with that. And then I want to curl up behind her beautiful body on this couch and hold her in my arms, telling her over and over again how much I fucking love her.

But instead, I slide into the office and quietly close the door behind me. Adoring the sweetness that is the angel on this new couch, I make my way over to her, lightly brushing her hair off of her face. Her breath shudders a few times, making me all too painfully aware that she had definitely been crying. I don't know what compels me to do it but I pull my cell phone out of my back pocket, turn the ringer off and snap a few pictures of her as she sleeps. Quickly I shoot a text to Rachel to let her know that Savannah is safe and to not expect her in for the rest of the day. I'll let her sleep and then I'll spend the day with her if she'll let me. Turning back to my computer I pick up where I left off with my inventory work, feeling more immeasurably whole than I've ever felt in my entire life.

An hour later I hear movement on the couch. Savannah's eyes open slowly and she blinks a few times before softly smiling at me.

"Well hey there Sleeping Beauty."

"Mmm…" She wipes her eyes and brushes her soft hair back from her face. "How long have I been asleep?"

"Only about an hour or so. I didn't want to wake you. You just looked so damn beautiful and you obviously needed it." Swiftly I step out of my chair and over to her on the couch. She scoots up enough that I can grab her legs and lift them on to my lap.

"Yeah, yeah I guess."

I slip her shoes off and begin to massage her foot. She sighs as her eyes close momentarily.

"Do you want to talk about it?"

She stares at me, unsure of what to say. Either that or she's holding back the words she wants to say and can't.

"What is there to say?"

"Well, do you want to tell me what happened at the salon?"

"Did you sleep with Jamie Henders?"

*Fuck.*

*She goes straight for the jugular.*

*Be honest, Bryant. No sugarcoating.*

"Yes."

"When? Recently?"

"Fuck no. I told you I haven't been with anyone since Samantha walked into the bar to tell me about Ivy. It was at least five years ago."

I watch her breathe in and out as she contemplates my answer and carefully crafting her next barrage of questions.

"How many times?" she asks curtly.

"Once."

"Why only once?"

Her question surprises me a little as if she doesn't remember how much my life used to revolve around fucking lots of women. Until one day it didn't anymore.

"Uh, Seven, I..." I run my hand up and down my face.

"Why only once, Bryant?" She's not letting it go.

"Why are you asking me this?"

"Was she married at the time?"

"Absolutely not," I answer her assuredly.

"Then why only once?"

*Jesus Christ.*

"Because I didn't want her, Savannah. She was another one-night stand as were a lot of women back then. I told you how I used to live. I fucked a lot of women. More than you probably want to know about and to be honest, I didn't keep notches on my bedpost. I just focused on living my life every day. I did what made me happy and that meant whatever made my dick happy. Jamie Henders never meant jack shit to me, Seven. She was never you."

She stares at my face for an awkward moment before she whispers, "Okay."

"Okay?"

"Yeah. Okay."

"Wait, what's that supposed to mean?" I ask confounded.

"Look, I'm not going to waste my time being upset about something you did years ago, but you should know that Jamie Henders makes no bones about having had you in her bed at least once. She just..." Her eyes avert mine.

"Just what?"

"She just made it seem like you two were an item at one point, that's all. This morning felt like I was back in high school all over again and the captain of the cheerleading squad was boasting about the blow job she gave to the quarterback of the football team."

I watch her for a minute, unsure of what to say. I wish I could say the right thing to make her feel better.

"Come here." I slide Savannah's legs off of mine and motion for her to come sit astride me on this couch. When she does so, I hold her face tenderly in my hands and make sure she's looking into my eyes when I speak again.

"Savannah I need you to hear me when I say this. Jamie Henders and I never, and I mean never fucking *ever*, were an item. She's been bitter towards me ever since the day she asked to see me again, expecting to get laid a second time, and I turned her down. I've never loved her a day in my life, not even in high school."

"I don't understand, in high school you guys were…"

"Never an item. Regardless of what she may or may not have said, we never dated. I never asked her out and she definitely never put her lips on my cock. A guy remembers those things, Sev. I wouldn't lie to you about that."

"But she told everyone you guys had…"

"I know she did. And I'm the douche who didn't put her in her place. I allowed the rumors to spread because back then it seemed like that's what was expected of both of us. But she was never the girl I wanted. Ever." Still holding her face in my hands, I softly brush my lips against hers before whispering "It's always been you, Sev. Nobody that I've ever been with can hold a fucking candle to what I feel for you."

I watch as Savannah's eyes begin to water and a tear slips down her cheek. I catch it with my thumb and softly wipe it away.

"Tell me what you're thinking," I request.

"She's a spoiled rich twat waffle who gets off on making everyone around her feel inferior."

I can't hold back my laughter. Leaning my head back on the couch I let out of hearty laugh. "Well there are two words I didn't expect to come out of your mouth." I grab her arms and pull her into me. She lays her head on my chest, sighing in comfort. "You're right though for what it's worth. She *is* a spoiled rich twat waffle and she *does* get off on hurting everyone around her. The sad thing is, everyone around this town knows it. She's not doing any good for herself or her friends. She's just digging herself a deeper grave."

"Good," I hear her say. "I hope one day she trips and falls head first into it and never returns."

"Hey." I rub her back until she lifts her head to look at me. "I'm sorry for what she said to you this morning. You didn't deserve that and it's my fault. I'm sorry."

She gives me a perplexed look. "How is any of this your fault? You weren't there."

"I didn't have to be there. One of her groupies saw me kiss you the other night during karaoke, so she knew finding you and putting you through the ringer was only a matter of time. She's done it more than once – tried to ruin any relationship it looks like I may be having that doesn't involve her."

"Ooh…" Savannah says. "So she's just green with envy because you're not interested in her."

"Yup. That's exactly it. She thinks I'll still allow the rumors to run through town but what I don't get is why? She's supposedly happily married and has been for a few years now, so I don't get why she still feels the need to flaunt herself around these parts."

"What does she do?"

I shake my head back and forth. "Nothing as far as I know. She sits at home with her little stupid yippee dog or walks around the town with her old friends playing *Mean Girls* all day."

"So that's why she does it then."

"What do you mean?" I ask.

"Because she's a nobody now. She doesn't work anywhere, she's inconsequential to anyone in this town apart from her husband who is probably rich enough that he can have whoever he wants…maybe he doesn't want her either…"

*She has a point.*

"Interesting theory. Regardless, I'm just sorry for today. If I had known she was in the area and out for blood, I would've told you to steer clear."

"It's okay. I'm a big girl and can handle a little mean girl. Besides…" she says, running her hand along the back of the couch. "I needed some retail therapy and you needed a new couch." She smirks.

I reach up to kiss her on her neck as she leans her body against me to touch the back of the couch. "Mmm…it's a nice couch too. You did a great job picking it out."

"You really like it?" she asks, rocking her head to the side to grant my lips better access to her collar bone. I continue grazing her skin as my hands slide up and down the sides of her torso.

"Yeah, I do. It just…" My hands slowly slide up the inside of her shirt. "…needs one thing."

I hear Savannah gasp as my hands fondle her breasts. "What more could it possibly need?"

She throws her head back and inhales deeply as I pinch her right where I know she'll be the most sensitive. My lips linger on her neck and chin as they wait to connect with hers…to taste her. "It needs your scent…our scent." I whisper in her ear. She responds in kind with a sexier than shit groan that makes my dick wake up and take notice. "Kiss me, Seven."

Like a lioness out for her hunt, Savannah's lips crash with mine, biting my bottom lip and swirling her tongue with mine over and over again. Hastily I pull her top over her head and literally rip her bra off of her body, paying no mind to any type of clasp. One look at her sheer beauty and I thirst for more of her. She tugs at my shirt which I help her take off and then immediately my lips are on her, sucking, tasting, licking, biting. She slowly rocks herself forward and back, causing my dick to scream for attention. I want her in the worst way. I want to lay her out on this couch and push into her until there is nothing left for me to give.

"Bryant..." She breathes. She covers my ear with her mouth swirling her tongue inside and out. It's all I can do to remain seated here as she teases me with her body. "I want you. Please, I need you." As she whispers to me her hands are on me, her right hand slowly tugging on the zipper to my jeans until she can reach inside to grab me.

"Mmmm Savannah..." I close my eyes and allow myself to feel her hands on me. Her strong grasp, the way she squeezes me, this girl is my personal heaven. Her touch lights my skin on fire, stirring a frenzy inside me that can only be calmed one way. While she holds me, I fantasize about her smooth hands, her warm lips, and her soft moan. The lust-filled expression she gives me is priceless, like she can read my mind and I've just said the magic words. She shimmies off my lap, leaving me bereft of her warmth but proving a stellar floor show as she unabashedly steps out of her leggings and panties. She kneels on the floor between my legs.

*Holy fuck this is hot.*

She pierces my eyes with hers as her mouth slowly devours me.

*Shit.*

My eyes want to roll back into my head while I experience the ecstasy of her mouth, but I'm also a man who likes to watch his woman work. I grab her hair with my right hand and pull it back so I can see her lips around me. "Good God woman, you know how to make a man lose control."

I hear her moan while I'm in her mouth. The vibrations causing me to harden even more than I already have. "That's better," I hear her say. I watch in anticipation as she licks the length of me before sliding her mouth back down over top as far as it will go. When she finishes I practically drag her back up onto the couch so she's straddling me, ready to take the ride of a lifetime right along with me. As she lowers herself onto me, we both shamelessly sigh into each other. She initiates the rhythm as she raises herself up on her knees and lowers herself back down.

"Christ, Savannah. You feel…"

"I know." She kisses me once, twice, three times. "Take me, Bryant. Please. Take all of me."

Her need for intimacy with me not only reassures me of her love for me, but makes me feel like she looks at me as the one person who can give her exactly what she needs. Her complete trust in me is all consuming as I wrap my arms around her, loving her, protecting her. Quickening the pace between us I thrust into her again and again until the inevitable explosion is near.

"Ahhh" Savannah cries out as she wraps her arms around my neck, meeting me thrust for thrust. My hands work their way under her, my fingers dangerously close to being able to tease all of her most sensitive areas. The mere proximity of my fingers to those spots causes her to scream out one last time before her body convulses against mine, her arms squeezing me tighter. Her body, warmly caressing me, causes me to lose control with her.

Sitting on this beautiful new couch, the girl of my fucking dreams wrapped in my arms and panting down my neck, squeezing my body between her knees, it's more than I could have ever asked for. We sit like this for minutes, both of our bodies calming in tandem. I feel her shiver slightly before grabbing the throw blanket beside me and tenderly covering her so that she stays warm.

"Do you love me okay, Bryant?" she asks sweetly. Immediately a smile comes to my face as she takes Ivy's phrase and turns it into her own.

"I asbofuckinlutely love you okay, Sev. Do you love me okay?"

I feel her before I hear her. She nods her head up and down. "Yes. I love you more than okay. I hope you like the new couch."

I chuckle, lightly feeling both of our bodies move as I laugh. "Babe, it's the best fucking couch in the whole damn world, and I don't ever want another one."

# Chapter 26

# Savannah

"Red sky at night, sailors delight. Red sky at morn, sailors take warn." I look out my apartment window at the beautiful hues of pinks and reds in the sky as I lay in my bed. It really is stunning even though I know it'll mean gloom and doom later in the day. My mother used to tell me that when the sky was red at night, that meant the next day would be a beautiful one, but if the sky was red in the morning, that meant rain. Of course today would be a rainy day. Why wouldn't it be? It's one of the days out of the year when I wish I could just stay in my bed all day, not talking to anyone.

It's July seventh.

It's Peyton's birthday.

I hate the number seven. Everyone says it's a lucky number, but for me, it's the bane of my existence. It was my nickname for years in school thanks to Bryant Wood. It was my age when I fell and broke my leg. It was the one answer to the only question I missed in the school math league tournament as a freshman. It was the number of final papers I had during one semester of college. It was also the number of days late Peyton was before she was born. She was due June thirtieth, but of course she took her little old time arriving. I should've known she would be seven days late, but then again, when she did finally arrive I gave up on the notion of seven being my unluckiest number. After all, my baby girl was born on the seventh day of the seventh month. There was nothing but happiness and joy that day and forever after. My curse had been broken…or I just had a new perspective on life. Either way, life was grand…until it wasn't anymore.

I can still see the clock on the dashboard flash seven o'clock right before our car flipped in the air and landed in the median. It was like a piece of me knew right then, that if something bad was going to happen, it was because I had taken notice to the time on the clock. Sure enough within twenty-four hours I would be without both of the people I loved the most in my whole life. Fast forward a couple of years and I'm lying in bed wishing the day away. Nothing good can happen on July seventh. Not anymore.

My phone dings on the night stand alerting me to a text message. With a grunt I roll over and grab it swiping the screen to see who it's from.

> Bryant: Good morning beautiful.
> Me: Red sky at morn, sailors take warn
> Bryant: Uhh…that's very…chipper of you this morning.

I close my eyes and breathe. Do I really want to go there right now?

*He doesn't know…*

*He doesn't know…*

*He doesn't know…*

*I should tell him.*

> Me: Today is Peyton's birthday.

I hold my phone in my hand waiting for his immediate response but it doesn't come. In fact, I lay in bed for about ten minutes before I see his reply pop up on my screen.

> Bryant: Ok

*Ok?*

*What the hell is that supposed to mean, "ok"?*

I don't get any other response from him and have no idea what I'm supposed to say to his last text. In frustration I just decide honesty is the best policy. At least he'll know how I'm feeling today.

> Me: Yeah. I kind of want to just stay in bed. Nothing good ever comes of this day except a good hangover to make me forget.

In less than two minutes I receive a reply.

> Bryant: Put some clothes on. I'll be there in ten minutes.

"What? Noooo…" I say out loud to nobody in my room. Ugh! What doesn't he understand about wanting to just stay in bed and wait out the inevitable rainy day? I close my eyes and pout for at least five of the ten minutes Bryant said it would take him to get here. I have a half a mind to answer the door buck naked just to spite his instruction, but knowing Bryant that's only going to cause bigger distractions. Rolling off the bed, I scoot to the bathroom, throw my hair up into a messy bun on the top of my head and pull on a pair of shorts and a tank top sans bra. Screw the make-up and the perfume, it's just Bryant. He knocks on the door just as I'm making my way down the hall. I answer the door with an eyebrow raised and a hand on my hip.

He takes one good look at me from head to toe before smoothly wrapping an arm around me in the doorway. "Well good mornin' to you too Seven." He says, picking me up and kissing me on the mouth as he backs me away from the door. I squeal as I have no control over where he's going.

"Bryant! Put me down!" I laugh. "What the fuck are you doing here?" I straighten out my shirt that twisted when Bryant picked me up and pull my hair a little tighter on my head.

"I have a question for you."

I huff. "And you couldn't have just texted me? What could be so damn important?"

"You're important, Savannah. Today is important, and whether you feel like it's a day to grieve or not, I need to know one thing."

"What?"

"Have you ever done anything to celebrate Peyton's life?"

"What do you mean? Like…a balloon send-off or something? You want me to sing songs in the streets? Ding-dong my baby's dead? What?"

Ok maybe I'm being a bit melodramatic, but still. This is my day…because it's Peyton's day.

"No Sev, I mean have you ever done something *good*…good for your soul…to celebrate Peyton? Something that commemorates her and makes you feel a little more at peace by the end of the day?"

I shrug my shoulders. "Not really, no. I can't do that stuff alone, Bryant. I'm just...not strong enough. I only just rolled out of bed like...five minutes ago. I couldn't even do that on my own. You had to tell me you were on your way."

He smiles sincerely. "You could've just not answered the door."

"No way. You knew I was in here. You would've never left and most likely would've made a scene."

Bryant winks at me, nodding his head in agreement. "Point made. You're right. I would've. At any rate, I'm here now Savannah. And I have a great idea if you'll just trust me. I would like to share this day with you to help celebrate Peyton and celebrate you...if you'll let me." Bryant holds his hand out for me to take.

I could easily say no. I could back up, chuck this all in the 'fuck-it' bucket and spend my day in bed, but that would mean disappointing Bryant. Why does he have to make this all so complicated yet comfortable for me?

"You just gave up your entire day for me?"

He nods. "It's nice to be the boss once in a while. I've got people who know what they're doing. I don't always have to be at the bar so yeah, when you told me what today was I made some calls and here I am. I promise you this day is going to be a great day, but you have to trust me first."

I take a deep breath, releasing it as I reach out for Bryant's hand. He immediately pulls me into him holding me against his warm inviting body. "Thank you, Bryant," I whisper.

He kisses the top of my head and holds me quietly for a moment before saying "You're welcome. I'll always be here for you, Sev, Always. Now before we go I need you to do one thing."

"What's that?"

"Put on a bra."

I raise my head from his chest, scowling at him. He laughs and rubs my shoulders. "Babe, believe me, your tits are the most beautiful things I've ever seen and if we were staying here all day I would be beggin' you to take things off instead of put things on, but this is why you have to trust me. Where we're going, you'll thank me, I promise."

I reach up on my tippy toes and kiss his lips swiftly. "Okay. Black lacey bra it is." I wink at him as I turn to walk back to my room knowing all too well how much he loves my black lacey bra.

In the next ten minutes we're hopping in his truck and heading for the freeway.

"Where are we headed?" I ask him.

He looks over at me smiling behind his sunglasses. "Trust me."

Less than half an hour later we're in Louisville, pulling into Toys-R-Us.

"Bryant...I'm not buying my daughter a birthday present that she'll never open," I say quietly staring out the window.

"Nope, you're not. Listen. Every time I bring Ivy up here to the Children's Hospital she gets a toy from the nurses. A nice toy, that's donated by God knows who. Every kid there gets one, every time. It's just a little way to bring a smile to the faces of those kids who sometimes spend their entire lives within those walls. Think about it Sev, don't you think it would be great to donate a shit ton of toys in Peyton's name to the hospital. We'll make it her birthday present except she'll be the one giving the gifts to all the children. I have a thousand dollars burning a damn hole in my pocket right now and I sure would like your help using it in that store." He says pointing ahead of us. "What do you say?"

I can't hold back my tears. Though they're gliding down my face, I smile through them, leaning over to grab Bryant's face. I kiss him, hard, tasting the combination of his breath and my tears. I love this man for all he does for me.

"Let's make it two thousand. I'll match every penny."

*Something good should come from that insurance money.*

"That's my girl. I love you, Seven."

"I love you too."

He squeezes my hand. "Now let's go have some fun."

For the next couple hours Bryant and I have a blast walking up and down the aisles of the toy store. We don't plan out our toys, we don't talk about gender specific anything. We're like two new parents buying toys for the very first time, reliving moments of our childhood and laughing together the entire time.

In two hours we have three shopping carts filled with just about every toy imaginable. We found baby dolls, paint sets, costumes, stuffed animals, video games, Lite Brites, Rubik's Cubes, and an entire Wii U game system complete with a few games for one of the waiting room/lounges in the hospital. My heart grows a few sizes with every step through the store, knowing that we're about to make many children very happy, and they deserve a dose of happy. We check out all of our toys, load them into Bryant's truck – thank God it's big enough – and head for Kosair Children's Hospital. Bryant makes a few calls on our way, and by the time we arrive there is a group of people waiting for us at the loading dock to help unload. My heart is full, my body is exhausted, and to my surprise, my spirit is up. Today hasn't been the downer of a day I thought it would be despite the fact that rain is still in the forecast for the evening.

"Thank you for today, Bryant," I say to him as we hop in back in the truck to head home. "Seriously, you made what was going to be a miserable sad day at home alone, an uplifting positive celebration of Peyton's life. I don't even know what to say."

Turning the ignition on, Bryant smiles sincerely as he quietly turns towards me. "You just said all you need to say, Sev. That's what I wanted you to get out of today. You needed to be able to celebrate Peyton's life instead of continuously grieving it alone. Her life meant something…to a lot of people, and it will continue to mean something for a very long time."

"Yeah," I smile. "Yeah, you're right. I really needed this today." I lean over the console of Bryant's truck to lightly place a kiss on his cheek. "And thanks for making me put on a bra. What would I do without you?"

Laughing, he takes my head in his hands and studies my face. After a moment he kisses my lips with softness and sincerity. Something flips in the pit of my stomach as his pulls back. If I didn't know any better, I would've thought it was the most loving good-bye kiss I've ever experienced. "I hope you never have to find out. Now let's go home. Looks like a storm's coming. We can sit out on the porch and watch the rain come in."

"Sounds great."

# Chapter 27

# *Savannah*

Not wanting me to be alone tonight, Bryant and I decide to spend the night together at his place. A quiet night on the farm watching the storm roll in. He drops me off at my apartment so I can grab a few things and get my car since I need to be at work in the morning, and he needs to go pick up Ivy from his parent's house.

"How about grilled sirloin tonight? A little bread, a little wine," Bryant suggests for dinner.

"Mmm only if you add the balsamic glaze and the tomatoes and scallions." I love when he cooks for me. He's so good at it. There really isn't anything he makes that I don't like.

"Deal. I'll pick up some fresh steaks on the way home."

"Sounds fabulous. See you soon." I wave and head into my apartment for just a few minutes. I grab an outfit to wear to work tomorrow and a few essential toiletries. I already have a toothbrush and shampoo at Bryant's place so I never need to pack much. Since Ivy won't be there, there isn't really a need for me to pack pajamas. Smirking at the thought of what we may get into later, I swing my purse and my duffle bag over my shoulder, lock the door behind me and head out to Bryant's house.

The smell of imminent rain floats through the air as I step out of the car. I smile curiously because I can hear music playing loudly from the kitchen. Shaking my head, I grab my bags from the back seat and head into the house where I come face to face with Adele in male form.

*Oh my goodness, this man.*

I'm laughing when I enter the kitchen but Bryant only looks at me, a grin on his face, as he continues to sing "Set Fire to the Rain" at the top of his lungs. I'm not sure I ever would've guessed that he liked Adele's music but hell, I'll take it. He can play her music anytime he wants.

"Hey," he finally says when the song ends.

"Hey yourself," I say. "I never took you for the Adele type."

He gasps playfully putting his hand over his heart. "What? A man can't be just as musically eclectic as his girlfriend, huh? I see how it is."

*Girlfriend...that sounds nice.*

"Hahaha! No, I didn't mean it like that," I laugh. "Be right back, I'm going to throw these in your room."

Bryant has already started what smells like a delicious dinner for the two of us. Steaks are already on the grill and he's chopping vegetables for a salad.

"Can I help?" I offer.

"Sure. Why don't you finish this, so I can get the scallions and tomatoes to the grill as well?" He hands me the knife he was using, kisses my forehead and heads over to the refrigerator. I stand at the counter chopping veggies when the first bolt of lightning strikes. I jump slightly having not expected the loud clap of thunder that follows.

"Whoa!" I say laughing at myself.

"Yeah...I'm glad the steak is almost done. At least I won't get stuck in a downpour."

I finish my job chopping the veggies for our salads, adding them to our individual bowls, grab the French bread from the bread box slicing us both a few pieces, and then set the table for dinner.

"Do you want wine? I think I have some Merlot on the shelf." Bryant asks from the patio doorway. When I look up from setting the table he's pointing to the wine rack across the room.

"Absolutely," I answer. "That sounds great."

I grab the Merlot and two wine glasses from the rack above the shelf and carry them over to the island counter. It takes a couple drawers but I finally find a corkscrew to open the bottle. Bryant walks in with our steaks on a platter, filling the kitchen with that freshly grilled smell. My mouth waters in excitement; I feel like I haven't eaten in days. Filling one wine glass I move my hand over to the second one to be filled. I don't know how it happens but the bottle slips from my hand, landing on the second wine glass, both of them crashing into broken pieces on the countertop in front of me.

"SHIT!" I scream. I jump back from the broken glass and look around hastily for a towel or a rag to help clean up the mess.

"Savannah! Are you okay?" Bryant runs in from the patio where he was finishing our meal.

"Yeah, I'm fine. Sorry. The bottle slipped out of my hand and I just made a huge fucking mess." I grab whatever rags I can find near the sink and start to sop up the mess.

"I'll get it," Bryant says to me placing a hand on my shoulder. "Your shirt is dripping with red wine and as hot as it that you're wearing a wet t-shirt, it's not going to help you clean up very quickly."

I chuckle because he's right. My shirt is a damn wet mess. "Thanks. I'll go grab a shirt from my bag and change. Be right back." I step back from the mess and run down the hall, careful not to let the wine drip onto the floor on my way. Running quickly into Bryant's bathroom, I carefully remove my shirt and throw it in the sink.

*There's no way that stain's coming out.*

*Glad it's not my favorite shirt.*

I rummage through my duffle bag for a fresh t-shirt but realize the only thing I packed was my sundress for work tomorrow. Looking around for one of Bryant's t-shirts without success, I just decide to grab one from his dresser.

*He won't mind.*

Assuming the top drawer of his dresser is socks or underwear I pull open the second drawer. Nope, it's all jeans and work-out gear. I move down to the third drawer and bingo! T-shirts! Not even caring which one I grab, I take the top shirt and slide it on over my head.

It's soft and smells like him.

*So good.*

"Hey Bryant! I only packed a dress. I grabbed one of your shirts from your dresser, okay?" I yell down the hall.

I'm just about to shut the drawer when I see it. An envelope poking out from the side of the drawer. I wouldn't have even given it a second thought if there wasn't writing on the front that was familiar to me.

"Savannah, wait!" I hear Bryant say from the kitchen, but it's too late. I've already pulled the envelope out of his drawer, twisting it around in my fingers to read the writing clearly. It's from the Donor Family Services of Give Life, the organization that puts donor families in touch with recipient families. I know because I've received several letters from them myself.

*But he told me he didn't know who Ivy's donor was.*

Curiously, I pull the letter out of the envelope and look at the front page. Just like mine, it's a greeting from the coordinator. I fold the letter back up and put it in the envelope where a second envelope sits. When I pull it out and see the writing on the front my heart nearly jumps out of my throat.

*It's my handwriting.*

*What the fuck?*

I want to put everything back in the drawer. I want to erase the last two minutes of time from my life because there's no way in hell this can possibly be happening to me. There's just no way. It's possible that someone else makes their L's that way but what are the odds? It's too late though, I'm in this...I've got to see it through. I have to know. I pull the letter from the envelope and begin to read the words that I already know are written.

*Dear recipient,*

*My name is Savannah. My daughter, Peyton, was the little girl who donated one of her organs to you. She would have celebrated her second birthday on July 7th...*

My body is stone cold. My hand is shaking. Bryant running into the bedroom and knocking the door open stirs me enough to drop the letter from my hand to the floor as if it's on fire. I jump back, covering my mouth with my hand.

"Savannah..."

"No," I whisper shaking my head back and forth.

*This isn't happening.*

*Not to me*
*Not today.*
*Not ever.*
*It can't be true.*
*There's just no way.*

"No, no, no," I say over and over again. The room is spinning and my head is still shaking back and forth in denial. "It's not true. It's not true. It's not true," I chant. My eyes are wide as I watch Bryant walk slowly farther into the room. He walks toward me but I can't be near him. I don't want to be near him. I back up until my back is against a wall. I'm trapped but every feature of my face tells him not to come near me right now.

"Savannah, please, just listen."

"Listen to what, Bryant? Listen to what?" My voice is shaking. "You told me months ago that you never found out who Ivy's donor was. That's what you told me, Bryant. That's what you told me."

His eyes are desolate. "Yeah, I know I did but…"

"BUT WHAT BRYANT?" I shout. I point to the letter now lying on his bedroom floor. "What is that? Why do you have it? Bryant, tell me please…tell me it's not true."

The speechless defeated look on Bryant's face says all I need it to say.

I'm right.

Ivy has Peyton's liver.

"Savannah," he whispers.

"Just say it, Bryant. Tell me. Say the words or so help me God…" Tears are now rushing down my face as fast as the rain falls outside the bedroom window. It's ironic that it's storming outside, but that storm out there doesn't hold a candle to what's brewing in this room right now.

"Sev, I was going to tell you…"

"WHEN, BRYANT?! WHEN THE FUCK WERE YOU PLANNING ON TELLING ME?" I scream. I swear I'm having an out of body experience. The real me is sitting against the wall, a scared girl not wanting to have this conversation while the bitch in me stands up and fights.

"I don't know Sev. I just needed to protect you from all of this." He hangs his head in shame before looking back up to me like a sad puppy that just lost his bone. "I swear I wanted to tell you but there was never a..."

"Right time? How about the day you found out for Christ's sake? How about when you saw me that night in your bar? How about the day you took care of me while I was sick? How about our first date? How about before I..."

*Took my clothes off and made love to you.*

*I gave myself to you.*

*I tore down my walls for you.*

Immediately I cross my arms over my chest and sob. How could I have been so stupid? He doesn't love me. He just feels guilty! This was his way of making himself feel better for the guilt he's been living with all this time. I'm such a fool.

"Savannah, I love you. Please, I need you to understand something." He pleads with me but his pleas are just words. Most likely the same words he says to all the girls.

"If you loved me, Bryant," I point back and forth between the two of us. "You wouldn't have let this happen. You would've been honest with me from the get-go. I can't believe I was such a goddam fool."

"NO!" Bryant shouts, making me jump and hit my head on the wall behind me. I wince, bringing my hand up to rub my head.

"Oh fuck, Savannah I'm sorry. I'm so sorry. But you have to put yourself in my shoes."

"I don't give a fuck about your shoes Bryant." I cry.

"Then FUCKING LISTEN TO ME ANYWAY!" He finally releases his feelings, freezing me in place.

*Is he going to hurt me?*

*I've never seen him this upset.*

*Or maybe it's fear...he's afraid?*

*What does he have to be afraid of?*

*His kid is alive because of mine.*

He sighs heavily as he watches me. "What was I supposed to do Sev? Call you up and say 'Hey, I haven't seen you in years, sorry about your kid but thanks for the liver.'? Was I supposed to tell you I loved you back then? Should I have asked you out then? No fucking way! There was no way I could ever contact you to tell you because how would that have made any part of this better for you?" He raises his arms in question. "Damnit, I was going to try to forget the whole thing. I was going to let you live your life and I was going to live mine but then you walked into my bar that day and I...I couldn't do it Sev. I couldn't let you go. Not again."

Bryant raises both of his hands to the top of his head, pacing back and forth. "Shit Sev. I've fucked this all up. It's all my fault. I knew at some point the truth would come out before I was ready to handle it and I would lose you. I'm so damn sorry. I'm SO sorry Sev. I never meant to hurt you. I would never ever want to hurt you." He throws his arms out to his sides. "None of this was meant to hurt you."

Another clap of thunder sounds outside.

*I don't think I can stay here.*

*Time to go.*

*I need to get away from him.*

"I should go," I say quietly, stepping around him towards the door.

"What? Wait, no Sev. Don't go." He reaches for my arm but I pull it free, grab my purse and hurry from the room, wiping the never-ending stream of tears from my face.

"I can't do this now Bryant. I need to go."

"Are you crazy? It's pouring down rain out there and the storm is only going to get worse! I'm not letting you go."

"SHE WAS MY BABY, BRYANT!" I scream. "SHE WAS MY LIFE AND SHE'S GONE AND NOW YOU HAVE A PIECE OF HER LIVING HERE IN YOUR HOUSE AND WHAT DO I HAVE?"

"Savannah," he whispers to calm me down.

"Nothing," I choke on my whisper. "I have nothing."

I step backwards toward the door, grab my keys from the table and head towards my car. As soon as I step from the front door I'm soaked. The rain is heavy and the thunder is piercing.

"Savannah please don't go. Wait for the…"

I don't even hear the rest of his sentence because I slam my car door closed. He pleads one more time to get me to stop by pounding on my window, but his efforts are fruitless.

"SAVANNAH!" I hear him yell as I slowly step on the gas leading my car down his driveway.

*I have nothing.*

*He has part of my baby girl and I have nothing.*

I don't even know where I'm heading. I just needed to be away from Bryant and away from Bardstown for a while. Maybe I'll just drive until I'm tired and get a hotel somewhere so I can be alone. Maybe I'll circle town and go to Mom and Dad's for a while. I could go to Rachel's but I'm almost positive that's the first place Bryant will look for me. Within five minutes I see the entrance ramp for I62 west and decide to just take it. Who cares where I end up tonight.

My thoughts are running wild as I play back in my head everything that happened just a short time ago.

*"SHE WAS MY BABY!"*

*"I can't believe I was such a goddam fool."*

Tears are still flowing as I drive further down the road. Bryant is right. This rain is ridiculous. It's pounding on the top of my car. Already there are puddles forming on the roadways that I try my best to dodge. I can only barely see where I'm going between the rain hitting the windshield and the rain, in the form of tears, falling down my face. Everything is a blur. I hear my phone ding alerting me to a text message that I can only assume is from Bryant. Taking my eyes off the road to read it would be a huge mistake so I ignore it. I make it maybe a total of twenty miles down the road before I decide not to be an idiot. Turning on my emergency flashers, I pull the car over to the side of the road. At least here I can wait out the storm alone and in peace.

Grabbing a tissue from my purse, I wipe my face and blow my nose. I focus on breathing in and out for a solid three minutes to calm myself down. Why does this hurt so badly? Why is this affecting me so much? I warned myself months ago that Bryant Wood was a douchebag and like an idiot I chose not to listen and now here I am – broken, and alone.

I reach for the nob to the stereo, hoping that something might calm me down, but of course the world is out to kill me today. Sam Smith's voice singing "Stay with Me" flows through the car speakers drowning out the rain. All I can do is listen to the lyrics, thinking about how Bryant would be saying these words to me if he were here right now…that he was saying these words to me before I left. I'm so confused. Deep down, as hurt and as angry and as confused as I am, I still want him here. I miss him already.

*But he lied to me.*

"FUUUUCK! FUCK FUCK FUCK!" I pound on the steering wheel in front of me, taking out all of my hurt and aggression in the only way I can right now. I don't care that when I hit the steering wheel it honks. There's nobody here. I can cry as hard as I need to, because nobody is around to hear me.

"Okay Savannah. Time to play Devil's advocate." I say to myself in between sniffles. Questioning my own thoughts is the only way I've been able to survive on my own. It's the only way to work through my pain.

*What am I upset about the most? The lie, or the truth?*

This is a hard question for me to answer, which makes it the right one to be answering. Am I mad that Peyton's liver was donated to Ivy specifically? No. How can I be? It's not her fault. She was in a life-threatening situation and my Peyton was able to help save her. She was a hero to so many children who never asked for my child to die. It's not any of their faults. It's not their parents' faults. It's not my fault. I know all this. The fact that I can easily come to this conclusion tells me that what upsets me the most, obviously, is the fact that Bryant knew about it and never told me.

What upsets me the most is the lie.

Who does that to someone they love? Who hides an inevitable truth, one that will absolutely cause a certain level of heartache, from the person that they love.

*Someone who just wants to protect.*

*"Sev, there was no way I could ever contact you to tell you because how would that have made any part of this better for you?"*

Bryant's explanation plays over again in my head and for the first time I begin to understand. He's right. If he would've told me all of this right when it happened, looking back on the state my mind was in then, I would've succumbed to an even deeper depression. It would've ripped me apart knowing that my kid was dead but a piece of her was alive in a child that not only wasn't mine, but one that I would be running into around town.

Love is an ugly beast sometimes, I know. It makes us do stupid things. It rips out our hearts when we least expect it. It grows on us like weeds, sometimes killing us with its poison. It throws us into the fires of hell several times during our lifetime and for what? So we can stand up, brush ourselves off and start all over again from the beginning and then sometimes, sometimes when we least expect it, love morphs from an ugly beast into the thing our hearts desire most. Passion. Companionship. Loyalty. Comfort.

*What if I still love him?*

*What hurts more? Knowing the truth and staying with Bryant, or knowing the truth and leaving him?*

I swallow the lump in my throat, thinking about what Mama would say if I were sitting with her at the dining room table. I'm sure she would pull out her Bible and read me that "Love is patient. Love is kind" verse that everyone reads at weddings. But then she would probably pat me on the arm and tell me that I'm the strongest girl she knows and that it's okay to be scared because "Bein' scared means you're probably thinkin' about doin' somethin' really brave."

I miss my mama sometimes. We live in the same town, yes, but a lot of shit has happened in the past couple years and Mama has helped keep me going when I didn't want to. This is one of those times. As much as she annoys me with her southern Bible talk, like Annelle Dosoto from *Steel Magnolias*, she's still my mama. She's the one person I need to hug me tightly and put all my broken pieces back together. Pulling out my phone, I see that I've missed several texts from Bryant that I refuse to even look at right now. I send Mama a quick text to let her know I'll be stopping by this evening, and that I'll just stay there tonight and drive to work from there in the morning. Checking the GPS on my phone I see that I'll have to drive down to the next exit in Elizabethtown to turn around and come back this way. I take a deep breath to settle my frayed exhausted nerves. The rain is still coming down and the fog is rolling in, but it's not unbearable. I look through my purse for one last Kleenex to blow my nose before leaving but I don't find any there. I always keep a box in the back seat in case of an emergency, so I turn around to reach for it on the floor. I start to turn myself back around when the bright light blinds me.

Headlights.

Big headlights.

Coming right at me.

*Shit! There's no time...*

I hear the deafening crunch of my vehicle as my head hits my head rest behind me and pin-balls between both front seats. The car is being pushed forward with the force that only a semi-truck could provide.

*Oh my God!*

There's a flash of pain in my right shoulder that doesn't register until my body is tipped upside down, weightless, as the car slides down a hill I didn't know I was close to and flips. My arms automatically flail above my head, hitting the ceiling of the car.

"HELLLLLP" I scream in pain, from what I'm not quite sure.

My eyes are squeezed closed as I feel the car roll several times, knocking my body like a rag doll against my door, against the console and back before the car stops. My head finally hits the steering wheel with a hard enough thud that blood splatters from my nose.

"Bryant!" I'm calling to him but no sound is coming from my mouth.

"BRYANT!" I cry.

*Please hear me.*

Slowly I move my head but my eyes can't catch up. Everything is blurry. I taste the salty bitter taste of blood at my mouth. I don't know what just happened. All I know is that I'm alone and wherever I am, nobody knows I'm here.

Nobody is coming to help me.

The world around me is alarmingly silent. I'm growing tired and my head hurts, and it's getting harder to breathe. If I could just close my eyes…

*This is it.*

*I'm dying.*

*This is how it happens then.*

*July Seventh.*

*I should've known.*
$\qquad$ "You are my sunshine…"
*It's only a matter of time now.*

$\qquad$ "My only sunshine…"
*It's so easy.*

$\qquad$ "You make me happy…"
*Wait…Bryant…*
$\qquad$ "When skies are gray…"
*No! Breathe Savannah!*
$\qquad$ "You'll never know dear…"
*I can do this!*
$\qquad$ "How much I love you."

# Seven

*Don't you die, Savannah!*

                      "Please don't take my sunshine away."

*****

Beep. Swoosh…Beep. Swoosh…Beep. Swoosh.

# Chapter 28

# *Bryant*

She left.

I'm standing outside in the pouring down rain gasping for breath from running after her car down the driveway. I can't believe she left. I can't say I'm surprised. Her reaction is exactly what I knew would happen, yet I did nothing to prevent it from happening. This is all my fault.

"DAMNIT!" I shout as loud as I can, leaning my head back into the cold punishing shower above. I kick at the gravel at my feet and watch as several stones fly up ahead of me. How could I have been so damn stupid? We were doing so well, why couldn't I have just told her? And today of all days…she shouldn't be alone tonight.

*Fix this Bryant.*

I contemplate going after her but I'm not exactly sure where she'll end up. She probably headed back home, but could've headed to her parents' house on the outskirts of town. I could at least drive by and see if her car is there. Running back to the house I pull my phone from my back pocket sending a quick text to Savannah:

> Me: I love you. I'm so sorry. Please at least text me when you get where you're going. You shouldn't be driving in this weather.

I click the button to send the text and then immediately regret sending it to her in this weather. Her eyes will be blurry enough from crying and I just made matters worse by sending her a text while I know she's driving. I'm such an idiot. Once I'm back inside the house I pull my wet hair back off of my face and pace back and forth in the kitchen, praying that Savannah texts me back. Thunder continues to clap loudly outside. It's definitely not helping my fear for Savannah's safety. I send a text to Rachel and Sloan asking that they let me know if they see or hear from her.

Rachel: What did you do this time?
Me: Long story. I fucked up. Explain later.

I throw my phone down in frustration. I'm quite certain she wouldn't drive to the bar. Sloan isn't a bad guy at all but she wouldn't go to the one place she knows people would be looking for gossip. She had to have headed home. I know she thinks she might need space but I need to fix this. Before I can go anywhere though, I need to change out of these wet clothes. Running back to the bedroom I throw my wet jeans and t-shirt in the bathroom before pulling on dry clothes. I step into my cowboy boots that I are waiting for me by the front door, head back to grab my phone in the kitchen and run out the door intent on finding the love of my life and begging her to forgive me. I've never begged a girl for anything in my life, but I owe this girl everything. I can't imagine my life without her now. I don't even have to think about it. I need her.

The drive east into town is a ridiculous disaster. I'm lucky I didn't run off the road with all the hydroplaning I did along the way. How Savannah's little car isn't stuck in a ditch along the road is beside me. Her car isn't nearly as heavy as mine…though I suppose she drives slower than I do. Luckily, there were no accidents on the way into town. Deciding to swing by her apartment first, I hang a right towards Main Street. Immediately I have to pull the car over as a fire truck and ambulance speed past me in the other direction.

*Stupid drivers.*

Within minutes I'm pulling into Savannah's apartment complex but her car is nowhere to be found. There are no lights on in her apartment. She's not here. I swing the car back onto the road and drive by both the bar and the salon but don't see her car in either of those places. The only other place I could think of besides Rachel's house would be her parents'. I trust that Rachel would text me if she showed up there but just to be sure I head in that direction. It's on the way to where Savannah's parents live anyway. Twenty minutes later I've come up empty handed once again. She's not at Rachel's nor did I see her car parked in her parents' driveway. I suppose it's possible that she parked in the garage but I can't just walk up and knock on their door. I'm not even positive they know about me.

"FUCK!!! FUCK FUCK FUCK!!!" I scream as I punch the steering wheel with as much force as I can muster.

I'm helpless.

She's gone. I did this. My own stupidity and selfishness drove here away and now I have no idea where she is. So help me God if something happens to her tonight I'll never forgive myself. I don't know what to do now. I'm not the kind of guy who usually panics but I know what today is, I know what I've done, and I know that Savannah is now God-knows-where, and is most likely alone.

The rain is still coming down at a steady pace, though I haven't seen much lightening in the last couple minutes. Hopefully the storm will be over soon. It would make things at least a little bit more convenient. Continuing to hope that she texts me back I keep staring at the screen on my phone, swiping it with my finger and punching in my password just in case I may have missed her text.

Like that would happen.

Before I even know what I'm doing, I'm pressing Savannah's name in my "Favorite contacts" list. I don't even know what I'm going to say but I need to hear her voice. Four rings in a row I hear before her phone jumps to voicemail. She's not answering. She doesn't want to talk to me. Can I blame her?

No.

"Savannah, I'm sorry." I start when I hear the beeping following her voicemail message. "Listen, Please just…I'm sorry. I never wanted to hurt you. I was going to tell you. I wanted to tell you. I've wanted to tell you since the day I saw you. Please just…Savannah text me when you get to where you're going. You don't have to tell me where you are. I just need to know you're safe. I love you. Savannah, I love you." Ending my call, I grip my phone in one hand while holding my forehead in my other hand. Savannah was right. I tried to ignore her depressed state when I spoke to her this morning. I thought I was doing something fucking good for her today and now I've gone and fucked it all up.

*I don't deserve her.*

Deciding to head back home in case she decides to stop back, I turn my truck around. The drive home is slow and depressing. I've failed her. I failed her then and I failed her now. Driving home without her feels like a piece of me is missing. At least with Ivy away for the next couple nights I can try to focus on what the hell I'm supposed to do to fix this. It's not like I can take Ivy's liver and give it back to Savannah. Nor do I think that's what she would want. I have to imagine that what hurts the most is knowing that I knew this whole time and never said anything...because I'm a pussy who was too afraid of losing the one good thing to walk into my life to just be honest with her.

*****

The bourbon in my glass slides down my throat with ease. I revel in the burn, accept it as a punishment for all I've done. It's been hours and I still haven't heard from Savannah, or anyone else for that matter. I pour myself my third glass of bourbon and lift it to my lips when my phone rings.

Thank Christ!

"Hello?" I answer the phone breathlessly in haste to hear any news.

"Bryant. It's Rachel."

"Is she there? Is Savannah with you?"

"No. I haven't heard from her. And I hadn't heard from you so I thought I would call and see what's going on."

"Fuck," I whisper more to myself than to her.

"Bryant? Talk to me. What happened?"

I'm silent for a moment as my third shot of bourbon slides down my throat. My glass clinks on the table beside me with a louder thud than I anticipated. "I screwed up Rache, and I don't think I can fix it this time. She's gone."

"That's bullshit and you know it," she says. "Anything can be fixed with a little love and tenderness." There's silence from both ends of the line as I decide that I don't even know what to say. "Wow…you must've hurt her feelings pretty badly…want to talk about it?"

"It's Ivy's liver."

"What?" she asks, confused. "What's wrong with Ivy? Is she okay? Oh God, what happened? Did she get hurt?"

I'm shaking my head back and forth as the room spins. I know she can't see me doing it but it happens nonetheless. "No. Ivy's fine. She has Peyton's liver."

The silence on the other end of the line is deafening. "Rache? Are you still there?"

"Yeah. I'm here…I just…what do you mean Ivy has Peyton's liver? Savannah's Peyton? I don't understand."

"Yeah, Savannah's Peyton. The one and only," I say a little louder as I sloppily pour myself a fourth shot of bourbon.

"Expl…wait…" Rachel says. I'm not quick to answer her because my thoughts aren't coming as quickly as they were a few hours ago…when I was sober. "Are you seriously telling me that Peyton's organs were donated and that Ivy was the recipient of her liver?"

I swallow the shot of bourbon sitting in front of me, grimacing at the burn that attacks my throat. "Yep."

"Oh my God," I hear her say softly on the other line. "How do you know this for sure?"

I sit for a moment trying to decide the best way to explain it all to Rachel without her hearing that I'm certifiably drunk right now.

"She wrote a letter to the Give Life foundation after Peyton died. I've had one of those letters sittin' in my dresser drawer for years."

I hear her gasp on the other end of the line. "And you never told anyone?"

"Nope."

"No one? Not even your parents?"

"Not even my parents." I lay my head down on my arm still holding the phone with my other hand. My head is spinning but I lift it so I can reach for the bourbon anyway. Noticing that there isn't much left, I don't even bother with the glass, I tip it back and swig it right out of the bottle.

"Oh Bryant. How did she find out? She didn't hear it from you I assume."

"Nope. Found her letter in my drawer," I explain sheepishly. "Complete accident but still…it's on me Rache. This is all my fault. I've been tryin' to find a time to tell her but there was never a good time. I love her, Rache. I'm in love with her and I want her back but she doesn't want me."

"You don't know that," she assures me. "Maybe she just needs some space. Give her the night and see what happens tomorrow. A lot can change after a good sleep."

"Yeah…maybe." Maybe she's right. I can definitely feel the need for sleep pulling me under. Alcohol has stunted my brain for the night. I'm out of coherent thoughts except for one.

*I'm sleeping alone tonight.*

"Call me tomorrow if you don't hear from her first thing, Bryant, okay? I'll help you look for her anyway that I can."

"Yeah. Thanks. Night Rache."

"G'night Bry." I hear her say before I disconnect the call. I stumble over to the couch since it's a hell of a lot closer to me than my bedroom. I'll just sack out here in case a miracle happens and Savannah comes back to me tonight. Grabbing the throw blanket behind me, I fall onto the couch and cover part of my body with the blanket. I'm out for the count in seconds.

*****

"BRYANT!" She's knocking on the door. I've been looking for her for days, coming up empty each time.

Where the hell did she go?

Why wouldn't she at least text me?

I open my eyes a smidge when I hear the knocking, but my splitting headache tells me I'm not ready to get up. Last night's bourbon party was meant to erase my pain, stop the hurt, but this morning I'm one hundred percent sure I'll be regretting it.

BAM BAM BAM I hear on the door again. "BRYANT, It's ME! Open the door!" I hear her shout. I try to get up, to get to her quickly, but my body betrays me. I flail around in my bed, frustrated that my feet and arms are getting tangled in my sheets. I don't even remember going to bed. I'm pretty sure I sacked out on the couch so how the hell did I get here?

"BRYANT! PLEASE! OPEN UP!" She's screaming right now, banging on my door. I get my hands free and try my best to slide off the bed, anxious to get up and run to her. I've missed her so damn much. I just want my hands on her, to feel her, to kiss her, to hold her and tell her how damn sorry I am for hurting her the way I did.

"I'm coming, Savannah! I'm coming. Hold on!" I reach my hand out, assuming if I do so, she'll put her hand in mind and I'll have her. Instead I'm holding onto a pillow as my body slips off my bed and I land on the floor with a hard thud.

Immediately my eyes spring open. I'm awake, alert and laying...on the living room floor? I didn't fall out of my bed. I fell off the couch.

*It was a dream?*

*But it felt so real.*

I take a deep breath, trying to settle my anxiety over hearing Savannah's voice again. The clock on the wall says it's two o'clock in the afternoon. Damn...the bourbon knocked me out way longer than I anticipated.

KNOCK KNOCK KNOCK. "BRYANT!!! If you don't open this door right now I'm going to break a window!"

"Whoa, whoa, whoa." I say to myself as I lift myself up off the floor. I guess I wasn't dreaming about everything. "I'm coming. Hold on!" As soon as I reach the front door, I unlock it and turn the knob. Rachel pushes the door open quickly. It smacks me with force as it opens. "Ouch. Damn, Rachel." I rub my head. "What the fuck do you want?"

I don't make eye contact but I hear the tremble in her voice. "Bryant?" She sighs. "You've been drinking?"

"Last night...I..."

"We don't have time, Bryant." She's extra hurried and I'm still lethargic, so I don't understand. Finally, my eyes look to her face and that's when I see it. Her expression screams fear, pain, fear, anxiety, fear...

"It's Savannah," she says quietly.

Everything about her expression sobers me in an instant. "Where is she Rache? Where did she go? Is she ok?"

Rachel leans forward and places her hands on my shoulders. She challenges me to focus on her eyes when she speaks next. "Bryant, Savannah was in an accident. I don't know when. I don't know how. I don't know any of the particulars. Savannah didn't show up for work this morning, and you hadn't heard from her yet, and then..."

"And then what? Jesus Christ, Rachel, what happened?" I whisper.

*Please don't let her be dead.*

*Please, God, don't take her from me*

"And then I saw the paper this morning." Rachel shows me the front page of today's paper. The front headline reads, STORM and FOG CAUSES NEAR FATAL ACCIDENT."

*Near fatal?*

Something doesn't seem right as I glance through the article quickly. It doesn't mention victims or anything like that, nor does it tell me what kind of vehicle was involved in the crash. All the picture shows is a semi-truck jack-knifed along the side of the road. "Rache, this says it happened near Elizabethtown. She would've had no reason to go there. This can't be her. This kind of accident could've been anyone. What makes you think it was Sev..."

Rachel interrupts me, "Because I had this feeling in my chest when I saw the paper this morning, and since nobody has seen or heard from her, I needed to make sure that it wasn't her, so I called her mom and...and..." Tears begin to run down Rachel's face, confirming what I don't want to believe.

Everything in my stomach rolls. I look at Rachel with a blank expression. In my mind, I'm trying to decide which is closer, the bathroom or the front flower bed. My body makes my mind up for me when I swing open the front door again and hoist myself over the porch railing where all of the pain I tried to hide in bourbon last night comes right back to me. I vomit three or four times-I lose count-before I end up dry heaving. I hear Rachel's footsteps behind me and then see a towel hanging from her outreached hand.

"Thanks," I whisper.

"You're welcome. You okay?"

"Yeah. Too much bourbon. I'm good." I breathe. "I'm good."

Fuck.

Seven…

This is on me.

"It's all my fault Rache. I did this."

"You didn't cause her to have an accident Bryant."

"She left here because of me. If that wouldn't have happened, she would be lying naked in my bed right now." I point in the direction of my bedroom down the main hall.

"Let's not talk about faults right now, okay? Grab whatever you need and let's go."

"I don't need anything. Let me just lock up. Where is she?"

"Elizabethtown."

"What the hell is she doing there? That's west of here! Why would she have gone west of here?"

"I don't know, Bryant. I just know that's where she is. Go get yourself a bottle of water and some crackers or something and then come on, I'll drive. You're in no state."

She's right. My head is still spinning. Drinking so much last night was the stupidest idea I've ever had…besides the obvious. I mentally slap myself for spending my night in a self-loathing drunken stupor while Savannah was God-knows-where getting involved in an accident.

*Please don't leave me Sev.*

*I'm on my way to you.*

I can only pray that she'll want to have anything to do with me when we get there.

# Chapter 29

# *O'Bryant*

We're pulling into the parking garage of Hardin Memorial Hospital in just under thirty minutes. My heart is trying to beat itself out of my chest. Thank God Rachel offered to drive so that I could take the time to sober up as much as possible. I down my entire bottle of water and shoved as many goldfish crackers as I could into my mouth, as well as a few Advil. It wasn't my hangover remedy of choice, but Savannah is more important. Before we exit Rachel's car, I run my tongue over my teeth.

"Shit. You got any mints Rache? Or some gum? I didn't even get a minute to brush my damn teeth and now I'm going to be meeting Savannah's parents."

Although neither of us feel the urge to laugh, she smirks at me before diving into her purse. "Yeah I have Altoids in here somewhere." She shuffles through until I hear the familiar jingle of mints in a tin. She hands it to me and I open it pulling out no less than six mints.

"Those are curiously strong you know," Rachel says, raising an eyebrow in my direction.

"Don't care. Anything to help erase the bourbon breath. I don't need her parents thinking I'm a drunk."

Rachel tilts her head and looks at me sympathetically. "Relax. They're not going to think that. I'll vouch for you if I have to. You ready?"

"Yeah, let's go."

Together we walk into the main entrance where the smell of a hospital hits me right in the face. Immediately my mind flashes back to a few years ago when I'm sitting in a hospital, day after day, waiting on better news for Ivy's recovery. We stop quickly at the front desk where an older man and woman both sit, wearing matching vests over their clothes. Volunteers.

"Can I help you, dear?" the white-haired lady asks me as we approach. Her smile is gentle and warm and she seems eager to help.

"Uh, yes. You can actually. I'm looking for Savannah Turner. Can you please tell me what room she's in?

"Yes. Absolutely." She sees the urgency in my eyes but it doesn't make her move any faster. We stand waiting patiently, but I feel the anxiety rising the longer and longer I stand here. The older gentleman sitting at the desk types in Savannah's name into his computer and looks back up to me.

"Sir, she's in the ICU. That's on the second floor. Room seven."

"ICU? Are you sure?" Rachel said she was in an accident, but never in a million years did I think it would've been an accident landing her in the damn ICU. Immediately I'm sweating, my body threatening me to give me back the crackers and water I recently ingested.

"Yes, sir," the gentleman says.

*Fuck.*

*It's bad?*

"Room seven," I repeat in a mumble. A quick look to Rachel and I'm rolling my eyes at the irony. "Of course. She hates the number seven...thank you, sir," I say to him. "Come on Rache."

We run to the elevators and hastily press the button for the second floor. Once we arrive, Rachel leads us down a hallway to a nurse's station where she asks about Savannah. The nurse types Savannah's name into the electronic tablet she's holding and looks back to us.

"Are you family?"

"Uh…" I hesitate. I'm almost ready to lie just so I can see her but Rachel speaks up before I decide to.

"Not exactly, no. I'm a friend of Savannah's." She nods in my direction. "But this is…"

"My name is Bryant Wood, ma'am. Savannah is my…"

*Shit, what do I say?*

"Fiancé!" Rachel blurts out. I look to her dumbfounded but she only raises her eyebrows slightly at me.

*Right…only relatives…*

"Please, can you tell me anything about what happened to her? How is she? Can I see her?"

*How many people do I have to ask to just see her?*

I fear for a moment that she's going to tell me I'm not allowed to see Savannah. I'm preparing myself to either beg for admittance or simply push past her and find Savannah myself. Before I decide what I'm going to say, the nurse eyes me over quickly, throwing me her most empathetic smile.

"Let me walk you down. Her room is number seven. It's just down here, last door on the left."

"Thank you." We both follow her down the hall.

"My name is Helen. I'm one of the nurses in charge of Savannah's care. Before you enter her room I feel like I should give you the heads up on what you should expect. The doctor can give you more information when he arrives for his rounds."

I take a deep breath, blowing it out full steam as we walk down the hall. "Okay, I would appreciate that very much. Thank you," I tell her.

"Right now Savannah is unconscious."

"WHAT?" I ask a little too loudly. "Why? What does that mean?"

"That means her pain meds have sedated her to keep her comfortable and out of severe pain while she heals. She just hasn't woken up yet, but she will.  It's not uncommon for cases like hers, but the doctors say there was no evidence of swelling in her brain, despite the hairline fracture to her skull. Everything seems normal in terms of brain function. She just needs to rest now. She'll wake up when her body is ready. Once she's awake, we'll assess her and hopefully be able to move her from the ICU. She's just here now as a precaution."

"Oh thank Christ," I say as I bend over at the waist, my hands landing on my knees. I take a moment to breathe in and out a few times. Rachel rubs my shoulder in support. Damn if I'm not being the biggest pussy right now, but the girl I love could end up with part of her skull removed.

"Are you okay Mr. Wood?" Helen asks softly. Her eyes tell me she understands all too well my reaction. I suppose working every day in the ICU, where many people don't make it out alive, she sees a lot of people like me.

"Yeah, I'm good. Sorry." I stand up once again and step forward towards Savannah's room.

"She may not look the same to you right now as she's suffered many facial contusions and has a broken nose. It definitely looks like she took a beating, but in time and if needed, a little physical therapy, everything should heal."

"Can she…umm…can she hear me if I talk to her?"

Helen smiles. "We can never know for sure but if you're asking me my personal opinion, I say absolutely. Let her know you're here for her. It can only help with her recovery."

I nod.

"Thank you Helen," Rachel says.

"You're welcome." Helen steps back, retreating to the nurse's station and allowing Rachel and me to visit with Savannah.

When we open the door though, we're not alone. Two older people are seated at either side of Savannah's bed. Though it's been many, many, years, I recognize them as Savannah's parents, Mr. and Mrs. Sanders.

"Bryant Wood!" Mrs. Sanders says quietly with a pleasing smile, much to my surprise. "I haven't seen you in years."

"Hello Mrs. Sanders."

She gets up from her chair and crosses the room, her arms outstretched welcoming a hug. "It's so good to see you. Savannah told us that she's been seeing you a good bit these days. I'm so glad she found someone who cares for her after all she's been through."

Nodding I say, "I care for her very much, Mrs. Sanders. I'm so sorry I wasn't here sooner. I only just found out about her accident a little over an hour ago."

I swallow the damn lump in my throat, praying that the word GUILTY doesn't etch itself across my forehead. It's my fault Savannah's in here. Wait till Mrs. Sanders hears that one. She won't like me so much then. I turn quickly to Mr. Sanders who is already standing, and shake his hand.

"Mr. Sanders. I'm Bryant Wood. It's nice to meet you, sir."

"Good to meet you too, Bryant," he says calmly. I can tell by his inflection that he's worried about his baby girl.

I watch as Rachel hugs Mrs. Sanders as well. She's way more comfortable with Savannah's family than I am since they've been friends longer. While the three of them are catching up, I turn myself toward Savannah and silently study her, but I'm screaming on the inside. She looks so peaceful just lying there, covered in a white sheet, but everything else about her portrays a horrible nightmare. Her eyes are black and blue; her nose is swollen to at least double the size that it was. Her right arm is in a cast from her hand all the way up and over her elbow with a matching full leg cast on her right leg.

*Oh Seven.*

*What the fuck happened to you?*

*I did this.*

The chaos of sounds around her is unsettling. The woosh of the IV machine, the constant beeping of the heart monitor. It's hard to listen to.

"How is she?" I ask.

"She's stable for now." Mr. Sanders says. "The doctor said she has a broken nose, a broken elbow and a dislocated knee. They did whatever surgeries they needed to do and ran tests. From what they're telling us, only time will tell."

"How long has she been asleep?" Rachel asks.

"Umm…we got here last night and she was in surgery, so I would say maybe twelve hours now? They told us to not be shocked if she sleeps through most of today and part of tomorrow."

"I just don't understand it though," Mrs. Sanders says, running a hand up and down Savannah's leg. "She texted me last night and said she was on her way to our place to visit, but she ended up here in

Elizabethtown. What on earth was she doing here? She doesn't know anybody over here, does she Rachel?"

Rachel looks to me quickly before she says "Uh, no. Not that I know of at least. I mean, I don't know all of her friends so I guess I really couldn't say."

"It's my fault." The words slipped out of my mouth before I had the chance to catch them.

Damnit.

"What do you mean it's your fault?" Mrs. Sanders asks.

I take a deep breath closing my eyes before I begin to explain.

*The truth will set me free in one way or another.*

"Mr. and Mrs. Sanders, Savannah and I…" My voice trembles. "I screwed up. I kept something from her that I knew would hurt her *because* I knew it would hurt her and she found out last night and…"

"Are you sleeping with other women, Bryant?" Mr. Sanders throws his hands up in defense. "I mean I don't want think about my baby girl in that situation but if you're running around with someone else…"

"NO SIR!" I say almost too emphatically. "It's nothing like that. Please, you have to understand that I love your daughter. I love her more than anyone else, except for my own baby girl, Ivy Lynn."

"You have a daughter?" Mr. Sanders is surprised to hear this news.

"Of course he has a daughter. You knew that, James. We talked about it a while back." Mrs. Sanders comes to my aid, though her help doesn't make me feel any less uncomfortable.

"Right. Right. I remember now. You were married before?" Mr. Sanders nods.

I shake my head. "No, sir. Ivy's mother and I never married. We were stupid and made a mistake that we didn't want to further complicate with a marriage that meant nothing to either of us. The baby was our number one concern. Samantha passed away a few days after giving birth to Ivy. She had three blood clots in her lung that the doctors couldn't find fast enough."

Both Mr. and Mrs. Sanders look taken aback. I'm not certain if it's because of the fact that Ivy's mother and I never married or the fact that Samantha passed away and I'm now a single father. There's a moment of awkward silence where I don't know whether they're waiting for me to go on and tell them everything or if they just want to drop the whole thing. They deserve the truth though and if I'm going to have any chance reconciling things with Savannah, I'm going to need her parents on board.

"My daughter, Ivy, she's almost three years old, but she was diagnosed with Biliarty Atresia when she was about eighteen months."

"Oh heaven almighty, that poor babe," Mrs. Sanders says breathlessly.

I nod my head slowly. "It was a rough time for us both as we waited on the donor list for Ivy to get a new liver, but we were blessed with a perfect match donor back in January of 2013. Since then it's been one doctor visit after another making sure that she continues to be okay."

"Praise the Lord," Mrs. Sanders says smiling.

"Yeah well…that's the tricky part Mrs. Sanders. What eats away at parents whose kids receive perfectly matched organs is the fact that on the other end of that organ, is a life lost. I mean how can I be happy and grateful that my kid is alive and well because another child died?" My damn eyes are watering. I blink several times and look up to the ceiling in hopes that they'll stay in my eyes and not drip down my face. I feel like I'm about the make the worst confession of my life.

"Oooh, bless your heart, Bryant. Don't you go beating yourself up for something like that. Little Ivy's life should be celebrated."

*I can't.*

*This is too hard.*

*Shit!*

"Mrs. Sanders, it was Peyton's liver that went to Ivy that day." Fuck. I'm crying like a scared little baby. "Ivy's alive because Peyton didn't make it. I received a letter from Savannah about six months later through the Give Life Organization, but those letters are designed for the donor family to not know who they're sent to at first." Tears are shamefully trickling down my face. My chest constricts and I bend over slightly to try and catch my breath. "I didn't want to tell her because what are the chances that something like that would happen? That both families would at least recognize each other. I...I couldn't do that to her. I couldn't hurt her like that again. I'm so sorry. I'm so damn sorry. I wish there was something I could've done differently back then, but I just couldn't. I was too damn scared to approach Savannah about it."

I wipe the traitorous tears from my face, demanding myself to not be such a damn pussy. When I look up I see Rachel first, whose expression is one of befuddlement. When I glace at Mrs. Sanders, I see the glistening of tears run down her face just as it did me, except she doesn't seem sad. She looks...grateful?

"Praise God for whom all blessings flow," she whispers through her small smile.

"I'm sorry? I don't...understand."

"What are the chances is right, Bryant. Honey, I am a believer in miracles and in our Lord's divine intervention and this, this is the Lord's work," she says. "Your baby girl's life was saved because Jesus needed little Peyton and she didn't need her body anymore. God was able to provide for Ivy through Peyton and if you ask me, that's a miracle if I ever heard one."

What the hell do I say to that? Savannah told me a couple months ago that her parents were devout Christians but I had no idea. For once, I'm speechless. Grateful, but speechless. I shake my head slowly, the guilt of Savannah's pain still heavy on my shoulders. "I love your daughter," I say to both of her parents. "But she's lying in this bed because of this truth. She found the letter she wrote tucked away in my t-shirt drawer. I don't even remember putting it there. It was an accident but it was too late. I couldn't stop it. She read it and it upset her and...she...left. I pleaded with her to not go out in the rain but she was adamant. She didn't want to talk to me anymore."

Mr. Sanders clears his throat, which causes me to look in his direction. "Is that why you sought her out? Out of guilt? You feel bad for her? 'Cause I imagine that's what set her off, Son. She doesn't like anyone pitying her."

"No, sir. It's not like that," I say softly. I sit down next to Savannah, taking her chilled hand in my own, watching her body rise and fall with the ventilator. "I do feel horrible for her, because I vaguely understand the pain she went through, but I had a crush on your daughter all through high school. I kicked myself then for doing nothing about it. She was too smart for me, books and cleverness…I just played football. Now…she walked into my life again a few months back and since then I've fallen in love with her. And before last night I could honestly tell you that she loved me, but now…I don't…this is all my fault."

"Give her some time," Mr. Sanders says, prompting me to look at him again. His brown eyes are intimidating, but sad, like this life is exhausting him mentally, spiritually, and physically. "She'll come around eventually. She's stubborn like her father, but you've been good for her. We could see her old spirit coming back. I imagine you have a pretty large part in that."

"Thank you, sir. I would give her anything."

"Then that's all I need to hear. You're a good man, Bryant. You're good for Savannah. Her mother and I can clearly see that."

I nod silently with my head down because it's taking everything I have inside to not get choked up by his words. A silent tear defies me as it slips down my cheek and on to the floor.

"Bryant," Mr. Sanders places his hand on my shoulder, squeezing just enough to tell me he's sincere in his compassion. My body starts to tremble when he I feel the comfort of his hand. He could be punching me in the face, screaming at me to leave this room, to never see his daughter again, but instead, he did the opposite. He gave me his blessing to love his daughter. I'm the most unworthy man for this, yet overwhelmingly thankful at the same time. "Son, it looks and sounds to me like you need to understand something very important, so you hear me when I tell you that none of this is your fault." He squeezes my shoulder a little harder. "Do you hear me?"

Sometimes we refuse to realize how strongly something impacts our lives until it completely destroys us. The pressure of hiding an important truth from everyone in my life, the endless feeling of guilt every time I was with Savannah, the weight of knowing that Ivy's life rests in my hands, and now the fear of possibly losing the one woman who was meant for me – it's all too much for one man. Hearing Savannah's father tell me that none of this is my fault breaks me into pieces. I sit in the chair next to Savannah, her father's hand on my shoulder, and I sob silently. My body shudders as I try to wipe away the tears that just keep coming.

Damnit.

It was never my intention to come here and break down, but I suppose when the heart needs to speak we damn well better listen to it.

"Savannah is a strong-willed woman," Mr. Sanders says. "She's brave and she's compassionate and usually has a good sense of what she wants in this life. She didn't cause the shit storm she's been through and neither did you. I hope you understand that. You've both weathered your own individual storms over the past few years and neither one of you came out of those storms the same people you were when you went into them."

Through my tears I try to smile as I nod in agreement. "That is definitely a truth, sir. We are definitely not the same people we were."

"Well Son, as you get older, you'll only regret the chances in your life that you didn't take, so thank you for taking a chance on our daughter, for trying to protect her. For bringing her spirit back to us a little more every. It'll be another uphill battle for a while but I think you're well suited for the job."

I wipe another stray tear from my face as I stand up. I extend my arm to shake Mr. Sanders's hand but he pulls me in for a hug. He pats me on the back before letting go and then says, "Margie, let's go get some coffee. Bryant and Rachel will want some time alone with Savannah."

"Good idea. I could use a walk anyway. We'll be back soon. You two make yourselves comfortable."

"Thank you," we both say.

# Chapter 30

# *Savannah*

It's beautiful here. The field is so vast and open. It looks like I can walk for miles and miles and never walk out of the field. The wild flowers blowing in the wind create a vibrant splatter of color against the clear blue sky. I walk a little farther ahead, picking flowers as I go, wrapping them together into a crown. I've always wanted to wear a wild flower crown. Maybe I could make Ivy one the next time I see her. As I gather a few more flowers I hear the laughter of children playing. I follow the sound until my eyes reach a beautiful ranch house with a semi-wrap-around porch overlooking a gorgeous patch of roses. There are rose bushes of all kinds, but what surprises me the most are the purple roses growing amongst the red, pink, yellow, and white ones. Purple roses are my favorite. I can't remember if I ever told anyone that before.

Finally, when I make my way through the rose bushes, I feel a familiar pull in my heart to what I see before me. Ivy and two little girls are playing together, giggling as they trade roses of different colors, picking the petals off of each stem and throwing them in the air like colored confetti. Ivy faces me while the other two have their backs to me. I smile at Ivy and the girls as I calmly walk around their circle to see what the girls are up to.

"Mommy!" One of them yells. I watch as she gets up and begins to run excitedly to…me.

*Peyton?*

I look around quickly in case I'm wrong in thinking she's running to me. Perhaps there is someone standing behind me that I hadn't noticed, but it's just me. Bewildered I watch her as she runs to me. Her hair is longer with beautiful bouncy curls but those eyes…I would remember those eyes anywhere.

It's her.

"Peyton?" I cry out. "Oh my God! Peyton?! Is it really you?"

"Mommy!" she yells again. She runs right into my arms as I scoop her up and refuse to let go. Her smell, the feel of her wrapped around my neck, all of it…it's heaven.

Heaven.

Wait…

I squeeze Peyton's body a little bit and she giggles, thinking I'm playing a game with her. In reality, I'm squeezing her to make sure she's real. I shouldn't be seeing her like this. Something isn't right.

"Vannie?"

I gasp audibly. There's only one person in the whole world who has ever called me "Vannie." There's no way he could be here. Sure enough I turn towards the house and he's there, in the flesh, walking towards me wearing the most reverent smile.

"Shawn?"

"Yeah baby. Were you expecting someone else?" He walks out and hugs both Peyton and I together. We're all here, finally. Together again as a family. I can't take my eyes off of either of them. Peyton has changed so much but Shawn, he still looks every bit the good looking husband I married so many years ago. Time has been good to him.

"I missed you both so, so, so, much. Oh, God it feels so good to just touch you!" I lean up and kiss Shawn while holding onto Peyton. His lips are warm and comforting, but they don't quite feel the same. They don't feel like the lips I've kissed recently.

*Bryant's lips.*

Suddenly my body stiffens and I close my eyes, assuming that when I open them again I'll realize that this was all a dream. A not too shabby dream, but a dream nonetheless. My eyelids lift and I'm still in Shawn's arms, holding tightly to my beautiful baby girl who still smells of strawberries and birthday cake…just as I remember her. Guiltily, I glance at Shawn, who is watching me with understanding in his eyes.

"Let's take a walk," he says.

"Mommy can I go play?" Peyton asks me. I don't want to let go of her for fear of losing her again, but I can't just keep her to myself either. She's so happy with her friends.

"Sure baby. Who's your other friend?" I nod to the third girl in the circle. Her beautiful hair is holds similar bouncy curls to Peyton's except that hers are blonde. She looks up and I catch a glimpse of her face. Big brown eyes, soft rosy cheeks, and a smile that could light up a room. She's a beautiful little girl. They're all beautiful little girls.

"That's my friend Rose. Love you, Mommy!" She kisses my cheek and runs off to play.

I watch in awe as she rejoins her friends. "How did she get so big?" I ask, shaking my head.

"She's beautiful, isn't she?" Shawn asks.

When I turn back towards him he takes my hand and leads me away from the girls so that we can be alone. "Are you okay?" he asks.

"Yeah, I'm okay. God, I've missed you. I never thought I would see you again." I wrap my arms tightly around his body, savoring his warmth.

"It's good to see you too." He is quiet for a moment before he continues. "Vannie, listen. I'm sorry we left you. I'm sorry I wasn't strong enough for you. I never meant for any of it to happen, but you've been so strong…"

"Whoa, whoa, whoa, wait a second." I interrupt. "What do you mean you're sorry? You're right here, Shawn. I don't…" I shake my head nervously. "I don't understand."

"The accident Vannie. Remember? We were in a car accident. It was black ice, remember? Our car flipped and went over the median. I'm so sorry Vannie. I couldn't stop it and I wasn't strong enough for you. Peyton wasn't strong enough for you."

Visions of our car accident flood my brain.

*Car accident.*

*Again.*

*Bryant.*

"Where's Bryant?" I ask cautiously.

Shawn shakes his head. "He wasn't in an accident, Vannie. You were."

I look around where we're standing again. In front of Bryant's house…which is surrounded by fields of wild flowers and bushes of purple roses. No horses, no farming fields, no woods to the side of the house.

"So am I dead now? Is that why I can see you?"

"I don't know babe. Looks like you were beat up pretty badly."

"I don't feel like I've been beat up," I say matter of factly.

"Look, I don't think we have much time." Shawn says. "So I need to say a few things to you, okay?"

"What do you mean? Why are we running out of time? Tell me what's happening," I plea.

Shawn holds my face in his hands and looks into my eyes. "Savannah Turner I need you to understand that no matter what happened to Peyton and me, or what happens to you soon, none of it is your fault. It was a tragic case of wrong place, wrong time and it is what it is. I don't want you dwelling on the past. You have too much to live for."

"What do you mean, Shawn? I don't want to live without you, or Peyton. You're scaring me."

"I'm not trying to scare you Vannie. I'm trying to tell you that it's okay. If you make the right choice, you're going to be okay and then you can spend the rest of your life with Bryant and Ivy and whoever else might come along in your future."

I watch in horror as he mentions Bryant's name, like he's known all along that I've had an affair, but he answers my expression with sympathy. "Savannah, Bryant loves you. Ivy loves you. I love you too, but I don't want to see you give up. I don't want to see you throw everything away when everything you've ever wanted is right in front of you. You only live once, Vannie. Take the chance on love again and don't look back. You deserve to be happy and he can make you happy."

"But I'm with you now. Why can't things just go back to the way they were before? You're here. Peyton's here…"

"But you can't stay here," Shawn says quietly.

"What? Why?"

"Because it's not your time Vannie. One day, we'll all be together again and when that day comes we'll be here, Peyton and I, to welcome you home but for now...Vannie, it's not your time. You have to go back."

Weeping, I shake my head and say, "I don't want to go back. I don't want to go back. I can't do this again. I'm not as strong as everyone thinks I am."

Shawn's hands smooth over my head and my face. "Yes you are baby. You're the strongest woman I know. You can do this. Your body will heal. Your spirit will heal and Bryant will be there with you the entire time. Let him help you. Let him love you. Trust me when I tell you that I want you to let him love you. Your life isn't over yet, so go live it. Don't wait for moments to happen. Create them. Live and laugh, play and love, and do all those things that those inspiration posters are always telling us to do." He smiles.

"I'm scared," I look deep into his eyes, allowing him to see my fear completely.

Fear that I won't heal physically.

Fear that I won't heal spiritually.

Fear that Bryant will be mad that I left him.

Fear that I'll forget about Shawn and Peyton.

Shawn smiles tenderly and leans forward to softly kiss my forehead. "It's okay to be scared, Vannie. Being scared means you're about to do something really, really brave, and I'm so proud of you for taking that step."

"What if I forget you?" I cry.

"You won't forget me babe. Peyton and I will be with you forever, right here." He says laying his palm over my heart. I place my hand on top of his and close my eyes momentarily, basking in his warmth.

"I love you, Shawn," I whisper.

"I love you too, Vannie. I'll always love you."

*"I'll always love you."*

*"I'll always love you."*
*"I'll always love you."*
Beep...beep…beep…beep…

# Chapter 31

# *Savannah*

"I wish she would wake up. How much longer do you think it'll be?"

*Mom?*

"Depends. Could be a few hours, could be a day."

*Dad?*

*Mom, Dad, I'm here!*

I want look at her and tell her I'm okay, but my eyes are heavy. My body feels like dead weight lying here. I want so badly to open my eyes but I just can't. Sleep is calling to me again, pulling me under into oblivion.

*****

"I miss you. I'm so sorry about everything, Sev. I never meant to hurt you and now look at you. You don't deserve this. It should be me in that bed."

*Bryant? He's here?*

*Wake up Savannah.*

*Open your eyes.*

Once again I slide into sleep, unable to communicate with anyone.

*****

The haze starts to lift from around me for a short time

"She can stay with me when she's out of here. I mean, if it's okay with you guys. You're always welcome at my house. It's a huge ranch house. There's plenty of rooms for anyone who wants to visit, and everything Savannah would need is on one floor. She wouldn't have to worry about steps."

*Stay? With Bryant? He wants me to stay?*

"Don't you have responsibilities at the tavern?"

"I've spent a lot of time with Ivy," Rachel says. "I'm more than happy to step in when Bryant needs to be away."

Consciousness wanes as I'm pulled under once more.

*****

Music. There's music playing. In and out of consciousness I can hear her singing one of my favorite songs. Adele's *To Make You Feel My Love* is being played through some sort of speaker. Even though my eyes don't open I can feel Bryant's presence near me. Plus, I recently learned of his small obsession with Adele...something I remember teasing him about a few days ago. Perhaps this is his attempt at waking me up with humor.

*****

"How long has she been here now?"

*That sounds like Audrey.*

"Couple days," Bryant says softly. I feel him squeeze my hand and wish so badly that I had the strength to squeeze his back.

"She still hasn't woken up?"

*Fight Savannah. Open your eyes. You can do this.*

"Not yet," he sighs.

"You really love her, don't you?" she asks sweetly.

"I've never in my life loved a woman more than I love Seven."

*Come on Savannah. Fight.*

Bryant squeezes my hand again,

*Stay awake!*

And for the first time...I squeeze back.

"Whoa!" Bryant jumps letting go of my hand. I feel it fall back onto the bed. "Shit, sorry! Savannah can you hear me?"

"What the hell just happened?" Audrey asks.

"I swear to God she just squeezed my hand. Savannah..." He tenderly puts my hand in his again and squeezes it gently. "Can you feel that?"

I squeeze his hand back, holding on tighter to his warm hand as I listen to him rejoice. "Oh thank Christ! You can hear me. Savannah, I love you. Do you hear me? I love you. It's okay if you can't open your eyes. I'm right here baby and I'm not leavin'." I feel him bring my hand to his mouth and kiss the top as he lets his lips linger there.

That was a lot of work for my body. All I can do now is…sleep.

*****

When my eyes finally open, it's dark in my room, except for the light of the television on the wall. I would assume that it's night time given the television show that's on, but then again *Say Yes to the Dress* is on a lot more often these days. My throat is dry, my head is pounding, and my teeth feel like a wooly mammoth lives in my mouth. I wonder if there's a toothbrush around here. My head hurts and my face feels like it's been beaten. I try to pick up my right arm so that I can touch my face, but it's extremely heavy. Slowly turning my head, I look down to see that my arm is in a bright blue cast with a matching blue cast running down my entire right leg.

*What the hell?*

*I'm broken.*

*And so thirsty.*

I can't see a water bottle anywhere around me, no cup of ice. The room is dark except for the television hanging on the wall that is on. The sound is turned down though, so I can only barely hear what's happening on the show. I'm sure there's a nurse call button around here, but hell if I know where it is. I roll my head back to the other side, smiling to myself over the person I see asleep in the chair beside me. Bryant's hand rests on my left leg. My heart leaps a little at the sentiment that he just wanted to be touching me even if he was sleeping. I try to clear my throat, thinking that might wake him up, but I can't make any sounds. Maybe I need to go about waking him up some other way. I focus on my left leg since it's not in a cast and try to wiggle it from underneath Bryant's hand. Lying in a bed for so long has weakened my muscles immensely. I have a hard time, but eventually I can bend my leg up to me knee, but that doesn't wake him.

*Ouch* – I wince. My entire body feels like it's one huge bruise.

*Damnit.*

The only other thing I can do is try to reach out and touch him. Raising my left arm slightly, I lay my hand on his forearm and rub my thumb up and down his arm near his wrist. In his sleep, he reaches over to scratch his arm. I want to laugh at him, but at the moment I'm so thirty. I just want him to wake up. Instead of rubbing gently I use all of my might to grab a hold of Bryant's arm and squeeze as tightly as I can.

*Please wake up, Bryant!*

He jerks awake suddenly like he's being attacked, but looks down to see my hand grabbing his arm. Startled and awake he puts on his biggest, yet cautious, smile as he leans over the bed closer to me.

"Seven! You're awake! Your eyes…they're…" He exhales heavily. "They're beautiful. I've missed seeing them this week, you stunningly beautiful girl."

I smile weakly and open my mouth to try and respond to him but I can't get words out.

"Seven? Are you okay? Can you hear me okay, Baby?"

I nod slightly so he knows I can hear him. With my left hand I make a drinking motion towards my mouth and try to say "water".

"You want a drink? You need water?" Bryant asks softly as he holds on to my shoulder. I nod my head affirmatively.

"Okay. Yeah. Water. Right…uhh…" Bryant looks around. For what, I have no idea. He turns back to me and says "Let me get the nurse and make sure it's okay for you to have a drink." He holds my face tenderly in his hands and looks into my eyes. "I'll be right back okay? I'm not leaving you. I'll be right back." He kisses my forehead and smiles. The dimple in his cheek peeks out. "God, it's good to see you awake." Quickly he turns and heads for the door to flag down a nurse.

In what I'm sure was less than sixty seconds he's back with a nurse following right behind him carrying a Styrofoam cup of water with a tiny straw.

"Well hello there, Savannah. My name is Helen and I'm the nurse on duty this evenin'. I'll be checkin' in on you every few hours, but this guy here tells me you're thirsty."

I try to say "yes" but again, no words come out. I sound like I have a nasty case of laryngitis. Helen smiles at me, nodding in understanding. "It's okay, honey. Water will help. I'll bet your throat is sore from the intubation and the fact that you haven't been able to physically drink anything in a while." She holds the cup up near my mouth and places the straw between my lips. I sip eagerly. "Not too much at one time. Let's make sure it's going to sit okay in your stomach before we give you lots to drink, okay?" I take that as my cue to stop drinking. I swish around the last sip I took in my mouth for a second, wetting as much of my mouth as I can before swallowing.

"Thank you," I say a little more clearly. I try again to clear my throat but Helen was right, it is a bit painful.

"You're very welcome, Savannah. While I'm here do you mind if I just do your check-up now?"

"Sure." My eyes slide to Bryant's. Looking at him again...his body...his face...the hat he wears backwards on his head. He's gorgeous. He winks at me before grinning slightly. I'm pretty sure I wink back, but my eyes feel so heavy it's hard to tell.

"Great," she says, pulling out her electronic table. "Can you rate your pain for me on a scale of one to ten?"

I look to Bryant and immediately laugh out loud remembering the first words he said to me not too many months ago.

*Well on a scale of one to four I would give that little dance of yours a perfect ten.*

"Umm, on a scale of one to four I would say my pain is a what the fuck happened to me?" Bryant snickers standing next to me, but only because he knows why I answered the way I did.

"That's my girl." He says placing a sweet kiss on my forehead. "Sorry, Helen. You'll have to excuse my trucker-mouth of a girlfriend here. She's not well...and the way she just responded is a bit of an inside joke. Sorry about that." He smirks.

Helen at least has a nice enough sense of humor that she can let my comments roll off her back easily. "Well it's good to see you feeling okay enough to joke a little bit. So your pain isn't too bad?"

"Well..." I pause trying to focus on how my body feels. "I don't really have much feeling in my right arm or right leg. But left side feels like it's been beat up pretty good but it's manageable. It's a little hard to breathe through my nose. It hurts too, and I have a huge headache."

Helen nods as she jots a few notes down in her tablet. "Good. Okay. Your pain meds are starting to wear off, so we can give you another dose of that. Your head will be in a little pain for a bit because you broke your nose. You also have a small hairline fracture to your skull. The pain meds should help that a good bit though."

*Damn.*

*No wonder it hurts.*

"Also you can see from your casts that you have a broken elbow and a dislocated knee. Your surgery went smoothly when you arrived here which is good. Now you just have to rest and heal." Helen reports.

"When I was brought in here..." I repeat. "How long ago was that?"

"Just a couple days ago. Now that you're awake and alert I imagine we might be able to downgrade you from the ICU. I'm just going to check your vitals and then send the report to the doctor," Helen explains. She excuses herself from my room, reminding me of the nurse call button and that she'll be checking in with me twice every hour unless I need her in between. She also lets me know that the doctor will be in first thing in the morning for rounds unless he comes to see me before that.

I thank her but frown, a little confused. It doesn't feel like I've been asleep for that long. I must've been really messed up. Pictures of what happened to me flash through my head every once in a while, but I can't seem to recall everything on my own. Nervously I glance at Bryant, hoping he'll be able to provide a little clarity and comfort for me. I'm a little scared to hear what he may tell me.

"What happened to me?" I whisper.

Bryant swallows hard before speaking. "You had a fight with a semi, Sev. I'm not sure exactly about the details but you were hit from behind by a semi-truck on the highway. Your car was…" I watch as he rubs his hand behind his neck, a clear sign that he's not telling me everything.

"What? My car was what?"

He sighs. "Your car was pushed down an embankment. You rolled a few times babe. Firefighters had to use the Jaws of Life to get you out. Doctors said you were only barely responsive when you got here. They said you kept wanting to fall asleep. You're in Elizabethtown right now." He says delicately.

*Elizabethtown?*

*The truck.*

*The headlights.*

*Tissues.*

"Too fast," I mumble.

"What's that?" Bryant asks.

"Too fast. I couldn't get the…" I swallow as I wince from the pain. "The tissues. They were in the back seat and I couldn't quite reach them. The truck was coming up behind me too fast. I was…pulled to the side of the road because it was raining so hard. I thought I would be safe there." It all feels like a blur yet so damn clear at the same time.

"Baby, you did the right thing." He says, sitting on my bed next to me. He holds my hand, gliding his thumb over my knuckles. "You couldn't have known that would happen. You did everything right, and more importantly, you're alive." He kisses my hand. "I'm so damn grateful that you made it out of that nightmare alive, Savannah. I'm so sorry. I'm sorry I didn't force you to stay with me at my house, I'm sorry I hurt you. I'm so damn sorry…for everything. This is all my fault."

My head hurts from trying to recall everything that happened. I remember very clearly everything that took place at Bryant's house that night before dinner…and damn, now I remember not getting to enjoy dinner.

"The food…what did you do with all the leftover food? We didn't even get to eat it."

Bryant frowns, not understanding what I'm talking about. As soon as it dawns on him, he shakes his head smirking. "Well I sat down and ate it all, obviously." When I look at him in shock he laughs lightly and kisses my hand again. "I'm kidding, Sev. Don't worry. I took care of it."

"Aww, I just feel badly that I left like I did, and you made such a beautiful meal, and Bryant, this isn't your fault. None of this is your fault."

"I should've told you," he whispers. The sadness in his eyes is devastating.

"I understand why you didn't," I say. He doesn't move or respond. "Hey." I squeeze his hand. He looks at me with glistening eyes that break my heart all over again. "Bryant, I get it now. I understand why you didn't want to say anything and it's okay. You weren't trying to be malicious. You were just trying to protect me from hurting."

He shakes his head slowly, his lower lip quivering. "Yeah."

A tear slips out of my own eye as I watch him almost fall apart in front of me. It looks like he's been taking this all so hard…and I wasn't coherent enough to help him. As I watch him, visions of Peyton and Shawn and Ivy and their friend all smiling and playing amongst the roses flutter through my mind. They were all so happy…peaceful.

"Bryant?"

"Yeah?"

"I need to tell you something…and…you're probably going to think I'm mental and maybe I am, but I need to tell you anyway."

"You can tell me anything Sev. I assure you, nothing you say is going to change my opinion of you."

"I saw Peyton." I smile when I say her name. "And Shawn, and Ivy and another little friend of theirs…all playing outside a place that looked just like your house. Bryant, I got to hold her and talk to her, and smell her."

"When did…" He clears his throat. "When did you see them?"

"I don't know. I mean it was while I was in here, asleep, so it must've been some sort of dream, right? But Bryant...I hadn't seen Peyton or Shawn in a dream ever since the day they left me. Not once."

Bryant peels his eyes away from me as he adjusts his hat down over his eyes. He hasn't said anything yet. I'm not sure what he's thinking.

"Well that's great." He nods. "That's really great." He looks up at me and smiles, though his smile doesn't match mine.

*Something is wrong.*

"What's wrong?" I ask him.

"Huh? Nothing at all, sweetheart." He never calls me sweetheart. "Did you...you know, talk to Peyton or...Shawn? In your dream, I mean?"

"Yeah, of course I did. Peyton showed me all the fun she was having...she was older in my dream though...Ivy's age, I guess. They were playing together and giggling...throwing rose petals in the air like it was confetti." I laugh...and then wince, because it hurts my head to laugh.

Bryant's eyes glisten as he listens to my story. I have no clue what could be going through his head right now, but he isn't making eye contact with me.

"And Shawn? How did that...make you feel?" he asks anxiously.

I decide not to answer him at first, pausing my story until he looks me in the eye so I can tell him exactly what Shawn said. It takes almost twenty-five seconds for him to finally look at me, his eyes worrisome. Reaching out to touch him, I brush my hand over his chest. I want him to hear me.

"He told me that everything I've ever wanted is right in front of me." Bryant's eyes grow bigger as if those weren't the words he was expecting to hear. "He reminded me that we only have one life, this one life, and that I should take a chance on love again because..." I sniffle through the tears that are sliding down my cheek. "Because I deserve to be happy, and he knows you make me happy."

Bryant blows out a huge breath of air. He holds his forehead in his hand for second before looking back to me. "Really? I mean...really?"

"Yeah..." I say through my tears. "Really. I love you Bryant. I'm so sorry I did this to us. I broke us. I knocked us both down, and I'll always feel terrible about that because you didn't deserve it. It wasn't your responsibility to put my broken pieces back together again. I needed to do it all on my own, but it sure was nice to know that every time you touched me or held me, or hugged me, you were gluing another piece back into place."

"Savannah." He slides into my bed, tenderly putting his arm around my shoulder and pulling me into his chest. I missed his body so much, his warmth, his comfort. "I love you too. So damn much it hurts. It broke me knowing that I had anything to do with this; I never ever wanted to hurt you. I'm so grateful you came back to me." He kisses my head as I nuzzle into the side of his chest.

"Stay with me," I whisper grasping his t-shirt in my fingers.

"I'll never leave you, Sev. I'm right here."

"Bryant?"

"Yeah?"

"Why were you watching *Say Yes to the Dress*?"

I feel his body tremble as he laughs quietly. "I wasn't. I turned it on hoping you would hear it and wake up. I know how you like those girly shows."

*If it's possible to fall even more in love with Bryant Wood, I just did.*

# Chapter 32

# *Bryant*

Holding her while she sleeps is my new favorite thing. It's better than an ice cold beer. It's better than driving down a dirt road with the windows wide open. It's better than sex. Feeling her body lying comfortably on mine, her arm wrapped in a cast lying across my stomach, her fingers clutching my shirt like she's afraid I'll leave her…she makes me feel like the goddam king of the world. I didn't think I would ever love someone as much I love Ivy. God knows my life has been nothin' but mountains and canyons, but for the first time in a long time, I finally feel like life is working its way back to solid ground. I've got my two best girls in my life. I'll love them. I'll protect them. I'll care for them. I'll provide for them. And I'll enjoy every minute of it.

"Good morning." A stout looking nurse, who kind of reminds me of Mrs. Potts from *Beauty and the Beast*, waltzes in with her tablet in hand. She catches my eyes when she sees that I'm lying with Savannah, her body comfortably curled into mine. For a moment I think she's going to sternly tell me to get my ass out of the bed at which point I would've told her to go fuck herself. Instead she sweetly smiles and softly says "I need to check her vitals. I hate to wake her up, she looks so comfortable. My name is Ruth. I'll be your nurse through the afternoon."

"Bryant." I smile back at her and nod. "It's a pleasure to meet you." Delicately I smooth Savannah's hair on her head a few times until her eyes open.

"Morning gorgeous," I say to her. "Ruth here needs to check your vitals. You okay to do that? I'll need to move so she has access to your good arm."

Savannah yawns and stretches a little bit before answering. "Yeah. Sure."

"Thank you." Ruth thanks me with a smile. She's a bubbly lady for such an early hour. I guess it's better than having a cranky bitch for a nurse. She must be just starting her shift. She walks swiftly over to Savannah's left side to check her IVs, and her blood pressure as well as her other vitals, all of which seem to be good.

"Um…" I hear Savannah say. "Do you think I could get rid of this catheter?" Her cheeks blush when she says it like she's embarrassed to say the words in front of me. Maybe it's a bad time to tell her I've been watching her pee fill the bag for a couple days now. Girls and their modesty.

"Sure thing dear," Ruth says. She turns and looks to me expectantly and I hear her loud and clear.

I clear my throat and tell Savannah "Hey I'm going to walk down the hall and grab a coffee. You need anything?"

"Ohhh a coffee sounds so good right now. If it's okay with Ruth, maybe you could get me a small cup?"

"Of course sweetheart, that's fine." Ruth confirms. "Oh…" She points her finger up in the air as she turns to face me. "Not too much caffeine though. It's bad for the baby."

"Will do. Be right back," I say as I head for the door.

Except I don't make it through the door.

I run right into it instead.

*Did she just say baby?*

My feet shuffle back a few steps until I can see Savannah's face. Her expression will tell me what I need to know. Maybe I just heard everything wrong.

"I'm sorry," Savannah says. "But did you just say…"

"Baby?" I finish Savannah's sentence for her.

*Fuck. I wasn't wrong. She heard it too.*

"Yes, Dear. That's what I said. Too much caffeine can be bad for the baby during a pregnancy."

Savannah's eyes dart to me and she shakes her head clearly confused. "But I'm not…I can't be…there's no way I'm…"

Ruth looks taken aback as she stops what she's doing to look at the befuddled expression on Savannah's face, shocked that it seems as though she told a secret that nobody knew. "Well dear me, you mean you didn't know? It's right here in your lab work. They even did an ultrasound…oh."

"Oh, what?" Savannah and I both say together.

For the love of Christ, Ruth better not give her bad news now that she's told Savannah that she's pregnant.

"Oh, I just see that they did your ultrasound when they had you back in the operating room to fix your knee and your elbow." She looks at Savannah and then says quietly. "I'm sorry, Dear, I just assumed you knew and that this man was the father."

"Ahem." I clear my throat having had enough of this woman. "First of all, I'm right here. You don't have to be secretive. If anyone's the father of that baby, I assure you, it's me. And secondly, she only just woke up a few hours ago. Of course she wouldn't know. We haven't seen a doctor yet this morning."

"Bryant, calm down." Savannah says to me. "It's okay."

Bullshit. It's not okay. She's laying there in that bed with her hand on her stomach, clearly shocked beyond all belief that she's pregnant and once again, it's all my fucking fault. She's quiet for a moment and it's killing me. I have no idea what she could be thinking. Is this even true? What if Ruth, the dumbass nurse, just got her confused with someone else? Then it's just more emotional shit that Savannah has to go through. On the other side, what if it is true?

"I want to see her chart."

"Mr. Wood, I don't…"

There's a knock at the door before it swings open and a team of three medical personnel walk in. "Good morning. My name is Doctor Cortina. These are my two interns following me for the day." He says as he motions to the people standing behind him, notebooks and pens in hand.

"How are you feeling this morning, Savannah?"

"Umm." She clears her throat looking to me before she answers. "Like I just woke up from the longest nap I've ever had." That's my girl. Always trying to ease the air around her even when she has to be panicking on the inside. "My head still hurts a good bit and my body feels sore but other than that, I think I'm okay."

"Good, good." Doctor Cortina says. "I'm happy to report that all your bloodwork has come back and it doesn't look as though there are any further complications, so now that you're awake and alert, we'll watch you for a few hours and hopefully get you out of here by later this afternoon. Do you have any questions for me?"

"Yes, actually," she says quickly. "Ruth, here, just let it slip that I'm...I mean - that I might be - she says I'm...pregnant?"

Doctor Cortina smiles. "Oh, so you didn't know when you arrived here? Your parents weren't sure if you knew or not."

*WHAT? Her parents fucking knew?*

*Her father knew and didn't say anything to me?*

Savannah shakes her head slowly. Her eyes in a trance. "No, sir." She gulps.

"Then congratulations are in order, Savannah. Yes, you are indeed pregnant. Your blood work and ultrasound put you in the nine to ten week range and as of now, I'm happy to report that the baby is doing just fine."

"Thank you...doctor." Savannah says unemotionally. I wish I knew what this girl was thinking right now. It's killing me that I can't read her facial expressions...or rather that she's not giving me any to try to read.

"You're quite welcome. You'll want to make sure you follow up with your Obstetrician when you get home. Since you haven't been on any prenatal care as of yet, it's important to get started right away. We'll make sure to set you up with some prenatal vitamins before you leave here."

Savannah nods her head quietly. Doctor Cortina turns to me and nods his goodbyes before leaving the room, Ruth following right behind. Savannah and I are alone for the first time since receiving this life-changing news.

A baby.

Our baby.

"Bryant, what's the date today?"

"Uh, July ninth. Why?"

"And what was the date nine or ten weeks ago?"

My eyebrows raise at her question. I pull out my phone and scroll back a few months counting the weeks as I go. "Umm, looks like the end of April or maybe beginning of May?"

She shakes her head. "I don't get it. We were always so careful. We used protection every time."

I swallow hard, knowing she's incorrect. "Not every time, Seven," I whisper. She glances at me questioningly. "The couch in my office…"

*Fuck!*

*I fucking knocked her up on the couch in my office.*

*The same way I did it with Samantha.*

*Fuck! Fuck! Fuck!*

"Oh," she says.

I feel the urge to scream, or cry, or…I don't even know how I feel right now. I need to take a damn breath for just a minute.

"I'm gonna…go…get those coffees now."

"Bryant don't…" It's all I hear before I hastily walk into the hallway. Once I'm out there I bend over at my waist, taking a huge breath of air.

"Sir, are you alright?" one of the nurses asks me.

"Yeah. I'm fine. Just needed some air." I walk down the hall to the elevators but can't get myself to push the damn button to call for one. Something in me tells me not to be far from Savannah, but I just can't bring myself to look at her right now. Instead I back track to the waiting room where the disgusting coffee vending machine is. I push a few quarters in and push the button for black coffee. It'll taste like shit but that's what I get for messing up Savannah's life again.

*"Jamie told her that the only reason she would want to be with you
is so you'll knock her up too, and give her another kid
to replace the dead one she no longer has."*

*"Savannah, not that you really want or need to know this,
but Ivy was conceived on the couch in my shit hole of an office at the bar."*

"Damnit!" I shout and kick the snack vending machine. To my surprise a package of Oreos slips out and lands in the tray. I stick my hand in and pull them out, placing of them in my pocket. I'll stress-eat them later. I can't believe I did this to her. She's got to be upset with me. Jamie was right, I knocked her up and I fucking did it on a damn couch in my office. I treated Savannah like a piece of trash, like another piece of ass. At least, that's the way she'll see it. How could she not? I didn't give her what she deserved. I didn't protect her. I wasn't honest with her. I'm the last guy she needs in her life right now.

"Bryant?" Mr. and Mrs. Sanders are in the doorway watching me pace the room by myself. "What's going on, Son? Is Savannah okay? Did she wake up?"

"Yeah, she woke up," I mutter.

Mr. and Mrs. Sanders look to each other frowning in confusion. "What happened then?" Mr. Sanders asks. Mrs. Sanders chimes in too. "Something must've happened because you look like you're about to..."

"You knew she was pregnant," I whisper. "You knew, and you didn't tell me?"

Mr. Sanders inhales a deep breath. It's not lost on me the way he puffs his chest out a little to show me that he's the boss.

"Sit down, Bryant."

*Fuck you dude.*

"I would rather stand if you don't mind."

"Sit...down...Bryant." He says more sternly. I stare at him, trying to decide if I want to push past him and run like hell, or follow his direction. Like a pouting child, I throw myself into a chair along the wall, of course, spilling some of my coffee.

"I'm...umm," Mrs. Sanders looks to her husband and me. "I'll just go check on Savannah."

Mr. Sanders is quiet for a moment when he sits down in the chair next to me. He leans his head against the wall, deciding on the words to say.

"Bryant, you're right. The doctor told us when we were here that night that it looked as if Savannah was pregnant. Assuming it's yours..."

"Yeah, it's mine, sir. Your daughter's not a piece of trash. She doesn't sleep around."

"Well I hope you'll understand then that when you were here with us that night and never mentioned a baby, I knew that meant that you didn't know, and it wasn't my place to tell you. For what it's worth though, from what I've heard these past couple days from people in the Bardstown community, and from some of your friends, you're a pretty great father. Probably more patient and stronger fighting than I ever was for my baby girl. For those reasons alone I know you'll be a good father to this child too."

"Sir, I can't even be certain that Savannah will want me involved. This is all my fault too. How could I have been so stupid?"

"Did you force yourself on my daughter, Mr. Wood?" he asks. I turn my head towards him, immediately offended that he would ever think I could hurt Savannah. "Never! Dear God, I would never do that to a woman."

"Then I think it's safe to say this isn't all your fault." When I make eye contact with Mr. Sanders, he winks at me. He fuckin' winks. "We're all adults here Bryant and everyone knows how babies are made. It happens. Do you love her?"

"More than the air I breathe, sir."

I see the side of his mouth rise up in what I'm sure is a tiny satisfied smile. "Then don't run away too quickly, Bryant. You two are in this together and she's going to need you now more than ever. I'm too old to deal with the hormones that are going to be coming your way…the hot flashes, and the late night pickles and ice cream runs. I'm just an old man trained and ready to spoil my grandchild with all the love in the world."

"But what if something happens to her, sir? Or the baby? She can't…I can't…"

"Perhaps it would be better for you to stop focusing on all the what-could-go-wrongs, and steer your thoughts towards the what-could-go-rights. It's okay to let your faith be bigger than your fear."

I nod my head slightly while I stare at my coffee. "I'll give her all that I can, sir. You have my word on that."

"I'm not the one who needs to hear those words, Son," he says. "Let's go check in on my baby girl." He stands up and walks out of the waiting room. I follow quietly behind him.

# Chapter 33

He walked out.

He left me here, broken and alone.

And I don't know if he's coming back.

This is all my fault.

It was that damn couch. We've always used protection but that day we were in the moment. It wasn't planned. Neither of us were really thinking with our brains. It was one of the best moments of my life. I needed him so badly that day and I hadn't even known it.

*"Savannah, not that you really want or need to know this,*
*but Ivy was conceived on the couch in my shit hole of an office at the bar."*

Damnit, what is it about the couches in his office. I can't imagine what he must be thinking right now. I walked out on him a couple days ago, landed in this God forsaken hospital and now this. A baby. Our baby. Another child, that I could've easily put in harm's way by driving through all that rain. Bryant has to be pissed with me. I've loaded a lot of extra stress onto his shoulders. Stress that he and Ivy don't deserve. I'm sure it's all too much for him.

"Knock, knock!" Mama stands in the doorway peeking in to say hello. As soon as I see her in the doorway I burst into tears.

"Savannah...what is it? Are you okay? Are you in pain?" She rushes to my side, checking me over quickly to see what the problem is.

"No, Mama. I'm fine. It's just...I...I'm..."

"Is this about the baby? Is that why you're crying?" she asks softly.

"He left me, Mama. Bryant left me here, and I don't know if he's comin' back." I cry.

"Baby girl, don't you cry. Of course he's comin' back. He was just in the lounge down the hall getting a coffee out of the vending machine. Your daddy's with him now." She lightly brushes my hair back off of my face leaning in to kiss my now pounding forehead. Crying does nothing to soothe a headache.

"He is?"

She chuckles. "Well of course he is, you silly girl. You didn't think Bryant Wood was going to walk out of this hospital and never look back now did you?"

"I…I don't know what to think. What if he doesn't want this baby, Mama? Ivy is a lot for him to handle with all of her medical appointments and all. I can't put this stress on him too."

"Yes you can, and yes you will." Bryant steps into the room with my dad. Immediately I feel the tears burn my eyes as they trickle down my cheeks.

"Bryant." I cry.

"Savannah. I'm sorry." He's at my side in an instant taking my hand in his. "I didn't mean to run out on you, I just…I needed to take a breath. This was all a little sudden and not at all how I thought it would go when the time came."

"What? What do you mean how you thought it would go?" I ask.

Bryant turns to my parents. "Would you guys mind giving us just a minute alone?"

"Not at all. We'll just slip outside."

Bryant is still staring at me with a pained expression when my parents leave the room.

"Bryant what is it?"

"I thought…" He breathes. "I thought that one day we would get here. I saw a forever with you. I could see us having a family together, but, I just never saw it starting on the damn couch in my office. Savannah, you deserve someone who lays you down on the softest mattress and makes love to you repeatedly. You deserve all the love a man can give you and I…I ruined that for you. I never meant to hurt you. I hope you can believe that. I'll do whatever you want me to do for this baby, but I'll also understand if you don't want me to be a part of the journey you're about to take."

"Whoa, hold up." Through tear-strewn eyes, I squeeze his hand. "Is that what you think? That I don't want you to be a part of this with me? That I don't want you in my life now that I've learned that we're pregnant?"

He clears his throat. "Well, I just thought…"

"I don't give a damn what you thought. Bryant Wood, I love you. You'll be a great father to this baby, just as you have been a great father to Ivy. I'm just sorry this was a surprise for both of us. I swear to you I didn't meant for this to happen. I wasn't trying to replace Pey…" I choke on my words as well as my tears.

"Hey, hey, hey." Bryant whispers, holding my face in his hands. He sits on the bed next to me and gently wipes the tears from my eyes. "Don't you dare put that on yourself. Don't you allow Jamie Henders to take over your brain and your heart. She's a bitch who knows absolutely nothing about what we have. I know it was an accident. Most pregnancies are, and I'm not the least bit upset about the fact that I'm fathering another child, because for the first time in my life I'm in love with that child's mother. I don't plan on you doing any of this alone. Do you hear me? You'll never have to be alone in this okay, Sev? I'm right here and I'm not going anywhere."

I study his face through my tears. I've missed him. I've missed him so much. The way I feel when he touches me, the comforting taste of him when kisses me. His warmth, his playfulness, his compassion. Looking at him makes me feel like I've been asleep for much longer than a couple days. I lean in towards his face a little and he meets me halfway, our foreheads touching. His hands still holding my face I see his eyes dart to my now parted lips. "Please, Bryant."

"What, Baby?"

"Kiss me. Please."

Delicately he brushes his lips over mine. They connect in softness moving together like slow, gentle waves. He tastes of coffee. The stubble from his unshaved face tickles my skin but I relish it.

"Do you love me okay, Bryant?" I ask in between kisses.

"Baby, on a scale of one to four…" he says. "I love you Seven."

*****

It's been four weeks since the accident, and since I found out I was pregnant. I'm through the first trimester and luckily for me it wasn't that bad. It's a humbling feeling every time – knowing that a woman's body can grow another human being inside it. From all the books I've been reading I should be feeling the baby kick soon, and in about four more weeks we have an ultrasound appointment to hopefully learn the sex of the baby. With any luck by then I'll be out of these damn casts and not bound to this fucking wheelchair. Nausea hasn't been a huge problem for me during this pregnancy, but my fuses are much shorter these days. I'm not nearly as patient as I once was. I'm tired of being broken. I'm tired of people needing to help me do everything for me, including helping me get to the bathroom so I can pee. I can't use crutches because my right elbow is in a cast so there's no way to move myself. This wheelchair is stuck to my ass all waking hours of the day, until Bryant lifts me and carries me to bed. Physical therapy is going well for my arm and elbow, but I still have to wipe my ass with my left hand, and that's not easily done for someone who is right handed. It's the one thing I refuse to let anyone help me with. I need some form of dignity left.

Bryant enjoys helping me out every morning and evening. He likes to help get me dressed because in his words, "It means I have to get you undressed first." He also likes the sponge baths he has to give me so that my casts don't get wet. I will admit though, it's nice to have someone else do my hair. A couple days a week, Rachel comes over and does it up nice for me so I feel like a normal human being. Even little Ivy gets to help me out some days by keeping me entertained. She reads to me, and by read, I mean makes up her own stories to every book she pulls off the shelf. She helps Daddy make me breakfast and dinner and tries to brush my hair for me after Bryant washes it. She and Bryant have been my biggest super heroes through all of this, and I'm forever grateful that he insisted I stay here since I can't live in my second floor apartment, nor navigate around my parents' two-story home. I just wish I could shake the frustrated feeling I seem to be getting more often. It's obviously the hormones.

"Hey. Let me help you with that," Bryant says. He just got Ivy to sleep, without me helping of course since I can't walk up the steps. I've wheeled myself around his bedroom to try and put some of our laundry away. Anything I can do to be of service to him, I try and do it if I physically can. It's just my little way of trying to pay back all he's done for me. This time though, I completely dropped the pile I had resting on my lap, watching helplessly as it fell to the floor. As much as I've tried to reach for it, I can't get to it.

*Damnit!*

"I can do it, Bryant!" I huff.

"It's okay, Babe. They're just socks."

"Yeah to you they're just socks. To me they're…they're another fucking reminder of the mundane things I can't do like put socks away." I blow the hair hanging near my eyes in an irritated fashion.

He stops and kneels down at my chair. "Hey. What's wrong? You're not normally this…edgy."

"Well I'm sorry if I can't do everything you can do as fast as you can do it," I retort.

"I never said any of that was a problem," he says gently.

"I'm sorry I can't make you happy."

"You make me extremely happy," he assures me with a smile.

"You haven't asked for anything…in a long time…from me, I mean. You don't want me anymore, I get it. I mean look at me!" I gesture to my whole sorry self, sitting helplessly in a wheelchair.

"Whoa little pony. Back the truck up. What do you mean I don't want you anymore? What is this all about Sev?"

"What do you think it's about?" I can feel the heat invading my cheeks.

His eyebrows shoot up in surprise, like I've called on the one kid in the classroom who hasn't been paying attention. "Uh…I…really have no idea. I mean, I'm crazy about you, Sev. You know that. I tell you every day, so you tell me. What's going on in that beautiful head of yours?"

I'm silent for a moment mulling over whether or not I really want to be honest with him.

*Fuck it.*

"You haven't asked me to touch you since we got out of the hospital."

Bryant looks at me for a moment, befuddled, before a smirk slowly emerges on his face.

"What?" I ask.

"Is that what this is about?"

"Is *what* what this is about?" I argue.

"You're frustrated," he snickers.

"Huh?"

"Sexually. You, my little sex kitten, are sexually frustrated."

I scoff. "As if."

*Ugh I can't believe how embarrassing this is.*

Bryant laughs. He can see the blush on my face and knows he's hit the nail on the head. "Admit it."

"What? No."

He leans in closer sliding his hand up my thighs. That spark I felt when I first met him shoots immediately to all the places I wish it wouldn't. "Admit it."

"Never. I'm perfectly fine," I pant.

"No, you're not," he says. His hands roam up my torso as he leans in to leave a playful kiss on the side of my neck. "You've been pent up in this wheel chair for weeks...void of a good release huh?"

"I don't need anything from you." My voice falters. There's no way I said that with any conviction whatsoever.

*I want it all from him.*

*Damn these casts.*

*Damn this wheelchair.*

"No, no, I get it. I've missed that connection too. It's been too long. Let me make it up to you." Swiftly he slides his hands under my legs as he does multiple times a day and lifts me, cradling my body against his. I close my eyes breathing him in, committing his delicious smell to memory. He carries me effortlessly to his bed where he lays me down. His eyes roam down my body and back up to meet my hungry stare.

"Lucky for me, we put you in a sundress today," he says with a wink.

"Yeah? Why's that?"

He kneels onto the bed, spreading my legs so that he can sit between them. He bends my left leg so that my foot is flat on the bed, resulting in the riding up of my dress. I can't help but roll my eyes when he looks at me like a damn kid in a candy shop, but when his left hand moves swiftly up my thigh, and he reaches the apex, I gasp much louder than I probably should.

"Easy access," he teases.

His playfulness makes me chuckle. Finally, I feel the tension start to roll off my shoulders, only to allow an entirely different kind of tension to take its place.

"You know I think I've done a damn good job of taking care of you these past couple weeks..." He states. "But I guess I have been neglecting some of your more...personal needs." He leans forward so that he's hovering over top of me, careful not to put any weight on my body. As he leans in he pushes my dress up and over my head, helping me carefully to take it off before admiring the half-naked body he sees lying before him. Swiftly, and because he knows I'm not much help, he pulls his shirt up over his head and throws it on the floor behind him.

"But your lips aren't broken." He traces my bottom lip with his tongue, prompting me to open them for him. He takes full advantage of my eagerness, kissing me until my lips are plump and swollen.

"Your neck isn't broken," he says as he trails his nose softly down my neck, kissing me up and around my ear before heading south.

"And these babies right here..." he says fondling my now swollen breasts. "These are *definitely* not broken." Bryant's touch on my blissfully sensitive pregnant breasts ignites my carnal need for him. I don't care about the lovey-dovey stuff. I just want his hands on me now. Right now.

"Bryant," I whisper.

"Shh, shh, shh." He answers. "I need to take care of you, Baby, and I'm not finished yet." He works his way down my torso, kissing and sucking along the way. My baby bump has started to fill out a little bit so there's a little more of me for him to play with. He looks up at me with his sexy brown eyes and in one startling move, rips the pink panties I had on completely off my body.

*Well that's one way to get them over my cast.*

I laugh out loud at my thought but quickly gasp when Bryant says in between licks, "And I don't think anything is broken down here."

"Oh my God!" I mewl.

"You like that?"

"Mmm hmm…" is all I can say. I'm breathing harder and grasping at the sheets around me.

"Good. Because you taste so good right now, I'm not sure I could stop if I wanted to."

It doesn't take long for me to find the release I so badly desired. And it doesn't take long for Bryant to figure out how to navigate around my broken limbs in search of his own release.

"Roll over on your side." He says to me as he unbuckles his belt. I hear him shoving his shorts down and stepping out of them. With my broken limbs resting comfortably he slides into the bed behind me. His left hand adjusts underneath my head where he now has easy access to my bare chest. His right hand coming around to play as well, Bryant spends the next several minutes exploring every surface and crevice of my body, his hands answering every one of my moans and groans.

"Are you ready for me?" he asks.

"Yes!" I spit out almost too eagerly. With his hands around my waist he pulls me back towards him so that our bodies line up perfectly. He guides himself inside me and with one hand resting on my pelvis pushes himself in as far as he can go.

This connection.

This is what I needed.

What I desired.

"Savannah…" he whispers in my ear as his breath escapes him. "Dear God you feel so…mmm…so good." He very slowly slides in and out, in and out, working himself up to what will be his inevitable explosion, but what I didn't anticipate was the overwhelming desire to explode with him. As his pace quickens, his fingers begin to latch on to me, pinching me, rubbing me, pinching me again until I can't hold back anymore.

"Bryant…" I warn. "I'm going to…"

"It's okay, Baby. Come with me," he says, accelerating his pace ever so much more. Realizing that my body is wrapped in all the love he has to give in this one moment, I turn my head and cover my mouth with my pillow to keep from screaming as we reach our climax in tandem.

# Chapter 34

# *Bryant*

These past eight weeks have been some of the best weeks of my life, yet the worst at the same time. Having Savannah here in my house, with Ivy and me, has been like a dream come true for me. Both of the girls I love under the same roof, day in and day out. There's nothing I want more than for it to stay that way, but all good things come to an end, I suppose. Savannah's elbow cast has already been removed and she gets her leg cast off today. She probably feels like it's been the longest, most unbearable summer and who could blame her? Two broken bones, three if you count her nose, and a pregnancy that's putting her body through hell – I'm in awe of her strength. She's been the best patient for me, and getting to play doctor for her has its perks in more ways than one. I've kept up with the rent on her apartment for her since she hasn't been able to work, but I imagine once the cast is off and she's okay, she'll want her privacy again. I wish that weren't the case, but I'm not positive there's anything I can do about it right now. She's definitely been eager to fly the nest, itching to be outside. In just a week or so, Ivy's off to her first day of preschool. I'll be alone, and fuck if that doesn't piss me off.

I left Savannah and Ivy at home for just a little while before Savannah's appointment. I told her I had a few things to check in on at the bar, but really I just needed to get away for a while so Savannah couldn't read my feelings. Instead of taking my sour mood out on her or Ivy, I'm taking it out on the glassware at the bar. I hate doing dishes. I pay someone to do the dishes here, but when I'm pissed, I clean. My mother would be proud, though I have half a notion to take one of these glasses and throw it against the damn wall just to watch it shatter.

"Hey man. How's it going?" Sloan asks.

I grunt in response because I just have nothing nice to say. My thoughts are stuck on my problems. I don't want to deal with anyone else's shit.

"Dude, who pissed in your beer, man?

"Shut up," I say.

"Don't think so Bry. I've known you too long. When your hands are in the soapy water, someone's about to get a new asshole, 'cause the Bryant Wood that I know hates to do dishes." He waits a minute to see if I'm going to react to his pushing of my buttons, but I don't.

"Your silence is deafening. You want to talk about it or do you want to just…maybe throw that glass against the wall?" he asks a little calmer but with a shit-eating grin.

I glance in his direction from the corner of my eye. "Actually, I have given that some thought." I run my towel over the glass one last time before setting it down and stepping back with my hands still holding tightly to the counter in front of me. With a deep breath I decide maybe it's not such a bad thing to talk this out. I can't talk to Savannah about it and Sloan's the only guy who gets me and doesn't give me too hard of a time.

"Seven's getting her cast off today."

Sloan's eyes shoot up in surprise. "Yeah? That's fantastic. I bet she's ready to be free of that shit."

The corner of mouth twists as I mutter, "That's just the problem."

"Come again?" Sloan says. "I don't see the problem here. What's the matter, you don't want to have to put away your kinky doctor costume or what?"

"More like I don't want her to give up the doctor's office." I try not to make eye contact with Sloan, afraid that I'll be an open book for him to read aloud.

"Ah, I see. You're afraid she'll go home."

Silence falls between us. I don't know what to say because he's right.

"Why does it bother me so much that she might want to go home? It's not like I won't still see her."

Sloan laughs and when I finally make eye contact he exaggeratingly rolls his eyes.

"What?" I ask "What's so funny?" Sometimes he pisses me off too.

"You are, you sad fuck. Don't you see it?"

"See what? What are you talking about?"

"You've in love with her, Bryant. She's your world. She's been your world since...I don't know...fucking March and shit. You've been crazy about her since the day she walked in here. She's lived with you for eight weeks and now you're just going to let her walk right out the door?"

"What the fuck am I supposed to do?" I yell, throwing my arms up in frustration. "I would propose to her if I could, but I'm not positive that she's ready for that. We've only really been together about six months."

Sloan purses his lips and shakes his head. "Bullshit. That's not the problem, Bry."

"Oh, for fuck's sake Sloan." I mutter as I step back to the counter and grab a glass. I shove it down in the warm dish water and run my rag through it roughly over and over again, scrubbing spots that aren't really there just to keep my hands busy.

"You're scared," Sloan states.

"I'm NOT...scared." My hands come to a halt and I drop the glass in the sink. Just like that I'm defeated. Sloan has called my bluff.

"You're not scared of losing her, Bry. You're scared of winning her."

I watch him for a minute as he stares at me. I want to push him down to the floor and nut punch him until he cries, but he's right. I'm scared.

"You're scared that the crush you had all those years ago has finally led to something bigger than yourself. You're scared of actually settling down with the one person in this world that you were obviously meant to be with in one way or another. You're scared of failing her after all she's been through. You're afraid you won't be enough for her."

"Yeah well, what if I'm not enough for her? What if I do fail her?"

"I don't have all the answers, man. But I'm pretty sure the only way you can fail her is by giving up on her, and I'm pretty sure you don't have it in you to do that. Look what you've done for this girl, after all she's been through. And look what she's done to you...how she's changed you."

I scoff. "You mean how she's put my balls in a box and turned me into a sentimental pussy?"

Sloan laughs so hard he starts to cough. "Well, I guess so, but damn if you haven't liked every minute of it."

I half smile. "Yeah. You're right. So what do I do now? I feel like I'm going to lose my window if I don't say something to her."

Sloan squints as he stands against the bar, thoughts running through his head. "Her cast comes off today?"

"Yep."

"You planning on celebrating?"

"Uhh...I really hadn't thought..."

Sloan interrupts me. "Let me say this again and not pose it as a question. You're celebrating. Tonight. I have a plan." He smirks.

# Chapter 35

# ✑ *Savannah*

"How does that feel Savannah?" Doctor Thile asks. For the first time in eight weeks I'm looking at a bare naked leg. Well, almost bare naked. Damn, do I need to shave.

"Wow! Lighter for sure. A little stiff but otherwise good," I exclaim. "I can't wait to walk myself to the bathroom! This pregnancy isn't doing me any favors in that department."

"Yes, I imagine you're right." He laughs. "Stiffness will be normal for a while and you'll feel a bit out of balance as you put your weight back onto it. Your physical therapist will help you through a lot of that and give you some tips on building the muscle tone back into your leg. Swimming would be a really good idea. All your scans are good though. The leg has healed nicely and I'm happy to say you've made a full recovery."

"I can walk up and down the stairs?" I ask him eagerly.

"Well, only you can know how the leg feels. It could take some time adjusting for a while. I have this cane for you to use…" As he holds it up I roll my eyes at the notion of using an old-person stick. "Yes, yes, I know. Canes are for old people, but I'm sure you'll find a way to jazz this up a bit to suit you a little better," he explains.

"I know a little girl who would throw glitter at that thing in a heartbeat if given the chance." Bryant whispers in my ear.

I smile at the notion. A girl can never have too much bling. "Great idea! She can help me with it this afternoon!" I lean over and meet Bryant's lips with my own.

"Thank you, doctor," we say together.

"You're most welcome, Savannah. Do give me a call if you have any questions or concerns in the coming weeks and like I said, be patient. Give it time, and before you know it, your leg will be back to normal."

# Seven

*****

Bryant and the girls from the salon insisted on going out tonight to celebrate the freedom of my limbs. I've loved every minute of living with Bryant and Ivy, but I wasn't about to say no to stepping out for a good time. I missed the entire summer and am eager to feel like a normal human being for the first time in a long time.

I'm dressed in my long pink strapless maxi dress that's belted right above my baby bump and covered with a denim jacket. I'm constantly hot but I also know that Bryant keeps the air conditioning up during the hot months…something about comfortable customers, equals heavily paying customers. Bryant comes down the hall in his jeans and a t-shirt that I've never seen before. It's a navy blue shirt, fitting tightly around his arms, as they all do, but it's the saying on the front that makes me grin like a giddy school girl. In big white letters it says DON'T ASK, I'M TAKEN.

I laugh when he steps towards me and picks me up in his arms to swing me around. "That's a nice shirt you got there, Mr. Wood."

"Yeah? You like it? I picked it out just for you." He teases.

"I love it…because it's true. And you're not only taken, you're mine." I kiss his lips softly at first but give him just enough more to let him know where my thoughts lie. It's a fantastic feeling to be able to lay claim to Bryant Wood. To know that he no longer feels the need to even look at another woman because of me is humbling and sexy all at the same time. I love him and if I have my way, I hope I'll have the pleasure of making him happy for years and years to come.

"Mmm keep that up Sev, and we may just need to stay right here tonight."

"No way!" I giggle. "I need to be out of this house and anywhere that isn't a medical office of any kind!"

Bryant's face falters a bit and I wonder if I said something I shouldn't have. He quickly recovers though and before I can ask he says, "Hey, before we go, I have something for you."

"Okay. What is it?"

Bryant dips his hand into his pocket and pulls out a square little box. Confused as to what it could possibly be, I take it from him and shake it in my hand. It rattles enough for me to know there's something inside but I can't tell what it is.

"What did you do?" I ask, graciously smiling.

Bryant shrugs. "It's not much, just something I thought you might like."

I open the lid of the box and gasp at the beauty of what sits inside. Delicately, I pull out the gold bangle charm bracelet, turning it over in my hands to see every detail. There's a sun and a small round gold charm that says *"You are my sunshine"*, but it's the other charms on the bracelet that bring me to tears. A gold charm with the letter P engraved on it followed by a small ruby birthstone, Peyton's birthstone. Another gold charm is engraved with the letter I, and sits next to a beautiful opal stone, Ivy's birthstone. The last round gold charm is blank. When I look at Bryant he answers my unasked question.

"We'll engrave it when we pick a name," he says softly.

My fingers touch the very last charm, a stunning diamond hangs next to the blank charm, the birthstone of our newest family member.

"Bryant..." I sigh. "This is..."

"Too much? I can take it back..." He says cautiously.

"Like hell you'll take it back." I clutch it to my chest. "I love it. Please don't take my sunshine away." I smirk.

"Sev, I would give you the whole damn sun if I could. You deserve at least that. Can I help you put it on?"

"Please." I say holding the bracelet out for him and turning my hand over. He slides the bracelet over my hand and when he does, I shake it so the charms all jingle together. It's a glorious sound.

"Thank you," I whisper.

He kisses me on the cheek before resting his forehead on mine. "You're most welcome. You look beautiful tonight. Now let's go have some fun shall we?"

# Seven

*****

I don't even mind that I can't partake in the alcoholic beverages tonight. Just being out in the open, surrounded by several of my favorite people, it's all I could've asked for and then some. Bourbon Creek has been playing for past hour or so and they're on fire tonight! Bryant has been waiting on me hand and foot to make sure I'm comfortable and, most of all, protected.

"Do you want something other than water? I've got orange juice or iced tea, lemonade..."

"Chocolate milk?"

He chuckles at my question. "You want chocolate milk?"

"Mmmm I've been craving it all afternoon but we didn't have any chocolate syrup at home," I explain.

"Well you should've told me. I would've run out to get you some."

"You've done enough. Besides, I know you have syrup here."

"I sure do. One tall chocolate milk coming up." He kisses my cheek and hops over to the bar.

"So how are you feeling Savannah?" Audrey asks. "It's so good to see you out and about. We've all really missed you."

Smiling I answer, "I've missed you guys too. A ton! One or two game nights doesn't cut it when I'm used to seeing you all every day, but I'm feeling much better. Elbow seems absolutely fine. Leg is stiff and will take a little while but the doctor says it has healed nicely so I should be back to my old self in no time."

"You mean your new self." Rachel says, motioning toward my belly. "Cause girl, your leg might go back to normal but nothing else about you will be."

"Ooh touché." I laugh, rubbing my belly out of habit. "You're right though. Nothing about me is normal right now. Just ask Bryant. My hormones are all over the damn place and I can't stop eating Trix cereal! And to think I gave him hell about even owning that shit six months ago."

Everyone at the table laughs as Bryant returns, tall chocolate milk in hand. "Here ya go, Baby."

"YES! Thank you!" I tip the glass to my lips and practically inhale the entire glass in less than ten seconds. Everyone at the table watches me in astonishment, mouths open, eyes wide.

"What?" I shrug. "I'm drinking for two." That earns me a round of laughter from the group.

Another hour into the evening and I'm surprisingly not tired. My ankles started to swell a bit so Bryant made sure to prop my feet up on his lap so he could lightly massage them throughout the evening. Every time I make eye contact with Rachel across the table she winks knowingly at me. As Bourbon Creek takes their break following their first set, Sloan opens up the floor to karaoke. Several customers lend their voices, or lack thereof, to the over-played party songs like *Piano Man, Love Shack,* and *YMCA,* but when Rachel gets up and heads to the piano I snap to attention eager to hear her sing…until Audrey nonchalantly lays a travel pack of Kleenex in the middle of the table.

*WTF?*

"Um, hi, everyone. For those of you who don't know me, my name is Rachel. I'm here quite often and have performed during karaoke night many times. I guess I'm sort of a regular. Anyway, I wanted to perform tonight for someone who I'm pretty sure would do it herself if she could, but there's no way in hell she would get through it, so that's what I'm here for." Rachel turns towards me. "Savannah, you're my best friend and you're one of the strongest people I know. You've been through more in one lifetime than I could ever imagine and I just thought you should hear this song. And um…yeah. Sorry, not sorry, for making you cry."

"What the hell?" I whisper to Bryant. He only looks at me and smiles lovingly. He shrugs like he has no idea what's going on, which means he knows exactly what's going on. Butterflies immediately start swimming around in my stomach, or maybe the baby is doing flips, but my emotions are creeping higher and higher as I anxiously await Rachel's performance.

I only have to hear the first six notes of the song's introduction on the piano to know exactly what's about to happen. My face falls into my hands and I sob quietly feeling Bryant's hand rub gently up and down my back. Rachel, sounding eerily just like Martina McBride starts to sing "In My Daughter's Eyes". The melody, the lyrics, it's all so overwhelming, but I know there's a greater reason for Rachel wanting me to hear this song tonight than to just make me cry, so I sit there watching her through my now watery eyes letting the words sink into my soul.

"But the truth is plain to see, she was sent to rescue me...
This miracle God gave to me gives me strength when I am weak..."

She's right. I needed to hear these words tonight. I may be sobbing like a hormonal pregnant lady who is up too late, but my soul is somehow lighter. Peyton has indeed rescued me, given me strength when I was weak. She's with me. In my heart always. Rachel's performance ends and I'm immediately on my feet bounding over to her, blubbery mess and all, to hug the shit out of her.

"I love you Rachel. Thank you so much for that."

"I love you too Savannah. I knew it would make you cry, but after all you've been through I needed you to hear the words. Really hear them and understand that Peyton was a miracle, she is a miracle and she will always be a miracle, and you're the strongest mother I know. I hope one day I can be as strong as you."

"Oh Rachel!" I cry as I squeeze her tightly again. Damn my hormones!

When I return to my seat, Bryant isn't there. I look around for him but Audrey tells me he just had to help Sloan in the back for a second. Bourbon Creek takes the stage once again and starts out with a set of Brad Paisley songs. I can't complain about that one bit. The first song they sing in this set is one that sounds familiar to me but I can't remember the name of it. It's the song I heard in Bryant's truck that day he took me on our first official date. He sang it so well that day...the day I knew I was in love with him. I almost wish he was up there singing now.

They take a minute to set up the next song as one of the musicians sits down at the piano. It's another relatively slow song, and also one of my very favorites. I know they're about to perform "Then" and I wish so much that Bryant would come sit and listen to it with me. The piano intro starts followed by the guitar but when the words are supposed to start, the lead singer isn't singing them. The voice that is singing is coming from somewhere else. I hear gasps coming from throughout the room as everyone turns to the back of the room toward the bar. To my surprise, when I turn around, Bryant Wood is standing on the bar, microphone in hand and he has eyes only for me.

*Oh. My. God.*

*Am I dreaming?*

*There is a man on a bar and he is singing...to me!*

He sings of being mesmerized and of not telling me that he loved me back then. It finally dawns on me that every word he sings to me is perfection. It's us. It's our story. He thought he loved me then but it's nothing compared to how he loves me now. Slowly he makes his way over to me. Holding out his hand, I place my hand in his so that he can help me up. He wraps his strong arm around me baring my weight while we dance slowly, gazing at each other eye to eye, mesmerized with one another.

*How did I get so lucky?*

When he gets to the part about getting down on one knee he takes my breath away as he literally gets down on one knee. Just when I think he might propose and I may actually faint, he pulls out a key and holds it up for me. I know from the look of it that it's his house key. It's the most endearing gesture and makes me both laugh and cry.

"Now you're my whole life, now you're my whole world..."

"We'll look back some day at this moment that we're in
and I'll look at you and say, I thought I loved you then."

During the guitar break he lays the microphone down on the table, and holds me tightly to him in a private dance, in front of the entire bar. "Savannah, I didn't want this day to come, for you to get that cast off because I've been so damn scared that you would leave me and go back home to your apartment and I don't want that. I want you with me. Always. My life doesn't feel complete when you're not with me. My bed is too big when you're not in it. My daughter needs a woman in her life who will treat her the way a little princess deserves to be treated. Please, Sev, will you move in with me and Ivy?"

It's happy irony that he asks because as soon as the doctor told me I would need physical therapy, I assumed I would continue to stay with him. Any excuse to stay there was one I was willing to consider. Fuck my apartment. I hate stairs anyway.

"On one condition." I smirk.

"Anything. Name it," he says eagerly.

I pause for a second and then with a twinkle in my eye I say "You'll have to teach me how to pee and brush my teeth in the shower at the same time while washing my hair with my non tooth-brushing hand."

I'm a ball of excited nerves as we enter the doctor's office today. All of my important stuff is getting moved to Bryant's tomorrow but first, we have to take care of our big ultrasound appointment. Today, with any luck, we'll find out whether we're having a boy or a girl.

"How about Finn if it's a boy?" Bryant asks in the waiting room. He's been fidgeting all over the place for the past twenty minutes as we sit here waiting for our turn. He's every bit as excited and nervous as I am. I think about the name Finn for a moment before shaking my head. "Nah, I'm not feeling it. How about Meredith for a girl?"

Bryant wobbles his head back and forth pursing his lips. "Not bad. Ivy and Meredith…hmm…nah. We need something that flows well."

We both sit quietly for a moment thinking of just the perfect name.

"Clyde," Bryant says proudly.

"What? No!" I laugh.

"Come on, he'll be hung like a horse, I just know it."

"Hahaha! I don't need to be thinking of how well hung my son might be and what if it's a girl anyway? Besides…Clyde and Ivy doesn't sound right. Sounds too much like Captain and Tennille."

"Good point." He nods.

The door in front of us opens and a nurse in pink scrubs steps out. "Savannah Turner?"

"Yeah, that's me," I say as Bryant quickly stands up to help me up, keeping his hand on the small of my back as I waddle down the hall. The ultrasound tech has me lay down on the table and lift up my shirt so that she can begin her routine.

"Okay, I'm going to take a few measurements of the baby's arms, legs, head, and stomach and then will need to measure the heartbeat. Do you know what you're having yet?"

"No we don't. We were hoping to find out today," Bryant explains.

"Well, there are never any promises that the baby will be in a good position to see but we'll do our best to try and find out before we finish up."

We both watch the screen in awe. It's a precious sight to behold. The tiny human we created is alive and kicking inside of me. It's a bond I'll never forget for as long as I live. For about twenty minutes the baby moves around as the technician gets the measurements she's looking for. At one point it even looks like he or she is waving at us.

"That's the baby sucking her thumb there, do you see it?"

"Her? Her? You said her…is it a her?" Bryant asks. "Are we having a girl? I have another daughter? Another princess?"

The technician smiles and turns her head towards Bryant and me. "Congratulations guys, you are having a girl."

Bryant's hand runs through his hair as his eyes grow large and watery. "We're having a girl." He chokes on his words. "A girl."

I close my eyes taking it all in for just a minute.

It hits me then.

My dream.

Peyton, Ivy and…the little girl.

My Past.

My Present.

My Future.

"Rose," I whisper, tears trickling down my face.

"What?" Bryant asks.

"Rose. Her name is Rose."

Bryant tilts his head, lovingly gazing at me. He leans over me, placing a soft kiss on my lips.

"Perfect choice. She'll be our Kentucky Rose."

# ACKNOWLEDGEMENTS

First of all, I never in a million gazillion years thought I would ever write and publish ONE book let alone two! Life just keeps getting more fun and I have many of you to thank for that. Don't for one second think that I'm not humbled by it or take it for granted. Writing has helped bring me out of a place I never want to have to return to again. You are all my sunshine!

Jen, I can't thank you enough for telling me that you knew two women, on opposite ends of the country, who were crazy about *Solving Us*. I'll never ever forget how giddy excited they both were the night we all chatted for the first time on Facebook. Now they're two of my bestest friends and reliable teammates. Had it not been for you, I wouldn't have either of them in my life...so THANK YOU for your gift!

Nikki and Shaniqua (see what I did there?), thank you from the bottom of my very humbled heart for being those two giddy excited ladies who couldn't believe they were getting the chance to talk to an "author". You make my world brighter every damn day. If this book receives any recognition, I'm pretty sure I can confidently say it's all due to both of you. Your excitement and passion for greatness is contagious! Nikki, thank you for jumping right in and editing the crap out of my terrible writing! I know, I already know I'm an ellipses whore and I sort of kind of used lots of extra commas this time on purpose. You're welcome. Also, thank you for not throwing up your hands and leaving me when I needed you the most. Your patience and work ethic are unbelievable and I owe you seven shots of something really yummy!

Samantha, I think you're the best damn graphic designer a girl could ever have the pleasure of working with. You made all those late night work sessions FUN and exciting! I love your creativity, and your work ethic, and your determination to make everything as perfect as possible. I can't wait to see Grothic Designs thrive BIG TIME!

Lauren, after the year you've had, you deserve the world. I hope one day I can have a part in giving it to you. Thank you, again, for putting up with all my inconsequential book talk while you dealt with pneumonia, flu, ear infections and drippy noses. You're stronger than pretty much anyone I know.

Kelli and Nichelle, I owe you both a TON for coming to my aid at the last minute. Seriously, Mexican food is on ME! THANK YOU for all of your help.

Doug, this is all your fault. *Seven* is all your fault…and I couldn't be more grateful. Thank you for loving me okay even when you didn't want to. Thank you for being my best friend, the one I giggle with late at night, the one who dries my tears when I'm frustrated and the only one who can help me with researching those steamy scenes. And most importantly thank you for being the best damn daddy in the world to our two children.

To all my new blogger acquaintances, fans new and old, and friends, colleagues, and supporters…thank you for letting me have the opportunity to fulfill a dream I didn't know I had. This is the life I want to lead, the life that makes me the happiest. Getting to meet and talk to so many of you is seriously a humbling experience each and every time. I hope you all understand that you are ALL my sunshine on a rainy day. I hope you'll continue to share your awesome encouragement and experience this adventure right along with me.

And last but never least…Amy Smith…if it weren't for you, Bryant wouldn't have ever learned how to pee and brush his teeth in the shower at the same time while washing his hair with his non-tooth brushing hand. You're a genius!

# About the Author

Susan Renee wants to live in a world where paint doesn't smell, Hogwarts is open twenty-four/seven, and everything is covered in glitter. An indie romance author, Susan has written about everything from lawn mowers to thick colossal bottles of wine, and has won a Snuggle Buddy award for her nonfiction book, *The Hula Hoop Tester's Guide to Jumping*. She lives in Ohio with her family and seven tiny donkeys. She's a Pet Whispering major from OMGU with a Masters in medical care for inanimate objects (a la Doc McStuffins). Susan enjoys crab-walking through the Swiss Alps, drinking Muscle Milk, and doing the Care Bear stare with her closest friends.

Website: www.authorsusanrenee.com

Facebook: www.facebook.com/authorsusanrenee

Goodreads: www.goodreads.com/SusanRenee

Instagram: authorsusanrenee

Twitter: @indiesusanrenee

Spotify: susan_renee

# Other Works By Susan Renee

## SOLVING US

Available now at

Amazon.com and Barnesandnoble.com

*****

"What scares you?"

"Love. Love scares me, Finn. Everybody I love I lose and," I let go of his face. "My past is…"

"Lonely? Dark? Confusing? Like your puzzle pieces don't fit?" he asks me.

"My puzzle pieces…" I ponder his thought for a moment. "Finn...my past feels like a fucked up Rubik's Cube."

"Mmm… Rubik's Cube, huh?"

"Yeah"

"Sounds perfect," he mutters.

"Perfect?"

*Did he hear me correctly?*

"I just told you my life is like a fucked up Rubik's Cube, and that's perfect?"

"Yeah." He smiles at me. "I know how to solve a Rubik's Cube."

Finn takes my hand in his and folds our fingers together, our hands now looking like a completed puzzle. The gesture isn't lost on me.

"Olivia, I understand exactly what you're saying; in fact, I could've used the same metaphor. You feel like your life is a cluster fuck of colored cubes that just don't seem to match up."

I look at Finn stunned. He sees me. He gets me.

"Yeah. That's exactly how I feel. So, I work hard to get one side to completely line up, and I love it, but as soon as I try to line up another side, I lose everything I had before."

"Yeah but, Liv, sometimes in order to solve a Rubik's Cube, you have to go backwards before you can move forward. And no matter what, I'll go backwards with you so that we can move forward together. You don't have to feel alone anymore. I *want* to be here with you. You have me. You have my heart. I'm giving it to you. Use it."